BLOOD

PRAISE FOR *BLOOD RED CITY*

'*Blood Red City* is both crime fiction at its gripping best and an all too believable portrait of a city under the sinister control of the oligarchs' Tim Baker

'Cannot recommend this highly enough to anyone who appreciates a pacy, realistic thriller that wrongfoots the reader time and again' G.J. Minett

'They say that London is the money-laundering capital of the world. Rod Reynolds shows how that is possible in this complex thriller ... Reynolds is as good at action as he is at the development of Lydia's character. She is brave, clever, sometimes silly and absolutely credible' *Literary Review*

'*Blood Red City* has an action-fuelled plot ... with each chapter presenting a heart-racing new turn of events ... This is brilliant. Highly, highly recommend!' Hooked from Page One

'Strikingly realistic with an exciting, serpentine plot' Hair Past a Freckle

'The premise is brilliant: a witness but no victim? ... I couldn't help but jump down that rabbit hole with Lydia, join her frantic search for the truth, all while trying to contact the witness ... Rod Reynolds takes his readers to the darkest parts of London and shows us that those who look squeaky clean may well be very dirty underneath their spotless veneers' From Belgium with Booklove

'London born and bred, Reynolds has always wanted to write about his home city and he's definitely done it justice ... portraying the vibrant, lively city in the summer heat. Definitely want more' Joy Kluver

BLOOD RED CITY

ABOUT THE AUTHOR

Rod Reynolds is the author of four novels, including the Charlie Yates series. His 2015 debut, *The Dark Inside*, was longlisted for the CWA New Blood Dagger, and was followed by *Black Night Falling* (2016) and *Cold Desert Sky* (2018); the *Guardian* has called the books 'pitch-perfect American noir'. A lifelong Londoner, in 2020 Orenda Books will publish *Blood Red City*, his first novel set in his hometown.

Rod previously worked in advertising as a media buyer, and holds an MA in novel writing from City University London. He lives with his wife and family and spends most of his time trying to keep up with his two young daughters.

Follow him on Twitter @Rod_WR.

BLOOD RED CITY

ROD REYNOLDS

**ORENDA
BOOKS**

Orenda Books
16 Carson Road
West Dulwich
London SE21 8HU
www.orendabooks.co.uk

First published in the United Kingdom by Orenda Books, 2020
Copyright © Rod Reynolds, 2020

A catalogue record for this book is available from the British Library.

ISBN 978-1-913193-24-9
eISBN 978-1-913193-25-6

Typeset in Garamond by www.typesetter.org.uk
City vector created by freepik – www.freepik.com

Printed and bound by CPI Group (UK) Ltd, Croydon CR0 4YY

For sales and distribution, please contact info@orendabooks.co.uk

For Elodie

CHAPTER 1

Up there, the city sprawled before her. Council estates and hulking tower blocks, a year on from the Grenfell fire. Glittering skyscrapers in the Square Mile and Docklands. A million lights. Faltering lives. The trains moving through it all with the slow grind of bulldozers on a landfill. London laid itself bare; eight million people eating, breathing, sleeping, fucking, dying. A muggy night, the air ripe with ozone, ready to spark. On the wall in front of her someone had ditched a cigarette butt in a champagne flute, and she stared at it as if it held meaning. Two drinks making Lydia philosophical.

The bar was on the roof of a disused council building in Elephant & Castle. Summer months, an arts fund laid out rows of weathered picnic tables and sold Prosecco and Aperol spritz at fourteen pounds per, from a tiki bar that couldn't have been more incongruous. In the lift on the way up, the new intern had described it as 'low-fi chic' – without a trace of sarcasm. The air smelled of lime and mint, undercut with weed – some dickhead thinking it lent cachet in a place where the only thing that impressed was the only thing that impressed anywhere: money.

The view was no bullshit though.

Lydia checked her phone, still unlocked from the last time. Two new emails: an overdue gas bill and one from an email address she didn't recognise. No texts or messages. That same hollow feeling, waiting for change to find her. As if the chance to start over would arrive in a WhatsApp message.

She looked at the second email. The sender's address meant nothing to her – aplofel159@gmail.com – but the subject read: *Lyds, please watch this*. Seemed like spam, but when she tapped on it to delete it, there was another line in the message body: *Please do not delete, I promise this isn't junk. Call you in a bit to explain*. There was a video file attached.

She stared at the screen, her thumbs hovering over the trash can icon. 'Lydia' was short enough for most people, very few called her 'Lyds', and she never used the nickname herself. Definitely not online, where a scammer would've scraped it from.

'Deep thoughts?'

Stephen Langham at her shoulder. He was holding out a gin and tonic in a plastic cup.

She smiled. 'Can't, I'm on my way in after this.' She raised the one in her hand, as if nursing an empty implied it was her first.

'It's only a single.'

'I've got a load on tonight.'

He set it down on the wall, a faint smile at recognising the code. 'Something big?' He nodded at her phone.

'On the graveyard shift? Come on...' She slipped it away in her bag, the email still on the screen.

He tilted his head, a hard-luck stare. 'It won't be this way forever, you know.'

'I wasn't complaining.'

'I didn't think you were.' He looked past her, eyes roving over the view; Canary Wharf blinking silently like a heart-rate monitor. 'We've talked about this – management know they've been heavy-handed with you.'

'Management' – distancing himself from it. She put down

her drink and regretted it as soon as she did, nothing to occupy her hands now. 'Surprised to see you here.'

'Here' was leaving drinks for Simone Hewitt, one of the online journos; Lydia knew her a bit, but she'd only been with the company twelve months, and it wasn't like they'd be swapping mobile numbers when she was gone. Truth of it was, Lydia had showed her face tonight for the same reason as all the others there – to be seen. The irony wasn't wasted on her: still playing the good corporate citizen.

'My turn with the company card,' he said. 'At the end of the night.'

'Shame I can't stay to take advantage then.'

He smiled, glancing at his watch. 'You on at midnight?'

She nodded, anticipating his next question. 'And I need to get going.'

'Let me order you a taxi at least. On the business.'

She started shaking her head, always wary of him perceiving her to be taking advantage. Then she thought about commuting to work on a sweltering Friday night, a Tube train full of party people heading out. The music and the gin eased the words *fuck it* into her mind. 'Thanks.'

The cab sped towards the river, passing Ministry of Sound; it took her back to her uni days: stumbling out of there with her housemates, the place they saved for really big nights – birthdays and breakups. The post-club ritual, searching for food, fags and a night bus. Fifteen years that'd passed in the blink of an eye. She wouldn't know what to do in a nightclub now.

The traffic was mostly heading the other way, out of town,

but everything snarled up around Borough Market. Lydia looked up from her phone and watched the people drinking on the pavement outside the bars and restaurants clustered under the tracks coming out of London Bridge. A few feet from her window, a girl in a floaty dress and red lipstick, chatting and laughing with a boy in skinny jeans and a T-shirt so tattered it had to be designer. The streetlights caught the sheen of sweat that coated their faces. Music came from everywhere at once, different tunes but the bass beats all merging into one, like she was hearing the city's pulse. A middle finger to the terrorists that'd run amok there the summer before.

A chime from her phone made her look down again. The video attached to the email had finished downloading and started to play. Lydia turned the screen to make the picture landscape and saw a Tube carriage being filmed through the emergency door of the connecting one. Two men were standing over a third, some kind of argument in progress. There was no one else in the shot. The man was shrinking into his seat, the other two clearly the aggressors. The train was in motion, and it was outside, not in a tunnel. From their gestures, it looked like they were telling him to come with them.

It carried on that way for a few seconds, then one of them punched the man in the face. It snapped his head in the direction of the camera, a spurt of blood leaking from his mouth. The picture moved sharply and the screen went black, a finger covering the lens – as though the person filming recoiled in shock. When it came back, it took a second to focus again, and the image was shaky now.

The victim got to his feet, but as he did, the taller of the two attackers hit him again, and the other slapped something over his mouth. They bundled him back onto the seat and pinned him there, one with a hand clamped over his mouth and nose, the other pressing his forearm into his throat. Lydia scrolled the video back five seconds and brought the phone closer to see. This time she saw it was duct tape they'd stuck over his lips. The strike that preceded it wasn't a punch but a thumb jabbed under the victim's Adam's apple, causing him to gag. It made her reach for her own throat.

She let the video play on. The victim flailed, tearing at his own face and the hands covering it, the weight of the two men on top of him keeping him in the seat. They were unmoved, staring at him as they pressed down with all their force. The man bucked a few times more, his eyes bulging, then his movements sputtered out until finally he was still.

One of the attackers glanced around, spotting the camera as he did. He grabbed the other one's arm and pointed, and Lydia felt a small well of panic, as if she was there. The image went haywire, whoever was filming it taking off with the camera still recording.

Lydia looked up and realised they'd come to a stop outside the office. The cab driver was turned around in his seat staring at her, as if he'd just asked a question.

'Sorry?'

'I said, are you alright?'

She glanced at her phone again, the screen reverted back to the email text now the video had finished. She hit the button to lock it. 'Yeah, I'm ... How much do I owe you?'

'Company account, miss.'

She blinked and put her purse away. 'Of course. Sorry.' She grabbed some coins from her pocket for a tip. 'Thanks.'

She climbed out at the foot of the tower and looked up, skyscrapers filling the night with coruscating light.

The lift sped her to the thirteenth floor. The indicator panel cued memories of the proposal that went round at the start of the year, suggesting the building be renumbered so there wouldn't be a floor thirteen. One of the country's leading media organisations, still riddled with superstition. People reaching for comfort in mumbo jumbo because the world was changing too fast for anyone to keep up.

She scrolled through the inbox on her work phone, trying to prioritise tasks for the night, but details from the video kept coming back to her. The victim's leather document bag, tumbling from his grip as he got to his feet. The man with the tape's long-sleeved black top, worn at the height of summer. The otherwise empty carriage. She surprised herself with how much had stuck from one viewing. The image of him struggling against the hands over his face was the most vivid of all. When she closed her eyes, it was right there.

She couldn't think who would send her something like that. Or why. The Internet was full of violent crap, but anyone who knew her knew she was repulsed by that sort of thing. None of her friends ever shared stuff like that on their WhatsApp groups, and even if it was just a gross-out thing, why the anonymous sender address? Still, it felt too random for spam.

Arriving at her desk, she checked her own phone again, then dropped them both by her keyboard and logged on. Straight to her inbox, new emails stacking up: a publicist trying to set up a 'candid' shoot with his reality TV star in Barbados; a reply from a former *X-Factor* contestant offering a threesome story; a pdf of an article about Prince William clipped from an

American scandal rag, a note underneath from her boss: *Make something we can use out of this.*

She slumped back, tilting her phone towards her but staring right through it. Twelve months of this shit already.

Early 2017, she'd stumbled into the biggest story of her life – and it swallowed her whole. It started with a Freedom of Information request about section 106 affordable housing provision on a luxury development in Camden. The paperwork that came back was mundane, but under scrutiny opened up a new line of questions. It proved to be the start of a breadcrumb trail that eventually led to at least three well-connected individuals who were likely to have profited from social housing exceptions negotiated on the deal – including the former deputy mayor for planning, a close confidant of James Rawlinson, recently departed mayor of London. The sums were six- and low-seven-figure amounts, but the opaque scheme employed was one that could be replicated on any similar development in the capital, and it had been, on dozens of projects just in the last decade. It went like this: as part of planning approval, developers were required to designate a percentage of the build as affordable properties – or make a cash payment in lieu. The big developers hated the policy because every affordable home they had to provide was one unit fewer they could sell as a 'luxury' London flat on the open market – denting their potential profits. Responsibility for agreeing and enforcing section 106 provision lay with local authorities normally, but on large enough developments, the decision could be referred to City Hall. On all the projects Lydia had identified, the rules had been loosened significantly – or even waived – through just that process. From everything she could glean, there was no justifiable explanation for why that should've been the case – leading Lydia to suspect that someone at City Hall was taking backhanders. When even a loosening of the rules could be worth more than a million in additional profit on any given development, it was hard to conclude otherwise.

She lodged similar FOI requests on eight projects in Camden, and made an approach through back channels to speak off the record to the former deputy mayor in question, Peter Goddard – now special adviser to Rawlinson's parliamentary bid. She worked eighteen-hour days poring over hundreds of pages of documents, begging help from experts who could guide her through the legalese generated when public policy met property legislation, in the process confirming her understanding that the exceptions granted were unjustifiable. The trail even led as far as various offshore investment vehicles, which she suspected were used to hide such illegal payments. She inched it closer to a story she could stand up.

The bosses beat her to the punch: early summer, a call out of the blue from the editor's number two, telling her to drop all of it. She'd argued her corner but couldn't shift him an inch. The biggest story of her career, canned in a forty-five second internal call. No explanation was offered.

Lydia did as she was told for a week; then she started digging again, urged on by Tammy Hodgson – the paper's no-nonsense investigative reporter, and her mentor-turned-friend. Working under the radar, the paperwork piled up, but the evidence did not – the secrecy around offshore companies stopping the trail dead. And no one at City Hall would talk to her. It came to a head when she confronted Goddard as he stepped off a plane at London City Airport – a stupid shortcut borne of desperation. He'd no-commented his way past her, and the next morning Stephen Langham was at her desk to tell her she'd been reassigned to the showbiz team. He'd handled her with kid gloves, but it hurt like hell anyway. More so because she'd screwed herself over through sheer frustration.

So now she spent her nights doing grunt work for the Botox Twins. A glorified assistant, appointed to dredge the digital gutters for click bait for the paper's website. Keeping it live through the night for the all-important American audience. She'd have given the bosses what they wanted and quit, if it wasn't for a bank account that was already on life support.

She went back to her monitor, continued picking through her emails: a retired footballer touting the details of his own affair. Monthly figures: traffic numbers going backwards in the UK and only just holding steady in the US. More pressure about to come from above, probably more job losses.

She brought up the video again, steeling herself to watch it on the monitor. A rustle came from the speaker and she realised there was sound; she plugged her headphones in and restarted. Mostly it was just the noise of the train – but as the blood spurted out of the man's mouth, the person recording cried out in a foreign language. She slid the bar back and listened again – a woman's voice, maybe Eastern European. Panicked, horrified – swear words at a guess. She watched the video through to the end, the bigger screen providing unwanted clarity: the look of helpless terror on the man's face as he suffocated, the dawning realisation that he was powerless to stop it.

It made her feel sick inside. She had the same thought she had whenever there was a senseless death in the news – overwhelming sadness for the people left behind. Whoever this man was, there would be someone who cared about him whose whole world had just been shattered. But seeing it happen in real time, with such disregard, brought on a bitter sense of anger as well.

There were two additional seconds at the end she hadn't seen first time, the footage mostly a blur as the woman taking it fled the scene. But as she ran, there was a flash of something Lydia recognised. She scanned back slowly, the still shot she wanted of the carriage floor only visible in a handful of frames. She paused on the least worst of them and leaned close. Then she got up and jogged across the office.

It was sparsely populated, only a skeleton staff in place once the first edition of the paper had been put to bed. Row after row of empty desks and black-mesh ergonomic chairs, captured in the forensic glare of overhead strip-lighting. There was a pile of newspapers on a bank of desks in the sports department. The one she was looking for was folded over on the top – that evening's *Standard*. She unfurled it as she zipped back to her desk, certain she was right. She held it up next to her monitor to confirm it: the newspaper in her hand was the same edition as the one on the screen.

The *BBC* had nothing, nor the *Guardian, Mail* or any of the wire services. She jumped onto Transport for London's website but there were no incident reports; most of the lines had shut down for the night, and those running the Night Tube showed no delays. A note on the contact page said the press office provided an out-of-hours service for urgent queries. She dialled the number and waited, hearing it click from a landline dialling tone to a scratchier mobile one. She brought up Google while it rang, flicking back to the email to see if there was anything to identify the video for a search.

A man answered. Lydia briefly described what she'd seen, but it was obvious this was the first he was hearing about it. He pressed her for more details, serving only to highlight how little she actually knew, and finally took her number so he could usher her off the line with a promise to look into it.

She tapped her nail on the desk, the still picture on the screen blurring as she let her gaze slip out of focus. Beyond the monitor, floor-to-ceiling windows reflected the office back on itself, only the red lights capping the skyscrapers piercing the black glass. An attack like that on the Tube, and no one had picked up on it. There were CCTV cameras everywhere; the men in the video acted without hesitation, and gave no outward impression of anger or impetuousness. If they were that calculated, why take a risk like that? And who was the victim to warrant that risk?

Her work mobile rang, vibrating into life on the desk. The number was withheld.

She snatched it up. 'Hello?'

'Lyds, it's me.'

Tammy.

'Did you get my email?'

'The video?'

'Yeah.'

'You sent that?' Lydia said. 'Why the anon—'

'Did you watch it?'

'Yeah. Yes. Are you alright?'

'Alright?'

'You sound a bit shaky.'

'I'm fine, I'm just ... Can you talk?'

'Yeah. What am I looking at here?'

'I meant in person. Can you get out?'

'Now? Where are you?'

'I'll meet you in front of the building in five. Okay?'

'You're outside?'

'I will be.'

Lydia glanced around the empty office, unsettled. 'Okay.'

She spotted Tammy across the plaza, standing against the inside flank of one of the pillars at the base of the office tower opposite. Her hair was coming loose from a ponytail and she was holding a cigarette. A flicker of guilt reared up at seeing her there; it was nine months since the paper had let her go in the last round of layoffs, and Tammy was still out of work. Coming out of the building, security pass clipped to her belt, it felt like the fact she still had a job there was rubbing it in her face.

Lydia offered a smile as she got close. 'I thought you gave up, missus?' She grabbed the cigarette from her hand, took a drag, and whipped it away across the plaza, the taste reminding her why she'd quit herself.

Tammy followed the orange tip with her eyes as it hit the concrete and rolled away down the gentle slope towards the street. 'It was so easy the first time, I thought I could do it again. Seems not.'

Lydia came around in front of her, a hand on her arm. 'Are you OK? What's going on?'

Tammy pushed her hair out of her face. 'You watched the video?'

'Who are they?'

'I don't know the killers.'

'Okay. But...?'

'The victim.' She looked up, meeting her eyes. 'I met him three days ago.'

'What the hell?'

'He contacted me a couple of weeks ago saying he worked in finance and had information on money laundering – would I be interested? He didn't give much away. I mean obviously I was, but I wasn't sure if he was serious or a timewaster, so I told him he had to meet me in person. I was a bit surprised when he turned up, to be honest.'

'Who is he?'

'He wouldn't say. He told me his name was Joe and he was a banker. He'd obviously done his research, because he asked me about my work on the Panama Papers leak and the financial crisis in 2008 and all that stuff. After that, I was the one doing all the talking, so I was thinking about sacking him off, but then he said he had inside knowledge about the biggest money-laundering scheme out there.'

'Jesus. And did he?'

'He talked around it. I think he was feeling me out.' Tammy turned sideways and pressed her back against the pillar.

'"Inside knowledge" – so that means he was involved.'

'I suppose.'

'Then why was he looking to come clean to you?'

She shrugged, shaking her head. 'The only thing I can say is that he looked like he hadn't slept for a year. I mean, he was smartly dressed and everything, but he honestly looked on the verge of a breakdown. Maybe the pressure...'

'Did he give you anything to go on?'

She shook her head again. 'We agreed to meet next week. He swore he'd elaborate and bring some evidence with him – that was my condition.'

Lydia puffed her cheeks up, blowing out a breath. 'And now this.'

'Someone didn't want him to talk.'

'Seriously? You think that's what this is?'

Tammy opened her hands, signalling her uncertainty. 'Either way, I didn't want to risk putting you in danger, hence the cloak-and-dagger stuff with the email and—'

'What, are you saying you're in danger?'

'No, no, not that I know of. But the timing makes me very nervous.'

Lydia steepled her fingers in front of her mouth, twisting her head to glance around. 'This is nuts.'

'I know.' Tammy opened her bag and took out a packet of Silk Cut, then seemed to forget she was holding them. 'It happened tonight.'

'Yep. Somewhere on the Northern Line.'

'You worked that out?'

'The pattern on the seat fabric.'

Tammy nodded in appreciation.

'You don't know where though?' Lydia said.

'No.'

'What about the police?'

'That's next. I'll take them the video.'

'Where'd you get it from?'

'Facebook. It was in one of those local groups, The Finchley Network. It was posted there...' She trailed off, as if she was embarrassed about something.

'You don't live in Finchley.'

Tammy hesitated, running her hands over her cheeks before she spoke. 'I've joined loads of them, all over London. They're good for finding stories. Local-interest stuff is easier to pitch sometimes.' Her face flushed as she said it, and Lydia looked away, pretending not to see. Tammy Hodgson had been a minor legend in the newspaper industry, at the forefront of some of the biggest journalistic investigations of the 2000s. Now she was reduced to trawling local Facebook groups for stories.

'I nearly dropped my glass when I recognised him,' Tammy said. She flicked her nail back and forth over the corner of the cigarette packet, building to something. 'The thing is, no one's reporting this yet.'

Lydia caught her meaning. 'You know I'm still stuck on the showbiz desk...'

'So? This looks like a professional hit on the Tube.'

'Then you should write it up. That's got to be worth a few quid.'

'If this guy was telling the truth, there's more than a one-off piece here.'

'And if he wasn't?'

'Either way, there's too much work for one person.'

'Tam...'

Tammy pushed herself off the pillar and circled around to face her. 'No one wants to look twice at a fifty-three-year-old woman. Every interview I go to, I'm in a waiting room with kids willing to work for nothing. I'm applying for jobs I was doing fifteen years ago and I get told I've got too much experience. I can't afford not to work, Lyds, and this is my chance to get back in. But I can't do it on my own.'

Lydia held her stare, the desperation in her eyes eating her up.

'Please?'

CHAPTER 2

The day's penultimate job was an easy one, comparatively. He'd ordered things that way. The self-help manuals he used to read would advise tackling the hardest tasks on your list first; fine in theory, not so easy when there were lives at stake.

So that came next. For now, Michael Stringer had the home of London Assembly member Nigel Carlton in his sights. A nice semi on a nice road in Finchley, the streetlights casting the bay windows in amber relief. He'd done business in worse places.

His skin itched, waiting. Carlton had arrived home ten minutes prior, the house unlit before that. Stringer's information was that Carlton's wife was in Brussels for business – a regular occurrence, in his estimation the cover for an affair. Not Stringer's concern in this matter, but professional rigour wasn't something he could just turn on and off.

Ten minutes was just long enough. Carlton had showed up in a cab, so the chance of anyone else arriving separately was slim – but not zero. A mistake he'd made once before: on that occasion, Stringer had tailgated a target into his flat after watching him arrive alone, only to have the man's secretary let herself in minutes later with her own set of keys, just as he was getting to it. Transpired the woman and the target took separate cabs from their office to keep their trysts under wraps.

But ten minutes was enough time to discount that possibility. Any longer ran the danger of a takeaway order showing up, or even the target leaving home again – a late-night urge for a bottle of Pinot or a bag of coke, or who fucking knew what.

Stringer rang the doorbell. The hallway light went on, and then the door opened without a sound. Carlton looked him over, the caution in his expression fading when he took in the wiry man in the charcoal-grey suit on his doorstep. Stringer didn't immediately speak.

'Yes?' Carlton said.

Stringer raised the blue plastic document wallet in his hand. 'We need to talk about these.'

Carlton squinted. 'Sorry, have we met? Who—?'

'The girl you've been emailing is fourteen years old. Did you know?'

'What? What girl?'

'Jennifer Tully – Jennycat18@hotmail.com. Her Facebook picture is her with glitter all over her face; I'm told it's something the kids are into these days. If you swore to me she was eighteen I'd probably believe you, but I wouldn't bet my career on it.'

Carlton dug into his pocket, produced his phone. 'I'm calling the police.'

Stringer waited, staring at him doing nothing. 'Well? You don't need my permission.'

'I don't know ... Look, you've got your wires crossed somewhere so why don't you bugger off before...' He swiped the phone to unlock it.

'"Assembly Member". That your title?'

Carlton looked up.

'Awkward as honorifics go, so I'll use Nigel. Nigel, have a listen to some of this.' Stringer dipped his head, mimicking reading even though he had it memorised. '"I've been thinking about you all night, I couldn't help myself, couldn't sleep ... I can smell you on my shirt and I just want to eat you up ... I haven't felt this way about anyone since I was a teenager ... I don't know what's come over me."' Stringer handed him the email printout, pointing to the sender details at the top. 'That's you, yes?'

Carlton skimmed the page, his mouth coming ajar. 'I've never … This is not me. I've never seen it in my life, I've never heard of this girl...'

'Let's go inside.'

'Who the hell are you?'

Stringer jutted his chin. 'Inside.'

Carlton backed up, staring at the printout as if he could wish it into thin air.

Stringer made his way down the hall and into a large kitchen, the rest of the house in darkness. The room was centred on a walnut-topped island unit and was straight out of a design catalogue: black bi-fold doors to the garden, brushed steel fridge, gleaming pans hanging above the counter. A cooker that looked like it'd never been lit. A faint smell of cleaning products.

Stringer took two glasses out of a cabinet above the sink and filled them with water. He set one down for Carlton and watched him inch down the hall, flipping the page to read the full email trail as he came.

'I've been hacked.' Carlton looked up, his face as pale as hypothermic flesh. 'Where did you get these?'

Stringer pushed a glass towards him. 'Word of advice: no one buys "I've been hacked" anymore. You're supposed to use WhatsApp for this shit, Nigel. Snapchat.'

Carlton set the sheet of paper on the counter, the spotlights in the ceiling so bright it gave off a glare. 'I've never seen any of these emails. Those are not my words, these are fakes.'

Stringer sipped his water. 'You didn't give me those, so where else would I have got them from?'

'How the hell should I...?' The penny dropped. 'The girl?'

He frowned in confirmation.

Carlton rubbed his face. 'Who are you?'

'That's irrelevant.'

'No it fucking isn't. Why are you doing this to me?'

'I'm just a fixer.'

'Then who are you working for?'

'You're asking the wrong questions.'

As he brought the glass to his mouth again, Stringer's shirt cuff gapped, flashing the melted skin on his arm. Carlton snapped his gaze to the counter, his discomfort a sure sign he'd noticed. Ten years ago Stringer would have made something of it; now he put the glass down and let his hand fall to his side. Not embarrassment; just taking away the distraction. 'The question you need to ask is what am I going to do with these?'

'I'm not having this.' Carlton snatched up his phone again.

Stringer took out his own mobile and tapped the screen twice, Carlton's phone vibrating a second later when the message came through. He stared at the image, his eyes flaring wide.

Stringer pointed to the picture, upside down from his viewpoint but more than familiar. It appeared to show a man and a girl at the start or end of an embrace. 'As you know, that's Jennifer Tully.'

'No ... no, I don't know her...' Carlton screwed his eyes shut, a memory coming back. 'She dropped her purse, I picked it up for her and she gave me a hug. A thank-you thing, I was as surprised as anyone. I was on my way into Pret, for god's sake.'

To Stringer, the snap looked too professional – the image a higher resolution than the average phone camera could manage, a red flag to anyone paying attention. But Nigel

Carlton was a newborn baby, wiping his own shit out of his eyes in the harsh new world he found himself in.

'There's a dozen emails here, Nigel, and the photos. My guess is the *Standard* will put you on page five, but you might make the cover. And then the nationals will grab it, and that will be that. Fourteen years old ... Christ.'

Carlton deleted the picture, visibly shaking. 'This is a bloody setup.'

Stringer took his time putting his phone away, then stretched the silence to breaking point, taking a sip of water. 'On Tuesday of next week, you'll meet a gentleman named Jonathan Samuels at an office in the city. You'll get a message telling you exactly when and where. Mr Samuels will have some suggestions for you to take back to your colleagues on the planning committee.'

'What do you want?'

'That's Mr Samuels' business. Miss the meeting and the story goes to the papers that afternoon. Speak to the police or anyone else about this and copies of everything go to your wife.'

Carlton planted his fists on the island. 'No one would believe this of me. Least of all my wife.'

Stringer put his hands in his pockets, calling time on proceedings. 'You sure about that?' He moved closer to Carlton. 'Absolutely sure?' He stepped around him and made his way out of the house.

The car was a hotbox, nowhere for the day's heat to go when the night wasn't much cooler. Stringer got behind the wheel and looked at the picture of Carlton and the girl on his phone.

For a second he felt pity for the man, but he let it go with the reasoning that it was on-the-job-training for a rising pol with ambitions of getting to parliament. Based on what he'd seen tonight, Carlton wouldn't make it anywhere close.

He checked his messages and opened Google maps. He'd overstayed at Carlton's, but he'd left slack in the schedule to cover that eventuality. He allowed his thoughts to turn to the next job – the envelope in the boot – and felt his guts lurch for the first time in years. The reasons were many, or so he'd convinced himself, but sitting there in the silence of the night, there was only one that mattered: it was the first time he'd worked for a killer.

The client was a reclusive Ukrainian financier, Andriy Suslov. Implicated in at least two suspicious deaths over the years, Suslov had the worst kind of connections. His instructions had been straightforward: rake up every piece of dirt Stringer could find on a London-based high-finance whizz named Jamie Tan. He didn't say why, and Stringer wouldn't ask – he never did. It was a standard sort of job, made exceptional only by the client.

He worked it for three months solid. Regular in-person surveillance on Tan, combined with a full data trawl into every nook of the man's life. He hacked his emails and his phones. He got a peek at his bank accounts. He ran background checks as far back as he could get. The picture he got was contradictory but unenlightening: a work-hard, play-hard city boy with a recreational cocaine habit, who went to church with his wife most Sundays and gave generously to an eclectic array of causes – Cancer Research, WWF, CAFOD – figure them guilt-payments for his lifestyle. Seeing Tan in person, there was nothing to mark him out as a target for this kind of gig. A man who wore sober navy suits and had his hair trimmed every two weeks. Quick to laugh, a face padded with puppy fat that belied his forty-two years. Wealthy, yes, but a pauper compared to Suslov – surely ruling out simple extortion as the client's motive.

Now, it all came to a head. Suslov's front man had called that morning: 'Today's the day' – reveal your work to Tan, make him understand that we own him now. Tell him further instructions will follow.

Stringer acquiesced without enthusiasm. Most of his gigs boiled down to money and power, but as serious as they were, no one died. Putting Tan in hock to Suslov, to unknown ends, felt like crossing a line. And the danger wasn't just to the target; he couldn't shake the thought that if Tan played it smart and ran to the authorities, the easiest way for Suslov to stay buffered was to eliminate the messenger – keeping his deniability watertight.

And all that was without thinking about his fuck-up. A slip of conscience that he still couldn't explain or understand. One that left him vulnerable.

He checked his route to High Barnet station, the point he'd intercept Tan on his way home. Google said it was twenty minutes away. Stringer pressed himself into the seat and took a deep breath. He let his mind drift, taking him to Islamorada in the Florida Keys. He'd holidayed there once, before this life, and he held on to the idea of going back someday. The water was so blue and so still there, on a cloudless day you couldn't tell where it met the sky. It used to be a simple escape fantasy – sitting in the sunshine with a large drink and nothing to do. These days it was darker; in his dreams, he imagined drinking up his courage all day on the white sand, until there was nothing left of himself to save, and he could stand up and walk into Florida Bay and just keep going. The water over his head, filling his lungs until it dragged him down into its depths. Finding closure in the place his life came apart.

It came and went. But some days, the only thing stopping him was the thought of all the people he'd have to kill before he'd allow himself to do it.

CHAPTER 3

The Tube crawled into Woodside Park station in the dead of night. The line ran above ground this close to its terminus, but it felt airless all the same.

Lydia was alone in the carriage. She picked her way along its length looking for bloodstains or any sign of violence. It was pointless, she knew that; knowing the video was shot on a Northern Line train did little to pinpoint anything. There were more outdoor stations at the northern end of the line than the southern, so she went that way first, but even that only narrowed it down to two branches and more than a dozen stops.

She started on the High Barnet branch, the one that ran through Finchley – a possible connection given the Facebook post. But even if she'd picked the right branch, there might be ten trains per hour running in each direction. She felt foolish being there, but her loyalty to Tammy trumped it – and was bolstered by her guilt.

No one ever said they'd got rid of Tammy because she'd encouraged her to keep working the Goddard story after the bosses shut it down. Tammy herself never hinted at it. Looked at objectively, she'd been an obvious candidate for redundancy:

commanding a big salary on the wrong side of fifty, at a time when all papers were slashing budgets and moving away from investigative work. But the timing felt more than coincidental – Tammy gone three months after they'd sidelined Lydia to showbiz. It felt like a vindictive move on the part of management – and it meant Lydia owed her.

The doors slid open but there was no difference in temperature inside or out, the night close and still. For a moment there was silence. She ducked her head out to look along the platform, but no one got on or off. No one waiting. No staff. A southbound train was slipping into the distance on the other side, blue sparks lighting up its undercarriage, marking its wake.

Back inside, she could see a man at the far end of the next car. She watched him for a few seconds, seeing no outward signs of life. She landed on the thought that it could be her victim – sitting there, dead or dying, somehow missed until now. He was huddled in on himself, head hanging, the kind of bloke you gave a wide berth – maybe a way to explain why he hadn't been disturbed. If they'd assumed he was just another drunk...

The man moved, making Lydia jump. He looked in her direction, holding her stare as her heart crashed against her chest. Then he turned the other way, half rising, the faltering movements of someone trying to work out where he was. He sat back down on the seat and rubbed his face.

Lydia closed her eyes and let her head loll back against the glass panel behind her. *Get a fucking grip.* The doors closed and the train moved off again.

She made it to the end of the carriage as they pulled into High Barnet. An empty Lucozade bottle rolled off a seat and clattered to the floor, snagging itself on a discarded *Standard*.

She looked through the window into the night and wondered what the hell she was doing. The driver came over the tannoy – tinny, muffled – to call all change.

The yellow tint to the platform lighting gave everything a jaundiced hue, feeding her sense that she was walking through a surreal dream. There were half a dozen new emails on her work phone – the time difference to the States kept them coming right through the night – to add to the pile already in her inbox requiring an action or a response. That was on top of the four sidebar articles she was supposed to upload by dawn; thousands of words of dross about celebrity holiday snaps.

The platform was an island, another train already waiting on the other side. She crossed over and walked alongside it, peering through its windows. She saw an older woman with wet hair, looking like she was on her way to an early shift; a man with paint marks on his work clothes; a city type in a pin-stripe suit. A stain on the ground drew her eye – a dark spatter across the white lettering that read *MIND THE GAP*. She toed it and saw it was dry.

She carried on to the end of the platform where the driver was standing outside his cab.

'Excuse me—'

'Leaves in three minutes.' He lifted his chin to indicate the dot matrix overhead.

'Actually, I wanted to ask about an incident earlier tonight. Did you hear anything about an attack?'

He screwed his face up. 'Where? Here?'

'Somewhere on the Northern Line.'

He was already shaking his head. 'News to me.'

'They'd notify you though – about something serious? We believe the man might have been murdered.'

'We who?'

'I'm a journalist with the *Examiner*.' She took out her phone and opened the video. 'I was sent this footage—'

He put his hand up and stepped back. 'I'm on a timetable, love. Ask them upstairs about it.' He pointed towards the station building, then slipped into his cab and shut the door.

She looked along the empty platform towards the staircase. A covered footbridge across the tracks led to the ticket hall. In her line of sight, a CCTV camera extended from the wall on a short bracket, spikes like needles sticking up from it to keep the birds off. The Underground staff at London Bridge had blanked her when she'd asked her questions, the same as the one at Camden Town. If the victim had been left on the train, chances were he'd have been found here or at Edgware – but surely a major incident would've been declared. So it seemed certain he'd got off somehow – or been taken off. But that didn't mean there'd be no trace.

She crossed the platform back to the train she'd arrived on and walked along until she found who she was looking for: a cleaner, moving carriage to carriage with a clear plastic bin bag and a grabber.

She waited by the door for her to step off. 'Excuse me.'

The woman stopped.

'There was a man attacked on a train tonight. Have you seen anything?'

'Like a fight?' She spoke with a clipped Caribbean accent.

'Yes, but serious. I'm thinking about blood on the seats or the windows or anything?'

The woman started moving again, stepping onto the next carriage. 'We get all sorts.'

Lydia followed a few steps behind. 'But tonight?'

'Tonight, I don't know. Go and ask the control room.'

'Does that mean there was something?'

The woman stopped and turned around, squeezing the grabber's claw open and shut by her foot. 'Please, I finish in ten minutes, I have to do this. Go and ask.' She turned and carried on.

Lydia stepped off the train and checked her phone – first for the time, then for emails; the latest was one of the digital subs chasing her copy. At the end of the platform, a pigeon pecked at a discarded Subway wrapper, spilling it onto the track and scaring itself enough to take flight. She jogged over to the stairs.

Stringer noticed her straight away. Passengers were sparse enough at that time of night, so the lone woman stepping off the train only to linger on the platform caught his attention. He kept one eye on her as she went over to talk to a driver. It'd been hours already, all that time trying to smother the rising tension in his gut.

He'd waited almost ninety minutes for Jamie Tan at High Barnet – but he never showed. He'd taken the precaution of putting eyes on him – Angie Cross, his runner, confirmed he'd left the pub next to his office near Bank just after 10.00 p.m. and gone to the Tube. When there was still no sign by midnight, Stringer raced to his house, on the off chance he'd missed him. Finding the place empty, he'd gone straight back to the station to keep watch while he figured out what was going on. He'd put in a desperation call to Angie, kicking himself for not getting her to follow Tan all the way home. She was in the dark.

So this anomaly almost brought relief – a chance to do something other than wait. He watched as the woman tried to show the Tube driver something on her phone. For a second he wondered if she was lost, asking for help reading a map on the screen, but the driver couldn't get away from her fast enough, and now his instincts told him to get a closer look at what she was doing.

Stringer took a picture of her with his mobile, but the distance and the light made it grainy. He'd guess her age as mid-thirties, light-brown hair worn in a ponytail, probably no more than shoulder length when down. She had a knee-length skirt on and a grey blazer over a navy blouse – professional clothes, but too neatly turned out to have been worn since the start of a nine-to-five; a point to chew on later if she proved to be relevant.

The woman took off across the platform and started speaking to a cleaner, disappearing from view when she stepped onto the train. He kept watching, seeing the other train leave and wondering if there was any chance Tan would show up on the next one to pull in. His concentration kept slipping, running through excuses and explanations he could offer to Suslov.

She got off again a moment later and nipped along the platform to the staircase. He moved away from his perch by the windows in the ticket hall and went around the corner so he could watch the top of the stairs, holding there until she popped into view again. She took big strides walking across the footbridge, coming in his direction, glancing around as if she was looking for someone.

She tried the ticket office but it wasn't manned. Checking around, she zipped over to a door marked *Staff Only* and knocked on it. An Underground worker in an orange hi-vis vest opened up, and she launched into him about whatever she wanted. He watched as she talked, assessing her as rushed but not frantic. Too harried to be police, not enough to be a friend or relative. Which left ... what?

He moved closer, staring at his own phone as cover, until he could just hear what she was saying.

'...an assault? Do the CCTV feeds from the trains come here?'

The hi-vis man folded his arms. 'Sorry, but I'm not going to stand here and discuss—'

'Can I just show you this?' She already had her phone up so Hi-Vis could look. 'Please?'

Stringer lingered a short distance away from them, looking distracted, as if he was waiting for his turn to ask the Underground man a question. At first he couldn't see her phone's screen, but suddenly Hi-Vis reacted to something he'd seen, tilting his head just enough to give Stringer an angle to get a glimpse. His skin went cold. Even at a distance, he recognised Jamie Tan being pinned to his seat.

Hi-Vis was shaking his head. 'It's got to be a prank.'

The woman shrugged, uncertain. 'You haven't heard anything about this then?'

'There's no way someone did that tonight. They'd shut half the network down.'

That seemed to derail the woman, and she looked away from Hi-Vis into the open doorway next to him, scratching her throat.

'Someone's mucking you about. Sorry.' He retreated into the office and closed the door.

The woman hesitated then put her phone away, moving off

as she produced another one from her pocket. She read something on it, swore under her breath, and turned down the stairs to the platforms.

Stringer let her have a few seconds' head start, then followed.

CHAPTER 4

Lydia finished typing the night's last story at 7.00 a.m., a fluff piece about Lottie M's latest beach break, her words just wallpaper for all the bikini shots, and a boxout on 'How To Get the Look'. Another Trump tweet was making headlines across the board, and it was no consolation knowing her article would get a higher billing on the website than the president's latest display of ignorance. Celine, the more senior Botox Twin, was fond of saying they were in the business of 'giving the readers what they want'.

She went to the communal kitchen to make a coffee. What she wanted was a glass of white wine. Waiting for the kettle, she picked up her phone and found Tammy's name on her recents log. She pressed call.

Tammy picked up on the second ring. 'Hey.'

'Didn't wake you did I?'

'No, I never made it to bed. My brain won't stop.'

Lydia launched straight into her dash to High Barnet. Daylight had been streaming into the office for a couple of hours, a disorienting effect that made the night before seem even more like a fever dream.

Tammy took a breath before she spoke. 'You're saying none of them know anything about this?'

'Nothing. Everyone I spoke to looked at me like I was mad.'

'Explains why no one's reporting it yet, at least.'

'Yeah, I've been keeping an eye too. What did the police say?'

'The British Transport Police are looking into it, but it was the first they've heard about it. Whoever Joe the banker is, no one's missing him yet.'

'What about the witness? The woman who shot the video?'

'Christ knows, poor cow.'

'They went after her, Tam. If they caught up with her...'

'Yeah, I know.'

Lydia picked up her coffee and headed back to her desk. 'What's her name?'

'I haven't got it to hand, I'll have to check Facebook again. I'll text you.'

'Have you tried messaging her?'

'First thing I did. She hasn't replied.'

'So what's your next move?'

'I want to go back over my notes from when I spoke to Joe – see if he gave away anything about himself that I missed. I'm struggling to concentrate though.'

'You should get some sleep, even if it's just an hour.'

'I will. Later.'

'Look, just ping me the woman's name and let me know if you hear anything from her. I watched the video again, and it freaks me out every time that guy looks down the camera.'

'Yeah, I will. And Lyds – thank you. I know you've got enough on your plate, I really appreciate what you're doing.'

The *Examiner* homepage was open on her screen, the top story a reality TV star in lingerie, headlined, 'Undie-believable!'

'No problem.'

The morning was bright and hot as Stringer made his way back to his car at High Barnet.

He'd followed the woman on the Tube to London Bridge. She'd been glued to one or other of her mobiles the whole journey, both iPhones, but favouring the white one that she'd showed to Hi-Vis. The train had been nearly empty, the woman sitting alone on her bank of seats, meaning there was no way Stringer could get close enough to see without being conspicuous. His frustration nearly boiled over a couple of times. He looked at his reflection in the black mirror of the Tube window and wondered what the fuck this job was doing to him.

When she got off, he'd trailed her as far as one of the new office towers that had sprung up in the footprint of The Shard. She passed through a security gate in reception and that was where he let her go, sticking around just long enough to note that the lift took her to the thirteenth floor and that there were three visible CCTV cameras in the lobby; enough to deter him from talking to the receptionist to determine the woman's name.

He flagged down a black cab and spent most of the ride back to his car Googling. It'd taken seconds to establish that the building was the home of *Certified News & Media* – owner of the *Examiner* and its trashy website, and a host of regional newspapers to boot. Which suggested the woman was a journalist of some stripe – a complication that didn't make sense from a host of angles. He'd trawled the corporate website looking for her, but there were no staff headshots to browse, so her identity remained unknown a little while longer. All the while, he'd kept an eye on the *Examiner's* main page for anything that might pertain to Jamie Tan – but if the woman on the thirteenth floor knew something concrete, she hadn't shared it so far.

When he picked up the car, he went straight back to Jamie Tan's place in Arkley. The house was one rung below a mansion: red-brick new build, Roman columns flanking the front door, a large gated driveway that homed an E-Class Merc and a Lexus LC with space to spare. The place had to top two million, even this far out of town.

Stringer looked along the windows, watching for movement inside. He'd been here before – only a handful of occasions but long stretches each time. The Lexus was Mrs Tan's, so its presence on the driveway was of note. A natural blonde ten years Jamie's younger, Alicia Tan had been a rising star in her own right at the American investment bank Cawthorne Probert – a role she'd seemingly given up when Jamie's career as an equities trader went stratospheric. That was three years ago, long before Stringer had ever heard of Tan, so this was all from his background work; but from everything he'd learned about her, she seemed too smart and too driven for a shift down into the role of gym-and-gin kept woman. The couple had no kids, so that couldn't explain the sudden end to her career, and a cursory sweep had turned up nothing to suggest she'd been forced out in disgrace. A low six-figure salary that doubled with a bonus wasn't easy to just ditch, no matter how rich they were. It was the kind of anomaly that cropped up in every life if you looked hard enough, but one that hadn't seemed germane at the time. Now, everything would be second-guessed.

He found a link on ExaminerOnline.com touting their tip hotline, and called the number from his throwaway. It rang for more than a minute until a man answered. 'News desk.'

'Yeah it's about that incident on the Tube. I heard there was a reward going or something?'

'Sorry, what?'

'A reward. That attack last night. I've got information.'

'You've lost me, mate. What attack?'

'On that guy, really nasty. One of your lot was asking the staff at High Barnet about it. You pay for tips, right?'

'Yeah, but ... look, can you hang on a minute?'

He heard the man shout across the office: 'Anyone know anything about an attack on the Tube?' Hold music came over the line – Pachelbel's *Canon*. Too soft and too optimistic for the moment. He waited, eyes on the house, the smell of pine oil coming to him – the trees lining one side of the property baking in the direct sunlight.

The line cut in again. A new voice – a woman, breathless. 'Hello?'

'Yeah, hi, who am I speaking to?'

'I'm one of the reporters here. My colleague said you know something about the attack last night?'

'They found out who he is yet?'

'I can't ... Sorry, were you a passenger?'

'I don't want to say.'

'What's your name?'

'Richard. What's yours?'

'Lydia.' A stunted breath, impatient. 'Can we start with what you saw?'

He brought his other phone up, Googled the name in conjunction with the *Examiner*. 'Just, you know, that fella being ... I mean it was sickening.' A list of results came up, a mixture between Lydia Wright and Lydia Sampson-Mills.

'Did you get a look at the men who did it?' she said.

He hit the images tab, scanned the results and tapped a picture from the top row. 'Yeah. You know, actually, I think this is a bad idea. Sorry.' He cut the call.

He stared at the image, a profile picture from a LinkedIn page for Lydia Wright. The woman wore her hair down and her face was fuller, but there was no doubt it was her. Even the blazer she wore looked to be the same. The latest entry on the profile listed her as a Showbiz & Ents reporter. Jamie Tan had no connection to either world.

His other phone vibrated with an incoming call. The one he'd been expecting: Suslov's man. He let it buzz four more times while he got his lies in order.

Then he answered. 'Yes.'

'I thought I'd have heard from you.'

'Why?'

'"Why?"' A hesitation. 'Is everything alright?'

'Did you call for a chinwag?'

'What? You know why I'm calling. What the fuck is this?'

'You gave me a job to do; let me do it.'

Another hesitation, startled this time. 'The job was last night. It's almost nine a.m.'

A movement in the house drew his eye; looking over, he saw Alicia Tan opening one of the upstairs windows. She was wearing a white vest top, her hair ruffled enough to be straight out of bed. 'Did you think it was open and shut? This stuff is messy.'

'What does that ... Something went wrong?'

Her image became a silhouette behind the frosted glass window one to the left – he assumed an en suite off the master. 'Admin. When it's over, I'll be in touch. Don't call me before.'

He hung up and dropped the phone in the console, jammed his head against the seat.

CHAPTER 5

Lydia's flat smelled of Thai. Saturday morning, the blinds doing little to stop the sunlight streaming in. She laid awake on her bed, time-fucked like she was jetlagged. She had the window open because of the heat, so it was as if every car and moped and bus passed right through her bedroom. But after two years in the flat, Tottenham's street sounds were like white noise – wasn't that keeping her from sleep.

She sat up and reached for the wine glass on her bedside table, drank off the last mouthful, fine with it because it was just a drink after work. The Thai was her flatmate's takeaway from the night before, but it had her craving one now. Ten o'clock in the morning, the taste of warm Sauvignon in her mouth, cereal and toast the last thing she wanted. Tired, wired, a thousand thoughts running through her mind.

Stephen Langham's WhatsApp foremost among them: *Are you awake?*

She looked at her phone, the message received half an hour ago. She plugged it into the charger and rolled back onto her pillow. The anonymous tipster call nagged at her. Nothing about it felt genuine, and her first thought was another paper had got a whiff of the story and was on a fishing expedition.

But who would've known to try her or the *Examiner*? Unless the caller was ringing around all the papers to glean who knew what – but that sounded a bit keen for a hack on a night shift. Still, it was naive to think she'd have the attack to herself indefinitely. Especially if it was true the video originally came from Facebook. Her searches hadn't turned up any sign of it, but that meant nothing.

Her phone buzzed. Stephen again: *Look out the window*.

She sat up, a smile curling the corners of her mouth. She crossed the room and split the blinds. He was leaning against the window of the Costa opposite, a takeaway cup in each hand. The only man on the street in a suit, handsome as fuck. He saw her looking and tilted one of the cups towards her – as if her answer was in any doubt. She let go of the blind and grabbed the wine glass to stash in the kitchen on her way to the front door.

When she caught her breath afterward, she slipped off him and the bed to retrieve the coffees from the floor by the doorway. Hers was lukewarm when she took a sip through the plastic lid.

Stephen shook his head when she offered the other one to him. Lydia set them down on the bedside table and went to pick up her clothes.

Stephen followed her around the room with his eyes. 'Are you OK?'

'Yeah. Why?'

'Seems like you've got something on your mind.'

'I'm just tired.'

'Sure?'

'Sure. I didn't get any sleep.'

'Sorry about that.'

'No, you're not.' She jabbed him gently in the ribs as she sat down next to him. He grinned, propping his hand behind his head.

'You always do that,' she said. 'I'm starting to think it's Freudian.'

'What?'

'You don't have to hide it away.' She held her ring finger up, gesturing to his.

He brought the hand out from under the pillow and waggled his fingers at her. 'Seriously?'

'I'm just saying I know it's not your style.'

'What? Marriage?'

'Yeah.'

'You'd run a mile if I turned up with a ring.'

She turned away, shaking her head. 'You don't know that.'

'Hold on, it's never exactly been your style either.' He gathered the sheet around himself and sat up. 'What's brought this on?'

She shrugged. 'Lack of sleep?'

He laughed. 'No, come on.'

'This thing...' She pointed to him and then to herself, flicking back and forth between them. 'You know I'm not in it for the money. It's not about climbing the ladder.'

'I know that.'

'I've never asked you for anything. Right?'

'Right.'

'Okay.' She slipped into a T-shirt in silence. 'Maybe I just wanted to hear you say it.'

'Why? What's going on?'

She stood up again, drifting across the room towards the window. She nudged her yoga mat against the wall with her toe, another new leaf from last year that'd gone untouched since she switched to night shifts. 'Sometimes I feel like I've boxed myself into a corner. I can't come to you in the office because it looks like I'm sleeping with the boss for the sake of my career.'

'To who? No one knows about—'

'To me. I have a hard time justifying this to myself sometimes.'

'I've never thought of you like that. The idea never entered my head.'

'I have.' She brought her hands to her chest. 'That's how it feels to me.'

He pulled his briefs on and put his arms around her waist. 'Things will change at the office. People have short memories.'

'How short? I swear to god, it feels like I'm losing it some days. I've written about every coked-up, manufactured nobody in this country.'

He pressed his lips together. 'I know. Look, they know how good you are, they'd have got rid of you if they didn't. And they've got me telling them.'

They again. 'I'm thirty-four years old and skint. I worked my backside off to get to where I did, and I never cared about the hours and the money and the fucking cavemen in that place because it was worth it. You couldn't pay me enough to do what I'm doing now.' She ran her hands over her face, breaking away from him. 'And now it sounds like I'm doing exactly what I just said I wouldn't.'

'You can vent without me thinking you're angling for something.'

She let her hands drop and met his eyes, nodding. 'I know. Sorry.'

'When I go in to bat for you, it's because you're an asset to the business. Things got screwed up – politics, whatever you want to call it – you are where you are; but I promise you it will come around again. It always does.'

He came to her again, and she kissed him softly on the lips. He reached down to pick up his trousers. 'Are you on tonight?'

She nodded.

'You want to do something tomorrow?' he said.

'Yeah – sleep.' She pulled a face to show she was half joking.

He smiled, pulling on his suit jacket. 'Message received.' His eyes dropped to the desk and she realised the teacher-training application pack was right there next to her laptop. If he noticed it he didn't say; he kissed her on the forehead and slipped out. She listened to his footsteps on the stairs, then went to the window to see him hit the street. She didn't hear him close the front door – never did; it made her uncomfortable to think how practised he was at this kind of thing.

She perched on the edge of the bed and picked up her phone, sleep now a lost cause. She scrolled through the BBC headlines, seeing nothing about Tammy's story, distracted, wondering whether she believed her own words to Stephen. Thinking about the lies we tell ourselves, and the things we want to be so – and the truths our actions reveal. Lack of sleep making her thoughts run fuzzy, the voice in her head someone else's.

She jumped around the web – *The Mail*, Facebook, Twitter, TfL – drew blanks all around. She brought up the video and watched it again, the victim's face too pixelated to be clear, but his desperate expression as he thrashed and bucked no less unsettling for it. She found herself wondering if the tape over the mouth held a significance beyond just cutting off his air.

Outside, one end of a shouted phone conversation rose above the traffic noise as the caller passed under her window. The woman was speaking Pashto or Farsi, the words accented with hard edges that jarred Lydia into action. She tapped a message to Tammy – *Any joy with the name?* – and went back to the video.

She paused it when a reply came almost immediately.

Yes...

She stared at the little notification bubble, waiting.

The phone starting ringing. 'Tam?'

'Thought I'd call, easier than trying to type it. Paulina Dobriska. That's the original poster.' She spelled out the surname.

Lydia grabbed a pen and scribbled it down. 'Okay, cool. Has she come back to you?'

'No. And the video's gone too.'

'Gone? As in taken down?'

'Must've been. It's not there anymore.'

Lydia pressed the pen against her cheek. 'Might be a good sign. If she's using her Facebook, at least we know she's still out there.'

'Unless someone made her delete it.'

Neither of them said anything for a second. Lydia shut her eyes and told herself not to let Tammy's fervour for the story colour her own judgement. 'Look, for all we know, the video got reported and Facebook took it down, or she just thought better of it. We shouldn't get carried away here.'

'Maybe.'

'So what now?'

'Hassle the transport police and Transport for London. I get the impression they don't know much themselves, and I doubt they'll tell me even if they do, but unless and until this Dobriska gets in touch, I haven't got much else to go on. Are you working today?'

'Tonight.'

'Okay. Do me a favour and keep an ear to the ground, will you? I still can't find any mention of this anywhere, even the locals – I don't understand it.'

'Well ... I think someone's got a whiff. I had a call last night, felt like someone was fishing for details.' She told her about the supposed anonymous tipster.

'Shit. OK, you don't have any idea who it was? The *Standard* are all over anything to do with the Tube. I keep assuming they'll get a whisper. It wasn't Fergal Lynch from their mob?'

'No. Definitely not a voice I recognised.'

Tammy breathed out hard. 'He's not silly, though, he'd put someone up to it. I'm going to write up what I've got. Could you test the water at your place – see if there'd be any appetite?'

Lydia's first thought was to go to Stephen, an impulse at odds with her little speech to him before; she dismissed the idea, annoyed with herself. 'I don't know – it feels a bit early. Write it up first, see where we are then.'

'Yes, of course. You're right.' The sense of deflation wasn't hard to detect in Tammy's voice. 'I'll talk to you later.' She was gone before Lydia could offer any words of reassurance.

She looked at her phone, the paused image visible again now the call screen had gone. It was frozen on the moment when the attacker had first noticed the camera, the man's black eyes looking right down the lens. Unease settled in her stomach like mercury pooling: what if it wasn't another paper calling the office earlier? What if the fake tipster was staring her in the face?

Stringer used the rearview to watch Alicia Tan on the back seat as he drove. Everything was firing inside him now; not panic, more the heightened awareness that came with high-stakes improvisation.

She'd thrown on light-blue jeans and a cream blouse and carried them off like they were couture. She made eye contact with him twice, but went back to her phone screen each time without speaking. He noted details: she had a dusting of freckles across her nose, a feature she'd concealed in the older photographs he'd seen; her left eye exhibited a slight droop; she didn't bother with her seatbelt.

She looked up again. 'How long, please?'

His mobile was in a prop holder on the dashboard, an Uber decal stuck across the top of it. He tapped the map to bring up the summary. It showed their destination as Jamie Tan's office in the City. 'Saying twenty-five minutes.'

She lifted her phone to her ear and waited, pointing a haunted gaze out the window. 'Jamie, it's me. I got your email and I'm in the car you sent. For god's sake will you call me. I'm trying to stay rational here but...' She held the phone in front of her, the microphone to her mouth as if to say more. But then she hit the button to hang up. She slipped the phone into her bag and let go of a breath.

The email that he'd sent, from Jamie Tan's account. A snap decision born out of his own sense of guilt and obligation.

Snatching her based on an instinct, but one that her reaction seemed to validate: she was in danger.

In truth, the flat was thirteen or fourteen minutes away. He would've preferred longer to get his story straight.

CHAPTER 6

Paulina Dobriska's Facebook picture was of a woman Lydia pegged as forty, but could've been ten years either side. A crop of the original photo, Dobriska's head was leaning to one edge of the image, as if it was pressed against someone who'd been cut out. She was smiling, the drink in her hand, the pose and the lighting making it look like a snap taken on a night out.

Lydia skimmed the profile; only the public information was visible, and it was light on detail. It said she lived in Whetstone and was originally from Warsaw. No employment or other details were shown. The five photos on display were selfies, solo shots all – three in bars or clubs, the other two seemingly taken in parks or similar. Lydia sent a friend request on the off chance, then sent her a direct message as well, mentioning the video and asking her to get in touch.

The part about Whetstone stood out. It was the penultimate stop on the Barnet branch of the Northern Line, and a theory formed: Paulina Dobriska goes out for drinks on a Friday night and then makes her way home late, getting caught up in this horrific situation. And if that was the case, it narrowed down the possible crime-scene locations – somewhere between East Finchley, where the line popped out of the tunnel for the last time, and the terminus at High Barnet.

She went back to the profile and scrolled further, but it was just as bare: her last post was from 2016, a semi-automated thing saying she'd been watching *Love Island*, and before that a series of profile picture changes dating back to 2014 – the ones Lydia had already seen.

She pulled up Google and searched the name. The Facebook page was the top hit, followed by links to various websites in Polish. She clicked through two pages of results, not really reading them, then switched over to the images tab. The profile pics were there, surrounded by a slew of Internet junk, no apparent connection to the other hits – people on beaches and soft furnishings and a small crowd and a dozen other irrelevances. The woman had barely left a mark. A search of an online database that scraped details from the electoral roll came up empty.

She pushed her hair back and felt sweat in her hairline, the room starting to bake. Spotify was open in the background so she turned a playlist on and maxed the volume so she could hear it in the shower. She went along the hallway, passing Chloe's bedroom. The door was halfway open, the smell of green curry at its most potent there. Two plastic tubs were sticking out of a takeaway bag in the wastepaper basket – the flat had no living room so Chloe had taken to eating on her bed when she wanted to have a night in. A sparkly top was slipping off the bed to join a pair of black jeans on the floor; a Friday night outfit, but there'd been no sign of her when Lydia arrived home at nine that morning.

She carried on to the bathroom and set the shower running, then stood under the water, thinking about the call at the office, the man who'd hung up on her. If it was another journo fishing he would've kept her talking longer. She tried to recall the specifics: the man had hung up right when she'd asked if he got a look at the attackers. As if he was spooked. And before that…

Before that he'd asked for her name.

She snapped her eyes open. The shower curtain was moving. She whipped it across, revealing the empty room she knew would be there but needed to see anyway. Shampoo stung her eyes as water cascaded onto the lino, puddling by the toilet. She turned the taps off and snatched her towel from the rail to wipe her face. The curtain was still flapping, steam causing it to billow gently as it rose to the ceiling.

She left wet footprints on the carpet going back to her bedroom, brought up Google as soon as she got there. She typed 'Lydia' and '*Examiner*' into the search box. There she was, right at the top of the results.

She killed the music and stepped back from the computer, her name on the screen seeming to pulse.

CHAPTER 7

Saturday night and the streets around London Bridge were teeming; there were crowds all along the approach to the station, and the narrow road outside the pub was a stationary file of Range Rovers and Uber Execs, queuing for the drop-off point outside The Shard. Stringer could make out the main entrance a hundred metres distant, the outside coated with white lights as if to give the impression the whole thing was a manifestation of pure incandescence – rather than an investment vehicle owned by a Gulf state even the Saudis called extremists.

A phone call earlier that afternoon established Lydia Wright's shift started at midnight – an overeager colleague only too happy to provide details. His watch showed 11.00 p.m.

now. He'd been there forty minutes already, making sure. Patience was a fundamental requirement of the job, but the sense that avenues were closing every second was putting his under strain. He'd spent a good part of the afternoon beating himself up for not staying on Wright when he'd had the chance that morning. But still the question of how to go about matters tore at him.

His phone vibrated, the same caller it'd been all day: Suslov's man ignoring his instruction to wait for him to call them. He put it in his pocket, feeling it stop and then immediately start again.

He was stationed in a pub over the road from Wright's building. A window seat looked out across to the lobby, the brightly lit reception as vivid as a TV screen from his vantage point. There was only one man visible at the desk: a black guy who looked barely out of his teens. Money or force could get Stringer past him easy enough, but the cameras were another proposition, as was the prospect of what waited for him on the thirteenth floor. Stepping out of the lift into an office full of witnesses was amateur hour.

His phone buzzed once more, a message this time. He took it out.

You will be collected from home at 10.00 a.m. Mr Suslov expects a positive debrief.

He swore under his breath. He started to type a reply, stopping and starting again. Finally he gave up, accepting that anything he said now would only make things worse.

He glanced at his watch without needing to, already doing the sums. Eleven hours to work with, less the travel time. More avenues closing off. He looked up at the building again; dim lighting showed on every floor, but the thirteenth glowed like a beacon, daring him to fuck things up worse than they already were.

He'd moved back onto the street by the time Angie showed up at ten-past. She brought supplies – a bottle of water and a packet of Mini Rolls. He ate them two at a time. He'd slept for one hour out of the last forty-eight and now it was starting to tell. If the cavalry had been anyone else, he'd have asked her to bring a gram of coke too.

'How come your shit's always middle of the night?' she said.

'You bring coffee?'

'No – do you know any twenty-four-hour Starbucks?'

There was mischievous humour in her face, but that wasn't what he was checking for. Without the glitter, she looked older than in the picture they'd used to create Jennifer Tully's Facebook profile for the Carlton job, but even so he figured she couldn't be older than early twenties. He'd asked her once, and she'd lied and said she was twenty-eight, so he'd never seen a point in repeating the exercise.

What he couldn't see were blisters on her mouth or fingers, and her eyes were clear. She seemed level. She clocked him looking her over, so he made his thoughts explicit. 'Good.'

She rolled her eyes. 'Been clean four months. I told you, I'm done.'

He nodded, taking his wallet from his pocket, the old conflict rearing up in him again. When he'd first met Angie Cross she was the favoured trick and sometime punching bag for a corporate-insurance big shot with more habits than his salary or health could sustain. It made the man an easy target, and Stringer had taken him apart penny by penny over a period of months. Angie was an unintended consequence; the man had been her main source of income, the severity of the beatings she put up with at his hands evidence of her dependence on him. 'Occupational hazard' she'd called it, in answer to a question Stringer had never asked.

He'd found he couldn't just walk away. He siphoned off what he could of the score to keep her afloat, but by the time he'd paid his clients, it was only a cut of a cut, so he'd resorted to finding jobs for her to do. The conflict came from what she might spend the money on; among the various physical and psychological scars the cunt had left her with, a crack habit was the most immediately debilitating – one he'd apparently nurtured to keep her coming back to him.

Stringer counted off five twenties and passed them to her. 'I'll go the same again when the job's done.'

She took the notes and folded them. 'You're three quid short. Costcutter take the piss this time of night.' She pointed to the empty tray of Mini Rolls in his hand. He flipped his wallet open again, but she was already putting the money into her jeans, giggling. 'Don't be a twat, I'm winding you up.'

He shook his head, trying not to smile, and opened the bottle of water to take a sip.

'So ... what's the plan?' she said.

'Wait until she shows.'

'Which is when?'

'About now.'

She leaned forward to look up at the office tower. 'How long you been here?'

He took a drink of water and watched the approach.

When he still didn't answer, she said, 'Isn't there an easier way to do this? Can't you get an address off the Internet or whatever?'

'The fuck do I know about ... I'm not a hacker.'

'No, I know, but people sell this stuff, don't they? Personal details and that. The dark web – I thought you'd have a contact.'

In fact he had two – but the moves he was making now were better kept out of those circles. 'Someone with public profile's a different story, but she's a nobody. This is the quickest way.' That part was true.

And then, there she was. She had her hair down, a different skirt but the same grey blazer on, and it had him wondering if it was her favourite, or just the only one Lydia Wright owned. Journalists earned next to nothing, and he wondered if that was a sign she'd be susceptible to a payoff if things went that way. He nudged Angie, but she was already following his gaze.

'Pretty,' she said.

True to form, Wright was walking towards her offices studying her phone, the light from the screen a white glow on her face. He couldn't tell if it was the one he needed, but she had a handbag on her shoulder as well. He nodded his head in her direction. 'We're on.'

Angie took off in a fast walk without saying another word. He watched as she raised her phone to her ear and started jawing as if she was having a row with someone as she went. One strap of her bag was already off her shoulder.

Wright didn't raise her eyes once. Angie was a good actress; she looked back just before impact, yelling into her phone as if she was oblivious to anything but her own conversation. Then she steamed right into her.

Angie sent herself sprawling, the contents of her bag scattering all over the pavement, her phone skidding off the kerb into the gutter. She got to her knees quickly, hands flailing and mouthing apologies.

Lydia Wright had stayed on her feet but quickly crouched down to check on the other woman. Angie was on all fours now, making a mess of scrabbling for her belongings. Wright took her own bag off her shoulder and set it on the pavement so she could try to help.

Angie got to her phone and cranked up the histrionics, playing up a crack in the screen. A passing couple stopped to see what was going on, one of them gathering up lipsticks and coins for Angie, only adding to the confusion. He saw Lydia Wright say something to Angie, and then she moved around her to help pick up the rest of her stuff. She only turned her back on her own bag a second, and that's when Angie dipped it.

After that, Angie found her composure with lightning speed. She grabbed up her stuff, apologised again, and moved off down the street. Stringer lost sight of her even before Wright had started walking again. He waited a second, watching the journalist as she looked around, dazed, before she carried on towards her office.

The car was two streets away, a shortcut around the back of Guy's Hospital taking him there, dark pavements washed in blue when an ambulance passed behind him, making him quicken his pace. He hit the unlock button on the fob and as the car lights flashed, Angie stepped out from behind the bin shed of a low-rise council block over the road. She darted over and whipped the door open. 'What took you so long?' She slammed it shut before he could reply.

He climbed behind the wheel. 'Got them?'

She put a purse and a mobile phone in the console, then handed him a second phone, the screen lit. 'This one was unlocked, I kept it open.'

He picked up the iPhone Wright had been using coming down the street and recognised it as the white one she'd shown to the Tube staff at High Barnet station. 'Good work.'

He went straight into the photo library. The most recent item was a video, dated to the day before. He pressed play.

Angie started to say something but he didn't catch it. Jamie Tan was on the screen, the image of him fighting for his life shutting everything else out.

CHAPTER 8

Lydia waited for the lift in the empty reception area. All the marble and chrome had an oppressive quality at night; coupled with the uncharacteristic silence, it made the place sombre and ominous. Colliding with the drunk woman outside played into it; the initial shock had passed, but her nerves were still jangling.

The lift doors opened and she stepped inside and pressed the button for the thirteenth floor. As they closed she reached into her bag for her phone.

It was gone. She set the bag down and spread it wide, digging right to the bottom. She remembered having her phone when she left the station, had it in her hand when...

Her work phone was gone too, and her purse. 'Shit. Shit, shit, shit...' She jammed the button to go back to the ground floor, just as the doors opened on the thirteenth.

She stepped out and then back in again, caught in two minds

until the door obstruction alarm sounded. She stabbed the button for the ground again, holding it until the doors closed. She couldn't think what the woman looked like. Dark hair, dark jeans, dark eyes...

The lift opened and she ran out across reception, drawing a look from the night man on the desk. 'You alright, miss?'

She carried on through the exit to the street, warm air enveloping her as soon as she stepped out of the aircon. She stood there, looking towards London Bridge station, then the other way towards The Shard. There were people drinking outside the pub opposite, chatter and laughter carrying over the queue of traffic, every other girl with dark hair and dark jeans. She took a few paces towards the Tube and stopped, turning around the other way as if she was unravelling. People swarming around her in either direction, oblivious.

'Fuck.'

She called the police from her desk. She changed her email, Facebook and Twitter passwords while she was holding for someone to answer.

She flushed when the first thing they asked was if she'd set up the Find iPhone app; another piece of life admin that she'd never got round to. They gave her a crime reference number and advised her to check her home contents insurance to see if she was covered. They said they'd look into it, but that they had to be realistic about their chances of finding the thief. 'Your purse might turn up in a hedge or a skip in a couple of days – they normally only keep phones and cash. So it's worth keeping your eyes open. Cancel your cards anyway, of course.'

She'd done that even before calling them.

She sent an email to IT, reporting her work phone stolen, and went to the kitchen to make coffee. Chris Barton wandered over from the sports desk. 'I'll have a brew if you're making one.'

She took another mug out of the cupboard and threw a teabag into it.

'Everything alright?'

'Just had my bloody phones nicked.'

'What? Where?'

'Right outside. And my purse.'

'Jesus.' He folded his arms and leaned against the counter. 'Druggie or kids was it?'

She picked up the kettle and poured. 'Don't know. I think just drunk.'

'You hurt or anything?'

She shook her head. 'I feel like an idiot. The girl bumped into me and dropped her shit all over the place. I was trying to help her.'

He tutted, reaching for his tea and looking at something on his phone. 'Nightmare. You must be shaken up.'

'I'm fine. Just pissed off.'

He took a sip and turned to go, fully concentrating on his mobile now. 'Well let me know if there's anything I can do.'

She rinsed the teaspoon under the tap, staring at his back. 'You're welcome.'

She took her coffee back to her desk and spilled it setting it down. She flopped onto her chair and folded her arms, letting her head fall back and staring at the ceiling.

The video, the phone call, now this. Did linking the three make her paranoid, or was it paranoia making her think like that in the first place? She unlocked her PC and it came to life on her inbox, at least twenty emails unopened. One stood out but only because the subject line was all caps: KARDASHIAN SCOOP OF THE YEAR – WATCH NOW.

She ignored it and brought up Facebook, looking at Paulina Dobriska's profile again. No reply to her friend request or her DM. She went over to the Finchley Network's page; it was a closed group, but the information listed it as having over three thousand members. She hovered over the *Join* button, but the thought of jumping through more hoops just to be able to look took her irritation over the top. Why the hell did the group need to be private anyway? Instead she sent a DM to Tammy: *Can you send me your phone number asap pls?*

Tammy answered after a few seconds: *? You lost your phone?*

Lydia typed a one-word response. *Mugged.*

The reply was instant. *WTF? 07958 824154.*

Lydia snatched up her landline and punched the numbers in.

'Lydia? Are you—'

'I'm fine, I'm fine. Some bitch pickpocketed me while I was trying to help her.'

'Christ, I'm sorry. Did they get much?'

'Purse and phones. It was right outside the fucking office.'

'You're not hurt?'

'No.'

'Oh thank god. Do you think it could be connected?'

'No.' Lydia rubbed her face. 'I don't know. Did you speak to anyone else about this?'

'Apart from the police, only you.'

Lydia cradled the phone with her shoulder and pressed her knuckles into her thigh. 'Listen, I want to have a look inside the Finchley Network. Can I borrow your Facebook login? I don't want to waste time trying to get them to let me join the group.'

'Sure.' There was a pause, then Tammy started reading out a username and password, and Lydia grabbed a pen to note it down. 'What are you looking for though? The video's gone.'

She entered the login details. When Tammy's newsfeed came up, it felt like she was sneaking around someone else's house. 'It's like you said, Paulina Dobriska's the only witness to this that we know of. There's got to be a way to find her.' She clicked on the Messenger icon and saw two DMs Tammy had sent trying to make contact. The second made mention of the video. Dobriska hadn't replied to either, and somehow the silence felt ominous. 'You forgot about someone.'

'What do you mean?' Tammy said.

'When you said this was just between us and the police.'

'Who?'

'Paulina Dobriska knows you're on her case as well.'

When Tammy hung up, Lydia clicked on the groups tab and went into the Finchley Network. A search for instances of Paulina Dobriska's name threw up two results, neither promising – a comment about a traffic scheme and a recommendation for a local dentist. She clicked on the second and perked up when she saw the context. The original commenter was asking for recommendations, and someone had then tagged Dobriska into the thread – just her name as a comment, no explanation, as if it would be something she'd naturally be interested in. Dobriska had replied with the name of a clinic shortly after.

Lydia switched over to Google and searched the clinic's name. The results page showed its location on the map – near Finchley Central station – alongside what looked like its official website and various other local directory listings for the same place. Underneath was a selection of Google Image results, and one looked familiar. A group shot, but she couldn't place it. Then she looked closer and recognised Paulina Dobriska's face poking out from the back of the crowd. She clicked the link and it took her to the same clinic's website. The photo was a cheesy corporate shot on a page titled, 'The professionals at Premier Dental Care'. The caption underneath named each person shown. She realised then it was the photo that had come up when she'd first Googled Dobriska.

She flexed her fingers and jumped back to Facebook, clapping her hands together when she saw the comment was only a few weeks old and that she had Paulina Dobriska's likely place of employment.

Her elation sagged almost immediately. Premier Dental was closed on Sundays.

CHAPTER 9

The video was as bad as Stringer feared. An attempt on Jamie Tan's life, captured in digital clarity. The assailants unknown to him.

'What the fuck is that?' Angie said.

He snapped his head up, bringing the phone to his chest. In his rush he hadn't noticed her looking, hadn't even given her a thought. He looked sidelong at her, nudging his shoulder with his chin as he tried to process it all. 'Nothing.' He put the phone in the console, reached for his wallet and pulled out all the notes inside, dropped them in her lap. 'Here, you did well.'

She stared at him. She gathered the notes in her hands, fanning them to count. 'What's this?'

'A bonus.'

'There's like ... five hundred quid here.'

He started the engine and put his hand on the wheel, glancing at his watch. 'Where do you want dropping?'

'Just get me away from here. Other side of the river.' Her voice was washed out as she said it and she was staring a hole into the side of his head. He refused to look at her again.

He pulled off and took back streets away from Lydia Wright's offices. 'The police won't be doing anything, you don't have to worry about them.'

'I'm not. It's the look on your face.'

He said nothing, eyes wide and locked on the road. It was all running through his head. Who took the video? Where did the journalist get it from – and so quickly? Who'd she share it with—?

He braked and pulled over to the kerb, a Prius behind beeping as it had to swerve around them. He got his phone out and refreshed the *Examiner* website, trying to remember the last time he'd checked it.

'Mike?' Angie waved her hand in his peripheral vision. 'Mike? Hello? What the fuck's got into you?'

He scrolled down but there was no mention of the video. A very minor victory that might not hold. He picked up the stolen mobile again and sent the video of Jamie Tan to his throwaway via WhatsApp, deleting the sent message and the contact details as soon as it was done. 'I'll take you home. Where're you staying?'

'With a mate in Kilburn. You don't need to take me all the way, just get me to somewhere on the Jubilee.'

'Give me a post code.'

'I don't know the address, I'm just crashing. Go to Kilburn Tube, I can show you from there.'

He nodded and typed it into the sat nav. He didn't say it was less to do with chivalry than his worry that she'd find a dealer and blow the money he'd given her.

Angie guided him to a stop outside a scrappy row of terraced houses, the other cars around them parked half on the pavement. The road was darker than most, three of the streetlights out overhead.

She put her hand on the dash. 'Thanks for the money. Is there more coming up?'

'No. Job's finished.'

'Six hundred quid just to get a phone and a purse?'

'There might be something else on the London Assembly thing. *Jennifer Tully*. I'll let you know.'

She jutted out her lip and nodded. She reached out and tapped the stolen phone in his hand. 'There's an email in there. I think it's where that video you watched came from.'

He had the inbox open before she'd finished the sentence. She'd left the one she was talking about selected, a short message from what looked like an anonymous email account, the video attached. He snapped his eyes to Angie. 'Did you see the whole thing?'

She blanched under his gaze. 'I just thought you'd want to...'

'Yes or no?'

'No. I just thought you'd want to know. Fuck's sake, as if I care...'

He took a stunted breath. 'Seriously, tonight never happened. You forget all of it.'

'What're you worried about? Not like I'm gonna speak to the Feds, is it?'

The police were the last people on his mind. He reached across her and popped her door handle. 'Get some kip, I'll find you something else soon. Do me a favour and keep your head down for a couple of days.'

'Why?'

'Just because.'

She stared at him a long second and then got out.

He watched her cross the road and jink around a skip overflowing with old furniture, waiting to make sure she went into one of the houses. Once she did, he played the video on Wright's phone again. He let it run all the way through, but he wasn't concentrating, his head filling with questions, doubts, self-recrimination. Trying to order the moves he'd made and the moves he'd have to make. The vanishing chances they might've left Jamie Tan alive. The chance he might be next.

The video finished and he stared into the darkness outside the windshield. A ratty fox snuck between two cars and started tearing at a black bin bag left on the street.

He picked up Lydia Wright's purse and opened it to look for her address.

CHAPTER 10

Lydia split the night between working on two articles she was due to post and looking for another way to reach Paulina Dobriska. She combed the Finchley Network in forensic detail, going back through months of posts without finding another mention of her. She checked the members list, to find out who'd added Dobriska to the group and discovered it was the same user who later tagged her for a dental recommendation.

The woman's name was Amy Parker, and Lydia sent her a friend request and a DM too, from her own account, saying that she was urgently trying to get in touch with Dobriska. It was gone three in the morning when she sent the message. It felt good to have another lead out there, but Premier Dental was the one with real promise. Thirty hours until it opened its doors again. She imagined walking into the place, a tropical fish tank in the waiting room, the smell of diluted mouthwash – the dental surgeries of her youth – and finding Paulina Dobriska waiting for her. Looking embarrassed to be asked about the video, some kind of reasonable explanation for it all.

Something about that version of events left her deflated.

There was a haze almost thick enough to touch when she came out of Tottenham Hale Tube on her way home, the heat from a distorted sun boxing in the fumes from the bus station outside. The roads were quiet, even for that time of the day, and the water in the canal was still and stagnant-looking as she crossed over it; all of London too lethargic to move on a Sunday morning in late summer.

She reached into her bag for her phone without thinking. Its absence pissed her off all over again, but even that was fleeting now – tiredness smothering everything. She stopped to lean on the bridge's railing, looking at the black water visible in the gaps between the algae, trying to remember if she'd left any wine in the bottle yesterday, and where might be open to sell her a fresh one in case not. Then she remembered she had no purse, and she nearly shouted in frustration. A swarm of bugs shimmered over the bank, making her neck itch. Behind it, the concrete skeleton of another block of flats under construction stood silent.

Stephen crashed her thoughts, not for the first time. If he'd messaged her she'd have no way of knowing, let alone replying. The timing was bad – he'd think she was being moody because of the chat they'd had the morning before. Maybe even think she was sulking. They'd agreed at the start not to discuss anything personal over work emails, but a basic message telling him she'd lost her phone wouldn't breach that. She'd hold back the details for when she saw him in person.

She turned on to her road. The Turkish café was already doing good business, but the rest of her street was shut tight. There were three empty Corona bottles lined up along the kerb, the remnants of a Saturday night waiting to be put to bed for good. She took her keys out of her bag and slipped them into the lock, suddenly grateful for the small mercy; that whatever else that little shit had stolen from her, she hadn't taken away access to her bed.

Pushing the door open swept a pile of crap aside with it – takeaway menus and a minicab flyer. But there was something larger too, and it jammed against the wall. She closed the door, looked down, expecting a small parcel, and stopped dead.

Her purse was sitting on the doormat.

CHAPTER 11

Stringer went to work on Wright's second mobile just as daylight was turning the sky a murky grey. This one was black, an older model than the other iPhone and less well cared for. It was locked, but he held the home button down to activate Siri, then said, 'Mobile data,' into the speaker. It displayed the setting toggle for that option, and pressing it brought up the full *Settings* menu, bypassing the pin screen. It bemused him that people were willing to spend fortunes on a phone with a security flaw anyone with Google could discover.

It was quickly apparent it was a company phone. The last email she'd sent from her work account was at 7.07 a.m., so unless her IT department had come up with a replacement phone in the small hours of a Sunday morning, chances were she'd been at her desk until at least then. It validated his decision not to watchdog her overnight.

He couldn't find any trace of the Tan video on that phone. It looked like she hadn't sent it to anyone else within her company, and if that was the case, the story was contained. For now. That bought him time, at least – assuming Suslov didn't already know the truth.

There was no sign she'd forwarded it to anyone from her personal mobile, either, and he quickly deleted the original and its attachment. But there still existed the possibility that she'd downloaded the video to a desktop or laptop. Reading the email before he junked it, it became clear Wright had been unknowingly dragged into the Jamie Tan situation. He couldn't decide if that qualified as good luck, or outright fucking terrible, but if it meant she had no understanding of the wider context, it felt more like the former.

The sender was another question again. Their email said they'd call in a bit, and Wright's personal mobile registered an incoming call around thirty minutes after it was sent. The number was withheld, and chances were that was the sender making good on their promise. He started to think about ways he could crack their anonymity.

Alicia Tan hovered at the back of his mind. She was as safe as he could make her for now, but the arrangement had a short shelf life – too many questions he couldn't answer, too many lies already told.

At 9.00 a.m. he forced himself to shut out the other bullshit and focus on what would happen when Suslov's man picked him up in an hour. He raced around the North Circular to where it met the A1, then headed south towards Islington. The road dropped down from Highgate to Archway, and when he passed under Suicide Bridge, the skyline rose in the distance, faded and indistinct in the yellow haze.

The most pressing decision was whether he revealed the video or not. Either choice carried risk, but he veered towards no – at least in the initial debrief. Information was everything, and you didn't give it up until you could put a value on it. Accepting the risk that by then it might be too late. But if Suslov already knew what'd happened to Tan – maybe even orchestrated it – then he was leaving himself open to being caught in a lie.

He steered around Archway roundabout, the ugly tower

rising above the station covered in scaffolding and sheeting. Information flowed both ways: how much did he really know about Andriy Suslov? Despite being based in New York, the man eschewed publicity and hadn't given a press interview since the nineties. He'd never met him in person and they'd spoken only once, a phone call right back at the start of the job. Everything else had been conducted through Suslov's frontman, a shiny-faced suit who introduced himself as Dalton. Whether that was his Christian name or surname was never made clear.

Background details on Suslov were beyond troubling. He'd made his money in the Wild East era after the Soviet collapse, consolidating mining assets before establishing his own investment companies. He moved Stateside in the early 2000s and built up the private hedge funds that he still ran to this day. Best estimates put his personal wealth north of a billion dollars – the kind of client Stringer usually drooled over. But the rumours about him weren't hard to come by. A business rival who'd drowned in a boating 'accident' off the coast of Maine in 2003, and a murdered journalist who'd been investigating that death were the two most dramatic hints as to what he was capable of. The latter was gunned down on the streets of Moscow in 2006, amid speculation she was about to publish allegations of Suslov's involvement in the 2003 death. In the context of what happened to Jamie Tan, they weren't easily dismissed as smears anymore. And if these rumours were widely known, in his experience it meant there was always more under the surface.

But most worrying of all were Suslov's reputed ties to the Kremlin, via his friendship with Viktor Yanukovych, the former Ukrainian president that *Time* magazine called 'Russia's man in Ukraine'. Suslov had served as an informal adviser throughout Yanukovych's political career, and it was well known that the two remained close, even with Yanukovych exiled in Russia. US diplomatic reports branded Yanukovych's party a haven for mobsters and oligarchs; Suslov fit the bill on at least one of those counts.

Stringer swung the car into the underground garage. He'd always kept his home address closely guarded, but after their first contact, Suslov had sent a car to pick him up outside, unannounced – a show of power that had more of an effect than he would admit.

He took the lift to his flat on the seventh floor. It was quarter to ten, enough time to change out of a shirt clocking up its fiftieth hour, splash some water on his face. A shower was a distant dream. He stripped off his clothes and caught his reflection through the open door of the en suite across the room. The light from outside was coming at an angle that shadowed every ripple of the mangled flesh that ran from his wrist to the top of his back.

The Accident. Never spoken about, almost never broached in the years since. An instant that defined a lifetime. Aged twelve, his mother at the cooker, frying chips for dinner, Stringer buzzing around her. Whatever they were arguing about long forgotten, obliterated by what came next. The old man sweeping in from the pub, the same as always – Carling on his breath, fag smoke on his M&S suit. The 'quick drink after work' that always turned into half a dozen. A toss-up which mood he'd arrive home in – tipsy and cheeky, or drunk and angry. That day, the latter. Abi smart enough to vanish to her room when she read the signs, Stringer too full of early-teenage fire to do likewise. The escalation was fast – from 'Shut up, Michael' to the threat of 'a proper slap' in thirty seconds flat. Stringer feeding off it, pubescent anger that the world was against him. Telling his father to fuck off.

Knowing it was a mistake the second the words left his lips. The old man flying at him, his mother trying to get between them, always the peacemaker, Stringer half fury and half terror. And then—

And then scolding white pain. On the floor, in agony, his arm like it was on fire. Shouts of 'Jesus Christ' and 'Oh fuck'. His parents squabbling between themselves about whether to throw water on the burns, his mother shouting not to because it was oil and it would just spread it. His skin red, melting, burning – reaching for it but too afraid to touch it, his arm alien. Abi appearing in the doorway, her face ... her face in utter shock, a look he'd never seen before, making him panic even more. His mother wrapping wet tea towels around his arm, his shoulder, trying desperately to strip his T-shirt off but stopping when she realised it had been melted into his flesh. Chips scattered all over the lino, one next to his head still sizzling.

Abi on the phone dialling 999.

Afterwards the old man would say it was an accident. That he was protecting his wife from their rampaging son. That in the struggle they'd caught the pan's handle, tipping its contents over the boy. The old man stopped short of blaming him outright, but the insinuation was there – *you started it*. His mother telling social services the same – 'a terrible accident' – the social all too happy to buy that in light of Stringer's school record as a troublemaker. Bad shit happened to bad kids, close the file.

Stringer living with the truth all these years. He saw the old bastard reach for the pan. Thankful, eventually, that it wasn't worse; that it wasn't his face, or his mother or sister. But for years, through the surgeries and skin grafts, the painstaking rehab and beyond, feeling nothing but rage. His mother playing peacemaker for all time – saying she'd been facing the wrong way to see, but she knew her husband and there was no way he would've done that on purpose. In her mind, protecting her family.

Afterwards, the old man was different; less boozing, more withdrawn. No sense of what he was feeling – maybe shame, maybe just shocked at himself. Stringer resolved he'd kill him anyway, as soon as Abi was grown up. Years of silent fury. Then Mum got sick, and the old man got a reprieve through necessity. Stalemate; the rage never dissipating.

Stringer stepped out of view of the mirror. He pulled a fresh suit out of the dry cleaners' polythene and threw it on, grabbed his keys from the kitchen counter and went to the street.

The Range Rover was idling on a double yellow when he came out of the main entrance. As he passed the railings separating his development from the road, the rear door nearest the kerb was opened from the inside. Dalton was sitting on the back seat in a navy suit and red tie. He stared at Stringer, saying nothing and making no invitation to join him – the same tough-guy act he'd adopted from day one. Stringer walked over and climbed inside, the car moving off as soon as he closed the door behind him.

Dalton started to say something but Stringer spoke over him. 'I told you to wait for my call.'

'I did. And we heard nothing, so here I am. What did Tan say?'

Decision time. His lies, their lies. Stringer glanced out the window, watching the Tesco Express over the road as they passed. 'He didn't show.' He looked back to Dalton to catch his reaction.

'You missed him?'

He shook his head, slowly. 'He didn't show.'

Dalton silently mouthed the words. 'Thirty grand for "He didn't show"? So, what, you just packed up and went home to bed?'

Stringer leaned forward. 'Do I look like I've been to bed lately?'

Dalton leaned forward too. 'Yesterday you said it was just admin. That was your word.'

There was no guile in the man's eyes, no sense he was holding cards back; for all the world, it looked like he was in the dark. But that didn't mean Suslov was. 'I need to see the boss.'

'What for?'

'Tan didn't show and he didn't go home. There's...'

'So you did manage to do something then? Christ.' He ran his hand over his mouth. 'Where is he?'

'I'll discuss it with Mr Suslov.'

'That's the very last thing you want. I promise you.'

'I'll decide that.'

'Fuck you. You said *admin*. You implied it was done. You wasted twenty-four hours.'

Stringer braced his hands on his legs. 'Sit me down with him.' *So I can look him in the face.* 'Is he in the country?'

'Andriy travels frequently.'

Stringer stared at him, getting it. 'You don't know?'

'I'm not his PA. I don't need minute-by-minute updates on his movements.'

'Well, find him and get me half an hour of his time.'

'And what are you going to say to him? "He didn't show, sorry"?'

'I want to explain I did my job. And I want my money.'

'Are you fucking insane?' Dalton reached forward and tapped the driver's seat. 'Pull over, please.' He looked back to Stringer. 'You're deluded if you think he's going to hand over a single penny. If you had any sense, you'd pray he's on the other side of the world until you've got some answers.'

The car came to a stop and Stringer popped his door. As he climbed out, he turned around to lean inside again. 'I don't give a fuck who he is. I get paid.'

CHAPTER 12

Lydia woke up in the same position she'd fallen asleep. It was past four in the afternoon. Her ribs and shoulder ached, and she wondered if she'd moved at all while she slept.

A breeze rustled the blinds, a soft metallic sound as they scraped against the wall. Her purse was on the bedside table. She rolled onto her back and picked it up, holding it above her face to unzip it for the second time that day.

Not a single thing missing. A tenner, a fiver, and at least five more in coins. Her driving licence was tucked away behind the credit cards, her address there for anyone to find. The same question that was plaguing her before she'd passed out still lingered: had someone found it and done the Good Samaritan thing by returning it? What were the chances of anyone travelling from London Bridge all the way to Tottenham Hale to return a purse – and so fast? At best, they'd hand it in to a police station.

So this had to be a message. Some wanker with a subtlety bypass. Who nonetheless had her listening out for sounds in the quiet flat. All she could hear was the traffic noise on the street and the scraping of the blinds.

She climbed out of bed and pushed her hair out of her eyes. She turned her laptop on and went to the kitchen to get a drink. Chloe's door was ajar but she wasn't in there. Lydia poked her head inside; her blinds were open and the bed was made so she must've been and gone at some point. She tried to think the last time she'd seen her flatmate – Wednesday? Tuesday?

In the kitchen she filled a glass of water at the tap and flicked the kettle on. Opening the cupboard for coffee, all she found was an empty jar of Nescafé. She shuffled the cups around on the shelf to get to the other jar, but there were no teabags either. She let the cupboard door swing shut and left the kettle boiling.

Back in the bedroom, the laptop was open on the login screen. She tapped in her password and waited for it to come to life, her fingers straying to a pile of paperclips in the desk drawer, unconsciously searching for something to do in one of those moments when she'd normally reach for her phone.

She clicked the icons for her inbox and her browser, ready to jump on whichever loaded first. The *Writing* folder on the desktop taunted her as she waited. Unopened in months, it held the start of the novel she'd taken a break from and never gone back to, and the outline of the non-fiction book she'd planned to write, detailing her investigation into Goddard and the property scandal. After the *Examiner* dropped the story, she'd channelled her anger that way, determined that all that work wouldn't go to waste. The legals were dicey, but that wasn't what killed it – in the end she'd simply run out of steam.

Now it sat there, a reminder of her true failure: a story left to die because she couldn't get it over the line.

Chrome opened before her inbox, so she jumped onto BBC News and skimmed it. The Brexit negotiations dominated. She clicked through to BBC London, a subsection that couldn't run enough stories about the Tube. Still she saw nothing about the attack.

It did not add up. You couldn't suffocate a man on the Tube and no one notice. If TfL knew about it, someone there would've leaked it to the press.

When she was working the Goddard story, she'd burrowed so deep into the rabbit hole that there were times she saw shadow connections everywhere. A document that referenced contact with a then-member of the cabinet; a tangential link to the CEO of an investment bank; meetings with a secretive American financier. The suggestion that the scheme went beyond just the developers and the politicians who enabled it, a hint of wider corruption. A team of ten might've been able to trace every branching stream to its source, given the luxury of time; with neither to play with, her imagination had started running crazy in the gaps. What if the same thing was happening now?

But the bag-snatch. The mystery caller...

She toggled to her inbox to send the email to Stephen about her phone. As she thought through how to word it, she stopped, staring at the screen. Something wasn't right.

She couldn't pin it down. Something about the way her inbox looked, the shape of the email list on the monitor...

The video. She scrolled down quickly, looking for Tammy's original email. There was nothing there.

The Costa was where he stood out the least on that shitty stretch of high street, so Stringer took up residence at a window table and watched Lydia Wright's flat. A forty-something white man in a suit was conspicuous enough there, but it would've been worse in the Turkish café a few doors down, or the pub filled with football fans. The aircon that had it cooled like a fridge was an added bonus.

Her flat was above a Ladbrokes. He'd seen her at the first-floor sash window a handful of times, and no one else had come or gone in the hour he'd been watching. He had her phones in front of him on the table, but couldn't get into the emails on either anymore. The password change was expected, but it still left him feeling blind when it kicked in. He weighed how much longer he could afford to hold; sitting alone in that flat, out of sight, she could be doing anything.

He switched to looking for mention of Jamie or Alicia Tan, but neither had made the news yet, the one high point in a day that was plumbing new depths all the time. He drank some of his coffee, not even tepid now, caffeine's diminishing returns making him nauseated.

A glint from Wright's flat made him look over. The sash window jerked shut from the inside. And a few seconds later, the front door opened and she appeared. She was wearing faded jeans and a T-shirt, and had a canvas bag over her shoulder that looked empty. She locked the door and turned right, headed in the direction of the shops.

He stood up to sink the dregs of his coffee and went outside. She was twenty metres ahead of him, the high street a long straight road that was busy enough with people to make following her as easy as blending in.

He stepped off the kerb to cross onto the same side as her, waiting for a car to pass. As he did, a man approached her door and rang the bell. Stringer froze on the spot, watching. The man rang again, holding the buzzer down, and when there was no answer, he checked both ways along the street and then seemed to do something with the lock. The door popped open and the man slipped inside.

Stringer weaved through the traffic and hesitated. Wright was in the distance now, almost gone from sight. He fought his indecision. The clothes, the bag – a supermarket trip maybe. A waste of time if he ended up trailing her around Tesco. But the guy at the door – what were the explanations there? A flatmate wouldn't ring the bell, probably not a boyfriend either. The landlord? Unlikely. Which made the stranger a big fucking question mark. He leaned against Ladbrokes' window.

Five minutes went by. Stringer went back to the other side of the street and stood at the bus stop. He gave it a couple more minutes, eyes on the window upstairs, no sign of movement. He ran through the possibilities in his head, the one that worried him becoming more pressing with every second that passed: that the man inside was waiting for Wright to come back.

The other side of the road was a long run of commercial premises with flats above, but there was a break three doors down, between a Middle Eastern supermarket and a pawn shop. He crossed over once more and turned down the side street. It reeked of rotting fruit, fetid and cloying in the heat, the smell coming from a large dumpster pressed up against the right-hand side. He followed the alley to where it opened out into a small courtyard lined with lockups. There were cars crammed bumper to bumper, the space being used as a makeshift car park for a dozen or so cars.

He could see the back of Wright's flat. He slipped between two of the cars and used the bonnet of a Ford Focus as a step to get a handhold on the roof of one of the lockups. He hauled himself up and got to his feet, brushing crumbling felt from his hands and trousers. The courtyard was overlooked by the back of a council block; anyone looking out would see him. He ran along in a crouch until he was by her window and could peer inside.

He was looking into an empty kitchen. A kettle on the side, a bowl and two mugs on the counter next to the sink. A red tea towel hanging from a rail on the cooker. White walls and Ikea cupboards – standard landlord kit-out. He listened but couldn't hear anything from inside.

He looked around to check he hadn't attracted attention from the council block, but there were dozens of windows, too many to inspect. He faced front again and tried lifting Wright's window, but the sash wouldn't budge. He paused a second, then took his phone out and used it to tap on the glass.

Nothing happened. He tapped again, harder.

The sound of movement this time. Faint, but there. The kitchen door was open but from his acute angle he couldn't see beyond it. He inched sideways to get a better look...

A face appeared in the doorway. White man, brown hair, black T-shirt. He froze just long enough. Stringer flicked his thumb to snatch a picture.

The man bolted.

Stringer scrabbled back across the lockup roof, feeling the felt bowing under him. He made it back to where he'd climbed up and got a grip on the edge, lowering himself until he could drop to the ground. His ankle gave as he landed and he buckled against a car. He righted himself.

Someone hit him in the side of the face, sending him sprawling. Not a fist, heavier. His vision blacked out, came back blurred.

Lying on the ground, he heard footsteps, someone running off down the alley.

CHAPTER 13

Premier Dental's sign was blue lettering on a white background, like a cheap knockoff of Bupa's corporate branding. Lydia could see why they were trying to piggyback on some credibility; on one side of the practice was an off licence, on the other, a kebab shop with half its sign missing. Finchley Central Tube was just around the corner, and Lydia had walked up from there, wondering how East and North Finchley could be such a contrast to this rundown stretch of Ballards Lane.

She had to buzz an intercom to get inside the door from the street, and it led straight to a staircase. The Listerine smell got stronger as she climbed; at the top, it opened out onto a small reception office and waiting area, the white walls lined with sleek posters for cosmetic dentistry treatments. There were perfect white smiles everywhere she looked, the hard sell hard to avoid.

'Can I help you, madam?'

She set her bag in front of her on the counter. 'I'm looking for Paulina Dobriska.'

'Is she one of the dentists?' The woman on the other side of the desk rolled the tracker wheel on her mouse, studying her screen. 'I can't see her name.'

Lydia glanced at the back wall, a metal plaque showing the names of the dentists that worked there. 'I'm not sure. I don't think so.'

'Sorry, I don't ... I'm a temp, I don't know everyone here yet. Can you spell the surname?'

'When did they bring you in?'

The woman looked up. 'Saturday. It was chaos because—'

'Their receptionist hadn't turned up?'

She nodded.

'Is her name Paulina?'

'Oh – is that who you're looking for?'

'Could you check for me?'

The woman looked at the door to one of the treatment rooms. 'I can ask one of the nurses, hold on.'

'Thank you.'

She knocked and disappeared through the door, then came back with a nurse in a white uniform. She came and stood on the same side of the counter as Lydia. 'You're looking for Paulina?'

Lydia nodded. 'That's right. She's off work?'

'Her brother called in on Friday to say she's unwell. Sorry, who are you?'

'Have you heard from her since?'

'No, not that I know of. Maybe Mr Henshall has. Look, sorry but who...?'

'It's for a story I'm working on. I'm a journalist.'

'A story?'

'How long's she been working here?'

The nurse looked at the ceiling thinking about it. 'A couple of years.'

Lydia gathered her bag straps together. 'Do you know what's wrong with her?'

The nurse glanced away, a guilty look crossing her face. 'I didn't speak to her brother, so...'

'What's the best number to get hold of her on?'

'We can't give that out ... can we?' She looked at the receptionist, who turned rabbit in the headlights.

'Please,' Lydia said. 'I'm sure she's okay, but I just want to check for myself.'

'What do you mean "okay"?'

'To be honest – I'm not really sure, that's why I need to talk to her.'

'Is something wrong? I never thought to check. I just assumed.'

'No, I totally understand. But if you could...'

The nurse hesitated, her hand poised above the counter. 'Look, I'll phone her. If she wants to speak to you she can.'

'Perfect.'

She went around into the office and picked up the phone, touching the temp on the shoulder and gesturing to the computer. 'Can I...?' She leaned over and took the mouse.

A patient came up the stairs and over to the desk, and Lydia slid out of her way, watching the nurse drift to the back of the office with the phone to her ear. She turned away when she started speaking, immediate enough that Lydia assumed it'd gone to voicemail. She couldn't make out what she was saying. The nurse hung up and came back over. 'I've left her a message. If she's not well maybe she's not up to talking.'

Lydia looped her bag over her shoulder. 'Yeah, maybe.' She pulled out a business card and passed it to the nurse. 'If you hear from her, would you let me know? Or ask her to call me?'

The nurse took it and looked up sharply when she saw the *Examiner* logo. 'Seriously, what's going on?'

Stringer watched Lydia Wright come out of the dental practice and put his phone away. He'd looked the place up online while she was inside. There was nothing on its website to indicate why she might've gone there – but she was in and out in a few minutes, and that meant it wasn't for a checkup.

His face ached where he'd been hit the day before. Professional pride told him he deserved it. Not reckoning on a backup man was a glaring oversight; it could've got him killed. No illusions, no excuses. Almost worse was that he couldn't understand what he was doing up there in the first place. Keeping the journalist out of harm's way served his own purposes, but caution was the start and end of everything. He'd left himself exposed, and with that one mistake he'd given up so much ground: they knew what he looked like and who he was watching. And that fact became even more dangerous if they were working for Suslov. It'd be near impossible to deny knowledge of the video if Suslov had tracked its path as far as Lydia Wright and caught Stringer right outside her flat in the process.

Wright turned off the main road towards the station and he followed after her. Finchley Central was at the bottom of a short street that sloped to an end at the car-park barrier next to the station itself. It was a low-slung yellow brick building with baskets of pink and red flowers hanging down its front. It looked like a disused stationhouse from a sleepy village, not a Tube stop in zone four. A throwback to a smaller London, when the area around him was still fields. Hard to believe that was in his grandparents' lifetime.

He followed her through the ticket gates onto the platform. She stood close to the edge so he kept back by the wall, out of her line of sight. She was wearing black jeans, pumps and a plain white top. She looked strained and short on sleep, and when he recognised that fact, guilt made it harder to keep watching.

He tried to gauge how far she'd take this – as if her appearance could provide some clue. It hadn't taken much digging to establish she'd done serious news before the showbiz fluff, but there was nothing in her record to suggest she was the crusading type either. He'd diverted journalists plenty of times in his work, but usually by trading one piece of dirt for a bigger one. It was standard practice, and when that failed, there was always someone who could be bought. But this represented a whole new level of risk.

His phone rang and he saw it was Dalton's number. He started walking without thinking, moving further along the platform and away from Wright.

'Yes?'

'Where are you?' Dalton said.

'Around. Where's Suslov?'

Dalton coughed. 'Andriy will be in London at two o'clock. He'll see you then.'

He checked his watch. 'Fine. Where.'

'Battersea. Do you know the heliport?'

CHAPTER 14

Lydia stopped by the office to collect a new phone from IT. As much as she resented being in that place on her day off, having no mobile was hindering her. The bonus was that it could double as her personal phone until payday at least. With the new one pocketed, she went to her desk to DM her contacts the new number from her laptop.

The office looked different in daylight. The commercial teams, people she never saw anymore, were already in, and the editorial departments were starting to fill up too. But the atmosphere was flat and tense – a typical Monday morning, the kind she'd almost forgotten about. A crowd from the sales team skirted her desk on their way to one of the meeting rooms, and she clocked Ben Mottingham, one of the ad directors, pointing her out to his junior. 'Dress down Monday?' He winked at her as he said it.

She kept her eyes on her keyboard. 'Get your suit from an estate agent?'

Mottingham blew a kiss and the junior looked away, embarrassed.

She called the press office at the Met to ask if Paulina Dobriska had been reported missing – but they wouldn't say anything beyond suggesting she file a report herself if she had concerns. She tried to do just that, but the first question they asked was the subject's last known address, and when she couldn't supply one, the conversation hit a wall. The officer on the other end suggested she get a relative to call them.

Lydia turned her computer off and got up to go, with a detour to Stephen's office on the way out. She weaved through the different departments and passed through the doors to the executive corridor. It was nicknamed The Reptile House because of the all-glass offices where they kept the bigwigs and not, so the story went, because it was full of snakes who'd eat their own eggs if the need arose.

Stephen's was a corner office with no one on the opposite side of the hallway, giving him more privacy than most. She came up to his door and saw him inside, standing, talking on the phone. She waited to knock, but he turned and waved her over, holding up one finger to signal he was nearly done.

She looked across his office to the view outside: Canary Wharf and Docklands straight ahead, some miles distant; the sunlight was shining off the Thames, making it a ribbon of pure white lacing through the city.

He finished his call and came around the desk. 'Are you working late or ridiculously early?' He pushed a chair back for her to sit down.

The office smelled of his aftershave; not overdone, just a note of sandalwood, the same as she could smell on her pillow whenever he'd been over. She rested her hands on the back of the chair but stayed standing. 'I'm not working tonight. I just came in to pick up a new phone.'

'What happened to the other one?' He was smiling, waiting for a punch line.

'I was mugged on Saturday night. Outside.'

'What?' He glanced at the open door behind her. 'Are you okay?'

'I'm fine.' She batted the air with her hands. 'I'm fine. It was my fault really. Stupid.'

He pushed the door closed and came to stand in front of her. 'What happened?'

She told him, struggling to meet his eyes, retelling how easy she'd made it for the woman who did it.

'Don't be hard on yourself. These people are professionals. It's just bad luck.'

'Yeah...'

He looked at her, waiting for something more. 'What is it?'

It all rushed to spill out, like a bottleneck starting to clear, and she had to step back to stop herself. She went to the window to get her head straight before she spoke. 'When I got into my emails, something had been deleted.'

'Something? Did you change your pass—'

'Yeah. Yes. First thing I did.'

'What's *something*? Was it sensitive?'

She looked at him and then the floor. 'It wasn't from my work account. It was a personal email.'

'What're we talking about here?'

She laid a finger on the corner of his desk. 'A message from a friend.'

He screwed his face up. 'What? That's just bizarre.'

'I know...'

'Maybe just kids mucking around? It's not nice to think of them snooping in your emails, but better if that's all it is, no?'

'Maybe. They only deleted that one message though.' Her finger started tapping on the desktop. 'If I was looking into something in my own time, would you cover my back if it led somewhere?'

He tilted his head. 'Lydia, what exactly is going on?'

Deep breath. 'The email they deleted was something ... Look, I don't know what it was. Tammy Hodgson sent it to me...'

'Tammy?'

'But now it's gone, and there's more too – someone I think is connected to it has gone missing. And then on top of that I got robbed, and...' She pushed a hair behind her ear. 'Now you're looking at me like I'm paranoid.'

He folded his arms, but uncrossed them just as quickly and stepped towards her. 'I'm just wondering what any of this has to do with showbiz.' She dropped her eyes to the floor, but he ducked down so he was in her eyeline again, big eyes to show he wasn't serious. 'Is this related to the Goddard stuff?' he said when she looked up again.

Goddard again, a shadow looming over every conversation they had. 'No.'

He raised his eyebrows.

'Nothing at all.'

'Then why don't you start again at the beginning. What was in the email?'

'It was ... I don't know, a video of a guy being attacked on the Tube.'

'Attacked?'

'Two men – it looked like they were trying to kill him. Suffocating him.'

He frowned. 'I didn't see that anywhere.'

'That's just it. No one's picked it up yet.'

'That's a red flag in itself. You said Tammy sent it to you?'

'Yeah, why?'

'I know you were close, but you know what she was like towards the end.'

She put her hands on her hips, remembering the tinfoil hat some joker had left on Tammy's desk in her last week. 'No, I don't. I remember some juvenile wankers trying to get at her, that's all.'

'Has she authenticated what she sent?'

She turned away, walking across the floor. 'This is why I didn't want to tell you...'

His computer chimed and he went around his desk and flicked the mouse to bring the screen to life. 'I have to be in a meeting. Look, if you really want to poke around this thing, I've got no problem with it, on the condition that it doesn't interfere with the day job, and you keep me updated if it goes anywhere. But think about whether it's worth the risk...'

'I can handle it.'

'I mean the internal risk. You need to think about how you're perceived. Tammy's a lovely woman, but you don't want to be seen as her protégé. Not anymore.'

'Wouldn't want journalists turning up stories...'

'That's reductive and you know it.'

'So is what you said.'

He smiled, closing his eyes in a way that said *you got me*. When he opened them again, he said, 'Are you sure you're okay? Is there anything you need?'

She circled around to stand between him and the door. 'The missing woman I mentioned – she's a witness, I think she might be in danger. Could you get me a contact to help trace her?'

'What, a private eye?'

'Don't take the piss. A friendly name in the police. Just to tell me if she's been reported missing or not. I lost touch with my sources when you lot binned me off.'

He frowned and she inclined her head, as if to say, *we're even now.*

He pocketed his phone and picked up his notebook and pen. 'I'll find you someone.'

'Thank you.'

He crossed to the door and held it open for her. 'Shall I come over one night this week?'

CHAPTER 15

The helicopter made a steep descent from a clear blue sky, the downdraft flapping Stringer's suit jacket. Dalton was standing next to him, holding a leather document case, his red tie blown over his shoulder. The rotor noise echoed off the small terminal building and the Crowne Plaza hotel behind them, scattering the gulls on the Thames.

The helipad jutted out from the edge of the river, across the muddy bank and into the water. It was held up by a framework of wooden stilts that looked like the remnants of an old pier, a relic against the backdrop of expensive flats on either side of the Thames. A glimpse of what lay beneath London's veneer. The structure vibrated as the craft landed, Stringer feeling as if it was shifting under him. It taxied a short way and came to a stop, the rotors slowing. Then the door opened and Andriy Suslov ducked out, older than in the most recent images Google turned up, but recognisable nonetheless. He was followed by a second man, much more heavyset. Suslov looked over, saw Dalton, and came towards them.

Stringer studied him as he approached. He wore a navy suit, the cut too good to be anything but tailor-made, and a white shirt with an open collar. His hair was greying in places, but otherwise dark; he wore it neatly parted, and the downdraft barely disturbed it. He was lean, but he carried his weight more on his right leg as he walked – disguised, but there.

Dalton held out the document case and Suslov took it. He pointed over. 'This is Michael Stringer.'

Stringer offered his hand but Suslov just looked at it. 'I'm due in Canary Wharf; we'll talk on the way.' Suslov turned to Dalton. 'Bring the car.'

Dalton nodded and walked off towards the parking bays out front. Suslov and the second man headed towards the other side of the complex, and Stringer followed. They rounded the control office, and a steward in a fluorescent vest guided the group down a set of concrete steps leading to a pier where a luxury yacht was moored.

Suslov crossed the metal gangplank onto the deck, where the captain was waiting to greet him, looking ready to salute. 'Welcome aboard, sir.'

Suslov barrelled past without acknowledging him. The second man off the helicopter opened the cabin and Suslov went inside. Stringer nodded as he passed him, evidently a bodyguard; the posture, the bearing, vibed ex-military type. He noted the contrast: a different class of hired help to the men at Lydia Wright's flat. The bodyguard closed the door after him and stayed on the outside, the back of his head just visible through the porthole.

Stringer hung back by the doorway. The interior of the cabin was decked out in teak, walnut and leather. Seating lined both sides, and Suslov plumped down at the far end, opening his hand for Stringer to take a seat opposite. Then he unlatched the document case and took a set of papers out, laid them on his lap and looked down to read. 'So, Jamie Tan.'

Stringer lowered himself onto the seat. The engines powered up and the boat moved out onto the river.

When he didn't answer, Suslov looked up.

'Something changed,' Stringer said.

Suslov shook the paper he was holding to crease it towards him again. 'An ambiguous phrase. He's missing, I understand; you told Dalton he didn't go home.' The accent was a collector's item – Americanised English with a hard Slavic edge.

'Correct.'

'Dalton implied you would have more than that.'

He opened his jacket and took his phone out – slowly, the man's bearing demanding it. He laid it on the seat next to him, watching for a reaction. 'Mr Suslov, we need to talk about the money first.'

Suslov kept his face impassive.

He had his words planned out, but he was still settling on a figure when he started speaking. 'Tan's missing and I can provide some clarity on that. But I'll need full payment of the agreed amount first, and thirty more on top – most of which will be used to facilitate rounding off some rough edges for you.'

Suslov set the piece of paper back on the pile, staring at him now. The boat hummed, the smell of diesel fumes coming and going. The remains of Battersea Power Station passed by on the riverbank, its shell attended by the towering cranes working on its rebirth as luxury apartments. 'You brought me from Paris to tell me you didn't get the job done but you want double the fee.' He put the papers down and crossed his arms. 'You came recommended as a fixer, not a fucking thief.'

Stringer upended his phone on the seat, flipping it end over end like a deck of playing cards. 'I want to show you something.'

No reaction. He sat forward and unlocked it, started the video and held it out for Suslov to watch. A blurry reflection played out on Suslov's glasses, his expression unchanging. The reflection went still, and Suslov took the phone and watched it through again. When it was finished, he tossed it back to Stringer.

Suslov set his gaze on a point somewhere out on the river. His jaw muscles tensed, but he said nothing at first. Then, 'This is authentic?'

'Best I can tell.'

'He is dead?'

'Unknown. I assume so.'

'Where did you get it from?'

He put his phone back in his pocket. 'I need assurances on the money first.'

'Why do you fixate on the money? You believe you're in danger from me?'

'I wouldn't have shown you if I did.'

Suslov straightened in his seat, coming to a realisation. 'You think I am behind this.'

'I keep an open mind. I'd rate it unlikely now.'

'What reason would I have...?' Suslov waved his hand to dismiss the idea, annoyed. 'Jamie Tan has value to me alive, not dead.'

'Then I'm sorry it didn't work out. But I put too much time into him to be left out of pocket.'

'You don't know who did this?'

He shook his head. 'Bold, though.'

Suslov leaned forward. 'Maybe it was you? Now you come asking for more money...'

His lies, their lies...

'I'm more subtle than that.' He held his stare.

Suslov leaned back and crossed his left leg over his right. He looked towards the door, the bodyguard still with his back to them, then down at his lap. 'You've been working at this for months. The night I tell you to earn your money, he disappears.' He pushed the document bag onto the floor. 'Whoever did this, it's a shitshow, so it was arranged in a rush. Knowing who and why would earn your fee.'

'I've already earned it, Mr Suslov.'

'No.'

Stringer edged forward on his seat, a weak attempt at projecting confidence. 'It's not my concern who did this.'

'You're supposed to know more about Tan than anyone. You'd have the advantage on any police agency.'

'I don't do detective work.'

'Then you have no value to me.'

'I have my dossier on Tan. I have the video. If you don't want them, I'll find someone who does.'

'You wouldn't be the first to try blackmailing me.'

The threat was barely disguised. If it was supposed to prompt thoughts of the journalist killed in Moscow, and the rumours of Suslov's involvement, it worked. Stringer wondered if that felt like blackmail at the time too; if this was all the same thing to him. 'Not blackmail. But information has a value.'

Suslov got to his feet. 'You think you can sell it to the people behind this? If you are so naive, I wish you good luck. They won't negotiate, they'll kill you.'

The phrasing resonated; it didn't sound like a general statement, more like he had a known entity in mind. 'They'd still have the dossier. Your name as the client on the cover. Useful for whoever's coming at you. That's what this is, isn't it?'

Suslov whipped off his glasses, discarding them on the seat. 'If these people moved on Tan in a rush, it's because they knew about your work. So maybe you won't have to go looking for them.'

A trail of logic he hadn't considered; the implications hit him all at once. 'If you told someone I was working for you...'

'No one knows my business. My guess is you screwed up.'

He looked to one side, hearing it as a message: *I know about your slip. I still might punish you for it.* The boat rolled, buffeted by the wake from a Thames Clipper passing the other way.

'You're saying the same thing to yourself,' Suslov said. '*No one knows my business*. But here we are, and now we have the same needs, so I say to you again: find out who and why. There's money on the table, this is your last chance to earn it.'

Stringer stared at him, not a hair out of place, not the slightest reaction to being shown footage of a brutal attempt on a man's life. He put it back to fifty-fifty whether Suslov had ordered it. 'Thirty up front, the rest when I come up with a name.' *And more again to give it to you.*

Suslov looked at him, deep lines in his forehead. 'This is not a negotiation. I've told you what I want, now you go and fucking get it.'

CHAPTER 16

The café was halfway down Camden High Street, the walls decorated in a swirl of beige and brown that might have been of-the-moment half a decade before, but now passed only for dowdy. The table next to hers was empty but the people who'd been there when she sat down had left their plates and cups on a tray, and two flies were circling above. One landed on a dirty spoon that had a film of coffee on it. Lydia picked the tray up and carried it over to the counter, then went to sit down again.

She studied each woman that came in, only a vague idea of what she was waiting for. Stephen had passed her the officer's name, Sam Waterhouse, and contact number, and they'd spoken once, a brief conversation to arrange the meeting. Waterhouse told her she'd be wearing black jeans and a green blouse.

Her phone rang in her bag. She took it out and didn't

recognise the number. She answered it, distracted, watching another customer come in off the street.

'Hello?'

'Is that Lydia Wright?'

She craned her neck to get a better look at the new woman ordering at the counter, seeing the colours she was looking for. She started to get to her feet. 'Speaking.'

'This is Anna Kershaw, we spoke. I'm the nurse?'

She took a couple of steps towards the counter, searching for a sign of recognition. 'Sorry?'

'Premier Dental. When you came in yesterday.'

Paulina Dobriska. 'Yes, sorry, of course. Anna – I didn't get your name then. Is this about Paulina?'

The woman at the counter took her coffee and came towards her now, raising her hand in greeting as she approached.

'Yeah, I wanted to talk to you,' the voice on the phone said. 'Have you heard from her?'

'No. No, look, can you speak now? Is this a bad time?'

The woman stopped in front of her and Lydia mouthed *sorry,* gesturing to the phone at her ear. 'Actually I'm just in a meeting. Can I call you back in a short while?'

'Well ... I'm on my break at the moment so it'll have to be after work.'

'Okay, great. Can I get you on this number?'

'Yeah. But, actually, I'll call you.'

'Okay, thanks. Please do, try me anytime.'

The line went dead.

Lydia slipped her phone away. 'Sam?'

The woman held out a hand. 'Hi.'

She shook it, pulling a sheepish expression. 'Always goes off at the worst moment.'

'That's okay. Shall we sit down?'

Waterhouse unzipped a rucksack to take a notebook out. She kept the bag on her lap and opened the pad in front of her, flattening the spine with her palm.

'Thanks for meeting me,' Lydia said. 'You've dealt with Bill Roundler in the past?' Roundler had been the *Examiner's* crime guru since before the website even existed.

'I've dealt with Bill in a professional capacity over the years. Not so much since I left.'

'Left?'

'The force.'

Lydia shifted around in her seat. 'Sorry, I thought you were...'

'Still serving? Is that what Bill told you?'

'No, he ... Another colleague of ours got your details from him. I just assumed you were still with the Met.'

'Not for a while. I still have contacts though; I did fifteen years.' She clicked her pen. 'What is it you need doing?'

'I'm trying to find out if someone's been reported missing.'

'Right. And you've tried the press office, I assume?'

She nodded. 'I don't know much about her. Name, employer, that's about it.'

'Is this someone they'd classify as high risk?'

'I don't think so. It's complicated.'

Waterhouse drew two lines across her page. 'Why don't you tell me what you do know.'

Lydia hesitated, torn between telling everything and keeping the story close. 'It's better to keep it simple. Her name is Paulina D-O-B-R-I-S-K-A. She hasn't shown up for work since last Thursday.'

She finished writing it down. 'A name like that should be

enough on its own, but you don't have a date of birth or an address?'

'No.'

'Where does she work?'

'A dental clinic.'

Waterhouse looked up at her. 'I can't do my job without some kind of context.'

'Why? With respect, if you've got the name...'

She set her pen down, breathing in. 'What I do relies on trust. I need to retain that trust and to do that, people need assurances. Not specifics, but my word that, for example, I'm not about to divulge sensitive information to a journalist. Bill understood that. So for me to give my word in good conscience ... You understand?'

Lydia looked away, gathering her thoughts. 'She may have witnessed a murder. I can't say for sure.'

'If she was a witness?'

'No. If it was a murder. At the very least, a violent assault.'

Waterhouse's expression hardened. 'If she's a witness to a serious crime, it sounds like you're talking about someone in danger. You said she was not high risk. Unless you're thinking they've got her stashed away already?'

'Stashed away? As in, a safe house?'

'Protective custody. And if that's the case, there's no way I'm going to reveal anything that could compromise...'

'I'm not asking you to compromise anything. The British Transport Police are looking into it, all I want to know is if this woman's safe.'

'The BTP? They're a law unto themselves. That's an entirely different problem, and outside of my scope.'

Lydia rubbed her face. 'But if she's missing, chances are it'd be reported to the Met, right? Or they'd know.'

Waterhouse studied her a second, then nodded. She took a sip of her coffee and set the mug back down. 'This is a professional matter, yes?'

'Of course. Why do you...?'

Waterhouse shrugged it off. 'You seem very invested.'

'I'm worried she's in real trouble. I don't know how fast the BTP are moving on this and if they don't get to her quickly...' Lydia looked away, tugging at the pendant on her necklace. 'Believe me, if you tell me the police have already got her, whatever the circumstances, I won't push for anything else.'

'You'd be wasting your time if you did.' It sounded like a rebuke, but she softened it with a smile as she turned to a fresh page in her notebook. 'I think we should start at the beginning. I guess Bill didn't talk you through my fees then, either?'

The girl came down the slide, jumped up and went around the climbing frame to the steps on the other side. Stringer watched her go, at least the fifth time in a row she'd done it, hopping each time. He let that thought drag him away a moment as he tried to remember if she ever walked anywhere; when he pictured her in his mind, she was always hopping or jumping from place to place, never walking; too much energy in her legs for anything as straightforward as that. And always laughing as she did it. He watched her cross the wobbly bridge now, shaking and rippling its chains as she jumped up and down, so much life in her that her little body couldn't contain it all. He broke into a smile just watching her.

'Don't see that very often,' his sister said, staring at him as he looked on.

He shrugged. 'She's something else.'

'It's not as endearing at five in the morning, promise you.'

He thought about his version of five o'clock in the morning – yesterday parked on a dead side street near the North Circular, working his way through a pair of stolen phones. Trampling his own red lines. 'I'd live with it.'

Abi turned away, following the girl's progress towards the slide. 'You're quiet today. Even for you.'

'Tired.'

'That's all it is?' He didn't need to look at her to know the expression on her face.

The girl came running over. 'Mummy I found a ladybird!' She held her finger out. 'Look, Uncle Mike.'

'It's beautiful,' he said, bending closer. 'What're you going to call her?'

'Sienna Jessie.'

'Her two friends at school,' Abi said.

'Well Sienna is my friend and Jessie is my friend too, but sometimes she's actually not my friend and that's okay.'

Stringer gave an exaggerated nod to show the explanation had made it all clear. 'Make sure you take care of her.'

'Why?'

'Why? Well ... because she's little.'

She made a face like she didn't understand.

'She needs your help,' he said.

But his niece had already turned and hopped off. She shouted over her shoulder, 'I will!'

Abi leaned back against the metal bench. A rubbish bin next to her was overflowing.

'Why don't you go to the other playground?' he said, nodding at it. The one they were in was on a scrap of waste ground between a car park and the mainline coming out of Euston.

She shrugged. 'It's too posh there. The mums wear diamonds bigger than my bedroom.'

'Better than this dump.'

'Ellie likes it here.'

Checkmate. They both looked over at her, losing her balance as she tried to do hopscotch and keep the ladybird on her finger at the same time.

'I spoke to Mum,' Abi said.

He nodded.

'She's doing better. The doctor's got her blood pressure under control again.'

'Good.'

'She's still got to lose the weight, but she knows that.'

'The diabetes?'

'It's all linked. When one's under control it helps the other, so...'

'Is the old man helping?'

She looked at her fingers, tangling them. 'In his way.'

He watched her as a train flew by on the tracks, filling the silence. She had the old man's eyes, a resemblance he hated, even though he shared it. But where their father's projected coldness and a lifetime's disaffection, Abi's spoke of rectitude. 'I honestly think he's trying,' she said when the noise subsided.

He grunted, nodding once. 'Does she need more money?'

She shook her head, not looking at him.

'And you?'

'You do enough.'

'I can get more if you need it.'

'Things are going well, then?'

A boy running across in front of them lost his feet and crashed to the ground. There was a moment of silence, shock on his face, then the cries came, piercing.

Stringer was halfway to his feet, but a girl who looked about the same age as Angie Cross came over and scooped the boy up. He dropped onto the bench again. 'I don't want Ellie to go without anything, okay? I know what schools are like...'

'You know about schools?' She flashed a disbelieving smile. 'You're wearing a suit in a playground...'

'I see the news, I know it's expensive. You won't ask for yourself, okay, but she's different.' Talking the way only families did – covering the same ground every time they saw each other, as if it'd never come up before.

'She's fine. The last lot covered her uniform and shoes.'

'You'll get more anyway. But I mean it, about her.'

She put her hand on his forearm. 'Is there something I can help with? A problem shared...?'

He shook his head. She kept staring at him a moment longer before she gave up.

He got to his feet and walked across to where Ellie was waiting by the swings. 'Got to go, kiddo.' He picked her up and held her, and she flung her arms around his neck.

'Not yet!'

A swing came free and he slotted her into its seat. He pulled her forward to get her started, but didn't let go. Abi came up behind him. 'Be a good girl for your mummy, okay?' he said.

'Let go!'

He lifted the swing higher, still holding it, drawing a giggle. 'Okay?'

She nodded her head, up and down. 'Push me!'

He lifted her to the top of his reach, held her there. 'Promise?'

She nodded again, jiggling with laughter. 'Promise!'

He let go, watching her swing backwards with her head rolled back.

He turned and squeezed his sister's arm. Those eyes again, the juxtaposition that always worried him: how she looked like the old man but took after their mother in all the right ways – kindness, patience, fairness. He looked like their mother, but couldn't lay claim to any of those virtues; the fear that he was his father's son on the inside. 'I'll call you.' She covered his hand with her own before he moved away.

He checked the time and dug the car keys out of his pocket, his mood ebbing again as Ellie's laughter faded from earshot. He came through the playground gate thinking about Andriy Suslov and Lydia Wright and the men at her flat. Wrestling with what the outcome would've been if he hadn't been there. What it still might be if he did nothing.

CHAPTER 17

The call came just as Lydia was stepping off the bus at Tottenham Hale. She recognised the nurse's number this time. 'Hello? Is that Anna?'

She couldn't hear the voice on the phone, the roar as the bus pulled away drowning out the nurse. 'Hold on...' She crossed the concourse to get away from the road and turned her back on the traffic, a two-pinter of milk dangling in her free hand. 'Are you there?'

'Yes, hi, I'm here.'

'Sorry about earlier, thanks for calling back. You wanted to talk?'

'Well … thing is, if I talk to you, is it unofficial?'

'What do you mean? Off the record?'

'Yeah, but – like, can I get in trouble?'

'With who?'

'With the police. If there's something happened.'

'No, you can't get in trouble just for talking to me. If you want to be off the record, that's fine. But if you know something about Paulina, you should tell the police too…'

'It's not like that. I tried calling her brother – after you came in and I never heard back from her. The office phone keeps a log of all the calls, so I went back and found his number.'

'Okay. And what did he say?'

'He answered speaking Polish. When I told him I wanted to check on his sister, to see if she was any better, he said, "Who?" So I said to him, "Paulina?" And he hung up.'

Lydia clamped the phone to her ear with one shoulder so she could push her bag straps back in place on the other. 'Right.'

'And I thought maybe I just got him at the wrong time, so I tried again earlier and it goes straight to voicemail.'

'That's … Have you tried Paulina since?'

'Same. Always voicemail.'

She turned around, trying to decide what to do. 'Anna, have you got an address for Paulina? I spoke to the police but they can't help much without one.'

'Well that's what I was asking about. Getting in trouble.'

'I don't follow.'

'If I gave you her address?'

'You can give it to the police.' She looked at her watch. 'Look, I'll come and meet you and we can go to the station together.'

There was silence on the line. A thin cloud covered the sun, like a gauze over a light bulb.

'Anna? What do you think?'

'I was hoping there was ... Do you pay for tips like that? I've got it with me.'

Money. Not nerves, not fear, making her hesitant – just basic greed. Lydia closed her eyes before she spoke. 'Tell me and we can work something out.'

Lydia went straight there. She almost talked herself out of it, the idea of turning around two hundred metres from her door and trekking to Whetstone making her balk. But she knew she'd just end up dotting about the flat like a fly, and that overcame her weariness.

She called Tammy just before she went into the station.

'Lyds?'

'I've got her address.'

'Who? Paulina?'

'Yep. I'm on my way there now. It's in Whetstone, want to meet me there?'

'Bloody hell, how did you manage that?'

'I'll tell you when I see you.' She checked her watch to gauge how long it would take, surprised to realise impressing Tammy still lit her up. 'I reckon I'll be there in about forty minutes.'

'Shit – I can't, I've got my nephew tonight for my sister.' As she said it, Lydia heard a child saying something in the background. 'Have you tried calling her?'

'Always goes to voicemail,' Lydia said.

'Yeah, same as me. Look, be careful, all right?'

'I'll let you know when I'm done. I'll text you the address;

can you pass it on to the police? If there's no sign, they've got to start looking for her.'

Tammy said something away from the speaker, the nephew vying for her attention. 'Yep, of course. Talk to you in a bit.'

It was a fifteen-minute walk from the Tube to Dobriska's address, down one of those long residential roads of 1940s terraced houses that seem endless when you don't know where you're going.

Lydia pushed through a stiff gate to go up the path. There were two front doors facing each other at a forty-five-degree angle – a cowboy builder's way of turning one doorway into two when the house had been converted into flats. She rang the bell for 65b and waited.

No one came to the door. She opened the letterbox and called hello. She let it flap shut and stepped off the path onto the grass. Net curtains obscured the view into the front room, but she could make out a bed and a desk, no sign of anyone in there. She stepped back and looked at the upstairs window, but nothing was moving.

She scribbled *Please call me urgently* on a business card and posted it through the letterbox, then tried the bell for 65a. She looked at the time – twenty past six. A toss-up whether it was worth hanging around to see if the people in the adjoining flat might be arriving home from work soon.

She went through the neighbouring gate, finding the same front door arrangement there. She could see kids playing through the window of 67a so she rang the bell and waited on the doorstep.

An Asian woman in a hijab opened up, a toddler on her hip. She looked at Lydia. A boy and a girl came up the hallway behind her, hiding behind her legs to see what was going on.

'Sorry to disturb you. I'm looking for Paulina Dobriska, she lives next door?'

'Yes?'

'Do you know her at all?'

'Yeah, little bit. Why?' The woman had a north-London accent.

'Have you seen her the last few days?'

She looked to one side. 'I don't think so.'

The boy tugged on the woman's leggings. 'Mummy...' She cupped her hand around his head to draw him closer.

Lydia passed her a business card. 'I should explain, I'm a reporter with the *Examiner*—'

The woman started shaking her head. 'Oh no. Won't touch that rag. Racists.'

Lydia grimaced, nodding. 'I'm with the website, not the paper.'

'So? Split you up into racists and not-racists do they?'

'I'm not ... I'm just trying to make sure she's okay.'

'Why wouldn't she be?'

'She hasn't shown up for work for a few days.'

'What's that got to do with you?'

'Look, thanks for your time.' Lydia turned to go.

'Well give it to us, then.'

'Sorry?'

'Your card. If I see her, I'll tell her.'

She handed it over and waved goodbye to the boy and girl, who smiled but hid their faces behind their mum's legs. She was already set on calling it quits. She'd had a missed call from her mum, no doubt spurred by receiving the message about her losing her phone, retirement in Devon leaving her with too much time on her hands. That meant a chat to reassure her everything was alright, which meant forty minutes at least once her mum got talking. If she started back for the flat now, she'd be able to get it done and still have something of the evening left for herself.

'Excuse me.'

She turned around to see an older man coming across the street towards her.

'Excuse me, I saw you ringing the bell.' He pointed to Paulina Dobriska's door.

'Yes. Do you know the woman that lives there?'

'Blonde lass. She's lived there a while but I don't know her name. Pleasant enough.'

'Have you seen her today? Or yesterday?'

'No. She's run off I think. Are you from the police?'

'I'm a journalist.' She passed a card to him. 'Why do you say police?'

He took it, holding it at arm's length to read the writing. 'Because I phoned them about it. There were two lads watching her door. I didn't expect them to send a panda car or anything, but I thought they'd look into it.'

She turned to face him fully. 'What do you mean "watching"?'

'They were sat in the car just there.' He pointed a short way down the road. 'I saw them ring her doorbell. The Paki woman didn't tell you, did she? They don't, do they, their culture?'

Lydia winced. 'You're saying someone was looking for the woman who lives there?'

'Yes. Burly lads, looked like footballers. We try to keep the neighbourhood watch going on the street but there's just too many don't want to know nowadays. I asked the lass to join ages ago but she told me she couldn't. And the Paki was a waste of time.'

'Sir, could you stop saying that word, please.'

'What word?'

'"Paki".'

'Why?'

'Because it's offensive.'

'What am I supposed to call them then? It's always bloody changing. The Indian girl.'

She closed her eyes and took a breath to keep her focus. 'When did you see the men in the car?'

'Saturday. Again on Saturday night. That's when I rang the police. I was going to challenge them but the lass on the phone told me not to. I took down their number plate if you want it?'

She rummaged into her bag for a pen. 'Please.'

He took a notebook from his shirt pocket and started to read it out.

She scribbled it on her pad as he spoke. She looked up when he'd finished. 'You said the men looked like footballers?'

'Yes, you know how they have that hair.' He ran his fingers along the side of his head. 'Nothing here, long on top. Looks like they've had a bath in Brylcreem.'

The two attackers in the video had crew cuts; no easy answers there. 'What age would you say they were?'

'It's hard to tell, isn't it? Twenties or early thirties.'

The phantom brother? 'They couldn't be family or something like that?'

'God knows. But I've never seen them before if they are. Are you going to write about it then?'

'Maybe. It depends.'

'I don't take your paper usually but I'll look out for it. Henry Siddons – you can quote me.'

She thanked him and moved off, glancing at the number plate she'd written down. She pinged a message to Tammy: *No one home, no sign of her for days*. Then she started back towards the station, writing a text to Sam Waterhouse.

CHAPTER 18

Stringer kept a second flat in Finsbury Park. He'd owned it for four years, choosing that specific one because it met all his criteria: a one-bedroom on the third floor of a ten-year-old block that comprised eighty units in total – the definition of unremarkable. The building had two entrances: one on the street – a main road that was always busy; and one at the back that meant he could pull up right outside the door. The residents were mainly young professionals or Chinese students, so the turnover was huge and no one knew their neighbours – meaning no one paid attention to a new face in the lifts or the corridors. And with the advent of Air BnB, flat 307 was just one of dozens that seemingly changed occupier every week.

He pressed the lift button. Most of his guests weren't public figures; he'd had politicians and even a cabinet minister once, sequestered while he cleaned up whatever shit they'd gotten themselves into, but usually it was the people on the other side of the coin: the politician's mistress who needed hiding from the press until the story came out on whoever's terms was paying him; the battered wife of the CEO who needed space to plan a clean break; the lawyer who had to disappear until

Stringer could broker a deal with his former clients. He'd put Angie Cross up there when she'd first crashed into his life, until she decided it was too isolating and left, saying she wanted to sort something out for herself.

The lift opened onto an empty corridor. The lights flickered on as he stepped out, the motion sensors kicking in – supposedly an energy-saving measure that never seemed to make a dent in the service charges the management company billed him for.

He came to the door and knocked. He had keys in his pocket but he'd decided on day one that he wouldn't use them while she was here.

He heard footsteps inside, a pause. The spy hole darkened and cleared. Then the sound of the lock turning.

Alicia Tan opened the door.

'Can I come in?'

She stepped back to open up fully, holding her arm out but not looking at him.

His shoes clacked on the wooden floor down the hallway. He went straight through to the living room and stood by the window. He heard her locking the door. The view looked south, towards the City, the Arsenal stadium rising like a monolith in the foreground.

'Kidnapped anyone today?' She was standing across the living room, staring at him.

'Not yet. Mind if I make coffee?'

'Be my guest.'

She'd hardened again since his last visit, understandable with what she was going through. She'd shown admirable poise when he'd first taken her here two days before. The lies he'd told her then weighed on his conscience: that Jamie Tan had paid him to stash her away in the event of something happening to him. It was the only way he could think to gain her trust while he figured out where the threat was coming from – and if it extended to her as well.

He went into the kitchen and flicked the kettle on. 'Do you want one? Tea?'

She came and stood in the doorway behind him. 'How long are you going to keep me here?'

He spread his hands on the counter. 'We've been through this. You can leave any time you want.'

'Yes, so you said. But I gave that some thought, and telling me my life's in danger isn't much different to telling me you'll kill me if I try to go.'

'You walk out that door, you'll never see me again. If that's what you want.'

'And I'm expected to just believe that?'

He dropped a teabag into a mug and opened the fridge. 'Milk?'

'Did you come here to play tea boy?'

'I came to check you're coping.'

She folded her arms and leaned against the doorframe. 'Go fuck yourself.'

He stirred the tea and turned to give it to her. She shook her head so he reached across her and put it on the counter by her side.

'You lied to me, but now—'

'To get you here,' he said. 'I lied to get you safe.' One more in the mountain of lies he built his life on.

'If Jamie hired you why didn't he tell me? You never answered that.'

He went back into the living room and she followed him

with her gaze. He took a sip of his coffee, too hot to taste the flavour.

'Well?' she said.

'I don't know.'

'He must have told you something...'

'It's not a conversation anyone wants to have. *Darling, I've made arrangements to keep you safe in case something happens to me...*'

Her face changed and he stopped himself. She'd had eyes like glass up to then, enough to make him forget and slip into talking like an asshole.

She looked away and rubbed her cheek with the heel of her hand, a sharp movement that made him realise she was more angry that he'd fractured her composure. 'Stop saying "something". I'm under no illusions what's happened. For all I know it was you that killed him.'

'You suspected something was wrong, you told me as much.' The worst part of his lies: that they'd worked too well. In the midst of her anguish over her husband, she'd started confiding in him.

'And so he hired me a bodyguard without telling me.'

'That's not what I am.'

She waved him off. 'Whatever you fucking call yourself.'

'I'm a fixer. That's it.'

She lowered herself onto the edge of a chair. 'How long am I supposed to stay here? According to this plan no one deigned to clue me in on?'

He studied her – a red mark on her cheek where she'd rubbed it, the one frailty in an expression as hard as porcelain. He shook his head to say he didn't know, finally making his mind up about the video as he did. 'I want to show you something, but it's going to be hard for you to see. It's your call.'

'What?'

'There's a video surfaced of Jamie the night he disappeared. It's not good.'

'Show me.'

'You're sure? You can change your mind at any time...'

'For Christ's sake, show me.'

He placed his phone on the coffee table and pressed play.

She twitched when she recognised Tan on the train and snatched up the phone to get a better look. 'What's...?'

He said nothing, letting it play on. She started when the punch came, her breathing fast and light. Then the duct tape and his convulsions. She didn't blink, didn't make a sound, and he could see she was steeling herself to show no reaction, the effort making her head tremble. 'Oh, Jesus – Jamie...'

The video played out and she held the phone, staring past it, her eyes filming with tears. She was silent for more than a minute. Then she swallowed and focused on him. 'Is that all of it?'

He nodded. 'Do you recognise the other two men?'

'No.'

'You're certain?'

'Yes, certain. Where did you get this?'

'It came into the possession of a journalist. I don't know where the original came from.'

'Have the police seen it?'

'Not from me.'

She looked around at him. 'Why not?'

He took the phone from her gently and set it face down on the table. 'What were you afraid of, Alicia?'

She held his look, no attempt to hide her disdain. 'Who the hell do you think you are? You don't know me.'

'You told me that. I'm repeating your words from the other night.'

'I was in shock. That doesn't give you the right to ask me now.'

'Whatever Jamie was into, it went bad. I didn't want to get him or you into trouble.'

She looked around the room, the cheap IKEA prints the only colour on the white walls. 'This place ... I must be out of my mind staying here...' She stood up.

'The danger's real, isn't it? That's why you stayed.'

'Did Jamie tell you something you're hinting at? Because if you know something I don't, I'd rather you just said it out loud.'

His lies, their lies...

Her lies?

'Like what?' he said.

'Oh come on. He asks you to look after me, but you didn't have any questions at all about why? How long for? What to bloody do with me if he disappears?'

'Paid.'

'What?'

'He didn't ask me, he paid. That takes care of my curiosity.'

She picked up his phone again. His instinct was to snatch it off her, thinking she was about to rifle it for more information he didn't have, but he held back when he saw her looking at the video again. A woman that projected so much composure, it was easy to forget she was as much a victim in this. She screwed her eyes closed, shuddering as she stifled a sob. She looked again, attached the video to a message, then sent it to a number he didn't know – her own, judging by the beep that came straight after. Then she got up silently and walked to the front door and opened it, staring him down with red eyes.

He watched her a moment, then nodded an acceptance to himself. He walked over to her, scrabbling for a reassurance to offer. When none came, he continued out of the door.

'Must be so proud of the life you live,' she said.

CHAPTER 19

Her mum was ten minutes into an update about a cousin in Australia Lydia had never met.

She was using her free hand to scroll through a Google search for the registration plate Paulina Dobriska's neighbour had given her. The results weren't much help. Various sites carried the basic details: it belonged to a black 2016 Audi Q7, first registered in London. It'd changed hands once, in April 2017. Estimated mileage, estimated value; nothing that could help her locate the current owner.

'Anyway I'd better go,' her mum said. 'I want to put the dishwasher on before I go to bed. You're sure you're okay though?'

'Yep, promise. Just one of those things.'

'And you're alright for money?'

She closed her eyes. 'Yeah. Thank you.'

'Well you know where I am. Love you.'

'Love you, Mum.'

She ended the call and put her mobile on the desk next to her laptop, a screen full of Audi Q7s staring back at her. The cheapest one was listed at £45,000, and the search said there were 173 of that specific model within ten miles of her postcode. It seemed impossible, even in London, that so many people had that much money to spend on a car. In the real world it was a deposit for a flat.

'Hiya.'

Lydia snapped her head around.

Chloe had poked her face through the doorway. 'Sorry, didn't mean to scare you.'

Lydia flashed an embarrassed smile. 'I didn't hear you come in.'

'Thought I'd say hello; feels like I haven't seen you in ages.'

'I know. These hours are a nightmare at work. You okay?'

'Yeah, just knackered – long day. Was that your mum?'

She nodded.

'How is she?'

Lydia heard her phone buzz with a notification but didn't look over. 'Same old. "Your dad's driving me mad. When are you coming to visit"? She sees the headlines about knife epidemics in London too; they don't help.'

'I got your DM about the new number – did you tell her about your phone?'

'Only that I lost it. She'd freak out if she knew.'

Chloe smiled. 'My mum thinks it's a miracle I've survived this long in the warzone. As if Peterborough is some kind of hamlet.'

'Tell me about it.'

'I'm making a decaf tea if you want one?'

Lydia shook her head. 'Thanks.'

'You working? I'll let you crack on.' She started to back out.

'Actually, Chlo?'

'Yeah?'

'I meant to ask, did you use my laptop for anything yesterday?'

'No, why?'

'It's ... don't worry, it must be me.'

'No, go on.'

'I thought I left it closed, that's all. It was open when I came home last night.'

Chloe cracked the door wider. 'Definitely wasn't me. Promise.'

Lydia pulled a dizzy look. 'I must be losing it.'

Chloe shifted her weight onto the other foot, leaning on the doorknob. 'Sure it wasn't Mr Mysterious in the suit?'

'Stephen?'

'Is that what he's called?'

'He wasn't here. Was he?'

'Nah, I'm only winding you up. Got his name out of you, though.' Chloe threw her hands to her mouth, smiling. 'Hang on, it's not Stephen from work, is it?'

Lydia smiled, shaking her head and locking her eyes on the screen.

'Oh my god, it is. Lydia!'

She blushed, waving her off, breaking into a goofy smile. 'Piss off.'

Chloe waggled her fingers, still chuckling. 'Night.'

Lydia closed the browser window full of Audis. She thought back to the day before, remembered using her laptop in the afternoon before she went to Tesco. When she came back it was open, but she could've sworn she'd left it shut. She normally did.

Her phone buzzed again and she looked over at it and snatched it up.

The top message was a text from Sam Waterhouse: *Call me.* But it was the notification underneath that had her staring at it without moving:

Paulina Dobriska has accepted your friend request.

CHAPTER 20

It was past ten when Stringer parked the car a street away from Highgate Tube. The roads were quiet and dark walking back towards the station, the tall streetlights fitted with dim bulbs to appease the residents in the big houses.

The entrance was on Archway Road, but it was just a sign saying *Highgate Station* above a flight of concrete steps down a steep embankment through the woods. He could see the tracks at the bottom, glimpses of orange light coming through the trees from the entrance proper.

He waited four minutes for a train, checking his watch again when he got on: about the same time as Tan would've made the journey. Highgate was the last stop underground going north, seven above ground after it – and only five that mattered if he discounted High Barnet and the spur line to Mill Hill East. Tan had taken the tube back to High Barnet most nights when he was tailing him, and then either driven or caught a cab to Arkley from there, so logic dictated they'd got to him somewhere between those points.

The train thundered into the tunnel heading north, his face reflected in the window opposite. He tried to picture it, seeing through Jamie Tan's eyes: another commute home, nothing more routine, paying no attention to what was around him. A Friday night, a few beers in, dampening the senses further. Tan couldn't have been expecting what was coming; Stringer had seen him take Ubers home from town before; surely that would've been the minimum precaution to employ if he'd sensed a threat.

The train popped out of the tunnel, the sudden dip in noise level like plunging underwater. Stringer sat forward, alert now.

It pulled into the platform at East Finchley seconds later, and straight away he knew he could discount it. The train had been outside at the start of the video and the attack went on for longer than it'd taken to go from tunnel to platform. Four stops left in contention.

The doors closed and the train moved off, noticeably less busy now. See it through different eyes: the killers. They're waiting for it to thin out, for their opportunity. They know Tan's staying on all the way to the end, they've got a bit of time. Assuming they were on the train already; surely the only way to go about it, which would confirm his assumption – bolstered by what Alicia had said at the flat – that they were unknown to Tan.

The line ran at street level now, passing houses and commercial units on the way to Finchley Central, the rainbow bundles of cabling that ran alongside the tracks like veins holding the network together. They pulled into the station and he got up to stick his head out the doors.

Another easy no: the northbound platform was a wide island, the only way out via a footbridge accessed by stairs or a lift. He sat back down in his seat, his elbows propped on his knees. A man with white earphones in looked over from the next bank of seats. Stringer met his stare, and the man went back to his phone.

The train juddered forward again, pulling out slowly before it accelerated. The line was surrounded by embankments on both sides now, heavily wooded. There were three people in the carriage, including himself. He got up again to look through the emergency doors into the next one, saw another three passengers there. He turned around, picturing the killers making the same calculations, the window of opportunity opening at this stage.

They pulled into West Finchley and that window widened further. He looked along the dark platform, lined with a low wire fence backed with bushes and trees. He stepped off the train and walked along, examining it. No holes, no sign it'd been cut. Besides that, he couldn't see a path through the foliage behind it. He carried on to the station building and went out through the ticket gates – another strike against this one – and found himself in a narrow alleyway that ran maybe twenty metres to the main road. He walked through the caustic glare of a security light, looking back to see a CCTV camera pointed right at him.

The top of the alleyway came out on the main road, a narrow single lane in each direction. To his left there was a small parade of shops, only the mini-supermarket showing signs of life at that time of night.

He retraced his path back down the alley and onto the platform, another train arriving just as he got there. He stepped on, making the same observations – only one other person on the carriage this time, the one next to it empty, the last one before the driver's cab. He stayed by the emergency door and turned around to look back, seeing it through different eyes again: the witness filming the video.

The line was raised above the ground now, a sea of red roofs on either side, the 1930s terraces that once represented an aspirational suburbia on the edge of the city. The next station was Woodside Park and he'd all but discounted it as they pulled in, given the elevation of the track – no easy access there. But when the train came to a stop, right in front of him was a street-level gate to the outside. Wide open.

He jumped up and got off the train, looking around and seeing he was the only person who did. There was no staff along the platform. There was an Oyster touchpad next to the exit, but no barriers. He waited until the train pulled out; no one on the southbound platform either, neither staff nor passengers.

He went through the gate and came out in a bleak turnaround, the small roundabout at its centre just big enough to hold a dead shrub. Nothing more than a drop-off point. There was a small car park chained off next to it, signs saying it was for staff parking or mini cabs only, but currently standing empty. Behind him was a cab office, its lights off. A modern block of flats rose beyond that, only two or three of them with a sightline to where he stood, all of them with curtains over the windows as he looked.

The road into the turnaround led back to the street, no more than thirty metres distant. He took out his phone and snapped a dozen pictures. He looked back at the gate, saw a solitary CCTV camera. It was positioned at ninety degrees to the exit, so anyone coming out of the station would only fleetingly cross its field of vision. He took a shot of that too.

Off the train and into a car in fifteen paces. Jackpot bells going off in his head so fucking loud he could hardly hear.

CHAPTER 21

Lydia woke up on top of her covers with her phone in her hand. She brought it to her face even before she knew what she was doing, still half in the grip of sleep.

Her eyes wouldn't focus. Her bedside lamp was on and it was light outside. She blinked and looked at the screen again – 8.10 a.m. It was gone two the last time she could remember checking the clock, fighting off sleep as long as she could, waiting for a reply from Paulina Dobriska.

She unlocked the phone and opened Facebook Messenger. She bolted upright.

A reply had arrived: *I don't want to talk.*

The words seemed to fill the screen. If a Facebook message could shout, this one did.

She looked at the time stamp – sent twenty minutes ago. She rubbed her eyes and gripped her phone in both hands.

I want to help...

Her thumb hovered over the send button. Maybe only one shot to get the right words. She deleted it and typed again: *I can help you.*

The message went and she sat on the edge of the bed. There was a green dot on Paulina's profile picture, indicating she was still online.

Lydia put the phone on her desk and paced to the window. She split the blinds, came back, checked it again. She stood, patting her hands together gently.

Her phone buzzed: *I don't want help.*

She grabbed it: *I'm concerned for your safety. I saw your video. Can we talk?*

Nothing. She read her own words back over and over, doubting each one.

What did you do with it?

Lydia didn't understand. *The video?*

Yh.

Nothing yet. Been waiting to speak to you.

It was a mistake.

She tapped her reply: *Mistake how?*

Traffic was queuing on the street outside and she could hear the low hum of idling engines. She stared at the phone, seconds dragging. The lights at the end of the road must've changed because she heard everything kick into motion again. Her patience cracked. *Paulina?*

Another few seconds ticked by. Then: *Shouldn't have put on FB.*

But it's real?

Paulina's reply was instant. *What u think?*

Lydia frowned. *Where are you? Can we talk – phone or face to face?*

A bus sounded its horn right outside the window, so loud it boomed around the room.

No response. Again impatience overtook her. *Please, if you're afraid, I can help. Publicity the best defence. Big media company behind me, can have your back too.*

She watched the screen, bouncing on the balls of her feet. 'Come on, come on, come on...'

The green dot disappeared.

She let her hands fall to her side. Then another thought revived her. The telephone icon was next to Paulina's name; she pressed it and put the phone to her ear, the dial tone sounding like it was underwater. It rang for thirty seconds. Then it cut out.

'Fuck it.' She tossed the phone on the bed.

Lydia waited for Sam Waterhouse outside Hampstead Heath Overground. It'd been her suggestion to meet there, and Lydia agreed to it even though it wasn't the easiest place to get to from Tottenham Hale. The bill she was racking up with Sam was on her mind, no need to inflate it further with extra hours for travel time. The fact that Stephen had given her the contact in the first place she took as implicit agreement that he'd sign off the expense – but she was conscious of not taking the piss. His words played on her mind now – "think about how you're perceived". Nagging doubts about his doublespeak – was he saying that for management, or himself? Where was the line between the two?

The idea Tammy had turned into some kind of conspiracy nut towards the end was rubbish – and yet if you brought up her name around the office, that was the narrative that survived her. It was a smear that cut Tammy deep, in her own words "tainting a lifetime's work". She'd opened up to Lydia about it at the time, just after they'd let her go, Tammy certain it was a characterisation put about by one of the bosses to help justify pushing her out the door. Lydia had never voiced her own suspicion – that Tammy's support for continuing the Goddard investigation, no secret at the time, had given it credibility. The final nail.

She tried calling her again, a follow-up to two earlier attempts and the text she'd sent: *Paulina Dobriska made contact, ring me.* Her phone was still trying to connect when Sam Waterhouse appeared at the top of the stairs leading up from the platform. Lydia cut the call.

'Hope you don't mind walking,' Sam said as a greeting, already moving off. 'I get sick of being at my desk so I take the chance when I can.' She led them across the road and started up the path towards the ponds the heath was famous for. 'Okay, first things first: Paulina Dobriska, of the address you gave me, has not been reported missing. In fact, that name didn't bring up any flags anywhere, so far as my contacts say.'

'Does that mean she's not known to police at all?'

'Probably. Look, there's always the chance of a misspelling, particularly a name like that, or a file not matching up, or some paperwork getting waylaid. But she's not on missing persons or the main database, so it looks that way.'

'Would it be classified if they had her in protective custody?'

Sam screwed her mouth up. 'Very unlikely. I mean it's unlikely enough that they'd even have her in protective custody. I only mentioned that last time as an outside chance. But even if she was, she'd have to be involved in something incredibly serious to warrant that. So I can't say there's zero chance, but let's be realistic. She saw something on the Tube, she's not a supergrass.'

Lydia almost blurted out that Paulina had made contact.

The path became a narrow causeway between two of the ponds, both covered in thick green algae. The sky was overcast, trapping the heat under the clouds, the air thick with pollen.

'Secondly, the number plate you texted me about,' Sam said.

'Yes...'

'For a car used by some blokes supposedly watching Dobriska's place?'

'According to the neighbour over the road.'

'Who might be jumping to conclusions?'

'He was a neighbourhood-watch type.'

'Some of them have overactive imaginations. People have good reasons to sit in cars, regardless of what next door thinks.'

'I'm not saying it has to be something dodgy. I was thinking it could be family or friends. Someone saying he was her brother called in sick for her.'

'You don't sound convinced. Have you got hold of him?'

Lydia shook her head. 'The number's dead.'

'Dead?'

'Straight to voicemail every time.'

'Phones do run out of battery. They get switched off...'

'I know, but—'

Sam held up her hands. 'I know. If it seems like I'm playing devil's advocate all the time, it's because the simplest explanation is usually the right one. I'm speaking from experience.'

'Can you trace it? The phone number?'

Sam blew out a breath, the path getting steeper as they came to the top of Parliament Hill. 'This is getting more involved than I'm comfortable with. Look, the number plate is registered to an address in Surrey. I'm not turning cartwheels about handing it over to you, because if there is something here, the police are the ones who should be investigating it. And if there's not, then these people don't need you mucking around in their lives.'

Lydia took out her phone and opened up Paulina's messages. She handed it to Sam just as they reached the top of the hill.

'What's this?' Sam took a pair of reading glasses out of her bag and put them on. When she was finished, she gave the phone back, staring at the floor as if lost in thought. 'Okay, that's all very cryptic. Did you speak to her in the end?'

'No. But does that sound right to you?'

Sam looked out at the view that stretched to the city and beyond, all the way to the Surrey Hills, the reward for making it up the incline to get there. The neon display that wrapped around the top of the BT Tower was flashing and blinking like a warning light. 'It sounds like someone who wants to be left alone.'

'She's the key to this. I called the transport police this morning for an update and they aren't telling me anything...'

'I made some enquiries for you on that front. From what I can gather, they are investigating, but they've got very little to go on apart from your video. They haven't identified the victim or the crime scene, and they're still reviewing CCTV.'

'How long will that take?'

'Depends. But they're pressed for officers like everyone else, so it's whenever they can spare someone to sit in a room and sift through it all – but without knowing when and where, there's hundreds of hours' worth to get through. I wouldn't hold your breath.'

'This isn't a priority for them?'

'To an extent, of course. But so is everything else. They're understaffed, you can't blame them.'

'I don't.' She looked over, squinting in the light. 'But that's why I need her.'

Sam took her reading glasses off and put them back in their case. 'Look, I admire your persistence. Not to discount what I said earlier, but it does feel like there's something that's a bit off.'

'What would you have made of this? If this was a case that landed on your desk back in the day?'

Sam scratched the back of her neck. 'I'm struggling with why you don't have a victim. I find it hard to believe the man in that video, if it was real, walked away from that. And even if he did, he'd likely need hospital treatment – and anyone presenting in that state, the police would be informed, even if he hadn't done so himself.' The warm breeze tugged at her hair and she ran her hand through it to push it back. 'So let's assume he died. If they left him on the train, there'd be a report, and it'd be in the papers. Right?'

'It would make the news, definitely.'

'That means they took him away – so where is he? Even if they did get him off the train, they can't have got far with him on foot, unless...'

'Unless they had outside help?'

Sam nodded, shrugging. 'Then you're talking about something that was planned, not a random attack.'

'Like a hit.' Tammy's word, when they'd first spoken about it.

'I'm just thinking aloud; let's not get carried away.'

'Then who the hell is he to warrant that?'

'My thought too.'

Lydia started walking again. 'Maybe that's the way in. Someone must be missing him.'

'Yeah, that's worth considering. But you're looking for a needle in a haystack – there's a quarter of a million reported missing every year. Hundreds a day. Without some way of identifying him, it's just a name on a list.'

She looked along the path sloping down to the boating pond, Highgate rising beyond it, a muddle of spires and houses catching the sunlight. 'There's another way to do it.'

CHAPTER 22

An unplanned trip to lean on Assembly Member Nigel Carlton was the last thing Stringer needed.

The morning had been fruitless, a trawl through his material on Jamie Tan. He'd had access to Tan's email accounts for the past ten weeks, but Andriy Suslov's name hadn't come up once – no connection between the men, no pointers to why he'd have an interest in Tan. He double-checked it first thing, then rooted through Tan's most recent items again to see if there was any kind of clue to who might've wanted him dead. Messages were still coming in, both from inside and outside his work. The industry jargon made much of it hard to penetrate, but there was nothing that even hinted at a threat to his life.

From there, Stringer distilled months' worth of appointments from Tan's Outlook calendar into a list of contacts that cropped up regularly enough to warrant further investigation. It pissed him off because it was the tip of a vast iceberg of work that probably still wouldn't shed any light on who killed him. And if he did turn something up, there was always the chance it would lead back to Suslov anyway.

But then the call had come to say that Nigel Carlton hadn't shown up for the lunchtime meeting he'd instructed him to attend. His contact went full-on meltdown on the phone.

'I've rearranged for Mr Samuels to be there at five o'clock. Same office, same address. So now you get him to the cunting meeting, even if you have to drive the cunt there yourself, right?'

It was the superficial aggression of a man out of his depth. The contact was a glorified estate agent called Ronald Simms, acting as go-between for a client who'd intended to stay anonymous. An information imbalance like that was a red rag to Stringer, so he'd run tails on the man until he led him back to the organ grinder: Sir Oliver Kent. Background on Kent revealed him to be a long-time local-government politician who'd spent the bulk of his career at City Hall, working on housing policy and planning, until he set up his own consultancy firm advising some of the UK's biggest developers. Seats on various company boards followed, and the picture emerged of a man leveraging a lifetime of public-sector connections to get private-sector projects off the ground across London – making himself rich in the process. Which explained his interest in Nigel Carlton – a politician with the power to influence all manner of planning policy and approvals through his committee role, and the ambition to go way beyond that. Kent had clout and connections, and that was the only reason Stringer put up with Ronald Simms and his bullshit tough-guy act.

Now he sat on a low wall on the plaza outside City Hall, waiting for a plenary session to break up. The building was nicknamed The Armadillo, but it looked more like The Gherkin had been driven into the ground at an angle, leaving only the top exposed. Even so, with the sunlight glinting off all that glass, the river and Tower Bridge in the background, the place radiated power and influence, and he understood its lure to small men like Carlton.

Members started streaming out into the lobby, and Stringer took that as his cue to go inside. He spotted Carlton at the top of a staircase and watched as he ambled down it, talking to another man he was in stride with. Stringer went against the flow and stood by the end of the handrail, Carlton not seeing him until he'd almost walked into him.

Carlton stopped abruptly on the bottom step, his colleague noticing the expression on his face and asking if everything was alright.

'Yes. Yeah, let me catch you up, Tom...'

The man nodded and carried on, a polite smile to Stringer as he passed.

'Shall we talk outside?' Stringer said.

'I think here will do. And you can save your breath, because it should be clear now that I won't be bending over for you.'

The show of composure was unexpected. 'The meeting's been moved to five p.m.,' Stringer said. 'Same place. You'll be there.'

Carlton stepped off the staircase and faced him. 'Do I look like I came down with the last shower? I know more people in the PR business than you can count. The second you move on me, your little story gets squashed and you're dead in the water. And then I'll come after you.'

Give the man his due, he'd grown a spine in record time.

'Do you recognise these, Nigel?' Stringer pulled a Ziploc bag out of his suit pocket. Inside were a pair of white knickers.

Carlton looked at them without moving his head. 'No, I fucking don't.'

'They're Jennifer Tully's. You sure you don't want to do this outside?'

'I'm going to speak to security.'

'You stand the fuck still.' Stringer crowded him. 'You go to that meeting today, or these get left in your bedroom at an opportune time for your wife to find them.' He was angry enough to add a line about Mrs Carlton doing so when she came home from fucking her bureaucrat in Brussels, but he didn't need him getting sidetracked.

'I'm confident my wife wouldn't give a damn to learn I was screwing someone behind her back.'

Brass-necked motherfucker...

'Even a teenager?'

'We both know that silly bitch is nothing of the sort.'

Stringer blinked, a white flash behind his eyes. He took a slow breath. 'How is it you're always a step behind?'

'I think you're out of bullets and you know it.'

'I haven't even started. Who do you think I'll take with me when I leave these in your house?'

Carlton's eyes narrowed.

Stringer turned to look through the glass doors of the entrance, to the plaza outside. Angie Cross, in her hastiest Jennifer Tully makeup, was sitting on the same low wall. Carlton made eye contact and she lit up into a smile.

'What the fuck is...?'

'She'll be with me, leaving it all there. Fingerprints, hairs, DNA – you won't be able to move for traces of Jennifer Tully. Which is going to look bad for you when she disappears right at the same time. And then your love letters to her get leaked, and your wife finds the panties and ... oh fuck, you're the chief suspect.'

Angie waggled her fingers at him, making eyes across the plaza like a lovesick kid.

Carlton couldn't stop looking. 'It would never ... The police would see through it in a minute. She's not real.'

Stringer shook his head. 'It'll stick long enough to make sure your only way into parliament is on a guided tour.'

'Parliament? Who's talking about...?'

'Don't waste my time, Nigel, your ambitions are no secret. This is your career, in the shitter.'

Carlton finally tore his eyes away, shifting his document case into his other hand. He looked at Stringer again. 'If you ruin me, then I won't be able to do what you want anyway. You'll have shot yourself in the foot.'

'Are you slow? If you're not at that meeting in four hours, you're already no use to me. Which leaves me out of pocket and predisposed to do everything I've talked about, purely out of spite. Because you pissed me off.' Stringer checked his watch. 'Now, economists say we respond better to incentives than threats, so here's your carrot: when you play nicely, you make friends. Friends who can help you when the time does come to get yourself elected.'

'Don't pretend you have that kind of weight.'

'Not me, idiot. The people I work for.'

'And who the fuck is that?'

'People with deep pockets. The friends you need.' He laid a hand on his shoulder. 'Five o'clock.'

Stringer watched his eyes and saw the greed spreading inside them, like blood in water. He wheeled around and walked out through the glass doors. He broke his stride to take a breath, trying to get something clean inside himself. Then he saw Angie looking at him and he moved off again.

She stood up as he came close. 'That poor bastard's face. Looks like it did the trick?'

He took the Ziploc out of his pocket and tossed it to her.

CHAPTER 23

Lydia looked up the address in Surrey Sam Waterhouse had given her as she took the train back from Hampstead Heath. It was a place near the river, not far from Hampton Court – her only point of reference on the map, the area of southwest London displayed not one she knew at all. The TfL website said the journey would take an hour and a quarter each way, so she went home first to change, so she could go straight from there to work that night.

An incoming call displaced the TfL page on screen – Tammy. Lydia pressed *accept*. 'Where've you been?'

'I got your message. She Facebooked me as well.' Tammy sounded breathless.

'And?'

'She said she doesn't want to talk, that it was all a big mistake.'

'Same thing she said to me.'

'She sounded frightened, don't you think? I mean, as much as you can tell from a message.'

'I don't know what to think.' Lydia glanced around, feeling as if all the other passengers were watching her. She got out of her seat and walked to the central part of the carriage. 'Something's not right. I spoke to a neighbour, there were two blokes watching her flat at the weekend.'

'What for?' Tammy cut herself off. 'Sorry, stupid question. But what's that about?'

'God knows. So I'm going to ask. I've got the address the car's registered to, it's in bloody Surrey. I'm on my way back to my place then I'm going to head straight there. Fancy it?'

'Now? I can't, I'm on my way out myself. I might have a way to identify our victim: Joe the Banker.'

'How?'

'I put the word out I was looking for information on big-time money laundering – some of my old contacts. One of them's working on a story about dark money flows out of Eastern Europe, and he's put me on to a guy in the city who's supposedly plugged into that world, reckons if anyone might know the players involved it'd be him. I'm going to his office now.'

'Okay. Then we should get together later to compare notes. Can you do this evening?'

'I can but maybe you should hold off on the Surrey thing for a couple of hours. That way I can come with you?'

'I can't, I've got to be back for work tonight. I'll be fine. It's Surrey – it's all poshos down there.'

'Lyds, I'm serious. If these guys were watching her flat...'

'You're the one going to speak to the international money-laundering guru. Honestly, I'll be fine. About eight tonight?'

'Okay, if you're sure. I'll text you somewhere central to meet when I'm done.'

'Cool. Oh, Tam, one more thing – can you re-send me the video?'

'Why, what happened?'

'Someone deleted it.'

'From your phone?'

'I think so.'

'Shit ... So you were targeted.'

Lydia said nothing, the silence its own answer.

'I'm so sorry, Lydia, I had no idea...'

'Don't worry about it.'

'But how did they find you? That was the whole reason I sent it anonymously, so there'd be no connection to me. I thought I was being paranoid.'

'I guess not.' The train pulled in to her stop and she moved over to the doors. 'Just be careful, yeah?'

Lydia's room was sweltering when she went into the flat, and she stripped off her top straight away, new sweat marks blooming on top of the ones she'd made crossing the heath. She turned her computer on and left it loading up while she made a sandwich for the journey.

When she got back to her bedroom, Tammy's forwarded message was waiting in her inbox. She fired back a thank-you then downloaded the video onto her laptop and saved it to her cloud drive. Then she changed her email password again for good measure.

She played the video through, watching for the best image of the victim. His face wasn't totally clear at any point; he was in profile almost the whole time, and the camera resolution wasn't great. Still she spotted one that might work. She made a screen grab of the paused image, cropped and enlarged it, and then saved it to her hard drive.

Then she posted it to her Twitter, Facebook and Instagram accounts, writing a short message to accompany it: *Need to identify this man. Contact me if you have info. Can DM me in confidence. Please share #JournoRequest*

The Surrey address the car was registered to wasn't near the Thames – it was on it. Not a new build, but someone had spent big money updating it. It was hidden behind a sculpted hedge that masked the black iron railings protecting the front of the house, but through one of the driveway gates, Lydia could see the bottom storey was almost all glass. On display inside, lots of clean lines and high-spec furniture, the look of a show home. There was more glass at the rear of the property so she could see right through the ground floor to a wide lawn outside that ran all the way to the riverbank. A small boathouse clung to the end of the garden, right next to the water.

There was an intercom system built into the wall next to the entry gate, its plaque engraved with the property name – Withshaw. She couldn't see anyone inside and there were no cars on the semi-circular driveway. The place radiated a stillness that made her think no one had been there recently. She pressed the button anyway, on the off chance it was one of the new ones that connected remotely to the owner's phone.

No one answered the muted ring. Looking again, she saw there weren't even any tyre tracks in the gravel out front. There was a small camera above the speaker, the black lens giving her the feeling someone was watching her. She pressed the buzzer one more time, but moved away before it rang out.

She tried two of the neighbours, but no one was home at the first, and a cleaner opened the door at the second. The man didn't even know who owned the house he was cleaning, let alone the one two doors down – which on this street was two hundred metres away. She thought about the relative ease with which she'd tracked down Paulina Dobriska's address – not to mention how someone had left her purse on her doormat. Anonymity was at a premium in 2018, the preserve of the rich.

She found a coffee shop on the way back to the station and took a seat next to the windows, folded open to one side so the room was open to the fresh air. She ordered a double-shot Americano and checked her phone. Her post had been shared several dozen times across the various platforms, but no one had replied. However low her expectations when she'd arrived, hitting another dead end sapped her. A converted flat in Whetstone and an empty mansion on the Thames: locations a city apart, tenuously linked by a flash SUV – but what was the connection?

She Googled the property and its name, Withshaw, looking for its occurrence on the electoral register. A commercial website came up offering data scraped from the official database; it showed some basic anonymised details about the house's occupants over time, but the names and other specifics were hidden behind a paywall. Turned out it didn't matter –

the last listing for the house ran to 2015, meaning the current occupant had removed themselves from the open version of the roll.

She went back to the search results. The next one down was a link to Companies House. Clicking on it, she found that Withshaw Ltd was a private company whose registered address was the one she'd just been to; its business was shown as property management. She clicked another tab that displayed the directors; one was Simon Shelby, a solicitor with an office in Bloomsbury, and the other was a company itself – Arpeggio Holdings, based in the Isle of Man. She clicked the last tab, showing appointments and filings. Shelby and Arpeggio had been appointed directors in 2015 when Withshaw Ltd was founded – presumably when the current owner had first acquired the house.

Her coffee arrived and she sat back in her chair. A property bought by a company, presumably set up as an investment vehicle, itself run by a solicitor and an offshore corporate director. It was a lot of trouble to go to just to own a house, even one worth a small fortune. But of course, it could be one of many; and besides, it didn't have to be anything more sinister than a legal tax avoidance structure.

She swiped her phone and opened Facebook Messenger to re-read her conversation with Paulina Dobriska. A witness but no victim; a crime but no crime scene; too many questions without answers. She typed a message: *What the fuck do you know, Paulina?* She couldn't work up the courage to send it.

CHAPTER 24

Sir Oliver's go-between phoned Stringer at 5.30 that evening. He took the call on loudspeaker as he cruised down Camden Road, driving back from dropping Angie at her crash pad.

'Nigel Carlton showed up for the meet this time,' Simms said.

'Good. When can I expect payment?'

'Let's see what he does first. My client is not impressed that you couldn't get him there first time.'

Stringer thought about Carlton's value to someone like Sir Oliver Kent. A man who'd spent a lifetime building connections, networks, influence; Carlton surely just the latest in a long line of useful pols he'd have cultivated over the decades. 'A few hours' delay doesn't derail anyone's plans.'

'That's not the point.'

'Exactly, it's a wrinkle. So when can I expect payment?'

'The client has bought a result, not a service.'

He braked hard at a red light, seeing it late. 'He got his result.' He nearly dropped Kent's name, just to fuck with the man. 'What happens next is in your hands.'

'They could've paid for a taxi if all they wanted was to get him there.'

'He showed up at the meeting, he's in your pocket.'

'Maybe. But you don't pay your builder when he's just torn your old kitchen out, do you?'

'You've got your incentives backward. You don't pay me, I'll rip up the measures that brought you Carlton. Then see how co-operative he is.'

'You're not that stupid.'

'Don't ever fucking threaten me.'

There was silence on the line. The traffic light turned green and Stringer hit the accelerator.

'See the job through and you'll get your money,' Simms said. 'Anything else is a mistake.' He hung up.

Stringer dropped the phone into the console but noticed there was a notification on the screen. He tried to read it as he drove – a Google alert. He'd set one for Lydia Wright's name, to tell him anytime she published anything new. There was a bus lane running alongside him, nowhere to pull over. He slowed down to let the next set of lights turn red, then grabbed up the phone again.

New posts to Instagram, Facebook and Twitter. He clicked the Twitter link. Right there on her timeline, a picture of Jamie Tan's face, filling his screen, out there for the whole fucking world to see.

Stringer found the pub at the top end of Caledonian Road, opposite Pentonville Prison. The outside was newly painted, a half-hearted attempt to make it look like a gastropub, but inside was another story. A dark room on a bright day, it was dominated by the elongated horseshoe bar. The furniture looked like it hadn't changed since the eighties – flimsy wooden tables, stools covered with dark paisley patterns, now faded. Half a dozen were occupied, mostly by women; wives, girlfriends and mothers, on their way to or from visiting time across the road.

Milos was at a table in the corner, playing with his phone, his eyes masked by the peak of a Golden State Warriors cap. He only looked up as Stringer pulled out a stool. 'Sorry, man, didn't see you come in.'

Stringer sat down and waved a hand to indicate no offence taken. 'You want a drink?'

Milos pointed to his glass, a J2O bottle next to it. 'Nah, I'm good. So what we doing?'

'CCTV.'

'That's a new one.'

'On the Underground.'

Milos bulged his cheeks. 'Not my ends. You talk to Freddie? He can—'

'Not Freddie. I need this to go outside, can you find someone?'

'Sure, but...'

'It'll cost.'

'Yeah. And, uh...'

'You can say the words "finders' fee".'

Milos' face relaxed. 'Okay, cool. Don't wanna piss you off but I gotta get mine, you know?'

'I want my name kept out of this.'

'Always. Not a problem.'

'How much am I looking at?'

'Depends what it involves.'

'I want the footage from Woodside Park Station, last Friday night, eight p.m. till three a.m. All cameras, including the ones covering the car parks, and entrance and exit approaches.'

Milos nodded along, typing a note on his phone. 'Looking for something in particular?'

'Just the raw footage.'

'Cool.' He finished typing and looked up. 'Done. Let's see what comes back.'

'What?'

'I posted it. Someone wants the gig, they'll ping me.'

Stringer looked around, the 1970s surroundings dissonant with a hacker advertising jobs on the dark web in real time. 'How much?'

'We'll see. Guessing two, three grand?'

'What?'

'Easy. More if it's tricky.'

'I thought you outsourced to kids in Latvian basements?'

'Stakes are higher. Everything used to be wide open, but companies are more savvy to it now. Them Russians fucked it up for everyone. And there's pride – now everyone's watching, no one wants to be the wasteman gets caught. You don't want them to know they been done, either, right?'

'Who?' Stringer said.

'The Underground.'

'No. Of course not.'

'So that's more dollar. Anyone can get in and leave footprints. You want clean, it costs.'

Stringer bowed his head. 'Knock them down as much as you can. And I want something else thrown in.'

'Thrown in?'

'I need to know who's behind this email address.' He showed him the aplofel159@gmail.com handle that'd first sent the video to Lydia Wright. 'A name and address would be ideal, a name the bare minimum.' He got up to go.

'Course, Rob. Whatever you need.'

His tone of voice distracted Stringer as he got to his feet, enough that he toppled his stool by accident. It made a crack hitting the floor and the barman looked over. Stringer righted it and toed it back under the table. Milos was already reading his phone again, his face hidden by his cap.

He walked to the door with the name-drop ringing in his

ears – said with a sly wink, as if the fucker knew it was an alias. Every wall he'd built, turning transparent.

CHAPTER 25

Tammy's first suggestion to meet had been a place in King's Cross, but it was the wrong side of town for Lydia to get back to the office after, so she managed to get her to switch it to Southwark.

She came out of the Tube dead on 8.00 p.m. She stood so she was partially hidden behind one side of the entrance, looking along The Cut towards the Young Vic and the bars and restaurants that lined the street around it. It was still light and hot, the outdoor tables at the pub next door all filled, the carefree atmosphere at odds with the sense of foreboding she'd carried in her chest ever since she left Withshaw. A summer evening under a black sun.

She checked her phone and looked around again, no message, no sign of Tammy. She waited five minutes and checked again, this time sending her a WhatsApp message: *Are you here?*

The single tick came up to indicate it had been sent, but not the two blues to say it had been read. The most likely explanation: still on the Tube.

But ten minutes later, it wasn't holding up. The tick was still a single and two phone calls had rung out before going to Tammy's voicemail. She tried one more time, hitting the same wall, so she left a message saying she'd be at the office and to call her if she was still going to show up.

The night was an exercise in distracting herself. Lydia got her work out of the way early; she churned out two articles in an hour on the same American singer and fired them off to the digital sub in the States. She wrote on autopilot, one eye on her phone for word from Tammy. Nothing came. She had dozens of emails that needed responses, but she ignored them and set about her own business.

It was Internet grunt work, the kind she used to hate but now relished by comparison. Her mum's voice in her ears stopping her feeling too sorry for herself: *Be thankful you've got a job at all.* She looked up Simon Shelby, the solicitor listed as director of Withshaw Ltd, but all she could find was that he was a tax lawyer – no surprises there. She wondered if he could be the ultimate owner of the Withshaw property – and therefore the Audi Q7 registered there and seen at Paulina Dobriska's place. But she couldn't come up with a scenario to explain why a tax lawyer would be interested in Paulina – let alone having her flat watched. She called his office number and left a message on his secretary's phone, not expecting she'd get a call back.

By 7.00 a.m. the sun was back above the horizon, making the skyline a silhouette, the skyscraper warning lights only dimly visible in the glare. Still no contact from Tammy, the churning feeling in her guts like alcohol hitting an empty stomach. She was checking her Twitter account when she saw Stephen Langham coming towards her desk. She flicked to a different tab too late, knowing he'd seen it and knowing she made herself look more guilty by doing so. 'Morning. Early start.'

He had his bag in his hand. 'Can we have a word?'

He started towards his office before she'd even got up.

She grabbed a pen and notepad and followed in his wake. When she got there, he was holding the door open for her. He closed it as soon as she went inside.

'Everything alright?' she said.

'This expense form you put in.'

'Yeah?'

'A hundred and fifty quid for what?'

The money she'd had to fork over to Anna at Premier Dental to get Paulina Dobriska's address. 'It was for a source.'

He kept looking at her.

'For information,' she said.

'Okay. Relating to what story?'

'The one I told you about.'

'The one you were going to work on in your own time?'

'I was. It was my day off.'

'Don't be obtuse, Lydia.'

'What're you talking about? I told you what I was doing.'

'You can't incur expenses on a story you're not supposed to be working.'

'Since when? You gave me Sam Waterhouse's details.'

'Who?'

'Bill Roundler's ex-copper.'

He leaned against his desk. 'You wanted to check about a missing person or something? Bill said fifty quid, tops.'

Her insides dipped.

'What?' he said.

'It opened up more avenues, so I asked her to check a couple of extra things.'

'How much?'

'I don't know.'

He pushed off the desk and stood rigid. 'Finger in the air?'

She shook her head, mouth open. 'Five hundred?'

He threw his hands out by his sides.

'Why is it a problem? You put me on to her.'

'Fifty quid I can slide through as a couple of cab receipts. You've run up six-fifty in two days. It's harder to make that vanish.'

'You should've been clearer.'

'I shouldn't have to be.'

'What does that mean?' The unspoken end to his sentence: *if you were more professional.*

'I'm not going to spell it out.'

She clicked her pen over and over, words trapped in her chest.

'Is this Goddard again?' he said. 'You swore to me it wasn't...'

'No.'

'No?'

'Nothing to do with it.'

He looked at the floor. 'So that's something at least. Is the story ready?'

She shook her head.

'Is there even a story?'

'They left my fucking purse on my doormat.'

'Who did?'

'I don't know. Whoever nicked it.'

'What the hell? Did you go to the police?'

She looked at him and then away at the view to Docklands.

He swore under his breath. 'I want to see the video.'

She hesitated, afraid of what he was going to make of it. Slowly, she took out her phone and put it in front of him, pressing play.

Stephen watched the screen, recoiling slightly in his chair as it progressed. When it was finished, she looked at him, waiting for his verdict.

He opened the top drawer of his desk. 'Okay, this is dropped as of right now. Get rid of this copper – make sure she doesn't lift another finger on this thing. And email me a copy of this, please.' He pulled out a Moleskine daybook and a pen. 'I've got a meeting with Evan.'

'Wait, there's something to this.' She threw her hands up, steeling herself. 'Tammy says this guy approached her about being a whistleblower.' She pointed to her phone to indicate the victim, holding Stephen's stare.

'Tammy says this.' He said it in a flat tone.

'He told her he had information on serious money laundering. I know what you think of her, but...'

'You're taking the piss out of me, Lydia. I don't appreciate it.'

The lift beeped as it passed each floor on the way to the underground car park, the sound louder and more grating on two hours' sleep.

Stringer took his phone out of his pocket and found a WhatsApp message from Abi that must've arrived while he was in the shower. A new set of pictures – Ellie playing in a row of dancing fountains that he recognised as Granary Square, by the Regents' Canal behind Kings Cross. In the first she was stretching her toe as far from the rest of her as she could get it, trying to touch the water. She became more adventurous as the series progressed until the last picture, where she was bent over double, hair and clothes soaked, letting the fountain hit her in the face.

He typed *love her* and hit *send*, not seeing his phone had added the emoji with heart eyes after the word "love". His sister would think he was cracking up.

The lift opened and he walked towards the car. When he looked up from his phone, he saw Dalton leaning against the bonnet. 'Andriy sent me to get an update.'

Stringer stopped short. 'Tell Suslov he can call me anytime.'

'That's not how it works when you're worth a billion.'

Stringer took out his key fob and blipped the car. The lights flashed, orange and white reflecting off the bare walls.

'Have you made any headway?' Dalton said.

'I'd make more if you'd let me get on with it.'

'So no, then.'

He shrugged. 'If that's what you came to hear...'

'I told Andriy I thought he'd made a mistake with you.'

'I bet your opinion carries a lot of weight.'

Dalton cracked a rictus grin. 'He doesn't think you can be trusted, but he's wary of you. He seems to think you're some kind of operator. I think you're a cheap blackmail merchant.'

'I've been called worse.'

'It should worry you. What he thinks, I mean. He's unpredictable, but if he thinks you're any kind of threat...'

'Then what? Another little boating accident?'

Dalton came a few steps towards him. 'Tan's wife is missing. Did you know that?'

Stringer stuck his bottom lip out, one of Angie's mannerisms rubbing off on him. 'Is it relevant?'

'Whatever I think of you, you're better than a question like that.'

'Did you go to the house?'

'Of course not. Not personally.'

Stringer put his hands in his pockets. 'What was Jamie Tan to Suslov?'

Dalton shook his head slowly.

'His value to Suslov explains his value to someone else,' Stringer said. 'It leads to motive.'

'You're wasting your time, Andriy's a fucking black hole when it comes to information.' Dalton scratched his cheek. 'He told me to tell you the wife thing has him wondering if it was something personal.'

Stringer squinted at him. 'You haven't seen the video, have you?'

'No interest.'

'The men who did this were serious.'

'They got him in public. I can think of more professional ways to go about—'

'That was necessity. Bold to go after him like that – shows confidence. They know they're not getting caught. And no one's found a body yet either.'

'I have no opinion. I'm telling you what Andriy said.'

'I've told you what I need to know. And money – I need cash.'

'You agreed the terms of your compensation with Andriy.'

'Not for me. A tip fund.'

'For what?'

'Suslov doesn't want to know what I do. Deniability.'

'How much?'

'Ten grand. And when he says no to that, push him for eight.'

'I'll relay what you've said. But you've got to give me something.' For the first time, a crack showed in his front, a flash of genuine discomfort at the prospect of going back to Suslov empty handed.

Stringer looked off to the side, seeing the grain of the pillar next to him, the tiny air bubbles and imperfections in the concrete. 'I know where it happened.'

'Where?'

'Get me the money.'

Lydia marched out of Stephen's office and straight across the newsroom, eyes dead ahead on the lift the whole way. She jammed the button and waited as the indicator showed it creeping up the shaft, the quiet on the floor behind her building in her head. They weren't talking about her. Their eyes weren't trained on her back. No one knew she'd been humiliated.

The lift opened and only when she was inside and the doors closed did she finally let go. 'Fucking twat.'

She pulled out her phone and texted Sam Waterhouse. *Sam – please stop all work on my behalf immediately. Problems this end. How much are your fees to date?*

She stared at it, tapping the screen with her thumbs. Wanting the immediate answer. Then she remembered the time – ten past seven in the morning. Ridiculous working hours, as if anyone needed 24/7 access to bullshit celebrity gossip. She'd seen the presentations from marketing about website traffic spikes at four and five in the morning UK time, fuelled by Americans on the east coast reading their phones in bed. Didn't make her feel any better about leading this twilight life, always out of time with the rest of the world.

She opened Twitter and logged into the *Examiner's* official account. Two million plus followers. She found her own post asking for the identity of the victim in the video and retweeted it, then dropped her phone in her bag before she could regret it.

The lift doors opened and she beelined for the street. A decision becoming clear – she'd fill in the teacher-training pack when she got home, then write her resignation. She could freelance to cover the rent in the meantime, and write the Goddard book – from the story that should've fast-tracked her career, to becoming its full stop. She could cut her spending to nothing, live on porridge if she had to. Anything was better than this, even embracing that most tired cliché: the lost thirtysomething who thinks the classroom is the way out.

At the back of her mind, barely acknowledged: amazement at the righteous anger she could muster to avoid confronting her own feelings of guilt.

She had the bottle of Tesco Sauvignon open but hadn't poured it when Sam Waterhouse replied.

Sorry to hear that. So far £800 + VAT – should I speak to you or Bill Roundler for payment?

Lydia brought her hands up, clasping them behind her head and squeezing. She took the bottle and poured a large glass, then grabbed it off the counter and carried both to her room.

She set them down on her desk and opened the teacher-training pack. The ads used to say 'Get £10k just to train', an outdated slogan that'd stuck in her mind. It was more nuanced now; the leaflet talked about possible bursaries and scholarships, and tuition-fee loans. She filled out her name and date of birth. Stopped to take another sip, imagining the conversation with her mum when she told her about her career change: *But you were always so keen...*

Her parents had helped put her through university to get her journalism degree. The cost then was nothing compared to nowadays, but their contribution still ran to thousands that they'd never asked for back. They'd support her in changing tack but Mum would have that tone that straddled concern and disappointment. Dad was an engineer all his working life, Mum an accountant – their only child was never supposed to go into words. They'd encouraged her anyway, never been less than supportive, and now it felt like she was throwing it in their faces.

The form wanted her National Insurance number and she didn't have it to hand. She got up from her desk and lay on the bed, holding her phone above her face, staring at her last message to Tammy, the words blurring. She tapped out a new one: *What happened to you last night?*

She let her hand drop to her side and stared at the ceiling, following the line of a thin crack in the plasterwork. A dozen years since she'd graduated. Starting out on trade magazines: *Design Week, Marketing Week*, the jobs as dull as they were badly timed – just as the Internet pulled the plug on the classified ad revenue that kept the magazines afloat. From there, catching on in local papers – but having to abandon London for Kent to do so. Years spent working local beats, all the time trying – and failing – to find the discipline to write her novel. Distracted by a series of relationships, none of which went anywhere, and nights in the pub trying to play office politics. Then, six years ago, her big break at last: the job with the *Examiner.* A move back to London, a redemptive comeback that quelled restless thoughts she'd wasted her twenties, even as she realised how many of her friends she'd lost touch with.

So what did it mean if she turned her back on all that? That she'd been right in the first place?

Lydia brought up Facebook Messenger and opened her chat with Paulina Dobriska. She typed: *Talk to me. Please talk to me.*

CHAPTER 26

Stringer sat at the same table as before in the Costa. There were others with a more direct view of Lydia Wright's flat, but he'd made peace with his compulsive tendencies years ago. He had a coffee in front of him, a half-eaten sandwich that doubled as breakfast and lunch, and a napkin he'd torn in half.

He scribbled a list on the back of his receipt – open leads: first, Milos, for the CCTV footage. He'd come back with a quote of three and half thousand, plus five hundred for himself. It was brazen and it pissed him off because he was certain the grasping fucker was taking a cut of the principal too. Second, Jamie Tan's business. The fragments he knew about international equity trading did nothing to help him penetrate Tan's world. Alicia was his best point of entry, but every visit to her put both of them at risk – and made him feel worse about his lies. Third, Premier Dental, the clinic in Finchley Lydia Wright had visited. He still couldn't find a connection, and it had him worried that he was missing something obvious. The situation with Nigel Carlton compounded the feeling. He'd misread the man badly after the first approach, underestimating him. His judgement was the foundation of everything and if it was slipping, it left him exposed – especially with predators like Suslov circling.

His phone sounded. A new email. He opened it to look; it was a discount offer from Azure, the boutique hotel where they'd stayed when they visited the Florida Keys ten years before. He was ruthless at keeping his inbox free from marketing junk, but he could never bring himself to unsubscribe from this mailing list.

The email was touting a late summer sale on room rates, but it wasn't the words that captured his interest, only the images. It showed the hotel, right by the water, separated from Florida Bay by a private beach no more than ten feet wide. A pier stretched out from the shore, doubling as a boat dock. He remembered sitting on it the evening they'd arrived, fetching two loungers off the sand and up onto the jetty, the feel of the wood, dry and weathered, on his bare feet. They'd shared a bottle of wine with the sun dissolving on the horizon, in a breeze as warm as a steam bath.

It was the holiday of a lifetime, and the one that was supposed to save a marriage that was petering out after eighteen months. His work was the main point of contention, but not the only one – money, stress, family all had a stake. Against the odds, the plan succeeded – but not how they'd expected. In the months that followed, he'd romanticised that first night as being the one they conceived, even though there was no way to be sure. It was unplanned but not unwanted; the result of a pill that'd been forgotten, or straight up didn't work – who could say. They came to joke about it as their miracle baby.

At twenty-one weeks they lost it. He'd moved out a month later – her choice, but a relief for both of them once it was agreed. The baby had been a sticking plaster that might have been strong enough to let the wound underneath heal; but ripping it away made them weaker than they had been at the start, and it was more than they could overcome. He hadn't seen her, hadn't spoken to her in eight years. He heard from Abi she'd remarried and had a family with someone else.

He didn't let himself dwell on it much anymore, save the times in the dead of night when he'd find himself trying to picture what their child might've looked like.

He lifted his eyes just as a man approached Lydia Wright's door. He had a suit on and salt-and-pepper hair, and a watch on his wrist that was big enough to see from across the street. He recognised him from somewhere, but couldn't isolate the memory. He got up to go outside and get a better look. He stood on the kerb, squeezing his car keys in his pocket like a stress ball.

He watched as the man pressed the bell, then stepped back from the doorway to wait, looking up. A few seconds later, Lydia Wright answered the door looking woozy.

Lydia opened her eyes with a start, still half in a dream. She was alone in a Tube carriage, speeding through a tunnel, when the tracks fell away, dragging her down into blackness. The echo of the sound was still in her mind, screams drowned out by the sound of rushing air. She rubbed her eyes, trying to shake it off. The doorbell rang again and she lurched off the bed to go to the window.

Stephen was on the street below. He looked up when she cracked the blinds, because he never missed a single bloody thing.

She went along the landing and ducked her head into the kitchen to check the time on the oven. She couldn't remember falling asleep, but she'd been out for four hours. She jogged down the stairs, only remembering the application form spread across her desk as she got to the bottom. She could see his shadow through the frosted glass in the door.

'Hi.'

'What are you doing here?'

'Can we talk inside?'

She glanced back down the hallway. 'I'm not ready for another dressing-down.'

'That's not what I came for.'

She thought about it, gently tugging at the hem of her top. 'Come up.'

She led him along the hallway and climbed the stairs, ending up in the kitchen. She flicked the kettle on, suddenly conscious of the wine on her breath, thankful she hadn't left the bottle on display. 'Make you a tea?'

'Just a water. Please.'

She filled a glass and gave it to him. 'I thought you'd be chained to your desk.'

He drained half. 'I felt bad about the way we left things.'

'Same.'

He put his drink down and pulled open his suit coat to reach for the inside pocket. 'Here.' He produced a wad of neatly folded money.

'What's this?'

'Take care of the police woman's fees. Just make sure no paperwork comes into the business.'

She stared at his outstretched hand.

'There's a thousand there, in case it was more than your estimate.'

'Is this ... Where's this from?'

'Doesn't matter. You were right, I should've been explicit.'

'Is this your money? I can't take it.'

He put it down on the counter, the top note unfurling. 'It all gets squared in the end.'

She wrapped both hands around her mug and held it by her mouth. 'I swear to god I wasn't trying to take advantage.'

'I know. It just felt like it earlier.'

'I wouldn't do that to you.'

They stared at each other, some kind of unspoken truce settling between them. His eyes were a watery blue, the first thing she could remember noticing about him.

Stephen took half a step towards her. 'Look, I came over because I'm worried about you. I had Sasha in my office before lunch complaining about your work.'

The other Botox Twin. 'Saying what?'

'That it's been choppy lately. The quality's uneven.'

She put her mug down and stood up straight. 'Cheeky cow. What do they expect me to do with the crap they give me?'

'The subject matter isn't the issue. She was saying that your stuff seems rushed. Sloppy.'

'Rubbish. That's absolute—'

'I'm not saying I agree.'

He toyed with his water glass, dragging it back and forth across the counter. 'Tell me one thing – you're not trying to get yourself sacked, are you?'

'Sacked? No.'

'I know how unhappy you are, but that wouldn't be the answer.'

'That's not what I'm doing. The opposite, in fact.'

'What does that mean?'

'What it sounds like. Show people what I'm capable of.'

'You don't have anything to prove. It was never about that.'

'What then? What happened with Goddard?' She regretted it as soon as she said it, a breach in the Chinese wall they'd constructed around the subject. A silence followed, proof he'd recognised it too.

He picked up his glass and set it down again, very gently. 'The story wasn't there.'

She closed her eyes and turned away.

'There was good reporting in what you did; it didn't go unnoticed. But you took a shortcut.'

'And I've been kicking myself for it ever since. That doesn't mean there was nothing to it.'

'Maybe there was, maybe not – but the story was nowhere near ready to publish, and certainly not ready for you to go after him. I saw it with my own eyes.'

'Then you saw the evidence. Everyone from Goddard down stood to profit directly or otherwise. They were taking bribes, it's the only explanation. They were in bed with the developers and now he's special adviser to a soon-to-be MP with well-known leadership ambitions, and no one gives a fuck.'

'That's an inference from what you had. The proof was missing. You have to be watertight with these people, they eat us alive otherwise.'

'So why pull the plug? You could've given me a slap on the wrist and put me back on the case.'

'You're talking as if it was my decision alone. Evan, Meredith, Gavin, they're all involved in these conversations...'

'That's what I meant. *Management.*'

He drew a breath. 'There was a thought it might teach patience.' He stepped closer again, his hand on the counter to tap the pile of cash. 'That's why this bothered me so much. Today felt like another shortcut.'

'So that one mistake defines my whole career? How am I supposed to prove anything to anyone when I'm producing filler for the white space around the bloody pictures?'

'You're still not getting it. Professionalism, maturity. Patience. That's what the business looks for. Not some blockbuster exclusive.'

'That's not how it works anymore. People are on Twitter all day for news – look at the *Guardian* lot, they tweet every bloody thought that comes into their heads. People want to follow a story as it develops, not just see the end piece.'

'We're talking about two different things, and you know it.'

'I spent six years being patient.'

'There's a vote of confidence in what happened. They might have binned anyone else altogether.'

She raised her eyebrows. 'Do they ask you to keep reminding me that?'

He rubbed his mouth, about to say something, when she put her hands up. 'Sorry.' She took his hand on the counter and kissed him. 'Sorry.'

'Forget it.'

'I'm grateful for this. Really.'

'I know.' His eyes slipped to his watch. 'This thing with Tammy – how far have you got with it?'

'It's coming along.'

'Truthfully.'

'I've got a few things live. I found the woman who took the video, I'm trying to convince her to speak to me. Tammy's got a lead on who the victim was. Her whistleblower.'

'She doesn't know who he was?'

'They only met once. He wouldn't tell her.'

Stephen was shaking his head as she said it.

Lydia leaned against the counter. 'She was trying to get him to trust her.'

'She was sloppy. Is she sure it's the same guy? The video's not exactly clear.'

'She says so.'

'She would, she lives for that kind of thing.'

'Not this again...'

'Do you trust her?'

'That's a leading question.' Lydia cocked her head. 'Why?'

He looked away as if it was nothing.

'No, go on.'

'I was just surprised she came to you,' he said. 'I didn't know you were still friendly.'

'We've always been mates. That didn't stop when she got let go.'

'No, not you. Her.'

She stared at him. 'I don't follow.'

He checked his watch again, but it didn't seem to register. He ran his fingers over his chin, as if deciding whether to say something. 'Look, you can't ever repeat this.'

'Just tell me.'

'When the Goddard thing blew up – the first time – Tammy was lobbying to take over the story. She wanted us to pull rank on you for her.'

Lydia splayed her hand on the countertop. 'She fucking what?'

'She wanted you off it. It was part of the reason Gavin told you to leave it alone – Tammy was driving him and Meredith mad about it. So you can understand why I was surprised when her name came up.'

'Why didn't you say something?'

He shot her a look that said *be reasonable*. 'I shouldn't be saying anything now.'

She looked away, nodding an acceptance at his explanation. It felt like she'd been tricked.

'Anyway. I just thought you should know before you take anything on trust from Tammy.' A final glance at his watch. 'I've got to go.'

When he was gone, she went back to her room and gathered the application papers into a slapdash pile, leaving the pen on top as proof to herself she'd go back to it. She simmered doing it, feeling betrayed, lied to, undermined, a dozen questions burning in her mind. She thought about calling Tammy to have it out with her right then, but she stopped herself, just enough self-control left to realise she'd be betraying Stephen's confidence in doing so.

She picked up the wine bottle and glass, and an empty mug, and ferried them all to the kitchen, then went back to her room and plugged in her phone. The screen lit up as the charger connected, and there was a notification showing – a missed call via Facebook from Paulina Dobriska.

She jumped up and hit the button to call her back, yanking the charger cable out so she could pace to the window with the phone to her ear.

It made the warped ringing sound and then she answered. 'You saw my call?'

'Yes, Paulina, hi. I'm so glad you got in touch.'

'You can help me?'

'Yes. Yes, I hope so. Where are you?'

The line went quiet, background noises on the other end that sounded like rushing water, but might just have been the connection. 'I need to get some money.'

'What for?'

'A plane ticket. I have to leave.'

'Where are you going?'

'I just have to leave. I don't feel safe here anymore.'

'Paulina, has someone threatened you? Because of what you saw? Your video, did you know any of the men?' It was too many questions all at once, eagerness getting the better of her.

'Can you get me money or no?'

She stared at Stephen's pile of fifties, sitting on the desk. 'Maybe some. Look, before anything else, can you say a bit about yourself?'

'What? Why?'

'So I know for sure who I'm talking to.'

'What you want me to say?'

'Well, can you confirm your address?'

'No. No way I'm saying that to you. I don't live there no more anyway.'

She realised then why the question spooked her. 'I already know where you live, you don't have to tell me the whole thing, what about just the flat number?'

'65b. How do you know...?'

'What about the nearest Tube to your work?'

'Finchley Central. Why you wasting my time? You want to know who I am? I the one saw a man get killed right in front of my fucking eyes. If you seen the video, how much more you want to hear?'

She stood on her tiptoes, afraid to move. 'Okay that's fine, thank you. Last thing: did you speak to my colleague, Tammy?'

'She's working with you?'

'Yes, sort of. She's a friend.'

'No. She message me but when I called her she didn't answer. So I call you.'

'Look, why don't we meet? How about—'

'If you bring the money I see you tonight. Five hundred pounds.'

'Okay. Where?'

'Ten o'clock. You know Brent Cross station?'

Patience. Professionalism. 'Yes.'

A link from Milos arrived via WhatsApp while the man was inside Wright's flat. The accompanying message told Stringer he'd need to use the Tor browser to access the website, which would slow the download speed because of the huge size of the CCTV files, and the server-jumping involved. On its heels came a second message, containing an address in Kentish Town.

This is where that email came from. Woman called Tammy Hodgson lives there. Tell her ain't no point using a fake email account if she's gonna do it from her home IP address.

He banked the name and looked up the address on Google Maps. Forty-five minutes from where he was now, with traffic. He went back to the search on his phone. It'd taken him a few minutes to place where he'd seen the man inside before: at the journalist's office in London Bridge. So what was he doing at her flat now? And why did it niggle him?

The man emerged again after fifteen minutes, leaving on his own. Stringer watched as he rubbed his neck, a faraway look on his face. It was fleeting, the man taking his phone out and pressing it to his ear while he flagged a cab. The blinds in the upstairs window twitched, and Stringer could make out her shadow behind them.

He crumpled the two halves of napkin on the table and threw them in his empty cup.

Tammy Hodgson's flat was a single-storey modern annexe tacked onto the side of a Victorian semi. It had its own entrance on a side street, around the corner from that of the main building. Stringer parked in a bay across the road from her door.

He'd looked her up before he left. It didn't take long to get the picture. Hodgson was another journo, formerly with the *Examiner* – explaining the link to Lydia Wright. A skim of her bio was impressive: she was credited with being on to the Credit Crunch before it happened, and subsequently being among the first to expose the malpractice in the banking industry that had caused it. That'd cemented her place at the top table, and from there she was one of the select group of journalists to first receive the Panama Papers, the 2015 insider data leak from the Panamanian law firm Mossack Fonseca that exposed money-laundering schemes linked to a dozen heads of state, and laid bare the widespread abuse of tax havens by the global elite. He wondered why her career had seemingly come to a hard stop such a short time later.

He watched her place for half an hour before he decided she wasn't home. From where he sat he could see the large window of the front room; the main panel was frosted for privacy, but he could make out enough of the room behind it to see there was no one moving about inside. There was the chance she was in the kitchen or bedroom, but he rated it unlikely she wouldn't have passed through the front room at all in that time. And when a DPD driver pulled up with a parcel, but got no answer from the knocker, it confirmed it.

He slipped across the road and down the short path to her door. There was grass either side of it, but barely enough to call a garden. The annexe ran the width of the main house's flank, meaning there was no rear access. He checked there was no one on the street then glanced through the side panel of the window, seeing a long, narrow front room with two open doorways leading off the back of it – one was the kitchen, another that was dark and looked like a hallway.

He stepped to the side to get a different angle on the lounge. There was a sofa along one wall, a flatscreen opposite, and a desk with an oversized Apple monitor in the far corner. Two floor-to-ceiling bookcases took up the remaining wall space. The centre of the room was brighter than the edges; he looked up and saw a skylight in the ceiling.

He stepped back, deciding what to do. No way of knowing how soon she might return. He looked at the lock on the front door – new enough to be tricky. He tried the handle to see how firm its housing was.

It was unlocked. The door swung inwards.

He stepped inside on reflex, whipping the door shut so he couldn't be seen from the street.

His skin felt electrified. The flat was silent, and he stood motionless, feeling his heart thudding in his chest, listening for any noise. He was in a short hallway, another doorway ahead to his left, leading into the front room. He heard a car pass by outside, the most mundane sound, now magnified in his ears.

He took a step forward and paused, the air so close and still it felt like it folded around him. A second step and he was in the lounge. His gaze fell on the desk first. There was an empty space in front of the monitor, two unplugged cables snaking across the desktop – as if a laptop would normally be there. The top drawer was ajar.

He moved slowly across the room to the kitchen doorway, flinching a little every time his shoes scraped the wooden floor. He ducked his head inside, saw a plate, mug and bowl in the sink, a tub of Flora on the counter, the lid off, a butter knife sticking out of it, the contents melted almost to liquid. He waited again, breathing silently. He backed up and went through the adjacent doorway, into the rear hallway.

It was dark, no windows in the passage, the two doors at right angles to each other at the far end both closed. He walked along it, faster now, driven on by the tension knotting his gut. He used his knuckle to push open the door to his right – a bathroom. It was cramped but neat, a shower cubicle filling most of the space, a toilet and compact washbasin the rest.

He turned to the last door. He pulled his sleeve over his hand to turn the knob, then pushed to let it swing open.

Tammy Hodgson was lying on top of the bed. She was fully clothed. Her eyes were open, the whites turned blood red. He didn't need to go any closer to know she was dead.

A voice in his head shouted: *GO, NOW*. He resisted it. He took in the room without daring to move. A glass had been knocked from the bedside table, but the carpet around where it lay was dry. Either it'd been empty, or it was an indicator she'd been dead some time. A pillow had tumbled to the floor too, on the other side. There was a pair of flat shoes at the end of the bed, looked like she'd kicked them off, and a novel on the bedside table, laid open face down to keep its page. He couldn't see her phone anywhere, nor any telltale outline in her trouser pockets.

He checked his watch to see how long he'd been inside the flat – three minutes. He gave himself another two and went back to the lounge, the desk. A frame on the desktop held a picture of Hodgson with a boy, the pair smiling, a sunny day in a park somewhere. His stomach dipped at the thought she had a kid. He glanced around, realising there was no sign of a child living there, no second bedroom that could accommodate him. A grim reassurance the kid wouldn't be the one to find her. He forced himself to keep going.

The top drawer was empty apart from some loose change and a paper clip.

Second drawer – empty.

Bottom drawer – ditto.

In his mind he saw the killer or killers hurriedly dumping the contents into a duffel bag, along with her laptop. He looked along the bookshelves – a mixture of fiction and non, books on international finance, politics, banking, Russia, sharing shelf space with rows of rom-coms and crime.

He checked his watch, glanced around again. The TV was above a cabinet with two cupboard doors, the only other storage in the room. He crossed to it and opened both, glancing at the window as the fear made him feel like he was being watched. Inside were DVDs, a box of tangled AV cables, a sheaf of printer paper and a stack of magazines. He leafed through the top few issues, saw nothing of relevance.

He silently closed the cupboards and stood up, woozy. The dead woman on the bed. The signs they'd ransacked her.

The intruder at Lydia Wright's flat...

CHAPTER 27

Lydia left early, hoping to steal an extra half hour if Paulina Dobriska showed up sooner than they'd arranged. There was time to make the meet and still get to the office for midnight, but an extra thirty minutes could make the difference. Staring through the Tube window at the orange streetlights blurring across the north-London night, she wondered why she cared about punctuality anymore. Wasn't she quitting?

Stephen's money was folded away deep inside her bag. She'd make up the rest of Sam Waterhouse's fee out of her own pocket. Somehow. Waiting while the train crept north made her antsy so she tried to focus on her priorities. Most important: did Paulina know either the victim or the attackers? Lydia's assumption was not, but if it turned out she did, that blew things wide open. Second, what happened after the video ended? It seemed likely she'd fled, but what did she see? If Sam Waterhouse was right that there was someone else helping them, maybe Paulina got a look at a car or a person – people? – waiting somewhere. Third: had she spoken to the police? If not, why not? And maybe linked to question four: had she been threatened, directly or otherwise, in the aftermath? She sounded terrified on the phone, so maybe that was its own answer to both.

The automated voice announced Brent Cross was the next station. The train glided to a stop, the platform at rooftop level. The shopping centre was just visible through the trees, the glow from its lights seeping into the night sky. The train waited with its doors open after she stepped off, the unnatural quiet undercut by the rush of traffic coming from the North Circular.

Antsy to straight-up nervous. Her thoughts started to

unspool, speeding up with her heartbeat. She took her time going down the steps to the ticket hall, trying to bring back some calm. Half a dozen other passengers overtook her as she went. Behind everything, there was still her anger at Tammy. She'd held off from calling her, and the realisation Tammy hadn't even bothered to message her to explain why she stood her up at Southwark the night before only pissed her off more. So now being first to the punch with Paulina gave her a sense of payback.

She came out of the ticket hall into a gloomy car park. She was twenty-five minutes early. There was a light on in the minicab office to her right, a café, a dry cleaners and a newsagent next to it, all of them shuttered for the night. The other side of the car park was lined with trees and bushes, a glimpse of a row of mock-Tudor houses behind them.

She walked along the small parade of shops. A man behind a high desk in the cab office glanced up as she looked through the window, but went straight back to his phone. She carried on to the end of the parade, where it met the main road. Above her, a bridge coated in peeling grey paint carried the tracks above the street, an empty bus stop underneath it, one of its Perspex panels missing.

There was no sign of Paulina. She looked around and saw a tall pole holding two CCTV cameras, pointed at the car park and the station entrance. Back in the ticket hall, a man in a suit was talking on his phone, and one of the station staff was writing on the white board. She retraced her steps and went to stand near them.

After fifteen minutes, a woman appeared at the corner of the car park, alone. She stopped at the far end of the shopping parade and looked around, glancing in Lydia's direction. She made eye contact but Lydia didn't move. There was a resemblance, but it was hard to tell at a distance.

The woman took a few steps towards her again and curled her finger for Lydia to come over, her manner impatient, as if Lydia had missed a signal. She moved slowly in her direction, trying to get a better look. As she came close, she felt a flutter in her chest – it wasn't Paulina.

'You are Lydia?'

'Who are you?'

'Paulina is waiting. She's in the car.' The woman jerked her head to her right.

'Can you tell her to come here, please.'

'She will not come. She sent me.'

Lydia stared at her, and slowly started shaking her head. 'No. If she wants the money, I'd like to see her face first.'

The woman rolled her eyes. 'You come with me or I go home, up to you. You two playing your bloody silly games. The car's right there.' She inclined her head again, her hands in the pockets of her hoodie.

Lydia looked up at the CCTV cameras, then back towards the ticket hall. The Underground man had a panel open on one of the ticket gates, trying to fix it. *Do you want this or not?* 'Okay.'

The woman turned and walked on ahead of her.

'How do you know Paulina?' Lydia said.

'She's my cousin. She stay with me when she arrived from Poland. Now all this crap and she says she has to go back.'

Lydia sped up so she could draw level with her. 'Did she tell you about what happened?'

The woman guided them down a long residential street, heading away from the bridge. 'I tell her I don't want to know.

I got enough bloody problems with Brexit and all that shit, I don't need her trouble. She tell me she's leaving, I said okay.'

They made another left turn, down the road with the mock-Tudor houses. 'Where's your car?'

The woman pointed somewhere ahead. 'Up there. Red Kia.' She walked on again.

Lydia looked back towards the main road, ten metres away. Already thirty seconds from the station. She couldn't see the Kia she was talking about.

'You coming or no?'

She kept walking but her insides were crawling. She let the woman's voice bounce around her head, thinking it sounded like the one she'd heard on the Facebook call earlier. Almost sure of it. Was this Paulina after all, playing games? Or something else?

The woman was a short way ahead; she stopped and turned around again, beckoning Lydia to catch up, impatience returning. Lydia slowed as she scanned the cars in the darkness, trying to see the Kia—

A man burst out of the car next to her. He locked his arm around her neck, so fast she couldn't even scream. She clawed behind herself for his face, instinct taking over, but the woman rushed over and pinned her arms.

She couldn't breathe, starbursts in her vision. They bundled her towards the open door. She felt the man turning to force her inside; she got her foot on the frame to stop him, but he cinched his grip tighter and one of them kicked the back of her knee to buckle her leg. She was halfway inside the car—

His arm went slack. The man collapsed to the pavement, dragging her with him.

She snatched a breath. From the ground she saw the woman

turn and run. Lydia pushed the limp arm off her neck and scrambled to get up, but then she saw a new face standing over her. Through her panic she recognised him – the man who'd been talking on his phone in the ticket hall.

He reached his hand out to help her up, some kind of weapon dangling from the other one. 'Come on.'

Stringer watched Lydia Wright walk away from the station from the other side of the road. He'd hung around the ticket hall while she waited for as long as he could without being conspicuous, then moved to a bus stop under the bridge that gave him a line of sight to where she was standing.

He took photos of the woman she was following on his phone, catching her face in the light from the minicab office. No one he recognised. He heard her saying something about 'trouble' and 'not wanting to know' before they slipped out of earshot. He let them get a head start then followed after, Wright's evident unease spreading to him.

When they turned off the main road, he went as far as the corner and stopped, a tall hedge wrapped around the first house on the street providing cover. He saw the journalist hesitating, and the woman getting impatient ahead of her.

They walked on a few more steps and then everything went to shit.

He saw the door of a black Saab fly open and the man lunge out. Big guy, heavyset, dark clothes. Stringer started running, pulling his telescope baton out of his pocket. The woman was helping now, clearly in on it too.

He flicked the baton out as he came close and coshed the

man on the back of the head. He went to swing again, but the guy was already down. On the floor, he saw his eyes lolling. A snap take: not the same man who'd broken into her flat.

The woman took off down the street. Stringer reached his hand out to Lydia. 'Come on.'

She looked up at him, eyes wide and face taut.

'Let's go,' he said.

She scrambled backward and used the car to claw herself to her feet, gaze flicking between him and the man on the floor. Stringer had one eye on the surroundings, looking for the woman or anyone watching from the houses. He glanced at Lydia again and curled his hand twice, circling around the car at the same time so he could check the number plate.

'What the fuck is...?'

He memorised it and then knelt on one knee, using the pavement to jam the baton back into its handle. 'We'll talk. Not here.'

The man on the ground stirred and Lydia stepped into the gutter to get away from them both.

Stringer started moving off, eyes locked on hers, hand outstretched.

Lydia watched, frozen in place.

'I've seen the video.'

Her eyes flared again. 'What is ... Who the fuck are you?'

'Come with me.'

She shook her head, backing away across the road. She made it to the other pavement and then she turned and ran full pelt.

Lydia ran into the station checking over her shoulder. She

couldn't see the staff member from before anywhere. Her legs were trembling and she was covered in sweat.

She ran up the stairs to the platforms. There were a handful of people dotted around. The indicator boards showed three minutes for a train in either direction. She stood at the top of the staircase and realised she was trapped if they were behind her. She looked at the tracks, gauging if she could scramble across them – but then what? *Fuck, fuck—*

She reached for her phone to call the police. When she unlocked it, there was a notification on the screen – a DM from Paulina Dobriska's account:

KEEP YOUR MOUTH SHUT YOU LYING CUNT. WE KNOW WHERE YOU ARE, WE CAN GET YOU ANYTIME

Lydia dropped the phone. It crashed onto the metal lip of the top step and then cascaded onto the next one. She took a ragged breath, violent tremors shaking her whole body now.

'You alright, love?'

She looked around and there was a man with a baseball cap standing to her side.

He bent down to scoop up her phone and held it out for her. 'Christ, hate it when that happens.'

The screen was shattered but still working, the notification legible through a thousand splinter lines.

She snatched it from him and backed away, his expression turning to a question mark. She watched his face, wondering if he was part of it, waiting for his mask to slip. Instead he stayed where he was, looking at her like she was drunk.

She saw the white help point ahead of her on the platform and she ran towards it. She pressed the *Emergency* button and a ringing sound came from inside the unit. She looked over her shoulder but the man who'd picked up her phone had sidled off down the platform.

No one answered. She hammered the button, knowing it would make no difference.

Then the train pulled in behind her, an overload of noise and light. When the doors opened, she wheeled around and jumped on.

CHAPTER 28

Lydia slammed the communal door shut and ran up the stairs. She unlocked the flat and went inside, double-locking the door behind her before turning around and bracing herself against it. After a minute she let herself slide down, drawing her knees to her chest as she hit the floor.

The flat smelled of clean washing. Chloe's room was shut, but she could see the clothes horse covered in laundry in the hallway next to the kitchen. It should've felt familiar and safe. The tremors had stopped, but her neck and throat were starting to ache and she felt sick.

After a few minutes she gathered herself up and went to her bedroom, reaching around the doorway to flick the light on before she went inside. She sat on the bed still wearing her bag across her chest. *What the fuck is happening?*

Her thoughts jumped and short-circuited. The woman: not Paulina Dobriska. All their communication had been through Facebook, so these people must have control of her account. The man who'd grabbed her – one of the ones from the video? She couldn't picture him now, but her gut feeling was that he'd been more heavyset.

Then there was the second man. On the face of it he'd saved her life. But nothing about that made sense. What was more plausible – that a white knight had appeared out of thin air, or that he was part of it? Was she supposed to walk off with him and spill her guts? The whole thing was too insane to process.

No. He said he'd seen the video. She'd seen him talking on his phone when she was waiting at the station entrance. He looked like a lawyer or an accountant, or any other commuter heading home in a suit. But he said he'd seen the video. No coincidence – he'd been there because of her. Watching her.

What else did he say? Had he used her name? He'd said they should talk, she remembered that. Where did he go after? No, she hadn't seen. All of it so fast, memories dissipating like steam.

She took her bag off and let it fall to the floor, turning the light out before she went to the window. She stood to one side to crack the blind and look out. Past midnight. There were cars on the street but the pavements were empty. She rolled away to lean against the wall and took out her phone, but didn't look at it at first, thinking about the police again.

When she lifted it up, the DM was still on the ruined screen. A new tremor rattled from her chest down her arms as she typed her reply:

GO FUCK YOURSELF

Stringer ran the registration from the black Saab through a website and got the result he expected: nothing found. He had a contact who could get a proper DVLA check done, but it would take time and money to confirm the obvious: whoever they were, they were smart enough to use false plates.

He stood at his kitchen counter, the white-blue glare from the laptop the only light in the room. He toggled to another window, Milos' CCTV cache still downloading. The dialogue box said forty-three minutes to go – and had done for the last five.

He stepped away from the screen. Almost 2.00 a.m. He walked to the balcony doors that looked out over London. The sky was a grey-purple, light pollution ensuring the darkness was never complete over the city. His thumbs were poised over his phone, still hedging over how to word his approach. He had a draft email in the works, and he started typing again.

I was there tonight – the guy in the suit. I have seen the video. I'm no threat to you, and I don't know the people who attacked you. I realise you must be shaken but we can help each other if you'll talk to me. Don't stay on your own tonight if you can avoid it.

He pressed send and watched it fly off to Lydia Wright's work email address. He had a feeling she'd be awake still, unless the adrenaline had burned her out completely.

He wanted to warn her about her dead former colleague, but there was no way he could say anything without looking guilty. The last thing he could afford now was to spook her any worse. When he'd got clear of the scene in Kentish Town, he'd used a throwaway to call the police to report a disturbance at Hodgson's address. He reasoned now that he'd done all he could.

What it meant was another matter.

He went back to the laptop and started the protocol to access Jamie Tan's Outlook calendar – but a red cross flashed up on the screen, *Access Denied*. That was new; if Tan's bosses at the bank had locked it down, the police must have been in touch. That boxed him in more than he already was.

He opened up the archive version he'd downloaded to his hard drive. Tan had been a frequent traveller for business, mostly to Frankfurt, but also Paris, Moscow and Cyprus. He'd never shadowed him on one of those trips because there'd been no need – Tan provided plenty of material to work with on these shores, in the form of a fierce recreational cocaine habit. He'd found out about it early on. Far from unique among his colleagues, Tan's biggest problem was that he was generous with it – doling it out with gusto. Even though he rarely accepted money for his generosity, it was enough to fit him up for possession with intent to supply, which would cost him his Financial Conduct Authority licence, and therefore his job – especially if someone with Suslov's influence was the one dangling it over him. For any normal coercion sting that would've been sufficient, but Suslov's instructions at the outset had been explicit: 'I want him on strings'. So Stringer kept watching until he was told otherwise, setting up to ensure he had everything he could on Tan.

Somewhere in it all, he'd lost his way.

What he discovered was that Jamie Tan had a secret second life, one he kept hidden from his colleagues and friends: he volunteered at two homeless shelters, sometimes working through the night and going straight to the office the next morning, only stopping long enough to shower at the gym. He worked with a charity in Hackney, ReachOut, mentoring underprivileged kids in maths. He gave money to Christian Aid with increasing zeal, almost as if he sensed his time was short. On Mondays and Wednesdays, he put fake lunch meetings in his work calendar, a cover so he could slip into a nearby church to pray. Stringer followed him inside once. He sat in a pew at the back and watched Tan spend forty minutes on his knees, hands clasped and head bowed. On his way out, he lit half a dozen candles. Whatever Tan was doing, the toll it was taking on his conscience was plain to see.

It was a few days later that Stringer had fucked up. His own conscience the cause. He still had no explanations for it.

He'd fronted him after an all-night surveillance session. Blaming it on no sleep was a cop out, but there was no doubt his judgement had been impaired. He'd waited for Tan to come out of his office, then walked up to him in silence, his phone held out in front of him. The picture onscreen showed Tan in a bar handing a baggie of white powder to a colleague, neither man making any attempt to conceal what they were doing. Stringer said nothing at first, waiting until he was sure Tan recognised what the image showed.

'I've got hundreds more like it, enough to destroy you. The people I work for are coming for you. I don't know if you deserve it. Drop everything and disappear.' He walked away before Tan had a chance to say a word.

It didn't make him feel any better, then or now. Rash actions never did. And he'd fucked up Andriy Suslov's plans, and put his own neck on the block in the process.

His phone buzzed on the counter, rattling itself in a quarter-circle. It was a reply from Lydia Wright, the message so short it drew his eye immediately.

So talk.

CHAPTER 29

Midday in Soho Square, clear blue skies all over the city. Lydia found a bench half in the shade and sat down, sweltering from being on the Tube and the short walk after. Familiar streets that looked strange now, the heat blasting off the pavements.

The lunchtime rush was still gearing up, but there were pockets of people on the grass already, a mix of creative types in ripped jeans and T-shirts, and the office set melting in shirts with open collars. A man and a woman were playing ping-pong on the outdoor table.

He appeared from the Oxford Street side of the square, and she took a deep breath when she spotted him, as if she could crush the butterflies in her stomach. She watched him move cautiously into the square, scanning around for her. He was wearing the same suit as the night before, or one that looked the same, enough to make her wonder if he'd been home in the hours between. He was tall with salt-and-pepper hair worn short but growing out. Looking at him now, he looked too slight to have taken down the bastard that grabbed her, even with a weapon.

He noticed her from a way off and nodded as he approached. She kept her eyes on his, projecting a confidence that had nothing in common with how she felt inside.

He stopped in front of her. 'Can I sit?'

She nodded.

He lowered himself onto the far end of the bench, looking around the square. 'Were you hurt last night?'

'Who are you?'

He adjusted his watch strap. It drew her eyes, and she got a glimpse of heavy scarring around his wrist. 'My name's Michael.'

'Why were you following me?'

'Let's start with the video.'

'No, let's start where I fucking say we start. I saw you at the station, tell me why you were following me.'

He laid his hands on his legs, his fingers jumping. 'I understand your anger.'

'You understand? You condescending prick.'

'Look, we're both here because of the video. We don't need each other's life story.'

'And what do you know about it?'

He looked away a moment, then to the front again, squinting in the sunlight. 'The man who was attacked is an associate of mine.'

'What's his name?'

'I didn't come to share information. I want to suggest that your way forward now is to leave this alone.'

'Who were those two last night?'

'I don't know.'

'Fuck's sake...' She put one knee on the bench so she could turn towards him. 'You said we can help each other, so stop wasting my time or I walk.'

'We can. The victim's wife has authorised me to compensate you for your work so far. She'd like to ensure, though, there'll be no future publicity.'

'What?'

'I can provide you with a sum of ten thousand pounds. It'll be passed to you in various forms to make it legitimate. It won't tie back to anyone.'

She stared at the side of his face. '"Legitimate".'

'I should add that this conversation is off the record.'

'So it's ten grand to look the other way.'

'They're your words.'

She watched the ping-pong match, tracking the ball's movement back and forth. The players were languid in the heat, laughing and jokingly blaming each other every time they had to chase down a loose shot. 'What were you even doing, following me?'

He leaned forward, resting his elbows on his knees. 'Who were you expecting to meet last night?'

She made a sound under her breath. 'Yeah, I thought that might be it.'

'The woman who took the video, right? That's what you thought.'

She didn't answer. A group of teenagers passed them, and she eyed them as they spread a picnic blanket out on the grass.

'Did you go to the police?' he asked.

She nodded. 'I told them about you.'

'Good.'

She snapped her head around to look at him, wrong-footed at seeing no sign he was rattled. 'You'll talk to them then?'

'I couldn't offer anything useful.'

'You saw the man who tried to strangle me. That might be useful.'

'I didn't get a good look at him.'

'Bullshit.'

'You'd be mistaken if you think I'm afraid of their scrutiny.'

'Really? I'm not even convinced you weren't with those two last night.'

'I already told you I wasn't.'

'Counts for fuck all.'

'If you really believed that you'd have the police here now.'

There was no emotion in his voice, in his face, in his stillness. Whatever parts he was lying about, his confidence underpinned the façade, as if all of it was truth in his world.

'So what is it you do when you're not offering bribes to journalists?'

He shrugged. 'Sometimes I watch their backs.'

'Oh, do not even … I appreciate what you did last night, but don't for a second pretend you were there with good intentions.'

'I was there; isn't that what counts?'

He spoke quietly apart from the last word 'counts', coming out loud and abrupt, as if it was a thought he hadn't meant to articulate. He closed his eyes and she watched him a second longer, but when he opened them again, his face was blank. 'Are they assigning someone to protect you?'

She stared at him, trying to gauge the motivation behind the question. She couldn't, so she ignored it. 'Let's pretend for a second I believe the bit about the guy in the video being your client. Is he dead?'

He gave no answer – the one she expected.

'Because, missing or dead, surely his wife would want as much publicity as possible. To find him, and/or his assailants.'

'Privacy is important to her.'

'More than justice?' Her hand was laid across the back of the bench and she raised her index finger to point at him. 'This fiction is threadbare. Who's really paying you?'

'The police are investigating what happened to my client. His family don't want it in the papers. Last night should've been a wake-up call – let the professionals do their jobs.'

'Is that a threat?'

He turned to face her for the first time. 'If I wanted you cowed, I wouldn't have intervened.'

His voice was calm but hard, the implication enough to make her look away.

'Give me the name and take the money,' he said. 'You've done enough.'

She slipped her leg off the bench and stood up. 'I'll make it clear: you can't buy me off, and you can't scare me.'

He looked up at her, shielding his eyes from the sun. 'What happens when they come again? I won't be there next time.'

'I'm sending the police your way. If you feel like helping for real, get in touch.'

She left him alone on the bench, scorched by the sunlight.

Stringer let her walk away across the square, shimmering in the heat haze. He waited out an impulse to get to his feet and go after her. Except there was no way to reason with her without exposing his own lies.

Her turning down the money was no surprise. Nor was her evident rage. What he hadn't counted on was how resolute she'd be. In that sense, the test had done its job – a gauge of where her head was at. But it hadn't thrown up the result he wanted. He'd gone there hoping to find she was just scared enough that the money would make her drop it. A final nudge to move her out of harm's way. Instead it might have backfired.

And, besides that, he'd given up too much. The fuck was he doing trying to justify himself to her? Where did that come from? He got up and exited the square in the opposite direction, even though it meant taking a circuitous route back to the Tube.

He rode the Underground back to Highbury and walked from there, his shirt sticking to his back. Holloway Road was a canyon filled with exhaust fumes. The fug clung to him and he could smell it on himself when he took the lift up to his flat.

The laptop was open on the counter. He stripped his jacket

off and threw it on the couch, then went to get a drink of water. He Googled for mention of a body found in a flat in Kentish Town, then again for Tammy Hodgson's name. Nothing new displayed. Then he carried the computer to his desk and started reviewing the CCTV footage again.

The files were broken down by camera, and again by time. He picked up with the feed he'd started that morning – the one looking back from the north end of the northbound platform at Woodside Park. He ran it at double speed, trains pulling in and out on fast-forward, passengers spilling off like something from a music video. Nothing caught his eye. It was the first of seven viewpoints Milos had supplied. But the time stamp showed the footage had only got as far as 10.00 p.m.; he didn't expect Tan to show up until nearer eleven on the night he died.

The silent monotony sapped him. His thoughts drifted. Lydia Wright – rattled but defiant. Her refusal to back down torqued his sense of guilt. He thought about the man who'd broken into her flat, and if he'd come again. His own words about the night before echoed in his mind: 'I was there, isn't that what counts?' Hearing them for how hollow they were – no points for effort. If something happened to her now, he was just as culpable.

He sat up as a figure blurred across the screen. He scrolled back, played it again at normal speed. The train pulled in and a woman burst off it. She ran along the platform, then disappeared up the staircase leading to the footbridge over the tracks. He bent close, about to watch again when another set of figures came off the train. Three men, the one in the middle being propped up by the other two. They had his arms around their shoulders, so he looked like a drunk being carried by his mates, his feet dragging along the ground. Stringer paused it and although the faces were indistinct, there was no mistaking Jamie Tan. One of the other two pointed towards where the woman had run, then they walked Tan across the platform and out of the gate he'd seen. He checked the time stamp: 22.47.

He rewound it to watch one more time. The woman ran off the train. There was something in her hand, looked like her phone. She disappeared, then the three men stepped off. The light caught Tan's face and he saw the duct tape was gone from his mouth.

He minimised the window and clicked on the next few files, checking each viewpoint until he found one that covered the exit gate. He scrolled through but the file ended at 21.11, so he opened the next and then the next until he found one covering 22.47. He maximised it again and kept his mouse hovering over the pause button, waiting for the three men to cross its field of vision.

Then they appeared. All of them were in profile, Tan's head bowed and the man furthest from the camera obscured by the other two.

He froze it with the group in shot and studied the face he could see. The man had close-cropped hair, thick eyebrows and a nose with a big enough ridge to suggest it'd been broken at least once in his life. He was wearing a dark top and dark jeans, and Stringer put his age somewhere between thirty-five and forty-five.

The CCTV camera had a wide-angle lens that took in one side of the turnaround outside the exit. The three stepped out of shot, but a few seconds later, a black SUV sped around the small roundabout and off towards the main road, disappearing from view before it got there.

Stringer ran it back, his other hand distorting the laptop screen where he was gripping it so hard. He froze the image with the car in shot, the number plate legible. He typed it into Google but didn't wait for the result, toggling back to the image and running it back further, to where the three had first appeared. He took out his phone and compared the image to the photo he'd taken of the man in Lydia Wright's kitchen. But there was no resemblance.

He jumped back to Google, which was showing a hit on the number plate – basic info: make, model, year. Which meant he could get the rest. Back to the CCTV footage, still frozen on Tan and the two men propping him up. He zoomed in and cropped the image to get a close-up of the man whose face was visible.

Then he grabbed his phone and car keys and ran to the lift.

CHAPTER 30

Lydia sat at a high stool in the corner of the bar, her feet bouncing on the footrest. She laid her phone on the metal counter in front of her, next to her lime and soda, and read the message from Stephen again – *Is everything ok? I heard you didn't turn up last night?*

She hadn't replied.

Sam Waterhouse walked in right on the hour. She spied Lydia and made her way over, her expression becoming more serious as she came near. 'You look like you've seen a ghost.'

'Rough night.'

'You didn't have to bring the money in person, I'd have been happy to...'

'It's fine, I need to speak to you anyway.'

'Yes?'

'This ... thing is out of control. Someone tried to snatch me off the street last night.' She flapped the collar of her blouse to show the bruising on her neck.

'Good god, what happened?'

Lydia walked her through it, a skim account covering just the basics. She left out meeting with the man in the suit that lunchtime; even as she did it, she wasn't sure why. Adjusting his watch, the mangled skin on display – the image played out in the back of her mind as she talked.

Sam took a breath when she was finished and craned her neck, looking away. 'You could've been killed.'

Lydia stilled her feet. 'I know. And look at this.' She showed her the last DM sent to her from Paulina Dobriska's account.

Sam handed her the phone back. 'What are you going to do?'

'Actually...' She reached into her bag and took out Stephen's wad of money. 'I wanted your advice.'

Sam took it with a nod and tucked it away. 'Have you called the police?'

'They're coming to interview me this afternoon.'

'Okay.' She drew the word out.

'At the very least, they need to focus on finding Paulina Dobriska.'

'Sure, of course.'

'What?'

'Nothing, I think you've done the right thing. It just leaves me in an awkward position.'

Lydia shifted on her stool. 'They don't need to know anything about your involvement.'

'I appreciate you saying that.' She pulled out an electronic cigarette and took a drag, exhaling the vapour behind her and under the counter where the bar staff wouldn't see. 'If these people are posing as her, using her Facebook account ... When was the last time anyone saw her?'

'In the video, as far as I can tell.'

'Not encouraging.'

'Are you saying I shouldn't talk to the police?'

'No, and I wouldn't want you to lie to them either. It's just not a great look if I've been asking around about this woman – but that's for me to deal with.'

'What am I supposed to do, Sam? If she's alive, she must be in trouble.'

'Tell them what you know.'

'What about this message?' She tapped her phone screen. 'Can you get someone to trace the device it was sent from? Get a location? Or what about the CCTV from the station last night...'

'They'll look into all of that.'

'I'm trying to get a head start.'

'I'm sorry.' Sam gathered her bag straps together and stood up. 'But I really have to take myself out of this equation now.'

'What? I told you, I'll keep your name out of it.'

'I hope you get this sorted.'

'Sam, please?'

'My best advice is that you be careful. For your own sake.' She nodded once, as if it was a full stop, and then picked her way around the tables towards the doors.

Lydia watched her go, the only customer left in the place. She drained the rest of her drink and stared at the bottles of wine in the fridges behind the bar. They looked like a mistake. She picked up her phone and unlocked it, opened up her inbox.

The email from 'Michael' was already selected. His words were splintered and refracted in the shattered screen, muddled in her head with the ones he'd spoken.

'I was there.'

'Isn't that what counts?'

She pressed reply and stared at the blank email. The cursor blinked.

He'd dropped that massive bastard as easy as anything. No fear in his eyes.

The image of his mangled skin…

A nagging refrain at the back of her skull: *he saved my fucking life*.

She shook her head and closed it. She opened Twitter instead. Thanks to the *Examiner* retweet, she had more than two hundred notifications. She started to skim them, her concentration wrecked by thoughts of what to do now. It made her think of Tammy. Underneath the anger lay the feeling that she really needed her guidance. Before she could stop herself, she'd called her number. It went straight to voicemail. She sent her a text: *Call me asap*.

The replies to her tweet asking for help to identify the victim in the video were all crap – *Why u wanna bone him, come get with me;* and *Yeah – he used 2 play 4 Chelsea* followed by half a dozen crying-with-laughter emojis. She gave up halfway through and clicked on her DMs instead. She kept them open like most of her colleagues, so getting random shit was nothing new. Now was no different – two separate dick pics, and some racist prick rearing up out of the social-media sewer to call her a Chink-loving bitch. But then there was a three-word message from someone she didn't know. No profile pic.

All it said: *He's Jamie Tan*.

Stringer called his DVLA contact from the car. The man answered after a couple of rings, saying, 'Hold on a minute.' He could hear muffled background sounds, movement, as if the man was making his way across an office. When he spoke again, he was somewhere quieter. Presumably more private.

'Yes?'

'Two plates: AP17 EPK and LD16 XPF. First one is probably false – seen on a black Saab near Brent Cross, north London. Second's real, I think: black Honda SUV, also north London, but Woodside Park Tube. I need registered addresses for both.'

'How hot are these?'

'Unknown.'

'Then I'm not interested.'

'What?'

'Last one I did for you was a vehicle of interest – fucking red flags everywhere. So no can do.'

'I'm paying a grand. This is, what, thirty seconds' work?'

'A grand? That says it all, then, doesn't it. Sorry.'

'Someone will do it, when did you get so rich?'

'I said I'm sorry.' He hung up.

Stringer smacked the steering wheel with his palm. He took the next turning off the main road and pulled over with his hazards on. He typed a message to Milos: *Need to meet right now.*

Milos was at the same table in the same pub, wearing the same baseball cap. It irked Stringer, feeling like it was out of the same playbook as piercing his alias last time; another knowing jab that said: *I see through your bullshit and I'm laughing at you.* But the truth was more benign and somehow worse: they were more alike than he was comfortable with. Because admitting it opened up thoughts of all the liberties he'd be taking if the roles were reversed.

He dropped heavily onto the stool opposite.

'So what's up?' Milos kept typing on his phone.

Stringer's patience lasted one second before he reached his hand over the screen and forced him to lower it to the table.

Milos looked at him. 'What?'

'New job. I need addresses relating to two number plates. Can you sort it?'

'Don't know, bro – I can ask.'

'What about your man from before?'

'Think it was a chick done the CCTV for you, as it goes.'

'Okay, what about her?'

'Why's it have to be the same person?'

'She was fast.'

'She might fuck you on the dollar.'

'I'll go to a grand – including your cut.'

'Yeah, but if she knows you're desperate, like...'

'Then don't tell her I am.'

Milos flashed a fuck-you smile. 'Go on then, what we got?'

Stringer scribbled down the two plates and slipped them across the table. He waited for Milos to look up at him before he spoke again. 'That address you found for me...' He watched for his reaction. 'The one the email came from.'

'Yeah?'

'You give it to anyone else?'

He looked at Stringer like he was joking. 'Like who?'

'Like anyone.'

'Nah, bro. Why, who is she?'

He stared at him a few seconds longer, getting more and more wound up that he couldn't read him. He shook his head to dismiss the question. 'How long for the number plates?'

Milos opened his hands, eyes twinkling. 'I'll message you.'

Back behind the wheel, the same drive he'd been on before, throwing the car all over the road trying to blow off his frustration. East along Seven Sisters Road, passing the fruit-and-veg stalls and the pubs where time had stood still, old men in houndstooth jackets, ties and black trousers, drinking Guinness and reading the *Islington Gazette*. He followed it to Finsbury Park, stop-start through the bottleneck around the station, then running parallel to the park's boundary wall. Giant marquees filled the grass, setting up for some kind of music festival.

The block that held his other flat rose into view, and he looped around into the small car park at the back. He checked his phone before he got out, but there was nothing from Milos yet. Wishful thinking on his part.

He took the stairs to the third floor and knocked on the door. He heard soft footsteps on the other side and then Alicia Tan opened it halfway. She stood in the gap and looked him over. 'Come in.'

He followed her to the lounge and she took his spot by the window, turning to stare him down. The place was pristine, unchanged from when he'd first brought her there, as if she was living like a ghost.

'How are you doing?' he said.

'Just say whatever you've come to say. Good or bad.'

'I don't have any answers for you. I don't want to give you false hope.'

'Then what?'

'I'd like to show you a couple more pictures. They're nothing as bad as...'

'Let me see.' She bustled over to him, standing ready.

He opened his phone and brought up the picture of the woman Lydia Wright had met with at Brent Cross. She was badly lit, one side of her face in darkness, her eyes half closed.

Alicia Tan looked close and then shook her head, her mouth screwed up. 'Who is she?'

'Someone who might've seen something.' He swiped to the next image, the still from the CCTV that showed the getaway SUV at Woodside Park. 'This?'

She brought it close again, studying the registration number, but again shook her head. Her shoulders slumped a little, betraying her disappointment. 'Who are these people?'

'That's what I'm trying to establish.'

'You know what I meant. What's their relevance?'

'I can't answer that until I know who they are.'

She backed away. 'You show up with these pictures and videos and won't tell me anything. Can you see this is killing me? I sit here going spare and I don't even know what I'm waiting for. Who I'm hiding from...'

'Did you go to the police?'

'Yes.'

'And?'

'They're investigating.' She locked eyes with him, defying the silence between them.

'I get that you don't trust me, but the more I know, the more I can help.'

'Help? I thought you were just a fixer? Now you're going to catch his killers?'

He looked down at his phone, the blank screen somewhere to fix his eyes. 'Did you tell them about me?'

She sat down on the edge of a chair and shot him a murderous look. She drew out the moment, sensing his discomfort. 'And say what? That a stranger kidnapped me and told me it was for my own safety – and I went with it because my husband was murdered?'

'I didn't kidnap...' He closed his eyes. There was no sense defending his actions when her choosing to stay in the flat revealed the truth of her feelings – as confused as they must be. 'Did you tell them what you're afraid of?'

'What, *I had a bad feeling my husband was in trouble*?'

'I got the impression it was more specific than that.'

She dropped her head into her hands, her voice muffled when she spoke. 'You're desperate for me to tell you something I don't know. It doesn't matter how many times and how many ways you ask me.'

'Then what was it made you feel that way?'

'His behaviour.' She opened her hands in frustration. 'He changed in the last few months.'

His skin prickled; a timescale that fit loosely with Suslov's interest. 'In what way?'

'He was just pushing everything to the limit. Even longer hours, going out five, six nights on the spin, drinking more, not coming home. And everything else.'

There was a hint in the way she said it, an indication she wanted to say more. 'Drugs?'

She closed her eyes, caught halfway between a shrug and a nod. 'Everyone uses. The pressure is insane. But he was going beyond anything I'd seen him do before.'

'Is there a chance he was in debt to someone because of it?'

She shook her head, but it was half-hearted. 'Money was everything to Jamie. I monitor our finances, we never struggled.'

'Even so...'

'I would've known. He didn't rub it in my face, but he never tried to hide it either. He's used the same dealer for years.'

Mention of Tan not coming home made him wonder if she knew about his nights volunteering at the shelter. 'What caused the change?'

'Work. Always work. You have to understand, traders thrive on competition. It wasn't enough for Jamie to be winning, he had to know he was winning biggest. And that everyone else was losing by comparison.'

'So something had changed with his job?'

'He didn't like talking about it at home. When he wasn't in the office, he just wanted to blot it all out.'

'And he never told you what was wrong?'

She held out her hands, as if she wasn't sure. 'Like I said, it was just a feeling.' She dropped them to her lap, the toll the conversation was taking starting to show.

He drifted over to the window, seeing everything and nothing all at once. Andriy Suslov. Coke pushers. He should've taken the registration of Tan's dealer the nights he'd seen him pull up on his moped. Another slip. And then there was the police involvement; they'd be coming at it from two different reports, two different starting points – how long would it take to marry them up? His chance to thread the needle getting tighter all the time.

He turned around and saw Alicia Tan holding her phone in both hands, swiping through her pictures. He could make out a shot of her and Jamie at a table with friends, both smiling. She stared at it as long as she could, then her head dipped and she dropped the phone on the floor. Sobs shook her whole body.

He wanted to tell her about the mentoring, the charity work, the things her husband had seemingly kept from her. Only the sense that it would hurt her further kept him silent.

He crept out of the room and out the front door, an intruder in his own flat.

CHAPTER 31

The tweeter's office was near Liverpool Street, a modern glass-and-steel structure. Lydia stopped across the road and looked up at the letters emblazoned high above its entrance – *HFB*. She'd heard of it, but only today learned it was short for Hesse Frei Bank. Like BT or BA, another corporation that'd reduced itself to a set of initials to hide its national origins in a globalised world.

She'd made no attempt to contact the man after his Twitter message naming the victim as Jamie Tan. Nothing was to be taken at face value now; that was the one conclusion she'd come to after spending the pre-dawn darkness in a nightmare of introspection. Hours of self-interrogation that did nothing to make her feel better or safer, and finally made her throw herself back into the work as a means of shutting her own voice out of her head.

Googling 'Jamie Tan London' had brought up dozens of pictures of shoes – turned out it was a make of brogue. When she switched to a regular search, half a dozen Jamie Tans came up – a lawyer, a banker, a student, a DJ, and more.

She went about it the other way, going after the man who'd supplied the name – and it took no time to identify him. His twitter handle was generic – Adam0048512 – but he'd tweeted a picture the previous year and a reverse image search linked it back to a Facebook account belonging to an Adam Finch, a trader at HFB. A quick skim of his friends list turned up one Jamie Tan – who was a vice president at the same bank. She jumped onto Tan's page and was confronted with a photo of the man she'd watched being strangled.

At last, a name to the face. It was jarring to see him that way – a posed shot, the kind used for a corporate profile. It showed Tan suited and smiling, not quite looking at the camera, handsome in a clean-cut kind of way. It seemed impossible to marry it with the grainy image she'd seen so many times – a banker without a hair out of place, not the usual type to be murdered on the Tube.

His Facebook wall was sparse, just a selection of profile-picture updates, including an older one that showed him with his arms around a laughing blonde woman. Lydia clicked on it, hoping the woman was named or tagged, but all that came up was the date.

She Googled Tan's name in conjunction with the bank and found his LinkedIn page. It showed a limited CV; he'd started as an equities trader at HFB in 2004, preceded by two eighteen-month spells at smaller investment banks. The entry for his current role was several paragraphs long, but not that revealing; he'd worked in various sectors, concentrating on European and emerging-market stocks. He'd been promoted quickly and ended up running the London trading desk. He'd won various internal awards that seemed to mark him out as a rising man in the bank.

She went back to the Google results and tried the images tab again, now she knew what she was looking for. But nothing new came up; she couldn't find any mention of him outside of his work.

Two hours' research that'd all led back to this building. She walked down to the traffic lights and crossed, then doubled back into the bank's reception. It was a cavernous space, the receptionists stationed at the far end behind a long row of individual marble blocks that served as desks. Light poured in through the glass walls, stretching her shadow across the floor. She went to the only free desk, gave her name and asked for Adam Finch. The man in the suit asked if he was expecting her and she smiled and nodded.

She waited at a bank of seats around an oversized glass coffee table. She crossed her legs and had to make a conscious effort to stop the top one twitching. She opened Twitter and debated replying to Finch to tell him she was waiting, in case he needed a nudge. She thought about why he'd contacted her and what it said about him, and she kept coming back to the same conclusion – he had something he wanted to get off his chest.

A minute later, he stepped out of one of the lifts. He spotted her straightaway, coming to a stop as he did. He eyed her a second, glancing towards the receptionists, then came over.

'Lydia?'

She stood up and offered a handshake. 'Hello.'

He shook it as if it was red hot, whipping his hand away. 'What are you..?'

'You sent me a message on Twitter.'

He rubbed his face. 'Shit...'

'Can we talk?'

He looked down at his watch. 'Look, not here. There's a pub inside the station, upstairs. I can meet you there in an hour?' He was already stepping back from her.

'Sure. I'll be there.'

Ninety minutes later, she was on her second lime and soda and there was still no sign of Finch. The pub was from that unique subset of watering holes only found in stations – the same sticky marble bartops and brass taps as its high-street cousin, but a clientele that had one eye on the departure boards at all times; everyone jumpy, ready to run at the flick of a dot matrix.

She had her phone open, about to DM Finch, when he walked in. She got off her stool as he came over.

'Sorry, I got held up.' He pointed to her glass. 'D'you want another drink?'

She shook her head. 'I'm fine, thank you.'

He went to the bar and came back with a large glass of red wine. He drank off half of it before he set it down, keeping his hand on the stem. 'So what's with the picture of Jamie?' He stayed standing, shifting his weight from foot to foot every few seconds.

She perched on her stool. 'I was hoping you could tell me.'

'What's he done?'

Interesting choice of words. 'When was the last time you saw him, Mr Finch?'

'Adam, yeah? Makes me feel like I'm at school otherwise.'

'Okay, Adam.'

'Last week.' He put his glass down and picked it up again. 'Haven't seen him since last week. Your turn.'

'About the photo?'

'Yes. Any of it. What are we doing here?'

She stirred her drink with the straw, deciding how much to give. 'I was passed a video of a man who was the victim of an attack. I was trying to identify him.'

He kept his eyes on hers as she said it, the first time he'd been still. 'And now you have?'

She looked down when she nodded.

'Where is he?' he said.

'I don't know.'

'Is he alive?'

She spread her hands in apology. 'I'm sorry, I don't—'

'What do you mean? If you've got a picture of him...'

'That's all I have. I didn't even know his name until you told me.'

He had his mouth open to argue the point but he stopped himself when the logic of what she was saying hit home.

'Can you think of anyone who would have reason to hurt him, Adam?'

He picked up his wine and drank the last of it. 'I need another one.' He turned and crossed back to the bar.

She watched him go, calling out his order and waving his glass at the barman even before he got there. While he waited, he spread his hands on the bar and ducked his head, his suit jacket bunching between his shoulder blades.

She placed her phone in the middle of the table, the voice recorder app open but not recording.

He came back with another full glass, but put it down untouched this time. 'He hasn't been answering his phone. I've tried him a load of times.' Before she could speak, he had his own phone out and was showing her the call log. 'Look.' It showed five unanswered call attempts.

'Adam, do you mind if I record this conversation? It doesn't mean it has to be on the record.' Her finger hovered near the button on the screen.

'No. No way.' He pushed her phone across the tabletop towards her. 'What happened to him? You said an attack?'

'It appears he was strangled.'

'A robbery or something?' The question was a backtrack from his initial reaction.

'I don't know, but my feeling is not. I think he was targeted.' She left it hanging, for him to pick up the thread.

But he looked away, his mouth twitching, then shook his head. 'I don't get it. I don't...'

'You're friendly with Mr Tan?'

'He's my boss.'

'Outside of work I mean.'

He shrugged, nodding his head. 'We go for beers and that.'

'Do you know if there's someone I can contact? A wife, parents?'

'His wife's name's Alicia. I've met her but I don't know her. She must be doing her nut. Wait, where are the police in all this?'

'I don't know. They haven't been in touch with your firm?'

'No one's spoken to me.'

'Didn't anyone think it unusual that Mr Tan hadn't shown up for work?'

'I asked. The answer came back he was sick.'

She inched closer. 'And that made you suspicious?'

His eyes bored into hers. 'No. Personal matter, isn't it.'

He was in full retreat now so she changed tack. 'Why did you contact me, Adam?'

He shrugged again, his face starting to flush from the wine.

'Usually people talk to journalists because they want to tell their side of the story.'

He stepped back from the table. 'What's that supposed...? This is nothing to do with me.'

She threw her palms up. 'That's not what I meant. But if you were concerned for him or think you might know why this happened...'

He brought his glass to his mouth and watched her over the rim as he drank. When he was finished, his top lip was slick with red. 'I just wanted to know where he was, that's all. If you can't tell me, then we're done here.' He wiped his mouth with the back of his hand and walked off.

CHAPTER 32

Stringer ran down a long corridor in the Royal Free Hospital. It took him past the pharmacy and an M&S concession that stank of grease, through to the lifts. The waiting area was packed so he doubled back across the corridor and ran up the stairs two at a time to the seventh floor.

He came out panting in another corridor, signs pointing to three different wards, the one he wanted to his left. He pushed through the double doors and followed it around to the nurse's station, the lone woman at the desk on the phone.

There was a list of patients on a whiteboard behind her. He

scanned it, waiting, not seeing his mum's name. The woman finished her call and looked up at him.

'Looking for Mrs Howton. I'm her son.'

Before she could answer, he heard his sister's voice behind him. 'Mike.'

He turned and saw Abi peering out of one of the rooms. She came out and met him as he approached, wrapping her arms around him. He held her, cradling the back of her head.

'What is it?'

'They don't know.' She let go and stepped back to look at him, her hands on her cheeks. 'They're doing tests, the usual, but it could be ... God, I don't know.'

He stared down the corridor, the words he needed refusing to come. 'You told me she was doing better.'

There was a note of accusation about it and she looked hurt. 'Mike, she was. I'm not a doctor, I can't...'

'I didn't mean it to come out like that.' He reached out to take her hand. 'It's just...'

'I know. A shock.'

'When did you get here?'

'Just after I called you. She'd already been sent up from A&E.'

'Where's Ellie?'

'One of the other mums is picking her up from nursery for me. She's okay at her place for a bit.'

He stepped around her to go into the room, but she kept hold of his hand, pulling him back. 'Mike...'

He stopped still before she could say it. His mum was lying on the bed, an oxygen mask over her face, her eyes closed and her face pale and shrunken. She had a drip in the back of her left hand. On her other side, William Howton was sitting in a chair. His father.

'Michael.'

Abi came to stand next to him. He could feel her staring at the side of his face.

He ignored the old man and went to his mum. He touched her cheek with the back of his fingers, as gently as if it was a child's. It was warmer than he expected, her skin slack. He could hear her breathing, weak and slow.

'She's unconscious,' his dad said. 'Talk to her. She'll like hearing your voice.'

Stringer glanced over, then around the room, his mother's one of six beds. One was empty, two were hidden behind their curtains, and two were occupied – women about his mum's age. He turned to his sister. 'Can we get her in a private room?'

'I don't know. I'll ask.' She shuffled back towards the nurse's station.

Stringer traced the line of the drip up to a plastic bag that hung from a portable hook next to the bed, a silent monitor beside it showing numbers that didn't mean anything to him. 'What happened?'

The old man hunched forward in his chair, the hiss of air being squeezed out of the cushion as he shifted his weight. 'She was doing something upstairs. Heard something smash, and when I got up there she was on the floor.'

'She been feeling ill?'

His dad shook his head. 'You know what she's like. Wouldn't say even if she was.'

'Or you don't want to hear it.'

He frowned, looking away – water off a duck's back. 'It was a picture frame that broke. The sound. Reckon she knocked it when she collapsed. The one of you two she keeps on the dresser.'

'Has she been taking her tablets?'

'Yes.'

'But?'

'But nothing. She forgets, it's not her fault.'

'You remind her?'

'When I'm there.'

'You fucking saint.'

He caught one of the other patients flick her eyes onto him.

'I'm not a nursemaid, Michael. Are you there when she wakes up crying in the middle of the night? When she doesn't know where she is because she thinks she still lives in the house she grew up in?'

Abi touched his forearm. 'They can put her in her own room, but then she has to go private. It starts at five hundred a night.'

'I'll cover it.'

'They've got no idea how long she'll be here.'

'Doesn't matter.'

She opened her mouth to say something more but then she rubbed his shoulder and slipped off again.

'Generous gesture,' the old man said.

Stringer went to the end of the bed and reached for her chart. Her temperature was normal, her blood pressure high. It was at the best of times. 'What happens now?'

The old man curled his lip. 'Wait and see what the doctor thinks. Doubt they'll say much until she comes round.'

'You don't sound unduly worried.'

'Worrying won't help her, will it?'

'Might make her think you care.'

'She already knows that.'

Abi swept in again, typing on her phone. Stringer looked at

her, expectant. She lifted her head when she realised it. 'Sorted. You'll need to do the paperwork. They'll move her as soon as it's done and they can find a porter.'

He dipped his eyes to her phone. 'Everything alright? Ellie?'

'Yeah.' She nodded. 'Yeah.'

He went back to the top end of the bed and knelt down to say something to his mum. He brought his mouth to her ear, searching for the words. There was a beeping sound coming from the corridor, the whisper of the oxygen flowing into her mask. He could feel his father's eyes on him. Thirty years walking this line between love and hate; so much to say, and nothing that would help.

He touched his lips against her cheek and stood up to go to the desk.

The same woman was there and had a clipboard and pen waiting for him. 'Mr Howton?'

He shook his head. 'No, but that's for me.'

'I'm sorry, I thought you said you were her son? We have visitation rules...'

'I am.'

She looked at him for an explanation, but let it go and handed him the papers. He was fucked if he was going to explain to her why he'd taken his mother's maiden name.

He brought the paperwork over to a plastic chair and took his wallet out for his bank details, started scribbling everything down.

The smell was the first warning – the same scent he'd always known. Face balm, the one he used after shaving, and peppermint. He was almost next to him when he looked up.

'You leaving?' the old man said.

'I'll be back.'

'A flying visit then.'

Stringer concentrated on the form.

The old man put his hands in his pockets. 'It's easy to turn up and lob a few verbals around, isn't it? Point the finger and disappear.'

'Not now.'

'Still, shown your face, that's what counts. Appearances.'

He pressed harder as he wrote, the ballpoint digging into the clipboard.

'You'll be there at the funeral. Make sure a load of strangers can see how much you cared.'

'Don't wish her into the grave.'

The old man stood over him. 'Don't put words in my mouth, you little shit.'

Stringer got to his feet. He had maybe three inches on him now, time whittling away at the man he used to stand eye to eye with. 'I can't hear you. Nothing you say registers.'

'That's always been your problem.'

'No, I learned your lessons.'

'Here we go again.'

'Hard to forget, isn't it?' He brought his arm up between them, running his hand up and down it.

'It was an accident. I've apologised enough.'

'Takes a special kind of cunt to believe his own lies.'

His father looked at the floor. He stepped back, shaking his head. 'I've never understood where we went wrong with you. You look at your sister, and then at you...'

'Don't bring her into this. She's the only good thing you ever did.'

'We agree on something, then.'

Stringer picked up the clipboard and signed his name on the

form. Then he pressed it into the old man's chest to take. 'You better hope Mum makes it through this.' He pointed down the corridor towards her bed. 'Because the day she goes is the day you do.'

Lydia had just dropped her bag in her room when the police showed up. They introduced themselves on the doorstep – Detectives Wheldon and Singh. She invited them in and led them up to the kitchen. 'Sorry, this doubles as the sitting room. Can I get you a tea?'

Singh seemed to be the senior, declining for both of them. 'Just water, thanks.'

She turned to the tap and filled two glasses, concentrating on not coming across as nervous.

'Miss Wright, I'm sorry to hear about what happened to you.' She put the glasses down in front of them. 'I know it might be uncomfortable to talk about but can you walk us through what happened? You can take your time.'

She gave them a partial outline, starting when she came out of the Tube at Brent Cross. She went back to explain about the Facebook messages from Paulina Dobriska's account, mentioned the video, and finished with the man who'd come out of nowhere to help her.

Wheldon took notes while Singh nodded his encouragement to her. At the end, it was Wheldon who asked the first question. 'You didn't happen to get a look at the car's number plate?'

She shook her head. 'I didn't get a chance. I just wanted to get away.'

'I can understand that. What about the make? Or colour?'

'It was black but I couldn't tell you the make. Sorry.'

'No problem.'

'The woman I met said she was taking me to a red Kia parked up the street, but I'm guessing that was a lie.'

'Well, it's a useful detail to know. We'll review the CCTV around the area.'

'Can you describe the woman?' Singh asked. 'You said you spoke to her.'

'Only as we were walking. She was ahead of me most of the time.'

'Just tell us what you can.'

'She was about my height, five-six, dyed blonde hair. She had a hoodie on – sort of blue-green. Light-blue jeans.'

'How would you describe her face?'

She untangled her hands on the table, at a loss. 'She had thin eyebrows, that's about all I remember. Just normal-looking.'

'Eye colour?'

'It was dark, I'm not sure.'

'How old would you say?'

'Late thirties?'

'And she never gave a name?'

'No. Sorry. She said she was Paulina Dobriska's cousin, but...'

Wheldon offered a reassuring smile. 'That's fine. What about the man that attacked you?'

She looked at her hands, even the memory raising her heartbeat. 'He came from the side and grabbed me from behind, I never really saw him. He was big – stocky.'

'Anything at all about him?'

'He smelled of cigarettes.' She meant his clothes, but as she said it, she remembered it on his breath as well, the stench on her face.

'And you said the second man managed to get him off you?'

'Yes.'

'How did he go about that?'

'I don't know, they were both behind me.'

'Did he have a weapon of any kind?'

She looked from one to the other. 'I don't know, maybe.'

'Did he say anything to you?'

'I can't remember. He tried to help me up.'

Wheldon looked at his notes. 'But that was the point you ran off?'

She nodded.

'And you didn't recognise him at all?'

'No.' She held his eyes, feeling a rush as she said it.

'How would you describe him?'

'He was tall, quite thin. Brown hair, slim face. He was in a suit.' In her mind, she pictured his face. Haunted, angular, a sadness about him. Deceptive, secretive.

Wheldon looked at his partner and then back at Lydia. 'Talk us through why you were meeting this woman again.'

'I thought I was meeting Paulina Dobriska – the woman who shot the video. I think.'

'And this pair were seemingly communicating with you through her Facebook account?'

She nodded again. 'Mostly messages but once on the phone. At the time I thought it was Paulina I was speaking to, but I'm pretty sure it was the woman who met me.'

'Have you still got the written messages?'

'Yes.'

'We'll need to have a look at them.'

A small panic rose up as she thought about the emails to Michael. 'It's a work phone, I need it. I can show you them.'

'Okay.'

She opened Facebook Messenger and found the conversation. She put the phone down and turned it around for them to see. Wheldon scrolled down as he read, and Lydia got up to refill her water – anything to break the silence.

Wheldon slid the phone back to her when she sat down again. 'Thanks. We'll definitely need to take a download of these, but we can arrange for you to come into the office to do that. Don't delete anything.'

Singh put his hands together on the table. 'The obvious implication here is that these two were involved somehow with the video you've talked about. You said you reported it?'

'My colleague did, to the transport police. They were looking into it.'

The two men shared a look that said *bloody clowns*. 'We'll speak to them, see how far they've got. They might have a line on who these two are. We'll need a copy of the footage too, obviously.'

'Course. I can send that to you.' She locked her phone and put it on the seat next to her. 'What about Paulina Dobriska? I tried to report her as a missing person, but I didn't have any details at the time.'

'Do you have reason to suspect she's missing? The Facebook aspect is very troubling, but we can't rule out the possibility she's been hacked.'

'She hadn't shown up for work and her neighbours hadn't seen her, as of a few days ago.'

'Have you checked since?'

There was no accusation in his voice, but she flushed anyway. 'I haven't had a chance.'

'Okay. Give me her details and we'll look into it.'

Lydia recited Paulina's address. 'There's a neighbour across the road, Mr Siddons. He saw two men watching her house.'

Wheldon glanced at Singh.

'I know how it sounds,' Lydia said. 'Neighbour with too much time on his hands and all that. But speak to him. Please?'

'What number is he at?' Singh said.

'I'm ... I don't know. He came up to me in the street.'

Wheldon looked up from his pocketbook as if she was talking about fairies. 'No problem, we'll find him and have a word. Have you been to hospital, Miss Wright? It's always worth getting checked over.'

'I'm fine, honestly.'

Singh pinched his lips and looked away.

'Are you still planning to cover this story, Miss Wright?' Wheldon said.

'I don't know. I'm still trying to deal with it all.'

'Of course. What I wanted to say was that these are clearly dangerous individuals. I'd caution you to leave this with us from here on. I don't want to worry you unnecessarily, but what you've described is a very serious situation.'

Singh was watching her and she couldn't read his expression.

'I'd also advise you take extra care for the next few days at least, especially at night. If you see them again, or anything at all that makes you suspicious, dial 999. I'll ask one of the local PCs to check in on you too.'

'Thank you.'

The two men stood up, Wheldon taking his business card from his pocket. 'I'll be in touch to arrange a follow-up, but if anyone tries to contact you through the same Facebook account, call me soon as you can. The same if you think of anything else that might be pertinent, even if it seems like nothing.'

'I will.'

Wheldon moved to the door but Singh rested a knuckle on the tabletop. 'One thing: you said the man that helped you was wearing a suit?'

'Yes. Why?'

Wheldon turned to him before he could answer. 'You thinking he passed through the Tube?'

'Yeah, it's worth a look. Another CCTV job. We'll probably need you to review the footage.' He nodded at Lydia. 'Thanks again.'

CHAPTER 33

Stringer woke up to a message from Milos. He was disorientated; the living room, sunlight streaming in. He couldn't remember lying down on the couch and he was still in a shirt and trousers. He looked at the wall clock and saw it was only 6.30 a.m. The curtains were wide open, the reason it felt later in the day.

He thought of his mum. Abi had messaged to say they'd moved her, but she was still unconscious. He'd seen her unwell over the years, but never like this. At seventy-nine and with a litany of chronic problems, he had no expectation she'd go on forever, but her deterioration in the last couple of months had been steep. As much as he wanted her to pull through, if this was her time, then maybe it was better if she didn't wake up. No good could come from a prolonged end, especially if it meant her being aware and having to face it.

Or maybe that was just selfishness talking. He'd spent decades avoiding a reckoning – in the flesh and in his own mind; if she died now, the chance died with her.

He opened his phone and read the message from Milos: *Job done, nothing much – phone me.*

It'd been sent in the middle of the night. He hit the call button, expecting his mobile to be off, but it started ringing.

'Yeah,' Milos answered.

'It's me.'

'Yo. So yeah, it's done but it ain't a lot for your money.'

'Go on.'

'First one you give me, that's a false plate. It don't exist.'

The Saab at Brent Cross – as expected. 'No record at all?'

'Nothing.'

'And the other one?'

'That one's been reported stolen.'

No big shock, but a let-down nonetheless. 'From where?'

'Somewhere out of town. One sec.' Milos murmured something while he searched. 'Yeah, Surrey. I'll send you the details.'

'Okay.'

'Pay me the usual way, yeah?' He hung up.

He put the phone on the table but it buzzed again immediately – an email from one of Milos's dummy accounts showing screenshots of the Honda SUV's entry on the DVLA system. It noted that the vehicle had been reported stolen to the police on the morning of the attack on Jamie Tan. The car was owned by a company, and the registered keeper was one Andrew Pitt. The address it was listed to was a place he'd never heard of, East Molesey – the same as where the vehicle was stolen from. He looked it up but it was miles out, almost to the M25 in southwest London. He tried Andrew Pitt as well, and got pictures of hundreds of men who carried that name.

One step forward and five steps back. If the killers had taken the precaution of stealing a car, chances were they'd have ditched it at the first opportunity. Probably torched it or similar. He thought about what the differences in approach told him: false plates in one instance, a stolen car in the other. The former was harder to set up and took more time, the latter more opportunist. Seemed to confirm his impression that the attack on Tan was a rush job – but then why go all the way to Surrey to steal the car?

He thought about ANPR, the licence-plate tracking system used by the police. There were scores of cameras in central London, but how many would there be as far out as Woodside Park? The notion became more fragile; even if they'd pinged a camera somewhere – and even if he could access that data – it wasn't the same as knowing where they'd ended up.

He went to the fridge and opened it. The only things inside were a tub of margarine and a half-full bottle of orange juice. He went to pour a glass but noticed the use-by on the bottle – three weeks out of date. He tipped its contents into the sink.

He leaned on the counter, his thoughts fracturing. His mum, the old man, Abi, Ellie.

Jamie Tan.

He started combing through it all again in his mind, mining for leads he'd missed, but he found Lydia Wright creeping into his thoughts instead. He couldn't pin it down at first – his protective instinct kicking in maybe; a transference of his feelings of helplessness elsewhere in his life. But as he stared at her last email on his phone, it dawned on him it was simpler than that: she was the only person with as much invested as him.

Lydia came out of the Tube at Kentish Town and broke into a fast walk. She'd been to Tammy's flat enough times to get there on autopilot. She still wasn't settled on what she'd say. Part of her wanted to tear into her, get it all out of her system so they could try and get past it. Another part told her to let sleeping dogs lie. As angry as she was, it felt like she'd never needed Tammy more than now.

She walked along Kentish Town Road, past the bus stop where she'd caught the N273 home after all the nights they ended up at Tammy's for after-hours drinks. She turned off the main road, flanked by Victorian terraces on one side and a row of council blocks on the other. She carried on to the junction of Tammy's street, picturing herself coming from the other direction, dead of night, drunken invincibility pierced by the isolation she used to feel approaching the estate. She took the turning, the big house the flat was attached to just in sight. She pressed on, coming to the side street with the entrance to Tammy's—

Police tape across the gate, a white tent covering the path and the front door. Lydia ran towards it. A community support officer wrapped her up in his arms, pulling her away, frantically saying something into her ear that wouldn't register.

CHAPTER 34

Lydia went straight to the office when the police were finished with her. It'd taken forty minutes for a patrol car to show up and take her to the station to speak to the DS in charge of the case. She'd called Wheldon while she was waiting, but got his voicemail.

A DS Littleton had taken her statement, his focus naturally falling on the attack at Brent Cross and Tammy's appointment with the money-laundering guru in the City. Lydia told him what she could, her despair made deeper by the fact she hadn't even got the man's name from Tammy before she'd gone to meet him. Littleton was conciliatory, assuring her they'd find a way to identify him. After that she showed him Wheldon's card and explained about her involvement with him and Singh, and Littleton promised he'd speak to them as soon as possible.

Now she sat at her desk at the *Examiner* feeling numb. She couldn't stop thinking about Tammy. The local paper reported the story online and the BBC website had picked it up. Neither article offered any speculation beyond the official police line. Neighbours spouted the usual platitudes, expressing shock that something like this could happen.

The news hit the office like a missile strike: a suspicious death so close to home something the paper would always go big on. The two journos assigned to work it up were desperate to talk to her, along with a third who was writing the paper's obituary. She gave them ten minutes, tearing up as soon as they sat down at her desk.

Stephen called when he heard, apologising that he couldn't be there because he was stuck at an outside meeting. He pleaded with her to go home, offering to send a car to pick her up. She told him she'd think about it, but for now the paper felt like the right place to be.

Guilt and fear. Guilt and fear. Her anger at Tammy now a stick to flog herself with. Wondering if she could've done something to stop it. If it was something she'd done that triggered it. Maybe because they hadn't got her at Brent Cross, they'd gone after Tammy instead. Maybe now they'd come for her again.

It was pointless and self-destructive. Trying to divine motivation through the filter of her own grief and shock.

Eventually she set about reading every word she could find on Jamie and Alicia Tan. It was the closest thing she could think of to a penance.

The two of them remained enigmatic. She found nothing new on Jamie, and even reading the links she hadn't had time to check that morning didn't shed any additional light. As far as the Internet was concerned, he was a high-flying trader and nothing more. His Facebook was the only social-media footprint she could find. If he had much of a personal life, he didn't splash it online.

Information on Alicia was even harder to come by. She didn't seem to have a Facebook account, nor Twitter nor Instagram. She had a LinkedIn profile that looked defunct – the latest entry had her in a position that ended in 2014. Until then she'd worked in various analyst roles, but in different banks to Jamie.

But then she struck gold: an entry on the Companies House website showed Alicia was a director of Tan Financial – listed as a financial consulting business. The registered address was in Arkley – a small town it turned out was near High Barnet. Her fingers tingled over the keyboard as she glanced around the office, as if she was sitting on a secret. She looked up the address on Street View and saw it was a large house – not an office, definitely residential. Not that much of it was visible; the driveway was gated and the house was concealed from the road behind a dense hedge. The kind of place where two successful bankers might live.

The Tans' house in Arkley was more imposing in the flesh. The tall pines lining the left-hand side kept half of it in shade, and the electronic gates at the front only added to the sense the place was off-limits.

There was a video intercom mounted in the wall next to her and Lydia pressed it again. There was a Lexus parked on the far side of the driveway from where she stood, but no sign of movement from inside.

Still no one answered. She looked along the road, deciding what to do. The place reminded her of the house near Hampton Court – Withshaw. Another empty mansion that hummed with a menace that made her want to walk away. The reminder brought a connection into view: she'd gone there to track the Audi that'd been seen watching Paulina Dobriska's address; what if they were the same people at Brent Cross? It was a hard truth to consider – especially if the only difference was that she'd got away. She made a mental note to tell the police to check for an unfamiliar Audi Q7 seen in proximity to Tammy's flat.

The neighbouring house to Alicia Tan's had a similar setup – gated drive, video intercom. She pressed the button and a woman's voice answered. 'Yes?'

'Hi, I'm looking for your neighbour. Alicia Tan – have you seen her?'

'I don't know our neighbours.' *Click.*

It was abrupt enough to make her step back from the speaker. She looked along the street again, leafy enough to ensure privacy for all the houses. It felt like she was wasting her time. She crossed the road and tried one more – a smaller place than the others, diagonally opposite the Tans'. Unlike most of the houses, the driveway wasn't gated so she walked right up to the front door. She rang the bell and waited, a dog barking inside.

A woman opened it on a chain. 'Hello?'

'I'm sorry to disturb you, I'm looking for Alicia Tan. She lives over the road?'

'Yes?'

'It's just no one's home, I wondered if you've seen her. Or Jamie.'

'I don't really know them.'

A chocolate Labrador stuck its face through the crack, barking and bobbing around. Lydia knelt on one knee and stroked its nose. 'She's beautiful.'

'Oh, thank you.' The woman's face lit up. She took the dog by the collar and pulled it back. 'On your bed, Minstral.'

Lydia stood up again. The woman guided the dog away and turned back to the crack in the door. 'Sorry, she wouldn't hurt a fly; she just gets excited for new faces.'

Lydia matched her smile. 'My cousin had one just the same. Bet she keeps you busy.'

'Honestly – they never stop.' The woman rolled her eyes in mock horror. 'Anyway, I'm sorry I can't help but I really don't know them over the road. We've been here thirty years but this street has changed so much – it's all bankers and lawyers now. We're a bit out of time.'

'No problem.'

'The car hasn't moved for a few days, if that's any use.' She nodded towards the house. 'The sporty one's hers; he drives one of those big executive things. I haven't seen that for a while either, actually.'

'Is it unusual for her car not to go anywhere?'

The woman raised her eyebrows. 'I hadn't given it any thought, but I suppose so, yes. I see her in and out all the time. She's in her gym gear, morning, noon and night some days.'

Lydia smiled at her again. 'Sorry to disturb you.' She held up a hand as a goodbye and went back to the street.

She stared at the upstairs windows of the Tans' house. They'd got to Jamie, they'd got to Paulina, they'd got to Tammy. And now maybe Alicia as well. Lydia was the only one who'd walked away from these people – and even that was only thanks to some stranger selling himself as a saviour. His parting shot rang in her ears – 'I won't be there next time'.

'Michael'. He claimed he was working for Alicia. It felt for all the world like bullshit – so now was the time to call him on it. She took her phone out and found his email. She thought about the two detectives, Singh and Wheldon, the lies she'd told them to keep him out of it. She wasn't even sure herself why she'd done it, some grudging sense of gratitude the only thing she could come up with. If they saw him on the CCTV, hanging around the station at the same time as her, following her, it would raise questions. Better to put the pressure on while she was still ahead of them.

She pressed reply and typed her message:

I figured out your associate's name is Jamie Tan. If you really work for Alicia, now's the time to talk to me.

CHAPTER 35

It took Stringer an hour to get to Sir Oliver Kent's office in High Holborn, traffic at a crawl. He went there straight from the hospital, a visit that he terminated early when he saw for himself they'd moved her into the private room – and that the old man was still by her side.

The hospital bill played on his mind. He'd called Kent's go-between first thing to demand his money again for the Carlton job, but Simms shut him down. The prick needed cutting down to size, something to take care of if he ever came out the other side of the Tan shit, but right now it was time to go around him.

The office building was half a dozen stories tall, an index in the lobby listing the different companies that occupied each floor. There were Perspex security gates across the entrance, but the wider one for deliveries was open and Stringer tagged onto the back of a group of people who swept through it with the confidence of employees who knew they belonged.

He took the lift to the top floor and came out in a small reception area decorated in muted tones. There were three company logos behind the desk, including the one for Kent's consulting firm. The receptionist smiled a welcome when he came over.

'Can I help you, sir?'

'Nigel Carlton for Sir Oliver Kent.'

'One moment please.' She picked up a phone and dialled an internal number.

Stringer spread his hands on the counter.

The receptionist said, 'Certainly,' into the phone and hung up. 'He'll be out in a moment. Take a seat.'

He scoped the glass doors that bore Kent's logo and went to stand to one side of them, out of sight of anyone approaching from inside. Top-floor office in a flash building, expensively designed logo; he wondered how much consulting Kent actually did – or if he was just milking his developer clients for the real goods: access and influence.

He counted off sixty seconds until Kent appeared. He was sixtyish and grey, with a gut that spoke of years of lunching on someone else's money – and a suit cut well enough to diminish it. He came through the doors with a cautious look, ignoring Stringer at first as he glanced around.

Stringer stepped to him and offered his hand. 'We haven't met. I'm Michael Stringer, we have a friend in common.'

Kent stared at him. Give him his due, he showed no discomfort as they shook. 'You're referring to Nigel.'

'That's right. There's a small invoice that needs settling.'

'I have staff to deal with those kind of things. Speak to—'

'With respect, I already have.'

'Then I'm afraid you'll have to take it up with him.'

Kent pressed a security card to the reader and reached for the glass door.

Stringer stepped in front of him and took a grip on the handle. 'We can have this conversation now, in private, or we can have it somewhere more public. At a time of my choosing.'

Kent stared at him like he'd just pissed up against the wall. Finally, he put his card away and said, 'Come inside a minute.'

He followed the man down the corridor to a large office at the far end. A wide desk dominated the room, a glass-and-steel model backdropped by floor-to-ceiling windows that showcased a view across the rooftops towards Tower 42. Kent went around the desk and stood in front of his chair. 'As I understand it, the job is not complete yet.'

Stringer put his hands in his pockets. 'I don't know what you've been told, but I did what I was asked.'

Kent squared a pen on the blotter in front of him. 'Another

meeting's taking place next week; we'll be better placed to judge Carlton's appetite for cooperation after that.'

'It's fifteen grand you owe me. I imagine you've earned that kind of money just while we've been talking.'

'I was led to understand you were a professional. Discretion integral to the service.'

'So is getting paid.'

Kent took his jacket off and hung it from the back of his chair. 'If I may, how did my name come to your attention? I expected to be able to keep my distance.'

'Your errand boy is careless. Simms.'

Kent scoffed, nodding. 'Thank you for your candour.'

'My line of work depends on reputation. I'd like to make this the start of a business relationship, not the end of one. But that cuts both ways.'

'The implication being?'

'I'm a professional. Like I told Simms, without payment I'll be forced to withdraw my services. If Carlton were to be made aware of that fact, you'd be back to square one.'

'Yes, that would be unfortunate.' Kent folded his arms. 'You seem the type who wouldn't have come here without doing his homework first.'

'Your reputation precedes you.'

'Then you should know the sum you mention is potentially the tip of a rather larger iceberg. If you're serious.'

'I didn't come here lightly.'

'No. Quite.' Kent drummed his fingers on his arm. 'What else do you do, Mr Stringer?'

'In what sense?'

'What other services?'

'Broadly speaking, you could call it corporate intelligence.'

'There's no need for circumspection, speak freely.'

Stringer shifted his weight. 'Tell me what you want and I'll tell you if I can do it.'

'A useful man to know then. Who else do you do work for?'

'You'll appreciate that I don't divulge my clients.'

'Absolutely. The right answer.' Kent turned his head to look out across the city. 'Do you work internationally?'

'I have done in the past.'

Kent nodded, turning back to look at him but saying nothing more.

'So is there something you've got in mind?'

'Perhaps,' Kent said. 'But I prefer to engage on an exclusive basis – reduce the risk of conflicts of interest arising. How would you feel about working for me?'

'I'm not employee material.'

'No, on the same basis as now. A supplier, my firm as your exclusive client.'

Stringer laced his fingers in front of him. 'I'd have to think about it.'

'Of course. It's a hypothetical question at this stage anyway.'

'It would cost you. I'd be turning my back on a lot of work.'

'You risked coming here over fifteen thousand pounds.' Kent flittered his fingers, dismissing the amount. 'I think we could come to an arrangement.'

'How many more like Carlton do you need?'

'Nigel is more than enough – if he plays along. I'm thinking of other matters – we'll talk again.' Kent moved across the floor to open the door again, signalling his time was up. 'Anyway, give it some thought.'

'I will.' Stringer went over to him and shook his hand in the doorway. 'As soon as I get paid.'

Kent eyed him, a look on his face between affront and amusement.

Stringer left him standing there and nodded to the receptionist on his way out.

The lift felt smaller on the way down, the smoked glass crowding him. Something about Kent's offer screamed ulterior motive, and his instincts told him to get his money and get out. But with no prospect of more work from Andriy Suslov, he couldn't afford to alienate a client as big as Kent, and that meant the proposal needed time and thought.

The doors opened and he headed towards the Perspex security barriers. A face he recognised was coming towards him, and he slowed down. He placed it immediately this time: the man he'd seen at Lydia Wright's flat – and at her office. Sharp suit, expensive watch. The man breezed past him. Stringer whipped his phone out and held it up as if he was reading a message. He turned around absently so he could snap a picture of him while he was waiting for the lift.

The man was too busy checking his own phone to notice. Stringer patted his trouser pockets as if he'd forgotten something, then retraced his steps to the lift, standing behind the target. When it arrived, they stepped inside one after the other, and the man pressed the button for the top floor. He looked at Stringer for the first time, his hand poised over the numbers.

'Same, thanks.'

They rode in silence. At the top, Stringer let the other man out first. The receptionist smiled when he approached the desk. 'Hey, how are you?' She'd folded her hands and was looking up at him – big eyes, big smile.

The man rested one arm on the counter, putting his watch

on display. 'Much better for seeing you.' She rolled her eyes, but the smile grew wider. 'Is he in?'

'One sec.' She picked up the phone, still twinkling at him. 'Stephen is here for you, Sir Oliver. Okay, thank you.' She put it down again. 'He won't be a minute.'

Stringer patted his jacket when the receptionist noticed him standing there. He made a sheepish face. 'Thought I'd dropped my wallet.' He pulled it out of his pocket and held it up. 'My mistake.'

CHAPTER 36

Lydia crossed Soho Square at half-pace. He'd arrived first this time, was waiting on the same bench they'd sat on two days before, his posture angular and guarded.

Unrelenting sunlight, but the square was dead – the offices empty for the weekend, too early for the shoppers peeling off to escape the crowds on Oxford Street. She stepped over a smashed pint glass on the path, its shards undisturbed from where they'd first scattered, some of them reduced to powder. How brittle everything was; how easy to slip unnoticed past the point where things could still be fixed.

She came to a stop in front of him. 'Are you here to talk this time?'

Michael kept his gaze straight ahead. 'You've got his name now, so what else do you want?'

'Did you have him killed?'

He shook his head. 'You know I didn't, so how about you dial down the hostility?'

'I think we're beyond small talk.'

'You asked me here, tell me what you want.'

'I want to know why that fucker tried to kill me the other night and why you were following me. I want to know what's going on.'

'How did you get Tan's name?'

'How did you get hold of the video?'

He looked up at her then, resignation creeping across his face – a giveaway that he'd worked out what she was going to say next.

'You had me robbed,' she said.

He sat back, glancing at her but looking away again as if he was ashamed. 'You got your purse back.'

She laughed once, incredulous. 'Am I supposed to be grateful?'

'No. I'm making the point it was just business.'

'What business? Who the fuck are—'

'The same as you. Information.'

'You're not a journo.'

'That's not what I said. Information – what we're both interested in.'

'How did you know about the video? No one knew it even existed then, so I can only think of one way, and it says you're up to your neck in this.'

'I had nothing to do with the attack.' He was working his left thumb with the right. 'I was waiting to meet Jamie Tan the night he disappeared. I saw you at High Barnet station.'

She found herself taking a step back. 'You were ... How long have you been following me?'

He set his eyes on a point across the square.

She waited but he said nothing. She stepped forward again, retaking her ground. 'Why did you come here if you've got nothing to say?'

'To hear you out.'

'Then you need something to trade. I've got everything now, all I see on that bench is a suspect.'

He took his phone out and brought something up on the screen. Then he turned it around and showed it to her.

She couldn't make out the image in the sunlight at first. She cupped her hand around it, wary of getting too close to him, and saw a picture of a man sticking his head through a doorway. 'Who is he?'

He shook his head. 'I don't know. But does the room look familiar?'

She bent closer, seeing—

'What the fuck?'

'That's your kitchen.'

She felt the blood draining from her face. *They were in her flat...*

'I ran them off. You want another quid pro quo – how's that?'

She snatched the phone out of his hand, resizing the image to get a better look at the face. *They were in her fucking flat. Just like Tammy—*

'When was this?'

'Last weekend.'

Her legs were shaking. 'They could've...' She looked up at him.

'Yeah.'

'You could have warned me a week ago. They tried again at Brent Cross and you let them—' She stopped herself when she got it. His eyes were on hers and she realised he was waiting for her to catch up. 'That's why you were following me that night. To protect...'

He opened his mouth as if he was going to say something, but took a breath instead.

'This is too much.' She thrust his phone back into his hand. 'I can't...'

'We both stumbled into this mess, so maybe we can help each other out.'

Her eyes wouldn't focus. She saw the face in the picture, moving through her flat. The kitchen, her bedroom—

Her laptop. The day she found it open when she'd left it closed – thinking Chloe had done it. 'Who are these people?'

'I don't know. I'm working on it, but for now I don't know.' The uncertainty in his voice was plain, and his words rang true for the first time.

Her thoughts raced to another place: Neighbourhood Watch man on Paulina Dobriska's street, his description of the men watching her flat from their car. 'Let me see that again.'

He swiped and held it up, not letting go this time. She spread her fingers on the screen to zoom in.

The man's hair – a skin fade on the sides, longer on top and sculpted. A description that resonated.

'You recognise him.'

She shook her head, still staring. 'No.'

'But something.'

She didn't answer.

'I'm serious about helping each other,' he said. 'This runs deep.'

'How the fuck am I supposed to trust you?'

'After what I did?'

She started to move away, not sure which way to turn.

He called after her. 'Wait.'

'Send me that picture,' she said. 'Email.'

He held her stare a long moment. Then he nodded.

'Now, I mean.'

He tapped the screen quickly and looked up at her again.

She heard the chime for a new email and turned to go.

'Lydia.'

She stopped.

'Be careful. If there's somewhere else you can stay, you should.'

'It's a bit late for warnings.'

Stringer's car was parked a few minutes away, the other side of Oxford Street. He called Angie on his way there, checking his watch as the dialling tone buzzed. She didn't answer immediately and he felt his temper fraying, stoked by unfair thoughts that she'd got bored in Soho and found a dealer.

She came on the line. 'Yeah?'

'She's just left the square via Frith Street, you got her?'

'I'm right behind.'

'Don't get too close—'

'Shit, Mike, let me work, yeah?'

He darted across one lane of Oxford Street to the narrow safety island that ran down the middle of the road. He had to shout over the traffic noise. 'Alright. But remember the deal – you find yourself with company, call me. Anything more serious, dial 999—'

'Yep, yep. I gotta go, she's gone into the Tube.' She hung up.

Stringer walked against the flow of buses until he could slip between two double-deckers to get to the other pavement. He took the next turn off the main road and darted along the back streets to where he was parked. He jumped in and set the satnav for Surrey.

The Molesey address the stolen Honda was registered to was on a wide avenue lined with trees spaced at regular intervals. Stringer parked right outside the house, looking it over from behind glass before he got out. There were no signs of life from inside.

He climbed out and walked a few paces to stand at the gate across the driveway. It was one of two, the pair joined by a wide semi-circle of gravel in front of the house. He followed the hedgerow to the other gate, looking up at the railings that stood ten feet high. He came to a stop and looked through them to the house. Straightaway he spotted a camera – a small unit on a plinth extending from the far right-hand side of the property. It was positioned to cover a wide area, and prominent enough to be a deterrent.

A gated drive, a CCTV camera no one could miss. The men who killed Jamie Tan had crossed the whole of London to steal a car for their getaway – and then picked the most secure place they could find to do so. He went back into his emails and checked the DVLA report Milos had sent him, thinking he'd read it wrong, but the address was there in black and white.

He went back to the first gate and put his finger on the intercom system built into the wall. The bottom floor of the house was open plan, fronted almost exclusively with glass; he could see there was no one inside. The back was mostly glass too, and it opened out onto a large garden bathed in sunlight, the Thames running across the bottom of it.

He pressed the intercom anyway, waiting while it rang in muted tones. Touching the brass plaque above it, he traced his finger over the engraving of the property's name.

Withshaw.

CHAPTER 37

Lydia took the Tube direct from Soho to Whetstone, forty minutes apart but different worlds.

She jogged to Paulina Dobriska's flat, leaving her covered in sweat by the time she got there. She looked around, trying to orient herself. She remembered the man's name – Henry Siddons – but didn't know which number he lived at. He'd approached her in the street the last time she'd been there. She looked from house to house, hoping for a giveaway.

There – across the road, two doors down, a big neighbourhood-watch sticker in the front window. She crossed over and Siddons appeared at his front door before she'd even started up the path.

'Hello, back again?'

'Hello, Mr Siddons.'

'Still haven't seen her, you know.'

'Who? Paulina?'

'Yes, the lass over the road. I knocked, too, but I don't think she's been back at all.'

The words only stoked her adrenaline rush. 'I wanted to show you something, if you don't mind?'

She could sense him puffing up. 'Oh?'

She raised her phone, the image Michael had sent her on the screen. 'Do you recognise this man from anywhere?'

He had a pair of glasses dangling on a chain around his neck, and he squinted, fitting them over his eyes. 'Right, let's have a look.' He took hold of her wrist, jerking her hand closer to his face, shocking Lydia enough that she almost snatched it away. 'That's one of them. The lads in the car.'

'The ones watching the place over the road?'

'Yes. The same.'

'You're sure?'

He let go of her wrist. 'Definitely. He was sitting right there.' He pointed somewhere across the street. 'Where did you get that from?'

Lydia lowered her hand slowly, hearing the distant sound of a ball being kicked against a wall, a child laughing.

Siddons reached out to touch her forearm. 'Everything alright, love?'

Nowhere felt safe anymore, so Lydia went to the only place she could think to hole up – the office.

She sat at her desk with a two-sugar coffee and traced it out on a piece of paper.

Henry Siddons sees two men watching Paulina Dobriska's place last Saturday – the day after Dobriska took the footage of the attack on Jamie Tan. Dobriska hasn't been seen at home or work since – a phone call to Premier Dental confirming the latter. And now one of the men is photographed in her own flat the same weekend.

She drew another line on the paper, to a box marked Withshaw – the empty mansion on the Thames their car was registered to, according to Sam Waterhouse. From there, two more lines – to a box for the tax lawyer, Simon Shelby, and one for Arpeggio Holdings – the two appointed directors of the limited company that owned Withshaw.

She drew one more line, connecting it to a box holding Tammy's name. She started to trace a question mark, but kept staring at the name Jamie Tan – the one thing that connected all of it.

She pressed her hands into her eyes, trying to slow everything down. It felt like the recurring dream she had where she'd tripped and was falling; bad enough to know it was happening, worse to realise it was too late to do anything about it. They'd been there, in her own home. Lying in wait. When that went wrong, they'd lured her to Brent Cross. And killed Tammy.

She uncovered her eyes, reaching for her phone. She opened Facebook Messenger and clicked on the chat with the woman posing as Dobriska, the last message in all capitals making her heart race with raw adrenaline. She scrolled past it, finding Dobriska's first message to her. Sent at 8.00 on the Tuesday morning – but then she remembered her friend request had been accepted the night before. Twenty-four hours after they'd invaded her flat.

And he'd been there both times – Michael. Maybe saved her life twice. Fuelling the sense that she owed him, the gratitude maybe not so misplaced. Or was that being naive?

She felt cold, a sensation she couldn't remember experiencing before in the airless office, let alone in summer. It seemed to come from inside of her, spreading with each heartbeat. She closed Facebook and called Chloe, clamping her teeth around the pen lid as the phone rang.

'Hey, Lyds.'

'Chlo, hey. Are you at the flat?'

'No, I'm at Nathan's. What's up?'

She dropped the pen on her pad. 'I think ... I think someone broke into our place last weekend.'

'What?'

'Yeah. This is gonna sound crazy, but I think they were looking for me.'

'What are you talking about?'

'I know. It's this story I'm working. Look, I don't want to scare you but can you hang out at Nathan's for a few days?'

'Bloody hell, Lyds, what's happened? Did you go to the police?'

'Yes. Yes and no. I'll explain properly when I see you but...' She let out a breath. 'I know I sound like a nutter but things have just got a bit out of control. Please, please, don't go back there for now.'

'You're freaking me out.'

'I'm sorry. I'm freaking myself out. I'm really sorry. Please, just give me a couple of days, okay?'

'Where are you?'

'I'm at work. I'm fine.'

'So where are you going to stay?'

She felt the first traces of calm coming back to her voice. 'I'll figure something out.'

Stringer threw the door open and jumped out of the car. He had his phone to his ear, waiting for Angie to pick up again. He looked up, not even certain from down there which window belonged to his flat, the Finsbury Park block as bland and uniform as a council office.

'Alright?'

'Shoot,' he said.

'I'm by her work in London Bridge – she went inside a couple of hours ago and I haven't seen her since.'

'You're sure?'

'It's dead round here so I can't see how I'd have missed her. I don't like hanging round this way again, Mike.'

'Why?'

'After the other night.'

'No one could connect you to that.'

'Nah, it ain't that. It's just – dunno, feels like bad karma and shit.'

He stopped with the car fob held out to press. 'You know how the world works; don't tell me you believe in that rubbish. What happened when she left me?'

'We went on a daytrip to the country. Totteridge and Whetstone, it's at the end of the Northern.'

He had the Tube map in his mind – past Finchley, one stop before High Barnet. Bells ringing. 'What for?'

'I'd say she went to visit her grandad, but I don't think he was. She looked like she knew where she was going until we got there, then she looked lost. It was really weird. Then she goes up to this old boy's door, and it's like he knows she's coming. She showed him something on her phone, they both looked like they had a little moment, and then we was off again, back to the Tube. I walked for miles.'

'And that was it?'

'All of it. She came straight back here.'

He leaned on the car roof. 'You get the address?'

'Yeah. You want me to message you?'

'Just keep hold of it.' He looked up again, columns and columns of windows stretching into the sky. 'I'll call you later.'

He went inside and up the stairs. The corridor lights flickered on and for a second he saw everything in strobe lighting; an instant captured and lost. He knocked on the door to 307, listening for Alicia Tan's approach on the other side.

There was no sound.

He knocked again, harder, stepping closer to listen.

He waited a few seconds and tried the handle. It was locked. He took his keys out and put them in the lock, knocking again as he did. 'Alicia?'

He unlocked the door and wrenched the handle. 'Hello?' The air inside was musty, as if it'd been closed up for a while. He went down the hallway, calling out as he did, tremors hitting him as he got flashbacks from Tammy Hodgson's place. Trying to reassure himself: *No one knew she was here...*

He glanced around the sitting room, then ducked his head into the kitchen.

There was a mug on the draining rack. He picked it up and touched the inside – dry.

He went back along the hallway and looked inside the bedroom. The bed was made but there was no sign of her. He pulled his phone out to look for the message where she'd sent herself the video. He copied the number and dialled it. It was dead.

There was drizzle in the air when Stringer pulled up outside the house in Arkley, the first break in the weather in weeks.

Alicia Tan's Lexus was there on the driveway, its front wheels still at an angle, indicating it hadn't been moved. He tried the gates, knowing they wouldn't budge. He followed the railings to where they met the boundary fence, stepped up onto the low wall at their base and hauled himself over them.

He landed crouched low on the gravel. He held still a moment, checking for any sign he'd drawn attention on the street. When nothing moved, no faces appeared in neighbouring windows, he crossed to the front door and knocked.

The house was silent, the sound of birds chirping in the trees all around him. He thought of Angie, tailing Lydia Wright around – in hindsight, maybe detailed to the wrong woman. Another mistake. He went around the side of the house, looking for access to the back. There'd been no evidence of a struggle at the Finsbury Park flat – a glimmer of hope he was clinging to. But then they'd killed her husband on a Tube train and left almost no trace, so maybe it was naive to take heart from that.

He followed a passage to the back garden. There was a wide patio area kitted out with rattan sofas and chairs, and a large canvas sunshade; beyond that, a manicured lawn stretched thirty feet or more, edged by carefully tended borders filled with yellow and red flowers in bloom. He skirted the wall of the house, moving slowly towards the folding doors to look inside. A soft breeze blew across him, like a blade traced across his neck.

He craned his head to look through the glass, making sure not to touch it.

Empty. A large open-plan room that took in the lounge and the kitchen, three stools tucked neatly under the breakfast bar that divided the two. No sign she'd been there. He covered his knuckles with his sleeve and knocked on the folding doors.

No response.

He stepped back from the house to give himself an angle and looked up. It was twenty-five degrees outside and there wasn't a window or door open in the place. She could be upstairs, left in her bed like Tammy Hodgson. But would she have risked coming back here? He looked again through the glass and realised he could make out the alarm panel on the opposite wall – armed and activated.

He surrendered to the reality of the situation: alive or dead, she wasn't there, and he had no fucking clue where she was.

His phone beeped. The alert jerked him out of his spiral – but only for a second.

Dalton. The message on screen: *You will be collected from home at 10.00 a.m.*

CHAPTER 38

Lydia slept in one of the meeting rooms. It was a corner nook, too small for its purpose, normally only in use when someone needed a private space to make a call during the day – and never at night. She rested her head on her forearms and dozed on and off for a few hours, stiffness in her back and neck eventually forcing her to abandon her efforts.

She took a shower in the basement bathroom, feeling grim when she had to put the same clothes back on.

At her desk she tried to regroup. When she unlocked her screen, it was open on the database the International Consortium of Investigative Journalists had set up to facilitate searches of the Panama Papers. She'd run a search looking for Arpeggio Holdings, but it was a more common name than she'd imagined and the list of results ran to three pages –

different variations, but with nothing to indicate any of them were the shell company she was looking for. She tried Simon Shelby, the other Withshaw director, and even Withshaw itself, but each search came up empty.

She typed an email to Dietmar Stettler, a journalist with the German team who'd first received the cache of papers along with Tammy, and who she'd corresponded with over an aspect of the Goddard story. A disclaimer on the website stated there was material that hadn't been uploaded to the database, for legal and other reasons, and just as important, Stettler was more familiar with navigating the huge volume of information that was there. She sent him the list of search terms and asked if he could turn anything up.

The lift chimed behind her, causing her to whip around. The doors opened and Stephen came out looking over at her. He was wearing jeans and a white shirt, the unfamiliar casual look somehow ageing him.

He walked over to the edge of her desk, the morning sun coming through the windows lighting him up as if he was under spotlights. 'You're still working?'

She glanced at the clock on her screen, not realising it was already gone nine. 'Just trying to distract myself. What're you doing here on a Sunday?'

'Looking for you.'

'What for?'

'I'm worried about you. Can we talk?' He glanced in the direction of his office.

She locked her computer and pushed her chair back to get up. She reached for a pen and pad but he put his hand over it. 'You don't need that.'

They walked in silence, Stephen in the lead, never once

looking back at her. The empty newsroom hummed, a low buzz that made it feel like the air was being sucked out. A cleaner was wiping the glass of the office adjoining Stephen's and she looked up in surprise when they came down the corridor towards her. She smiled and said good morning with a Spanish accent and vanished around the corner.

She followed him in. He stopped immediately and leaned against the wall. 'How you holding up?' He reached out a hand to take hers.

She went to say something but she felt tears well up in her eyes. She looked away, trying not to break in front of him.

He leaned closer, looking at the bruises on her neck. She jerked back and he held his hands up to show he wasn't going to touch. 'What happened to you?'

She was shaking now, inside. If she spoke her voice would falter.

He wrapped his arms around her and she buried her face in his shoulder. He whispered something she didn't catch, his face in her hair. Then he broke off.

'What happened to your neck?'

'I just ... It's nothing.'

'I can't imagine how you're feeling right now but I promise you I only want to help. Talk to me, please.'

She dipped her forehead against his chest. 'I don't know what's happening.'

He cradled the back of her head – a gesture that was enough to tip her over the edge.

'They killed her. It could've been me.'

After that it came out in a rush. The attack at Brent Cross, the police, arriving at Tammy's place. She jumped around the timeline, telling things as they came to her because she didn't want to leave a pause for him to ask questions. She spoke the name Jamie Tan and it felt like catharsis.

When she was finished, Stephen was silent at first. He looked ashen, stepping backward slowly to perch against his desk. His first words: 'You've told the police all this?'

'Yeah. They're looking into it.'

'Okay, good. That's a start. What about protection?'

'They've asked the local bobbies to keep an eye on my place. Told me to dial 999 at the first sign of—'

'That's it?'

'What else can they do?'

He breathed out through his nose. 'I've spoken to Evan; he's briefed the rest of the senior team, and legal are involved as well. They'll need to speak to you – obviously they want to restrict your involvement as much as possible going forward.'

'Why?'

'It's a police matter and the risk is too great.'

'What? She was my friend, isn't that my choice to make?'

He straightened his shirt. 'I get your frustration, but aside from the fact that legal's word is god, I can't accept you putting yourself in any further danger.'

'Stop it. What we do outside of work doesn't give you a right to decide what risks I can or can't take.'

'I'm not. Take the personal out of this; can you imagine if I gave you the green light and something happened? I have a responsibility to the company and to its staff – I can't ignore that.'

She pointed to the bruises. 'I deserve to see this through.'

'At any cost?'

She stared at him, neither of them moving. She could see a vein in his forehead pulsing.

'There are more layoffs coming,' he said.

'That's not a surprise.'

'Yeah, but it's been signed and sealed now. Big headcount reduction.'

'What's the relevance?'

'It might open up an opportunity to move you.'

'Again?'

'Back, I mean. To the news desk. You've done your time.'

'Okay.' She said it with no emotion.

He spread his arms. 'I thought you'd be pleased.'

'I am. But it feels like a consolation prize.'

He drifted across the office again, finally anchoring himself by planting his hands on his desk.

She stood in front of him. 'You can't expect me to just forget what they've done.'

'I'm just asking you to leave it to the police. Please. We'll liaise with them, stay close to the investigation, make sure they can't let up for one second.'

'It feels like I should be doing more.'

'Whoever these bastards are, they don't get to kill one of our own and just walk away. I promise you that.'

She looked at his face, saw the wiry red lines snaking across the whites of his eyes. 'How soon are you moving me?'

CHAPTER 39

Stringer looked out his window at Dalton's Range Rover parked on the street below.

He took his time dressing, a protest he recognised as pointless. At five past, another text came to remind him they were waiting. He read it and threw his phone on the bed.

The morning was overcast, the clouds that brought the rain the day before still lingering. His mother would call it sticky, a word that fired a memory – the days from his childhood where he'd come downstairs to find her in the kitchen in her nightdress, wiping the sweat from her forehead with a piece of kitchen roll. All while drinking a hot cup of tea. The old man would still be in bed, the smell of a lit Benson & Hedges always the first signal he was awake.

The Range Rover door opened as he crossed the pavement, Dalton in his usual seat.

Stringer put his hands on the chassis and ducked his head inside. 'What do you want?'

'Get in.'

'Save yourself the trouble, let's talk here.' An open hand to point out the empty street around them.

Dalton picked up a phone from the back seat and held it out to him, the screen lit and showing a call was connected. 'Mr Suslov is eager to hear your progress.'

Stringer ran his tongue around his cheek and hauled himself up into the ride. There was a passenger in the front seat next to the driver, a new wrinkle from how it'd been all the other times. 'Who's he?'

Dalton ignored the question, reaching across Stringer to close the door. 'Well?' The car pulled into the road.

Stringer opened his hands on his lap. 'I'm following various strands.'

'Such as?'

'There was a getaway car. It looks like it was stolen for the job, but I've got a line on its address anyway.'

'And?'

'And I'm working on it.'

'If the car was stolen, what does the address matter?'

'There's something off about it.'

'Meaning?'

'Meaning I'm working on it.'

'Where did you get the car details from?'

'I told you I needed some money. Where is it?'

'Mr Suslov was reluctant.' Dalton flicked a nervous glance at the phone on the seat next to him, then fixed Stringer with a look and shook his head. He mouthed, *He was fucking furious.* 'You said you'd located the scene. Putting two and two together, am I right to think CCTV footage exists?'

Stringer cocked his head, staring through him.

'If you've been sitting on more information about what happened...'

'What are you going to do with it? Pass it to the cops?'

Stringer looked at the phone now, wondering if Suslov was simmering on the other end. Dalton clocked him doing it and shot him a middle finger. He looked out the window, seeming to check where they were. It prompted Stringer to do the same and he saw they were approaching Old Street roundabout.

'What about the wife?' Dalton said.

'You tell me.'

Dalton shifted in his seat. 'What does that mean?'

'It's only you and Suslov think she's relevant.'

'So you haven't even looked for her?'

'What for? She didn't do it.'

Another glance at the phone. The call timer ticked in silence. Stringer sat back in his seat. 'Where are we going?'

'Somewhere we can talk.'

'We can talk here. I thought that was the point.'

Dalton stared at him in silence. Something was different, a new tension about the man that Stringer should've picked up sooner. He glanced at the door, trying to remember if they'd locked them when he got in.

Without warning the car made a sharp turn into an unmarked entrance. They cruised down a slope, plunging from daylight into gloom. An underground garage. They cut right across a line of bays, the car park empty apart from them. Stringer released his seatbelt and flung it off. 'What is this?'

Dalton kept his gaze down, his eyes flitting between the phone and the footwell.

They came to a stop and the driver and passenger jumped out. They opened Stringer's door and pulled him off the seat.

'Get your fucking hands off me.'

The two muscled him against the bare concrete wall. Dalton dropped down from the back seat and placed the phone on the roof of the car. He reached back inside and produced an iPad. He watched Stringer as he came over, holding it like a clipboard. 'You've been meeting with a journalist.'

'What the fuck is this about?'

'Why did you meet with Lydia Wright?'

'None of your business.'

'Mr Suslov would like to know.'

'Get fucked.'

Dalton looked at the man on the left and nodded. The car boot opened, someone pressing a button unseen. The driver walked over and pulled out a golf iron. He came back to Stringer and raised it slowly to his face, clipping his chin. He rested the edge of the blade on his forehead, the metal like a cold finger on his skin.

'The journalist,' Dalton said.

'No.'

For a second nothing moved. All eyes on Dalton, disbelief that this was really going to happen. Then he nodded again.

The passenger grabbed Stringer's wrists and pinned them above his head. Before he could even struggle, the driver swung the golf club into his guts.

He buckled, folding into himself in the instant before the man pinned his arms again. There was a pounding silence in his head, the garage tilting.

'The journalist.'

Stringer spat on the floor to one side and gasped for a breath. It was all he could do to get a whisper out. 'She's irrelevant.'

Dalton swiped something on the tablet. 'She's irrelevant, the wife's irrelevant – is there anything that is relevant? Did you kill Jamie Tan?'

Stringer stuttered in disbelief. 'You know I didn't.'

'Let's be precise.' He turned to talk to the phone on the car like it was a jury. 'Did you arrange his murder?'

'No.'

The driver swung the club again, connecting with his ribs and stomach. Stringer retched and his legs gave this time, the other man letting him fall to his knees and then to all fours.

He scrabbled on the floor. A pipe ran down the wall next to where he'd been standing, water leaking from it, the grainy discharge under his fingers.

Dalton came over and crouched in front of him, turning the iPad around to hold it in front of Stringer's face.

His eyes were watering enough to blur the image, but recognition came anyway. It showed him marching up to Jamie Tan in the street with his phone held out. Dalton swiped and the next image came up – Stringer looming over him. The next

– Stringer looking as if he was yelling at him.

'You want to explain these pictures?'

A strand of drool slipped from the corner of his mouth, collecting on the concrete.

'Mr Stringer?'

Shit... 'The fuck are you doing watching me?'

'That's rich, coming from you. Now, do I need to reiterate who's asking these questions?'

Stringer closed his eyes. 'It was thirty seconds. The only contact we ever had.'

'The purpose being?'

Stringer said nothing, scrambling for a lie.

'Looks like you're threatening him,' Dalton said.

'No.'

'Then what?'

Stringer breathed hard.

'*What?*'

'I wanted to panic him, see if he'd fuck up even worse.'

'What were you showing him?'

'A picture. Him passing out class As. He didn't know anything about me.'

'Safe to say he'd remember you though.'

'It was thirty fucking seconds. A stranger on the street.'

'And yet shortly after, he's dead. Then you turn up asking for more money. Did he come looking for revenge? Did you kill him in self-defence?'

'No.' Acid bile burned in his throat.

'Did you kill him to blackmail Mr Suslov?'

'What? No...'

'Why are you talking to the journalist?'

'For another job. Unrelated.'

'You're lying.'

'Where is this shit coming from?' Stringer said.

'Were you blackmailing Tan on the side?'

'No.'

'That's what you do, isn't it?'

'Only when I'm getting paid.'

'Tan was a wealthy man. Easy pickings.'

'Not enough to cross Suslov.'

'You expect us to believe this bullshit? Where's the wife?'

The change of direction threw him. 'I don't know.'

'Is she alive?'

'I don't know.'

'When was the last time you saw Tan?'

He clutched his stomach, rearing slowly back to his haunches. 'Which one?'

'Don't be smart. Jamie.'

It took a second for his thoughts to clear. 'The day before.'

'Where?'

'On the train. I was watching him.'

'After you walked right up to him like that? And you think he didn't notice you?'

'I was careful.'

'You knew his movements then.'

'Of course I did.'

'You knew he'd be on that train that night.'

'For Christ's sake, I had more reason to keep Tan alive than anyone. He lives, I get paid.'

'He died and you asked for double.'

Stringer clutched his stomach, trying for one good breath. 'Bring the phone.'

'What?'

'The phone. Over here.'

Dalton let the iPad dangle by his side and came back with the mobile. He held it up to Stringer's mouth.

'I didn't kill him, Suslov.'

Silence.

He took a breath to gather himself and spoke again. 'Tell this fucking child to let me go.'

A sharp noise came from the phone, like Suslov was clearing his throat. Dalton hit the button to take it off speaker and brought it to his ear. He listened, moving on the spot, but then turned away from Stringer and the other men. He dipped his head, saying something in a low voice that seemed like a protest. At last he nodded, then said, 'Okay.' He put the phone back on the roof and stood in front of Stringer, holding the iPad to himself again. 'Get him up.'

The two men gripped his jacket and pulled him to his feet. Then the driver walked over to the car and tossed the golf club into the boot. He bent over to extract something from deeper inside, coming back holding a handgun.

Dalton glanced at it then looked back at Stringer. 'Where's the wife?'

Stringer stared at the phone, trying to block everything else out. The low ceiling was lined with fluorescent strip lights, a glare that seemed to penetrate him like an x-ray. They knew he'd been talking to Lydia, they had pictures of him with Jamie. Now the test they'd been building to: see if he'd lie again about Alicia, only to show him a picture of them together. A guess at what Suslov had said on the phone: *If he lies, kill him.*

Unless that was the bluff.

'Stringer?'

'I need my phone.'

'What for?'

'The address.'

'Where is it?'

He nodded to his trouser pocket.

Dalton signalled the passenger. 'Get it.'

The man patted his pocket and reached inside, producing the phone. 'It's locked.'

Dalton nodded and the passenger passed the phone to Stringer. 'Open it.'

Stringer turned it to grip one-handed as if he was unlocking it with his thumb. Then he swung it into the driver's mouth.

The metal rim smashed into his teeth. Blood spurted and the man dropped the gun to throw his hands to his face.

Stringer burst past him and ran towards the left-hand wall. He could hear the second man shouting behind him. Up ahead: an alarm panel, red light blinking. He smashed his palm into it, breaking the glass to set it off. A piercing siren bounced around the walls, filling the tight space.

He kept running, zagging around a column so they wouldn't have a clear shot, making for a door under a fire-exit sign on the other side of the garage. He could hear footsteps pelting after him. He didn't look back, his lungs burning.

He crashed through the emergency door and slammed it shut. He was at the bottom of a stairwell. He flattened his back against the door and braced his feet on the wall opposite, a metre off the ground. He grabbed for the baton in his pocket but it snagged on the way out, a desperate grasp catching thin air as it clattered to the floor.

The man crashed into the door and it jolted him violently, coming open a way before it snapped shut again, his legs just holding. He pushed until they were almost straight in front of him. He arched his back straining to get to the baton on the ground, but it was out of reach.

The door juddered again, but the man had no momentum now and it barely gapped. Stringer could feel him pounding on the other side, shouting something that was lost in the noise from the alarm.

He counted seconds, fearing a gunshot. How long until someone responded to a fire alarm in a building in the city?

The door moved again but held. His legs started to cramp. He tried to hold it but the pain got too bad and he had to drop his feet to the floor. He whipped around to plant his hands on the door to brace it again, stretching the cramp out of his calf as he did.

The hammering stopped. The door was still. He held his position a few seconds longer, weighing it, weighing it...

He grabbed the baton off the floor and darted up the stairs.

Two flights up he came to an emergency exit. He burst through it and found himself on the street, the daylight blinding him.

CHAPTER 40

Monday morning, Lydia finally grasped the nettle. Thirty-plus hours in the office had her at breaking point.

She came out of Liverpool Street station and made the short walk to the HFB building. There was a sense of safety being surrounded by crowds of people on their way to work – proof that the real world still existed, that other people were still living normal lives. The mundane something she could still claw back.

The receptionist at HFB said Adam Finch hadn't arrived for work yet. Lydia pretended she'd mixed up her times and said she'd wait for him. She took a seat by the entrance and studied the faces streaming in, feeling exposed sitting in Jamie Tan's place of work.

Finch showed up fifteen minutes later, with florid cheeks and his tie worn loose, the top button of his shirt left undone. Looked like the end of his week, not the start.

She jumped up to call after him. 'Adam...'

He stopped and turned around, the look on his face showing that he remembered her. He carried on walking.

'Adam, please, I really need you to talk to me.'

He reached the bank of lifts and pressed the up button half a dozen times.

She came close enough to talk in a hush. 'Someone tried to kill me last week. A friend of mine was murdered. Your friend Jamie's at the heart of all of this.'

He looked up at the lift indicator and went to press the button again.

She put her hand over it before he could. 'You didn't contact me on the off chance I knew where Jamie was, so why don't you just tell me whatever you wanted to say?'

He rubbed his forehead with the back of his hand, his document bag dangling from it. 'I don't know what you're on about.'

A lift arrived and he moved towards it. She went after him, holding out her arm so the doors wouldn't close. 'Whatever it is that's got you spooked, it's going to keep eating you up until you get it off your chest. I just hope to god no one else has to die before you do.'

A man and a woman filed around her into the lift. She could feel them eyeing her, but she kept her gaze on Finch.

'Do I have to call security?' he said.

'They killed my fucking friend, did you hear me?' She saw herself in the mirror at the back of the lift and got a flashback to Goddard at City Airport. Eighteen months on and still making the same mistakes. She looked at Finch, his mouth ajar, looking like he wanted the ground to swallow him up, people inside the lift and out staring at her like she was a madwoman. She put her arm down and stepped back, staring at him.

He couldn't meet her eyes.

Lydia walked into the police station at two minutes before eleven, trying to make sense of how her life could've been shattered at such speed. Even a fortnight ago, she couldn't have believed she'd be living a Monday morning like this. All the time she'd spent waiting for something to change, for her life to pick up again; her mother's voice in her ears now, *Be careful what you wish for.*

It was ten minutes before Wheldon showed up to take her through to a meeting room. He gestured for her to take a plastic chair and asked if she wanted anything to drink.

'No, thank you.'

'I'll be back in a minute.' He held up a hand almost in apology as he slipped out the door.

The room was bare, but not as intimidating as it could've been. There was a yellowed spider plant in one corner, a light-grey carpet on the floor. She was there at Wheldon's request, and ready to co-operate – but leaving her to stew seemed designed to make her nervous.

Wheldon came back a few minutes later, Singh in tow this

time. They took seats across from her, setting a file folder and a laptop down in between them.

Wheldon tapped his pen on the table. 'Thanks for coming in, Miss Wright, we'll try not to keep you. How've you been since we spoke?'

'Fine. I've been working a lot. Keeping my mind occupied, you know?'

'I was very sorry to hear about your colleague. It must've been a terrible shock.'

Lydia nodded. 'Do you know any more yet?'

'A murder investigation's been opened, as I'm sure you're aware, so I can't say too much while that's ongoing.'

'Have they figured out who she went to meet that morning? About money laundering?'

'I can't answer that, I'm sorry. We're liaising with DS Littleton's team. I'm sure they'll speak to you again in due course.' He squared the folder in front of him. 'Now, I want to state upfront that we haven't made an arrest in your case as yet. That's not why you're here.'

'I didn't ... I didn't expect you had.'

'Okay. I just need to manage your expectations. That's not to say we've made no progress, though. I'd like to show you a photograph if I may.' He flipped open the folder and slid out a stack of papers. He leafed through until he found it, spinning it around on the desk so it faced her. 'Do you recognise this man?'

The image was a grainy shot of Michael standing in front of Brent Cross station, a still from a CCTV feed. She put her finger on it to bring it closer. 'That's the man that helped me. The man in the suit.'

Singh nodded without saying anything. Wheldon opened

the laptop and positioned it so they could all see the screen. 'This is the CCTV footage from that night. The camera looks right at the station entrance, can you take a look for me?'

She nodded, a sick feeling blooming inside that she was about to see Michael working with the other two, before or after the attack. She started trying to conjure up a way to tell them about her contact with him.

The video played and she saw herself come out of the ticket hall, and then he appeared right after her. He looked in her direction and then took his phone out.

They let it continue. Lydia walked along the parade of shops and then back. Wheldon hit fast-forward while she waited outside the station, then brought it back to normal speed as Michael walked past her, towards the road. 'At this point he leaves, but not for long.'

She had her lips apart, shaking her head. 'I never noticed him.'

Wheldon fast-forwarded again, then pressed play when the woman appeared at the bottom of the picture. 'Now, here you are going to meet this character. She's one of the two that attacked you?'

'Yes.'

Singh took over. 'She barely comes into the shot and she keeps her back to the camera. Even here, when she looks around, she makes a point of scratching herself so her face is obscured.'

Wheldon circled her on the screen with his pen as she did it. 'So we've not been able to get a good look at her.'

The woman led Lydia out of the camera's range. Then a few seconds later, Michael came into view again, crossing from left to right, on their trail.

'So wherever he'd gone, he was waiting for you,' Singh said. 'Somewhere out of shot.'

'I suppose so.'

Wheldon paused the footage and interlaced his fingers. 'So it seems likely that this man was there because you were. Can you think of any reason why that would be?'

She looked from him to Singh and back. 'No.'

'And this man wasn't known to you?'

'No. I'd never seen him before.'

'Who else knew you were going to be there that night?'

'No one. I didn't tell anyone what I was doing in case they thought I was mad.'

Singh looked up. 'Not even Tammy Hodgson?'

Lydia shook her head. 'I couldn't get hold of her. I only agreed to go there a few hours before.'

'When was the last time you heard from Miss Hodgson?'

'Sometime the day before. Around lunchtime – we were arranging to meet that night.'

'And did you?'

Lydia looked down. 'She didn't show up.'

'But Miss Hodgson had been communicating with the same Facebook account.'

'Yes.'

Singh noted something down but said nothing more.

Wheldon nodded. 'Okay.' He pressed play again and fast-forwarded. 'Now, I want to show you one more thing.' He waited, all three of them staring at the screen. After a few more seconds, Lydia saw herself appear again. Wheldon slowed it down as she watched herself sprinting across the car park and into the station. Even watching it back raised her heartbeat.

'That was after, obviously. What are we looking for here?' She looked at Wheldon.

He kept his eyes on the screen and she looked back just as Michael appeared again. He crossed the car park, looking over his shoulder, then stopped outside the minicab office, turning to face the road. He looked like the world's skinniest bouncer.

Lydia edged closer to the screen. She watched him stand there, minutes passing by, not moving, apart from to glance over his shoulder into the ticket hall. This was when she would've been inside – dropping her phone and trying to keep herself together long enough to get on a train. The sense of terror came back to her, and suddenly she wished she'd known he was there. More than that: she wished he'd come inside to tell her she was safe.

Wheldon stopped it again. 'Now, what's he up to here, would you say?'

She looked up at him, running her nail back and forth along the edge of the table. 'I don't know.'

'Seems almost like he's keeping watch,' Singh said.

She shrugged. 'I mean ... why?'

'We've been through the rest of the footage immediately before and after; the woman you met doesn't appear again, nor does anyone fitting the description of the man that attacked you. Not really surprising, given how aware of the cameras the woman acted. There was also no sign of a red Kia, although from what you said, it does sound like that was always a lie.'

'Yeah.'

Singh leaned back in his chair. 'We've spoken to the gentleman working in the station that night; he had no recollection of any of you, and we've not turned up any other witnesses so far. So you can see why we're even more keen to speak to this man.' He looked at the screen again, Michael dead centre in the frozen image. 'You're absolutely sure you don't know him?'

Lydia shook her head, staring at the screen. Her emotions running haywire, feelings she couldn't put a name to. A debt to pay. 'Can you track where he went after?'

'He goes into the Tube but we lose him from there.' Both detectives stared at her. She kept her eyes on Singh, not certain she believed him.

Finally Wheldon looked down to thumb through the stack of papers again. 'You made a report last weekend that your phone was stolen.'

'Yes.'

'You didn't mention that when we spoke.'

'I didn't think it was relevant. It was a girl that robbed me.'

'Had you spoken with the woman you believed to be Paulina Dobriska at that point?'

'No ... Well, I'd sent her a message on Facebook but she hadn't responded.'

'Right.'

'So it is possible these people were aware of you and had already taken an interest. That there could be some connection between the two incidents.'

'I guess so. I don't know.'

'Given subsequent events, I don't think that level of coordination is out of the question,' Singh said. He moved forward in his chair again, bending low over the desk. 'Miss Wright, if this man has approached you, or threatened you, the best thing you can do is tell us about it. Whatever he might have said, we can help you.'

'Why would he threaten me? He stopped them.'

'Perhaps. But the only people who knew you were going to be there that night were you and the people you met. You said you didn't tell anyone, so how else would he have known?'

'You're saying he was working with them?'

'It's one possibility.'

'It doesn't look like it from this.'

'The things criminals do often don't make sense.'

'I don't know what you want me to say.'

'I just want you to be absolutely certain that you don't recognise this man. Not even someone you've noticed hanging around your office or your flat maybe?'

'I've already told you I don't.'

Singh kept his stare on her, hooded eyes that were half closed but alive with silent accusation. Eventually he looked at Wheldon, who closed the laptop.

'Okay, thank you for talking to us today, Miss Wright.' He pushed the photograph of Michael towards her. 'Take that with you; it might prompt something to come back to you later.'

She took it from him and folded it into her bag. 'What about Paulina Dobriska?'

'We've passed her details to our colleagues in the missing persons team. They're making inquiries.'

'Did you speak to her neighbour? That car he saw traced back to—' She stopped herself, glancing from one to the other and thinking about dropping Sam Waterhouse in the shit.

'Traced back to...?'

Sam could look after herself; Paulina was more important. 'I traced it to a house in Surrey. It seemed to be empty.'

'How did you do that exactly?'

'A source.'

Wheldon opened his hand on the desk. 'Miss Wright, I don't need to remind you that—'

'Leave the investigations to us,' Singh said. 'Not least because you're putting yourself at risk.'

'Fine. But did you speak to him – Mr Siddons?'

'We're carrying out our enquiries.'

They stood up and she found herself looking up at them like she was back in school.

'That man's presence on the night in question was clearly no coincidence,' Singh said, opening the door for her. 'And I'd consider him a danger. If he should approach you, you need to alert us immediately, whatever story he might spin you.'

She got up and stopped in the doorway to face him. 'I hear you.'

CHAPTER 41

Stringer sat at the table closest to the door, the breeze from the outside the only respite from the wet heat inside the cafe. The place was a few metres down from Kilburn Tube, a part of London he didn't know well. In front of him, a black coffee was going cold. He watched the street for Angie, looking down when his phone started to ring. A blocked number. He answered, thinking it might be her to say she was running late.

'Mr Stringer?'

Hearing Sir Oliver Kent's voice threw him. 'Yes.'

'I thought you'd want to know that I've settled the matter we discussed in my office.'

'My fee?'

'The same.'

'Okay.' He sat up straighter in his seat. 'Okay, thank you.'

'My inclination was to hold off until I was more certain of progress with Nigel Carlton, but I wanted you to know the proposal I made was serious. A show of intent.'

'I appreciate that, but...'

'But?'

'It would need further discussion.'

'Naturally. Are you free today?'

'I'm...' He saw Angie coming down the other side of the street. 'I can't today.'

The silence on the line spoke of the man's indignation, not used to hearing no.

'Look, I want to hear you out, but now's not a good time. Can we speak later?'

'You're working on something else?'

Angie came through the door and nodded to him, heading to the counter when she saw he was on the phone.

'Yes.'

'Of course. A man of many talents. Perhaps we'll speak another time then.' Kent hung up before he could say anything more.

He screwed his eyes shut. *Fuck*.

Stringer put his phone on the table next to his coffee as Angie sat down. He'd wiped it clean of blood and saliva, but there was a dent in the metal rim where it'd made contact with the man's teeth, and the glass above it showed a small fracture.

Angie rubbed her eyes, then stopped when she took a proper look at him. 'You look awful.'

'Rough weekend.'

'What's going on?'

He shook his head and looked away. It still hurt to breathe.

'Mike, you don't have to do the Mr Strong and Silent act all the time. Everything you've done for me...'

'It's complicated. I want you to stay away from the journalist now.'

She frowned. 'Why?'

'Better we don't get into it.'

'This is nuts. I never seen you rattled before all this.'

He took a wad of notes out of his pocket and dumped it in front of her. 'That's all I can do for now. I'll make it up to you later.'

She covered the pile with her hand to hide it, glancing around to see if anyone was looking. She let out a breath in frustration. 'It ain't about the money. I just don't get how you go from "don't let her out of your sight" to "stay away".'

'It's my problem.'

She slumped back in her chair, but sat forward again just as quick. 'Everything is. Look, so you know, she went to talk to the Feds this morning. That's where I was when you texted me.'

'Okay.'

'Doesn't worry you?'

'Not the police, no.'

'And there's something else.'

'Go on.'

'Before she went to the copshop, she went into town. She looked like shit – bit like you do.'

'Thanks.'

She smiled at her own joke. 'Nah, I mean like she ain't slept in a while or had a proper shower neither.'

'Stick to the point.'

'So I'm on her and we end up at this office with HFB written on it. I Googled it and it's like an investment bank.'

He moved his cup out the way to put his arms on the table. 'I know it. What was she doing there?'

'She literally lost it. First she's just waiting but then she sees this next man come in. She goes after him and she's like, "I really need to talk to you". Like he's her ex and he's been ghosting her or some shit.'

That didn't fit. Lydia Wright had no connections to Jamie Tan prior to the video – so this had to be a source. Someone Tammy Hodgson had put her on to? 'Then what?'

'Then nothing. He got in the lift and threatened to call security. She let him go.'

'What did he look like? Could you pick him out if you saw him again?'

She pulled a face. 'Dunno, maybe; them suits all look the same.'

He went to say something but she waved her hand to cut him off. She held her phone up for him to look. 'That's his name though.'

The photo was zoomed in on a security pass worn in a lanyard around his neck. Adam Finch. Stringer couldn't help breaking into a grin. He zoomed out again to look at the man's face, then passed it back to her. 'You're good.'

His phone started ringing silently on the table. Abi. He turned it over when he saw Angie looking.

'Answer it if you want.'

'It can wait.'

She put the money in her pocket. 'I like working with you, Mike. I know you're shady as fuck, but it's all good far as I'm concerned. And I'm serious about talking. I'm only about half as stupid as you think I am. I'm a good listener.'

'I don't think you're stupid.'

She winked at him, smiling. 'You always bite.'

Her eyes were bright and clear, crackling with energy. A different woman from the one he'd first met, somehow younger and more mature at the same time. It made him think of Ellie, a world of potential in front of them both – and how easy it was to veer onto the wrong path. Angie had escaped it once; there had to be hope in that.

'What you thinking now?'

He didn't have an answer at first, his train of thought freewheeling away from his control. Only when he traced it back did the answer come to him. He wanted reassurance that Ellie's future was safeguarded – even if he wasn't around to see it.

CHAPTER 42

'Hello?'

Stringer coughed. 'It's me.'

'Your name didn't come up on the screen,' Abi said.

'I lost my phone. This is a temporary number.'

'Okay.' The silence was pointed, disbelief evident.

'What?'

'You never lose things.'

'Well now I did. How is she?'

'I thought you were ignoring me. Where've you been?'

'I had to work.'

'Dad said you walked straight out the other morning.'

'I just stopped by to check she was comfortable.'

'Can't you two call a truce, just for a bit? For Mum's sake.'

'This is a truce. I had to go to work.'

She took a deep breath and let it out.

'How is she?' he said.

'Her blood pressure went haywire yesterday but they don't know why.'

'Are the doctors saying anything? What's the prognosis?'

'More tests. They're doing what they can, but I get the feeling they think it's a matter of time.'

He swore to himself. 'They don't know that.'

'Come on, Mike, let's not kid ourselves.'

He looked along the street towards Liverpool Street station, then the other way towards HFB. 'How's Ellie?'

'She's not sleeping so well. She was awake at half-four this morning, bouncing around the flat. It's a reaction to what's going on – kids are so sensitive to stress.'

'Have you told her about Mum?'

'She knows grandma's poorly. I sugar-coat it in a big way, but I'm not going to outright lie to her.'

'And you?'

'I'm coping.'

'Can you put her in for some extra nursery hours? I'll cover it.' He thought about Oliver Kent hanging up on him – a cash injection he couldn't afford to lose, especially with the looming possibility he'd have to disappear for a while to stay alive.

'It's not that easy, they're oversubscribed. Anyway, I don't want to feel like I'm pushing her away just to suit me.'

'Anything I can do, just tell me.'

'Why don't you come over one evening? I could use a sounding board more than anything. I'll cook something. Ellie will love it.'

Any explanation he could offer would have to start with why he didn't even dare go to his own flat. He wasn't about to dump his troubles on her plate that way. 'I can't right now. Work. Maybe later this week.'

'Okay.'

The phone vibrated in his hand and he snatched a glance at the screen. A reply from Lydia Wright: *I'm here. Where are you?* He put it back to his ear and moved along the arches separating the walkway from the street. 'I've got to go. I'll call you later.'

'Yeah.' The word laced with disappointment.

Lydia came up the escalator out of Liverpool Street seeing the City rise in front of her. Broadgate was almost all in shadow; the sun bathed the tops of the office buildings in brilliant white light, but its reach didn't extend to anywhere near ground level.

Michael's message was as abrupt as always – *We need to talk urgent. Meet me at HFB.* Those last three letters just tossed out there, the bait no less tantalising for being unsubtle.

She had no idea what she was doing. Hours since she walked out of the police station, that one image she couldn't get out of her mind: him standing outside the Tube, as if they'd have to go through him to get to her. Risking his life for her. Whatever he was and whatever he'd done, that had to be worth something. An unfair question crept into her head: would Stephen have done the same thing?

She put on the cheap pair of sunglasses she'd bought in Boots – ridiculous, unnecessary, but some comfort found in putting a barrier between herself and the world. She crossed the concourse in front of the station entrance and turned towards HFB.

'Lydia.'

She spun at hearing her name.

'Keep walking.' Michael drew up next to her and tugged her sleeve to pull her in step with him.

She snatched it away. 'What the hell are you doing? You scared the shit out of me.'

'Just keep walking.'

She got her feet going again, the shock levelling out but leaving her at a higher anxiety level, like a boat marooned on a hillside after a flood. 'What's going on?'

He guided her up a flight of steps into the shopping parade that ran along the side of the station building, the stone archways that fronted it making her hesitate. Deeper into the shadows with him.

'I didn't know if you'd come.' His eyes were still scouring the street.

'What are you looking for?'

'Checking you're not being followed.'

'Followed by who?'

He looked at her and away again.

She kept watching his face. It looked like he'd been awake for days – bags under his eyes and deep lines in his skin.

'Come on, I think we're okay.' He started walking again.

'If you're trying to scare me...'

'You should be scared already. Been home lately?'

'No, and that's exactly what I was going to say – you're too late. What do you want?'

'To put our heads together.'

'You must be kidding.'

He stopped and rubbed his face, then turned to her. 'This keeps going the same way, we both end up dead.'

She stepped back, recoiling from him and the words she

didn't want to hear. 'You say things like that to freak me out but you've been lying to me from minute one.'

'That's in the past now.'

'You get to just decide that, then?'

'It's necessity. They know we've been talking.'

'Who? Who does?'

He stared past her, over her shoulder. It felt like a door was closing and this was her last chance to get out. Just walk away.

'A client hired me to look into Jamie Tan. I spent months working the job. I was waiting for him at High Barnet that night, because it was time to twist his arm. He never showed, and then I saw you poking around.'

'What do you mean "twist his arm"?'

'Just that. To make him compliant for a meeting with the client.'

'You make it sound like you're a recruitment consultant. You were there to threaten him.'

'Not like that.'

'No? Like what then?'

'This is white-collar stuff.'

'Crime. White-collar crime is the phrase.'

'Corporate intelligence. That's what I do.'

'That doesn't mean anything. Anyway, last time it was your bullshit about working for his wife.'

'I was trying to protect her. And you.'

'By buying me off?'

'By steering you clear.'

'Rubbish.'

'My client made a move against me yesterday.'

'All these oblique terms – just speak in plain English.'

'He thinks I killed Tan, and he tried to have me killed.'

She threw her arm up and wheeled away from him, turning to lean on the granite balustrade fronting the walkway.

He came and stood a short distance along from her, eyes trained on the street.

'Why does he think that?' she said.

'It's a misunderstanding.'

'I can't believe I'm listening to this. If you're telling me you killed him by accident, I'm gone. I've seen the video...'

'I was trying to warn Tan off. The client saw me and they put two and two together and got a thousand. They thought I was threatening him, but I had nothing to do with what happened on the Tube that night.'

Lydia looked up at the sky, a white contrail miles above, one end of it clear and sharp, the other fraying to nothing. 'What's this got to do with you and me talking?'

'In their mind it's all evidence I fucked them over.'

'So here you are doing it again, and ... Shit.' She looked around, feeling eyes on her. 'That's why you're so jumpy. How do you know they're not watching you now?'

'I'm clean. I ditched them yesterday and I've stayed out of sight since.'

She kept looking away from him, her gaze fixed on Heron Tower. The new sunglasses were cheap, the lenses staining it a nicotine-yellow tone. 'Who's your client?'

He leaned into the balustrade and then pushed himself back again. 'Better you don't know.'

'Better for you.'

'No.'

'You want my help but it's always a one-way street with you.'

'We need the same thing. Getting to the truth about Tan is the only way to protect ourselves. That's our leverage.'

'What about the police?'

'Way out of their league.'

A group at the pub over the road burst into laughter, the sound carrying even over the traffic noise, making both of them look up. Men and women in business suits at a standing table loaded with wine glasses, one of them holding court.

'They never tried to contact me after Brent Cross,' Michael said. 'The cops.'

'And?'

'You didn't tell them about me, did you?'

She looked back at him, not giving an answer.

'Have you thought about why?' he said.

'Maybe I wanted something to hold over you.'

He tilted his head. 'Okay. It's a weak hand.'

'It's not weak at all.'

'So how does it play out?'

'I didn't tell anyone I was going to be there that night. Now, you and I know you stole my shit and you were at my flat, and you were tailing me for days before that, but the cops don't have that part of the story. So in their minds, all they see is a man in a suit watching me at the station, who must've been working with the other bastards. Accomplice, conspiracy – gives them plenty to throw at you.'

'You know that's not why I was there.'

'I don't know anything for sure,' she said.

'So what do you want then?'

'The truth.'

'Everything I've said today is gospel.'

'Then let's go from the start.'

'The start is Tan. Who gave you his name?'

'Why does that matter?'

'Was it this guy?' He took his phone out and showed her a picture of Adam Finch in a strip club, a topless woman sitting on his lap. Finch was chatting to the man next to him, both of them grinning.

The skin on her face went taut. 'How did you know that?'

'Lucky guess. There's more.' He turned the phone around to swipe to a different picture, then showed her again. The image on the screen was Finch with the same dancer, now bent over in front of him, her panties clamped between his teeth. Jamie Tan was on the edge of the shot, laughing and pointing with his bottle of Peroni.

'What do you want me to say?'

'What's Finch's part?'

'Nothing. He ID'd Tan for me but now he's not talking.'

'I can help with that.'

'I don't need your help.'

He hooked his thumb towards the HFB building. 'Then this should be easy.'

Finch came out of the lift, looking for someone that wasn't there, Stringer's message via the receptionists – *Jamie Tan is waiting for you downstairs* – having the desired effect.

He let Lydia lead the way, following at her shoulder. Finch spotted her coming and his face changed from confusion to anger. He started to turn away but then came right at her.

'This is harassment.'

'We need to talk,' Lydia said.

Finch looked at her, flicking his eyes to Stringer behind. 'I told you I've got nothing to say to—'

Lydia put her finger up to cut him off. 'You don't need to say anything, just listen.'

Stringer pulled his phone out and put it in front of Finch. 'Remember this?' The picture of Finch with the panties in his teeth was on the screen.

Finch leaned closer to look at it, then glanced up. 'So what?'

Stringer drew his finger across the screen to bring up the next image. 'This is one of the other dancers from that place. Jamie Tan took her to a hotel and this is how her night went.' The picture was of Angie Cross when he'd first met her, her face battered and bloodied.

'Jesus Christ.' Finch put his hand in front of it and pushed the phone away.

'Tan did that,' Stringer said. 'That's the man you're protecting.'

'I'm not protecting anyone. I never knew anything about it.'

'That's not what she says.'

'What?'

'Jamie paid her to hush it up – twenty grand.' Stringer clocked Lydia twisting her neck to peer at him as he spoke. 'She says you were the one arranged it.'

'Bullshit. That's fucking bullshit, I've never even—'

'Never what? Had her knickers for dinner? It would take five seconds for me to dress this up, Adam.'

'Who are you?' He looked at Lydia. 'Who the fuck is he?'

Stringer crowded him. 'The police might let you off with a slap on the wrists, but the FCA will take your licence in a heartbeat. That's you done for good in the City. Can you afford to never work again?'

'This is—' Finch cut himself off, checking who was in earshot. He drifted away, looking lost, but turned down a short corridor on the far side of the lifts, flicking his head for them to follow. He stood behind a column that meant he couldn't be seen from reception.

'This is a fucking joke,' Finch said when they got there. The corridor was empty apart from the three of them.

'What was Jamie Tan into that got him killed?' Lydia said.

'Jesus Christ, I should've never sent you that message.'

'Then why did you?' Lydia said.

He looked at his shoes, grimacing and waving the question off.

'Do you know his wife?' Stringer said.

'Not really.'

'What do you know?'

'I've only met her twice.'

'Where would she go? Have they got a house abroad, anything like that?'

'No idea.'

'Family? Friends? The name of her fucking gym?'

'No idea.'

Stringer clocked Lydia shooting him a look in his peripheral vision, and he knew he'd been too insistent. But then she looked away again and took up the thread. 'You told me you were friendly with him, this doesn't sound like it.'

'He was my boss. We'd have a drink after work with the boys, we weren't tight.'

Lydia planted her hand on the wall. 'What was he doing, Adam?'

He screwed his eyes shut like he was wishing himself away.

'Just give us the outline. We'll do the rest.'

'I don't know the rest. He kept it all close.'

'Start with what you do know.'

'It got him killed, for Christ's sake.'

'Then help us get the people responsible.'

Finch raked his fingers through his hair, leaving a tuft sticking up at the front. 'Jamie ran the desk. Most guys when they get to that level, they pass the day-to-day stuff over. It's client relations and managing the team and dealing with all the internal bullshit. But Jamie was still running his own book.'

'Meaning what?'

'He had his own positions in the market. He was still trading – day-to-day stuff, beneath his pay grade. I don't know the ins and outs and I don't know anything for definite, but I saw enough.'

'To know what?' Stringer said.

Finch pounded the wall lightly with the palm of his hand. 'I swear to you this is all I know. I don't want anything to do with this after.'

'Say it and we're gone.'

Finch slumped against the column, his brown hair splaying against the plasterwork as he lolled his head. 'Mirror trades. Look up mirror trades.'

CHAPTER 43

They sat opposite each other in the basement of a Starbucks behind Liverpool Street. Lydia had her phone in her hand, skim-reading as she scrolled the Google results past her eyes like the wheels on a fruit machine.

The first few hits for 'mirror trades' were companies offering amateur investors the chance to automatically copy trades made by their pros. No relevance there. She glanced up at Michael but his eyes were locked on his phone too. She scrolled on. Further down, a news article by Bloomberg, the financial information provider, from January 2017 – 'How Mirror Trades Moved Billions from Russia'. She stopped the page and tapped the link.

Michael clocked the suddenness of the movement. 'What?'

She ignored him to keep reading, ripping through the article. The numbers were astronomical: $10 billion laundered, more than $600 million in fines. At the heart of it, Deutsche Bank – Germany's biggest, and HFB's main rival.

'What is it?' he said.

'I'm still reading. Add Deutsche Bank to your search.'

He went back to his phone and Lydia finished the article. She jumped back to the results and scrolled further down, finding others from the *FT* and Reuters. It took her a couple of minutes to scan through but they only regurgitated the same details.

'I don't understand,' Michael said.

'It's money laundering, on a ridiculous scale. Moving money out of Russia into the western financial system without it being detected.' She kept reading as she talked, picking out key points. 'Deutsche Bank were allowing clients to buy shares in roubles through their Moscow desk, and sell the same shares, at the same time, for dollars in London. The trades are notionally done for different clients, because they hide the ownership behind offshore shell companies, but ultimately it's the same client buying and selling to himself.'

'Go back, I'm not following.'

'So company A in Moscow buys a hundred shares in Crime Inc. – in roubles. At the same time, company B in London places an order to sell a hundred shares in Crime Inc. – in dollars. If the same person secretly owns company A and company B, all they're really doing is taking their money out of one pocket and putting it back in the other. But on the way, the dirty roubles in Moscow turn into clean dollars in London. And once the money's in the western banking system, it can disappear offshore and none of the authorities are any the wiser.'

Michael nodded his head once, processing it. 'But that was at Deutsche. Tan was at HFB while all of this was happening.'

She held her finger up to tell him to wait. She was skimming a longer article, this time in *The New York Times*. Two lines jumped out at her. She read the first:

'"The scheme was in place 2011 to 2015".'

Michael flicked his eyes to the wall, coming to the realisation. 'So...'

'So are we supposed to believe that whoever was moving money wholesale out of Russia just gave up when Deutsche got busted?'

He set his phone down on the table, the movement so slow and deliberate it was as if it might shatter on contact.

'This is...' She shook her head, struggling for the words. 'Who moves money out of Russia on that scale? We're talking about people with connections all the way up.'

'State-connected?'

'There are capital controls on moving money out of Russia. The rules are it's fine to loot the place, but you have to keep the money in the country. The government was worried about capital flight, so no one could get that much out without someone's approval. It has to go to the top – oligarchs, Russian mafia. The FSB...'

'As in the old KGB? As in Putin?'

She sat back in her chair, picturing Jamie Tan coming to Tammy, threatening to blow the whistle on all of it. 'Fucking hell.'

She waited to see if he'd say something but he kept his eyes on the wall, a thousand-yard stare that gave away nothing. She stood her phone up to read aloud the second passage that'd jumped out:

'"Investigators believe the Deutsche Bank mirror trades scheme may be just one of several employed by wealthy Russians to expatriate their fortunes, which they estimate have been used to illicitly move up to a hundred billion dollars out of the country in the last two decades. The Russian central bank itself indicated the involvement of other international banks, which it declined to name."'

'Moscow and Cyprus,' Michael said.

'What?'

'Tan was backwards and forwards to Frankfurt all the time, but he made trips to Moscow and Cyprus too. It says there were Cypriot banks acting as middle men as well.'

She pushed her hair off her forehead, the drab walls a counterpoint to the rush that was gripping her – a place as mundane as a Starbucks basement to learn the extent of the shit she was caught up in. 'This is crazy – are we honestly saying Russia killed Jamie Tan?'

'After the Skripal thing in Salisbury? Litvinenko?'

Two KGB defectors, two state-sponsored hits carried out on British soil. Sergei Skripal and his daughter survived, despite exposure to the weapons-grade nerve agent Novichok. Alexander Litvinenko wasn't so lucky; suspected Russian agents laced his tea with radioactive polonium in a London restaurant, and he died three weeks later. A 2015 public inquiry concluded his assassination was an FSB operation – likely authorised directly by Vladimir Putin. 'But they were spies...' She trailed off saying it, a limp protest that didn't stand up to what she knew.

'The method was different but it's just as brazen as the others. They want the Brits to know they did it, even while they deny it.'

Michael tapped his fingers on the table, something moving behind his eyes. They stared at each other, the burble of conversations around them overlaid with the piped-in music coming from unseen ceiling speakers, a folksy guitar number in the requisite minor key. Lydia picked at the cardboard seam of her coffee cup to stop her eyes from straying to his mottled wrist. 'Why did you ask Finch about Tan's wife?'

He shrugged.

'She's missing, isn't she?'

He nodded, looking down.

'What's your real interest in her?'

'Her safety. I told you.'

She stared at him, trying to discern anything from his expression. He looked like he was fighting to keep everything bottled up. 'Was that stuff about the stripper true?'

He tilted his cup to study the side of it. 'Which part?'

'Any of it.'

He said nothing at first. Then he set his cup down and pushed it away. 'Jamie Tan didn't do that to her. She's separate to all this – but Finch doesn't know that.'

'So who is she?'

'A friend.'

'What happened to her?'

'Some asshole used her for a punch bag. She's got nothing to do with—'

'And what did you do?'

'Why does it matter?'

Because I need to know I'm right about you.

He reached for his cup again but she took it away, making him look up at her. 'What?'

'Did you buy her off for someone?' she said.

'No.'

'No?'

'No.' He picked a grain of sugar off the tabletop with the end of his finger, concentrating his gaze on it as he dropped it to the floor. 'The guy that did it – I took him for every penny. I gave her as much as I could.'

'His money?'

He nodded.

She picked up her cup but put it down again without taking a sip. 'You really did that?'

'Why do you say it like that?'

'Like what?'

'Disappointed.'

She reached out and tapped his phone screen. 'Because you'd let him buy his way out of what he did to that poor woman?'

'She didn't want the police involved. It was her call.'

'Sure. And now what's she got?'

'Enough to start over.'

She looked away, shaking her head. 'At least we're clear now about what "corporate intelligence" means.'

'I did what I could. Are you whiter than white?'

She could feel his eyes on the side of her face, like there was something more to say. She checked the time on her phone, buying herself a second. 'Why did you try to warn Tan?'

'I don't know.' He said it immediately, a faraway look in his

eyes that made it seem genuine. 'He wasn't … It didn't seem fair.'
He stopped himself, his jaw muscles pulsing as if he was still
trying to work it out. 'It was a fuck-up.'

'Why?'

'Because of how it looked. I should've realised...'

'What?'

'I gave them an excuse.'

'To kill him?'

'No. Me.'

She leaned in close. 'Who the fuck are you working for? That
they'd do that?'

'I told you, it's better not to know.'

She set her hands on the table to push her chair back. 'I've
got to go.'

'Go where?'

'I need to go to work.'

'That's a mistake.'

'I don't have a choice.'

'It took me three seconds to find out where your office is.'

'I'm safe inside the building.'

'After what we just talked about?'

She ignored him and got out of her seat. He watched her as
she turned to go.

'I know about Tammy Hodgson.'

She was facing away from him but the name froze her on the
spot. 'What?'

'Did she put you on to Adam Finch?'

She spun around. 'No. How do you know about her?'

'She sent you the video.'

'But it was anon—' She closed her eyes, the only possible answer
coming clear – that he'd traced it back to Tammy somehow.

'They murdered her. You know it as well as I do.'

'Who? You throw that out there as if it's nothing, just fucking tell me—'

'Whoever killed Tan. Hear me out: if she put you on to Finch, maybe she'd got as far as mirror trades to—'

'She hadn't.'

'You're certain?'

'About Finch, yes. And almost so about mirror trades.'

'Then there's no fucking way they leave us alive.'

She stared at him, her chest tightening, battling to keep her voice level. 'Why?'

'Because she didn't know a fraction of what you know – we know – and they killed her anyway.'

CHAPTER 44

'Fuck's sake.' Lydia slapped her keyboard and jumped up in a rage, sending her chair rolling across the floor until it crashed into the bank of desks behind her.

The email was from an agent representing the wife of a Premier League player. According to the pitch, her husband had beaten the shit out of her when she confronted him over messages she'd found on his phone, and now this agent was selling the woman's exclusive, including the chance to do a photoshoot to capture, what he described as, 'her shocking injuries, while they're still fresh'.

She pushed her hair out of her face, swimming in all the words she'd read about mirror trades overnight. Investigations in the wake of the Deutsche scandal indicated they were one of a number of similar schemes with exotic names – the Azerbaijani

Laundromat, the Russian Laundromat, the Global Laundromat – all aimed at moving and laundering the dirty billions flooding out of Russia and the former Soviet states. The money flowed into an impenetrable maze of shell companies around the world, facilitated by international banks and front companies with innocuous names like Indigo and Gabledown – many of them UK-based. The American trader implicated as the mastermind at Deutsche was last seen in Bali, a jurisdiction that – surprise – had no extradition agreement with the US. He'd gotten out in time, and she wondered how he'd been tipped off, and by whom.

She rubbed her eyes as if she could chase away her tiredness, then gazed across the open office, mostly empty. There was a flat-screen mounted to a pillar in her line of vision, showing one of the news channels. She caught a glimpse of a familiar face on the screen and got up to move closer. The sound was muted, subtitles running across the bottom. The pictures showed James Rawlinson, former mayor of London, in a hard hat being guided around a construction site somewhere in Haringey, a standard press op to remind prospective voters – and his own party – that he'd been a big hitter during his eight years in power. The grandee leading the tour looked equally ridiculous in his suit/hard hat/hi-vis combo; she recognised him as Sir Oliver Kent, the long-time politician and former council leader who'd jumped the fence to take up big-money consultancy gigs with corporate developers. The two were a natural fit – Kent and Rawlinson had worked hand in glove on various planning and regeneration initiatives over the years. But it was the group following them that drew her in – media relations people, advisers, hacks, all watching where they put their feet crossing the building site. And there at the front of the pack was Peter Goddard.

Seeing him now seemed like her own warning. Of course he'd been in the news since the day she'd approached him at City Airport, and more frequently since Rawlinson announced his bid to become an MP – but now he served as a reminder of past mistakes. Impatience; impetuousness; getting ahead of the evidence. It ran too close to Stephen's words about the business looking for maturity and professionalism. That was all well and good, but Goddard was dirty and she knew it, and one day she'd make him pay for it. Revenge the only emotion she wanted to feel right now.

She went to the kitchen and made a coffee, took it back to her desk. Checking her phone absently, she toyed with the idea of messaging Michael. All this tired energy, and no one to bounce it off. But the email waiting at the top of her personal inbox was one she wasn't expecting – Dietmar Stettler, the German investigative journo she'd asked about Arpeggio Holdings. The connection sparked as she read his name, and she couldn't believe she hadn't made it earlier: there was no one better placed to give her the German perspective on HFB.

She opened his email, just two lines:

Lydia, it's good to hear from you. I can give you some background in this instance, but better to talk on the phone, I think. Email me to say when is a good time to call.

She wrote back saying she could speak anytime – the sooner the better. She signed off with her mobile number.

As she put the phone down on the desk it started to buzz. An international dialling code.

'Hello?'

'Lydia, it's Dietmar.'

'Hi, how ... What time is it there? I didn't mean to disturb you in the middle of the night.'

'It's okay, I was awake anyway. I find I don't sleep so much these days. And the same for you, it seems.'

'I'm working nights. Hopefully not much longer.'

'Hmm. A good time to work, though, no? I always liked a quiet office. Anyway, you did not answer to discuss sleeping habits. How did you come to be interested in our friend Simon Shelby?'

'Shelby? I was expecting you to say you knew something about Arpeggio Holdings.'

'Arpeggio, no. It's in the files, but it's one of very many similar shell companies. There's nothing that makes it stand out. How does it link to Shelby?'

'They're both directors of an investment company that owns a property connected to a story I'm working. I could do with knowing who the ultimate owner is.'

'Alright. So, Simon Shelby is a name we used to see a lot – he was connected to numerous offshore tax and investment schemes of questionable legality. I wouldn't go so far as to call him a criminal, but it's hard to be a clean cloth in dirty water, you understand?'

'Who was he working for?'

'Anyone with money,' Dietmar said, 'the same cast as always – Chinese, Russians, Americans, and of course the Brits. A lot of his schemes were connected one way or another to the Ukrainian financier Andriy Suslov. Do you know Suslov?'

A bell was ringing somewhere deep in her memory, but it wasn't much more than an echo. 'I've heard the name.'

'He shies away from publicity, but I can never be sure if that's because of his dubious reputation, or the reason for it. You can Google him.'

'You said you used to see Shelby's name a lot. Not anymore?'

'Not so much, but what does that mean? The leaks we have are only glimpses of the whole.'

'Does he still work with Suslov?'

'Impossible to know.'

She rubbed her neck, planting one knee on her seat. 'What about the other term – Withshaw?'

'Nothing, I'm afraid. This is another shell company?'

'Yes. And the name of the property I was talking about.'

'This story – Suslov has significant business interests in Germany. If he is a part of it, you will let me know?'

'Yes, of course, absolutely. Listen, Dietmar, one other thing – what do you know about mirror trades?'

'The Deutsche Bank scandal?'

'Yeah. Sort of.'

'Well, I could speak all day on this, but maybe you have something specific you're thinking of...?'

'Did you hear anything about HFB being involved too? Or something similar?'

'HFB? No, this is new to me. A very staid bank, here in Germany, but then so was Deutsche believed to be. What makes you say that?'

She pushed back off her chair to stand straight again. 'I've got a source telling me – with no evidence, no corroboration – that HFB were mirror trading too.'

He laughed at her emphasis, acknowledging how shabby it sounded. 'A few years ago I would have told you there is no way. Now...' There was a pause, as if he was switching the phone to his other ear. She remembered him once telling her that he didn't like to 'radiate' one side of his brain for too long. 'If you want to know more about Deutsche, I'm happy to answer any questions you put to me. If, of course, you'll do the same for me with HFB.'

She laughed, rolling her head around her shoulders to work the kinks out of her neck. 'Of course. Thanks, Dietmar, I owe you a beer.'

'I'd prefer a glass of wine. And a story about HFB...'

'I'll call you when I know more.'

She set the phone down and looked up at the TV screen again, but the news had moved on to a sports roundup, a golfer making a putt on a course too vivid and picture-perfect to be anywhere but America.

Simon Shelby and Andriy Suslov. Where did she know his name from? She put Suslov into Google and sorted through what came back. Basic background on him and where he'd made his money, infrequent profiles from business magazines over the years, his ties to the Kremlin through ex-Ukrainian President Viktor Yanukovych. Buried further down, a link that made her click the second she spotted it: 'Was Ukrainian billionaire Andriy Suslov behind the murder of journalist Irina Voronova?'

She raced through the article, a piece for an online journal penned by an anonymous writer who claimed their identity had to be hidden for their own safety. Voronova's name wasn't familiar, but it was more than possible Lydia had heard about her murder over the years and that was why Suslov's name struck a chord. The piece detailed how Moscow-based Voronova had been investigating the 2003 drowning death of Leon Kozlov, a high-up at a Russian fund specialising in emerging markets – and a direct competitor of Suslov. According to the article, Voronova had evidence implicating Suslov in Kozlov's death and was on the brink of publishing her claims at the time she was killed – speculation that had been reported at the time.

Her own murder was unsolved, the Russian authorities attributing it to a botched street robbery. No one had ever been charged. The writer went on to allege that the actual culprit was an ex-FSB agent suspected of involvement in two previous contract killings and who could be placed near Voronova's apartment on the day of the hit. The author claimed the man had, until three months before, been employed as a security consultant for Andriy Suslov, and the report went into some detail substantiating its claims. Two weeks ago Lydia would've dismissed the author as another Internet nutjob. Now, it felt all too real. When she put the article's title into Google, it spat out another dozen pieces linking Suslov to Kozlov and Voronova's deaths.

She crossed the office to the windows and looked down at the streets. Lights moved everywhere below her, cars and buses, the city alive in the dead of night. She'd never felt scared down there before all this started; the one upside of working nights was seeing the city keep buzzing, keep moving, a machine always ploughing forward even while most people slept. Now all that was slipping, her sense of safety and confidence being stripped away from her.

The risk was worth it though. Through the tiredness and the anxiety, the flutters in her chest were firing strong. Billions and billions of dollars, a scandal with global reach, the chance she'd found her own Skripal or Litvinenko. A story that eclipsed Goddard ten times over. If she could grasp it.

She took her phone out to shoot a message to Michael: *Where are you?*

Stringer waited by the Tube at Belsize Park, a short walk from the hospital. He stood in a narrow access road that came off the main street, the other end letting out into a low-rise housing estate he'd recced on the way, itself a maze of walkways and dead ends with more than one exit point on the other side. He'd seen nothing to make him think he was being followed leaving the hospital, but Suslov's men had been on him for weeks without him realising, and that left him in no doubt he'd been careless. But for right now, he was more worried about who might be following Lydia.

The sky was swarming with red-rimmed clouds when she appeared. She looked around for him, then took her phone out. He didn't move at first, watching instead who came out after her. It was early but a decent crowd made its way out of the station, at a guess the shift-change at the hospital being the cause. Filipinos, Ghanaians, Portuguese, almost all women, flowing around Lydia as she inched towards the street with her face in her phone.

When everyone else was gone, he walked up to the railings separating the exit walkway from where he stood and stuck his hand through to signal to her. 'Let's go.'

She looked up, startled.

'Come on.'

She looped around the railings and he led her into the housing estate until they were in a dead-end alley behind a bin shed.

'Glamorous,' she said.

He looked at her neck, the faded bruises still showing. 'So I'm here, now what?'

'I need to make someone talk, seems like that's what you do.'

'Who?'

'He's a lawyer by the name of Simon Shelby.'

Stringer frowned. 'And?'

'The woman who shot the video – she's missing. He's connected to her disappearance.'

'In what way connected?'

'Does it matter?'

'Everything matters. You can't do this stuff blind.'

'There's more – Shelby's a fixture in offshore circles.'

'Money laundering?'

'Yes. Not himself, he's a facilitator others use.'

'Where are you getting that from?'

'I know people who do this stuff day in, day out. They tell me Shelby's name has been bouncing around for years.'

'Specifically in relation to mirror trades?'

'No. Not so far, anyway.'

He took his hand off the wall and paced a few steps, antsy. 'So his name came to you separately because of the woman?'

'Yes. But I've only just turned up his link to offshore stuff.'

'How long's she been missing?'

'Best guess, since she shot the video.'

'Then she's dead.'

She turned away, closing her eyes, and the look on her face made him press his fingers into his neck. 'Sorry. No sleep makes me...'

'Forget it,' she said.

'So what is the connection between her and Shelby?'

She pushed up the sleeves on her top, eyes locked on his.

'You want to talk about trusting each other – this is it,' he said.

She took a breath and held it, finally letting it out as she spoke. 'I spoke to a neighbour who saw a car watching her house. It's registered to an address that's owned by a company that's run by Shelby.'

He stared at her a second. 'That's it?'

'What, that's not good enough for you? I'm sorry, I thought I was dealing with an extortionist. I didn't realise you had standards of proof you had to satisfy before you'll blackmail someone.'

'I just meant—'

'No, fuck off, okay? You have no bloody right to tell me my work isn't up to it. I've got people trying to kill me; I'm not about to let you dictate what leads are worth following or not.'

'If you want my help...'

'I'll do this with or without you. Don't doubt that for one second.'

'You're not the only one in danger here. You're not the only one who hasn't been home for days.'

'Then why are we wasting time arguing about whether to go after Shelby?'

'It's not as simple as that. This stuff takes time to set up. That's why I was asking if there's more.'

'You came up with something for Adam Finch fast enough.'

'I'd done the legwork on him, indirectly. I had something I could use. All I've got on this guy is a house and that he moves money around.'

She stretched her arms out to brace her hands against the walls of the narrow passageway. 'The woman who shot the video, her neighbour identified the guy you photographed in my kitchen as one of the men watching her flat. He was watching the witness's flat.'

It fell into place then – Angie following her to Whetstone, right after he'd shown her the photo in Soho Square. 'That strengthens the link, but it still doesn't give us any leverage over him.'

'So you're saying it can't be done?'

He scraped his heel on the pavement. 'Have you tried knocking on the door?'

'Shelby's? He's not talking...'

'No, the address the car's registered to.'

'Yeah, of course. No one was home.'

'So we go back.'

'It looked empty.'

'A dirty lawyer's not going to give up client privilege just because we ask him to. The direct approach has to be worth another try.'

She opened her mouth to say something but hesitated, drawing a breath instead. 'Okay.'

'Where is it?'

'Miles away – Surrey.'

He froze. 'Where in Surrey?'

'Somewhere by Hampton Court, why?'

'Withshaw.'

She stared at him, the breeze tugging a strand of hair across her mouth. 'How the hell could you know that? Did you follow me?'

'No.'

'No?'

'I've been there. I went there myself.'

Her face went white. 'Why?'

'The men that killed Tan used a car registered to there.'

'What?' She stepped right up to him. 'What?'

'What do you want me to say?'

'How long have you been sitting on this?'

'The car was reported stolen. I went there and it was empty, so I put it on the backburner.' He kicked the wall. 'Fuck.'

She turned around with her hands clamped to her head. 'This is it. This is the whole fucking thing.'

'The car that took Tan away was a company car registered to an Andrew Pitt. Mean anything to you?'

'No. Should it?'

'No. It didn't to me.'

'So we find him.'

'Easier said than done. There's a million Andrew Pitts on Google.'

She took her phone out and put the name into the image search. 'Any that look like the guy you snapped in my kitchen?'

'Shit, I didn't have that part...' He came around next to her, his shoulder against hers.

She flicked her finger over the screen, scrolling quickly, shaking her head. She clicked through the pages until the results started repeating. 'Bollocks.'

'We've still got the address. We try there first, and if not, it's Shelby.'

The cab dropped them outside Withshaw.

Lydia was out first, gripping one of the driveway gates to peer inside. Stringer came to stand behind her. It was as still and brooding as the last time she'd been there, defying the bright morning sunshine.

Stringer stepped around her and pressed the intercom.

'What happens if someone answers?'

He looked at her, his finger still on the button. 'No one's answering here.'

'I never even thought this through ... What are we supposed to say: *Why did you kill Jamie Tan?*'

'If you're having second thoughts...'

'I'm saying we need to be prepared.'

'We find them, we get our leverage. Then we work out how we use it.' He took his finger off the button.

'No cars,' she said, looking at the driveway. 'Same as last time I was here. No tyre tracks.'

'Someone's spent money on it recently, otherwise I'd say it's vacant.'

'What about getting inside?'

He looked at her. 'You know anything about breaking and entering?'

'No, I meant...'

'What?'

'Maybe you knew someone.'

He took his finger off the intercom. 'I don't.' He looked away, sizing up the house again.

'You're touchy for someone who had me mugged.'

He flapped open the bronze letterbox built into the gatepost, underneath the intercom. He tried the door to the compartment but it was locked, so he slipped his fingers inside the flap, straining to reach for something.

Lydia checked both ways along the street. 'Anything?'

'Hold on...' He contorted his wrist, the scarred skin turning white with the strain. His hand inched in further.

He slipped his hand out, an envelope between his fingers. He held it out to read. It was addressed to Withshaw Ltd. 'No help.'

'Open it,' she said.

He put his finger under the seal, starting to walk. 'You ditched your ethics fast.'

'They tried to fucking kill me.'

He pulled the letter out and looked at it, then passed it over. 'Addressed to *Dear Sir or Madam*.'

She took it from him but it was a marketing letter sent by a wealth-management firm touting for business. 'We're wasting our time here.'

'Be the same if we go after Shelby without something to use.'

'There's one thing I've got.'

Shelby's office was in a converted Georgian terrace in Bedford Square. It was late morning by the time they got there, Lydia already feeling if she lay down she wouldn't get up again.

They stood on the wide boulevard that ran around the square. There were gardens at its heart, but no one using them. She saw then that the gates were locked; more important that the bent solicitors had nice views from their offices than risk regular people mucking them up. Lydia took out her phone and called Shelby's number.

'Simon Shelby's office.'

'Hi, it's Lydia Wright calling, can you put me through to Simon please?'

'Is he expecting your call?'

'Yes.'

'Thank you; one moment please.'

There was a pause and hold music came on the line.

Michael was looking up at the windows on the second and third floors.

The music cut out. 'Hello? I'm afraid Mr Shelby can't take the call at the moment, can I take a message?'

'It's fine, I'll call back.' She ended the call and faced Michael. 'Well, he's there.'

'So now what?'

'Give him till lunchtime. If he doesn't show by then, I'm setting the fire alarms off.'

Shelby made his appearance at 1.11 p.m., coming out of the door and down the four steps to the street. He was fifty-something with thinning hair around the temples and crown, even more pronounced than in the picture Lydia had found online, but there was no question it was him. He turned towards Tottenham Court Road, the harried gait of a man getting his own lunch as an excuse to snatch five minutes away from his desk.

They were standing in the shade alongside the gardens. Lydia clocked him and set off first, Stringer following without a word. Showtime made her tiredness evaporate. She crossed over to the same side as him, speeding up to catch him before he reached the busier pavements of the main road.

'Simon.'

He half turned on hearing his name. He was already sweating in his suit. 'Yes?'

'Simon, my name's Lydia Wright. I left you a message a few days ago.'

He shook her hand looking blank, his grip soft and clammy. 'Yes?'

'I'm with the *Examiner*, I wanted to ask you about—'

He let go of her hand. 'I'm afraid I don't speak to the press.'

'This is off the record. What can you tell me about your involvement with Withshaw?'

His mouth became a thin line. 'Again, I don't talk to the press.'

'Will you be talking to the police?'

He started to move off but stopped. He turned around again slowly, wearing a smile that said he should know better than to bite. 'Alright. Why would I need to do that?'

'My enquiries have linked two cars registered to the property known as Withshaw to the disappearance and probable murder of one man and the disappearance of a young woman who witnessed it. You are a director of the company that owns Withshaw, aren't you?'

He glanced at Michael and then back at her. 'I don't know anything about that. Am I supposed to assume this gentleman is a police officer?'

Michael shook his head slowly, staring at Shelby.

'I didn't think so. I'm not sure what your agenda is here, so if there's nothing else...'

'Is it linked to your work for Andriy Suslov, Mr Shelby? Is that why?'

She sensed a change as she said it. A charged silence, the air between them starting to crackle.

Shelby took a slight step backward, his tongue curled around his teeth. Michael was staring like he was about to run through him.

'Mr Shelby?' she asked.

He forced a smile. 'I really have nothing more to say to you.' He took another step back, then turned and walked off.

Lydia started to go after him, but Michael put his hand on her arm to stop her. 'Leave him.'

She watched Shelby go, jinking in front of a cab to get across the road and then fast-walking onto the opposite pavement and away.

Michael looked at her. 'What was that about Andriy Suslov?'

CHAPTER 45

Stringer left Lydia at Tottenham Court Road station. He couldn't ditch her fast enough. He'd seen she'd sensed something was wrong, maybe even that hearing Suslov's name had set him off. That would have to be unpicked later. For now, all he could focus on was buying himself some space to think.

Once she was out of sight, he doubled back and merged into the crowds on Oxford Street. Losing himself, losing his mind…

Withshaw to Shelby to Suslov.

To Jamie Tan.

A straight fucking line that said he'd been played. He drifted through the crowds like he was underwater, somewhere so deep down that no light could penetrate and he couldn't tell which way was up anymore.

Running from a Ukrainian oligarch with the power to eliminate anyone he wanted. Certainly Jamie Tan. As ruthless as Suslov was, the missing part had been motive. But with every piece of evidence pointing his way, one answer started to make sense: whoever Tan was moving money for, it wasn't state-sanctioned after all. There was one degree of separation between the Kremlin and Andriy Suslov; if they'd leaned on Suslov to shut down a rogue money-laundering network, everything else fell into place. Using oligarchs to do their dirty work was an established part of the Kremlin playbook.

The only part that hadn't fit was why Suslov had hired Stringer in the first place. Now it hit him like a spotlight had found him in the murk.

He was being set up.

That's why they were shadowing him while he was following Tan. Building an insurance policy. Tan disappears and hopefully the police get nowhere, but just in case they don't, here's a readymade fall guy to hand over. He'd made it easy for them by fronting Tan, and that picture had to mean there were more. Photos of Stringer staking out Tan's house, following him all over London – probably of him at High Barnet the night of the murder. They could've even planted evidence – Suslov had made a point of showing he knew his address.

Even as he was sinking, a new depth opened up beneath him: the most effective fall guy was always a dead one.

He looked up and saw he'd walked almost the length of Oxford Street, Marble Arch up ahead of him. He felt his phone vibrating in his pocket and pulled it out. Abi. He swiped to answer but he was too slow and the call ended. When the main screen came up, it showed she'd tried him four times already.

Stringer swept into the hospital room and found himself face to face with the old man, hovering by the end of the bed. Abi was in the chair next to her with Ellie on her lap.

Stringer raised the bouquet of flowers and pressed them into the old man's chest. 'Find a vase for these.'

His mother was watching Ellie with a sidelong glance, her head barely turned but the hint of a smile on her face.

'And then we played family and I was the mum and Jessie

was the sister and Martina was the baby but then Martina wanted to be the mum and I didn't want to be the baby and so we didn't play that game anymore and...'

Abi bounced her on her knee, trying not to laugh. 'Slow down, sweetheart. Look who's here...'

Ellie looked up at him. 'Uncle Mike!' She put her fingers in the corners of her mouth and pulled a face. 'I'm a monster, blargh!'

His mother's eyes followed Ellie's gaze slowly, turning by degrees rather than a smooth movement to look in his direction. She still had an oxygen tube under her nose.

He stepped closer to the bed. 'How you feeling?'

She closed her eyes, looking pained, and he glanced at Abi, but she shook her head to signify it was okay. 'She's having trouble getting her words out.'

'Can you ever imagine that of her?' the old man said behind him, smiling to himself. He laid the flowers on the window ledge.

Stringer came closer again and reached for her hand, and Ellie tugged at his suit coat. 'Uncle Mike, can we play a game?'

'Maybe in a minute, kiddo.'

Abi scooped her up. 'Come on, let's go and get a drink.'

Ellie wriggled out of her grip and threw her hands up when she landed on the floor, like a medal winner. 'Yes! I want a juice.'

Abi led her out by the hand. 'Dad, you coming?'

He shuffled past Stringer and sat down in the chair. 'No, I'm fine here, thanks.'

She shot Stringer a look to say *I tried* and went out the door.

'Mum, can you hear me? It's Michael.'

'She can hear you fine.'

'What did the doctors say?'

'They're monitoring her. Same thing they always say.'

She grimaced again, drawing her legs up towards her this time. He froze, not knowing what to do. Then her expression eased and she opened her eyes again.

He looked at the old man. 'Can't you even give us a minute?'

He stared back at him, saying nothing.

Stringer felt her move her hand, fingers curling a fraction around his. 'William.'

She said it so softly a breeze could carry it away. The old man leaned closer at hearing his name.

But she kept her eyes on Stringer, the smile coming back to her face, keener this time. 'William. I've missed you.'

Stringer sat on the plastic chairs in the corridor outside her room. Abi came out a few minutes after she'd gone back in, holding a can of Lilt. Ellie wasn't with her. She walked up to him and put her hand on his shoulder. 'Do you want a mouthful?'

He waved his arm to say no. 'Thanks.'

'She's sleeping again.'

He nodded.

'Don't take it to heart,' she said.

'I know.'

'The doctor said it's too early to tell if this is how she's going to be now. It might just take some time for the fog to lift.'

'She was already showing signs before.'

Abi looked at the wall. 'Yeah.'

'What happens next?'

'Give it time, Mike. It's only been a few hours.'

'Yeah, sorry. Of course.' He stood up and put his arms around her shoulders. 'Thanks for everything you've done.'

'It's fine.' He looked down to where she was pressed to his chest, but she wouldn't meet his eyes.

The door opened behind them and Ellie burst out. 'Mummy? Where are you, Mummy?' The old man followed after her. She came rushing over and Abi broke away to gather her up. 'I finished my juice.'

Stringer looked down and saw her tearstains on his shirt.

Abi carried Ellie back towards the room. 'Come on, let's go and say goodbye to Grandma so we can get you home.'

'I want green pasta for dinner.'

The old man hovered, coming to a stop a few paces short of him. 'Apple doesn't fall so far from the tree, uh?'

'I don't want to hear it.'

'The resemblance. That's what's confused her. You're the spit of how I looked at your age.'

'Get away from me.'

'Is it so unpalatable?' He took a step closer. 'To know the son is so much like his father?'

Stringer bundled him against the wall, pinning him with his forearm across his throat. 'There's one big fucking difference, though, isn't there?'

The old man bared his teeth, spittle flying, writhing to try and get free of his grip.

'Maybe that's the way we square this,' Stringer said. 'Maybe we pour cooking oil all over your arm and see what the resemblance is like then.' He heard a shout along the corridor as if it came from a mile away. He forced his forearm harder into his throat. 'I mean after all the skin grafts and the surgeries and the fucking hospital visits and all the other shit. Then we really will be the same, won't we?'

He felt a hand on his shoulder, prying him away.

The old man's throat rippled with tendons. 'We're not the same. You deserved everything.'

A second pair of hands grabbed him and he let go. He looked around and saw it was two porters pulling him away. They were saying something but the words weren't getting through. Then Abi appeared between them, trying to prise them off him. He wrestled himself free, backing off with his hands up in surrender. The porters stood between him and the old man, forming a barrier. Abi was gripping his face between her hands trying to get something through to him, but he was looking past her. A gap opened up and he saw Ellie bouncing a toy rabbit on the chair and staring right at him.

CHAPTER 46

Lydia stood on the Golden Jubilee Bridge, watching the crowds passing beneath her. Webs of giant cables held the bridge up, like metal puppet strings lofted above the river. Two minutes before ten but it was still warm, the people along Southbank in T-shirts and cotton dresses. Through the music and laughter there was an edge to the vibe, the urgency that came with every hot, late-summer night – one last chance to dance, as if the sun might never come back.

She looked down at the Royal Festival Hall and the concourse in front of it. She was surprised Michael wasn't early. But even as she thought it, she recognised what she was doing, projecting her assumptions onto him. The same thing she'd done from the start, building a version of the man in her mind that fell apart when it met reality.

An EE ad played on a digital billboard, green light dancing on the brutalist concrete architecture around it. A plane flew low across the night sky, its own lights lost in the battery of reds and whites and yellows of the skyline; one insignificant among the many. When she lost sight of it, she looked down again and he was there.

He was standing with his back to the river, scanning the crowd. She stepped away from the railing to keep out of sight, even though she was just another face at that distance. She gave it a minute more, then sent her message to him: *Been caught up, can't make it. Sorry.*

She watched him reach for his phone, the screen glowing bright in the dark as he read her words. He tapped something and then her own phone buzzed with his reply. *Are you okay?*

She hit reply. *Just work, can't get away.*

She watched him study his phone again and then slip it into his pocket. He set off as soon as he read it, heading away from the river, and she moved along to the end of the bridge and went slowly down the steps, keeping him in sight.

She followed him down the side of the Festival Hall and along the neon passageway approaching Waterloo. The station entrance was rammed and she lost him in the crowds for a second, only to spot him again on the concourse, half a head taller than most. She ran over to the Tube entrance and stepped onto the same down escalator he'd taken.

They rode the Northern Line in adjoining carriages. The Tube was just as packed as the station above, so it wasn't hard to stay hidden. Lydia watched, standing close to the glass in the connecting door, and couldn't help thinking about the parallels with Paulina Dobriska.

He spent the short trip staring at the train doors. Half of London got off at Tottenham Court Road, jostling him around, but he didn't react, didn't even seem to notice. He had a look on his face like he might have killed someone if he had.

And that was the problem. She'd let herself be suckered in, despite all the warning signs. Then she'd dropped the name Andriy Suslov in front of him for the first time, and it'd spooked him worse than Shelby.

The third spoke on that wheel: herself. What would link Michael to an oligarch suspected in the murder of a journalist? Coming into her life just days after someone tried to kill her. The pieces starting to fit no matter how much she didn't want them to.

So now it was time to turn the tables. See what he was hiding.

He got off at Euston and walked a short way along the main road before turning off. The streets were quieter there and Lydia had to let the leash run long to stay unseen.

Halfway down the side street, he turned again, disappearing between two monolithic council blocks. She broke into a run to keep up with him, slowing when she got close so he wouldn't hear her footsteps. She stopped at the corner and craned her head around to look, braced to find him waiting there for her, a trap to draw her out. But all she saw was his back, halfway across the courtyard between the flats.

She stayed where she was as he went up to the entrance door, the block's name in black letters above it – *Palgrave*. A few paces short of it, he stopped and turned. A streetlight above doused him in yellow light. He looked in her direction and she shrunk into herself, but his gaze kept moving, as if he was taking in the whole estate.

Then he threw his arms out, still looking around. It was like he was daring someone unseen to come at him. He took a step forward, his mouth moving now, the words lost to the night. He stood like that for a minute, his face set in an expression that was equal parts defiance and desolation.

Whatever he was waiting for wouldn't come. He let his arms drop to his sides, as if in defeat, holding that way for half a minute or more. Finally he turned around and went to buzz the intercom. He waited for the door to open and then he went inside.

Lydia felt her pulse throbbing in her neck as she tried to decide what to do. The block was eight storeys high, and as she counted she realised there was a communal balcony running along the front of each level, the flats at equal spaces along it. He reappeared on the fourth floor. A door halfway along it opened, expecting him, the silhouette of a woman backlit in the doorway.

She watched him walk up to the woman and she hugged him briefly and ushered him inside. The door closed and they were gone. It was another assumption busted – that he was a loner who wouldn't have any attachments in his life. But then why did he buzz the intercom? That suggested a girlfriend or booty call over a wife.

She thought about calling Singh and Wheldon. There was no easy way to explain it without giving up her lies. But what reason did she have to protect him anymore?

Stringer kicked his shoes off on the doormat – Abi's standing order so he wouldn't wake up Ellie, clattering down the laminate hallway.

Abi watched him, arms folded. 'You look terrible.'

'Yeah.'

'About earlier...'

'Was Ellie okay?'

She let her arms unfurl and fall to her sides. 'I told her you and Grandad were just playing. She said she understood, but they tell you what you want to hear sometimes.'

'I'm sorry. I didn't mean for—'

'I know.' She nodded, turning into the small kitchen. 'You want a drink? Kettle's boiled.'

'I'm good.'

She came back clutching a mug to her chest. 'Look, I don't want to sound like a cow, but when was the last time you slept?'

He thought about the question, but when the answer wouldn't immediately come, he just shook his head.

'You're not on the gear, are you?'

'No.'

'Because the way you were earlier...'

'No. It was him, he wound me up. It's what he always does.'

'Yeah but you know what he's doing; it's the same thing he's been doing for decades. You normally shrug it off.'

He walked down the short hallway into the sitting room, dropping onto the sofa. He sat forward, his elbows on his knees. The TV was on but silenced. The room was immaculate, Ellie's toys packed away in fabric crates in one corner, except for a small table that was laid out for a tea party, the guests three stuffed dinosaurs.

Abi followed him in but stayed standing. 'What's going on, Mike? I can't ever remember you like this.'

'It's just work. Something's gone wrong and I don't know how to sort it yet. I'll get there.'

'If you want to talk...'

'You're dealing with Mum. That's enough.'

'Still trying to protect me.'

'No. I just appreciate what you've taken on. I wish I could do more.'

She moved past him, bending her knees to rest them on the edge of the armchair opposite so she could stare out the window behind it. She put her hand on the windowsill for balance, an assortment of ornaments and empty vases spaced along the plastic ledge, some of them he recognised as hand-me-downs from Mum. He knew the view like the inside of his eyelids, looking out on the courtyard below and the scrappy grass next to it. From where he sat, all he could see were the lights of the block opposite, a grid pattern of yellow glare.

'Why can't you go home, Mike?'

'It's only for a few days while this blows over.'

'And you can't use the Finsbury Park flat?'

'Just a precaution.'

Her face was turned away from him but he could sense she'd closed her eyes.

'About that...' he said.

She brought her mug to her lips and took a sip.

'I wanted to speak to you earlier, but...' He set his eyes on the TV, some talking head gabbing on Sky News. 'I've signed the flat over to you and Ellie. There's a mortgage on it and taxes to pay, I'll cover all that. There are some papers you need to sign—'

'Mike...'

'I just want some certainty.'

'I thought we'd settled this? I don't want to move. Ellie's friends are here, I know the schools, I know the area...'

'I'm not saying move. Especially not right now.'

'Well, what are you saying then? You're scaring me.'

'I just want to know you're both taken care of. If you don't want to live there, you can rent it out and sell it when the mortgage finishes.'

She slipped back off the chair. 'And what happens the next time you need to stash someone?'

'I'll deal with it.'

'Mike, fuck off. You're talking like you're ... God, I don't even want to say it.' She knelt on the floor in front of him. When he kept his eyes on the TV, she thumped him on the arm to make him look at her. 'Seriously, what are you into?'

He didn't answer, but she wouldn't look away.

'I took a job,' he said at last. 'I thought it was the same stuff as usual, but the guy wound up dead.'

'Dead?' She searched his face. 'Wait, you didn't—'

He put his hand up to stop her. 'The fuck? Of course not. Who do you think I am?'

'Sorry, sorry. I just...'

'I don't know for sure who did it, but it's starting to point one way. And this guy was into some serious shit.'

'So you walk away. You just walk the fuck away.'

'It's not that simple. And there's someone else I have to think about.'

'Who?'

'A journalist. She got dragged into it and...' He rubbed his face. 'Fuck.'

'Are you involved with her?'

He snapped his head up. 'No. Not like that. It's just ... I feel responsible. She doesn't know the extent of it.'

She unfolded her legs from under her and pulled them to her chest. 'Can you go to the police?'

He shook his head. 'Anyway, I'm not out of moves yet.'

'Don't do anything stupid. Please.'

'Never.'

In his mind he saw the turquoise waters of Florida Bay stretching in front of him. Tranquil and quiet, a place to erase himself and lifetime of regret. Choosing his own end. He meant what he'd said, but if the moves ran out, that was how it would finish, not with Suslov's hands around his throat. He deserved that much, if nothing more.

CHAPTER 47

Lydia kept her eyes open as she showered. The bathrooms were in the office basement, next to the generator room; in the mornings, when there were queues for the four cubicles that served hundreds of people, there was nothing sinister about the place. But gone midnight, alone down there with her brain already in overdrive, the hum of a working building was playing tricks with her mind.

Her hair was still wet when she came out of the lift. She saw the Post-it note stuck to her screen as she walked over, but she couldn't make out what it said until she got close. Just one word: *SLAG*.

She peeled it off and looked around, maybe a dozen people dotted around the vast office, none of them looking in her direction.

She switched on her computer. When the screen came to life, it was showing the page of search results about Andriy Suslov she'd had open earlier. She stared at it, thinking about the links between him and Shelby and Michael.

Play it back: Michael hadn't reacted when she'd mentioned Shelby to him. There was no sign they knew each other when they'd doorstepped him earlier. She tried to pin down when she'd first spoken his name to him and realised it was only that morning. It felt like it was a week ago. Contrast that to how he'd come off when she dropped Suslov's name. Her instinct was to confront him about it – but he'd lied to her over and over, so what would be different this time? She kept thinking about Tammy, the way he'd let her name slip – so knowing. She'd watched for him outside the council flat in Camden for more than an hour, but when he still hadn't reappeared, she'd retreated to the safety of the office. But it wasn't a wasted trip; she had something now – an unknown personal contact that offered a glimpse inside his privacy.

Andriy Suslov kept buzzing around her head. She switched to her email and clicked to open a new message before the latest slew of bilge could pump into her inbox. She typed in Dietmar's address but then her desk phone started ringing. It rarely rang anymore and she didn't recognise the muted tone at first. She grabbed it up when she saw Stephen's name showing. 'Hello?'

'Have you got a minute?'

'Now? What are you still doing here?'

'Working late.' He coughed away from the phone. 'So?'

She looked at the Post-it note where she'd dropped it next to her keyboard. She picked it up. 'Yeah, sure, I'll come round.'

She locked her computer and crossed the floor with the Post-it stuck to her index finger, there for anyone who wanted to see it. The Reptile House was dark apart from Stephen's office, the light blazing at the end of the corridor. He was sitting at his desk, focusing on his computer.

He gestured to the chair opposite, frowning as he finished reading something on his screen.

She dropped the Post-it note in front of him and sat down.

'What's this?'

'Someone left it for me.'

'What?' He lifted it up by one corner. 'Seriously?'

'Guess we should've expected it. Amount of time I spend in here.'

He stared at her, his eyes alive as he processed it. Then he crumpled it into a tight ball. 'Fuck's sake. They're like children.'

She watched him drop it into the bin. 'I thought you'd be more worried.'

He clasped his hands together and lifted them up to his chin. 'It's idle gossip. No one knows.'

She brought her thumbnail to her mouth and chewed the corner. 'So? What's up?'

'Is it raining?'

'What?' She followed his gaze to her wet hair. 'Oh. I came straight from the gym.' She crossed her legs. 'And look, I know I was a bit late tonight, but—'

'I didn't get you in here for a bollocking.'

'Okay.'

'So Sasha was due to fly to LA tomorrow to cover the MTV Awards. She's had to drop out.'

'Why?'

'Schedule conflict.'

The words were loaded, inviting questions, but she couldn't read where this was going, so she waited for him to carry on.

He picked up a pen and twirled it. 'I want you to go in her place. You'll be gone for five days.'

She sat back slowly in her chair. 'I'm not exactly MTV's audience.'

'And Sasha is?'

'No, but, she's willing to play that game.'

He took a sharp breath. 'It's basically a jolly. The work off the back of it is only a couple of pieces; it's all pictures and video. You go to the parties, you hang out ... The company covers all of it.'

'I know, but...'

'But?'

She thought about where she'd been two hours before, tailing a man who may have saved her life to a council estate because she couldn't trust him. Mirror trades. Andriy Suslov. Paulina. Tammy. 'It's a bit sudden.'

He tossed the pen onto his pad. 'I picked you because I trust you and I thought you'd be able to go on short notice. Do you know how many of that lot out there would jump at a chance like this?' He tipped his head towards the newsroom.

'Yeah and I don't want to sound ungrateful. It's just with everything...'

'I told you, the lawyers said you've got to leave it alone.'

'You knew I wouldn't just walk away.'

He leaned forward over his desk. 'That's exactly what I expected you to do. And I told you why, and the wider implications. Two days ago you were in here, in tears, because someone tried to kill you. I'm bending over backward to take you out of harm's way.'

She uncrossed her legs to plant her feet on the floor. 'That's why you're sending me? To get me out of the way?'

'Would it be the worst thing in the world to be somewhere else while things blow over?'

'Is that what we do now? Just wait for things to blow over?'

'Are you fucking kidding me?'

'Are you?'

He got up and went around behind his chair, gripping the back of it, his head bowed. 'I'm doing this for you, and I make no apologies for it. I care about you, and I don't want to see you get hurt.'

She was halfway to her feet, but the sincerity in his voice stopped her dead.

'When did you last go home, Lydia?'

'What?'

'There's a roomful of journos out there, did you think no one would notice?'

'Are you talking about me or us?' She pointed to the crumpled Post-it.

His cheeks hollowed.

'Why has anyone else got a right to my fucking business?' she said.

'Something's gone very wrong when one of my team is afraid to go home. I'm not just going to stand by and watch.'

'Would you be treating me like this if I was a man?'

'If the danger was the same, absolutely.'

She looked at the windows and the lights beyond, breathing, letting his words sink in. 'Can I have some time to think about it at least?'

He bent down and opened his drawer, then pulled out a small plastic folder and tossed it across the desk to her. 'Sure. Flight leaves at half-two this afternoon.'

The street leading from Tottenham Court Road to Simon Shelby's office stank of piss. The Grange Hotel backed onto it, and its recessed back doors and fire exits were apparently a magnet for the caught-short.

Stringer waited a little way along from where it met Bloomsbury Square. It was just past seven in the morning and he'd been there thirty minutes already. The Tottenham Court Road Tube was the closest station to Shelby's offices, so chances were he'd come from that direction, but he had one eye on the far side of the square, in case he made the longer walk from Holborn.

His phone rang. Milos's number.

'You got my message?'

'Yeah, bro, you keep some funny hours.'

'One more job for you.'

'I'm listening.'

'I need records for a mobile number – specifically a list of calls made and received. Can you do it?'

He sniffed. 'Same answer as always: lemme put it out there and see what comes back. Who you after?'

He read out the number he had for Dalton, praying it was his only phone. 'I only need the last week.' In truth, he only needed the last few days – but it was cleaner to ask for a week. 'How much?'

'Dunno, never had this one before. Leave with.'

'Thanks. Call me soon as.'

'Yeah, look, there's something else.'

'What?'

'We done some biz together, so I ain't gonna front you on this.'

'On what?'

'Your name been pinging around.'

'My name?'

'Yeah, your real name.'

He thought back to the pub, Milos's verbal wink when he'd called him Rob, the alias he'd always used with him. 'What are you talking about?'

'Don't take it personal, but I ain't get dirty with mans without knowing who I'm dealing with, feel me?'

'Go on.'

'It's just a thing, you know? Precaution.'

'Make your point.'

'Someone's looking for info on Michael Stringer. Financials, emails, phones, personal, everything that's going.'

He pressed the phone to his ear, turning to speak into the wall. 'Who?'

'Come on, man, it's all anonymous. Some username. And even that's probably someone playing middleman, same as I do for you.'

It was a stupid question, Suslov the only answer. 'How long's this been out there?'

'Day or two, but I only seen it last night.'

'Why didn't you fucking tell me?'

'Easy, bro, I just did. This shit supposed to be on the down low – but I figure you put a decent amount of green my way.'

'Can you shut it down?'

He sucked in a breath. 'Nope. Anyway, job might've been done already.'

His emails. Exchanges with Lydia Wright – times and places. Her no-show the night before... 'Speak to them. Take the job, then sit on it.'

'I can't do that, bruv, people know it ain't what I do.'

'Then subcontract it to someone who can.'

'Would you take a job if you knew you had to screw it up, your line of work? Ain't no one wants to have their rep busted that way.'

He turned around, checking the other approach. 'So there's nothing I can do?'

'Change your passwords, man. Your pin numbers. Guessing you ain't a social-media cat, but if I'm wrong, delete your accounts. Don't know what to tell you outside of that. Someone's coming for you in a big way.'

He planted his hand on the wall, steadying himself. 'Alright. Let me know about that other thing, yeah? And thanks.'

He cut the call and Googled the switchboard number for Lydia's office. He tapped it into his phone and listened to the dial tone. 'Come on, come on...'

Someone answered and put him through. Another dial tone. A glance along the street.

'*Examiner*.'

'It's me. Are you alright?'

Silence on the line. Then: 'What do you mean?'

He swallowed. 'After last night. When you didn't show, I thought...'

Another pause. 'What?'

'Listen, someone's trying to hack me. My emails and everything else. I just got a tip-off.'

'Who?'

He almost said *Suslov* without thinking. 'I don't know. I've got to go, I just wanted to warn you because of how they did Brent Cross. Take my number, if you get an email from me, call me to confirm it's genuine.'

She didn't say anything, and he knew then it was falling apart. He read out his number anyway. 'I'll be in touch.'

'Okay.'

'Be safe.' He went to end the call but she spoke again, faint.

'Michael?'

'Yeah?'

'You too.'

Lydia put the phone down and stared at the screen again, his voice ringing in her ears: 'Be safe.' All the doubt crowding her; her trust as a rope, frayed to the final threads – but still she couldn't bring herself to cut them.

She had a dozen tabs open, each one linked to the previous, none of them read through to the end. The type blurred when she looked at it.

No answers. No clarity. The travel papers Stephen gave her were on the side of her desk. She was due at the airport in less than six hours. Five days away didn't sound like much, but it was more than just the time; it was final acceptance she'd drop the story. Call it what it was: an ultimatum from the business. Bundling it with flight tickets and VIP passes didn't change that truth.

She shut her browser down, leaving just her inbox on the screen. Half an hour until she finished for the night, ordinarily a cause for minor celebration, now a prompt to remind her she couldn't go home even if she wanted to.

Dietmar Stettler's old email was open on the screen. Her eyes moved over it without thinking, but then something started resonating.

The words he'd used. She reread the message, but it was just the one telling her to email him with a good time to call. Something else...

'Financier'. The word he'd used to describe Andriy Suslov when they spoke. The scales falling away from her eyes at last. 'Secretive American financier' – a phrase from her notes on another story. She double-clicked to open her Goddard file, sitting in the documents folder just one step removed from its former location, dead centre on her desktop. It contained hundreds of files; she ran a search for 'Andriy Suslov' and watched the bar inch across the screen. It finished and threw up one result – an email chain from the mayor's office from a few years before, as innocuous an exchange as could exist: Goddard swapping emails with go-betweens at an American bank, arranging a meeting with their client who was flying in from New York – Mr Andriy Suslov. She sent the document to the printer, but the gist of it was already coming back to her. Dietmar had called Suslov Ukrainian, and that was what'd thrown her off the scent; in fact he held dual nationality and was based in the States.

Suslov meeting with Goddard three years prior. She ran to the stuffy alcove where the printers were stashed, four big machines that made the windowless room reek of toner. She snatched the papers off the tray and stood, not knowing which way to turn. Screaming to tell the one person left who might care. Feeling as alone as she ever had in her life.

Shelby came from the other direction after all. Stringer spotted him on the far side of the square and set off towards him at pace.

He intercepted him a few doors short of his office. Shelby didn't notice him until he was almost in his face, looking startled when Stringer stopped hard in front of him.

'Hello, Simon.'

The shock showed in his eyes, along with signs of recognition.

'Yesterday. I was with the journalist.'

Shelby concentrated on putting his phone away, as if success might mean he could crawl into his own pocket next to it. 'Yes?'

'Simon Felix Shelby. Age fifty-three, home address, twenty-seven Park Road, Twickenham. Divorced, lives alone, in a house that's way too big for one. Two grown-up children, Megan and David. Attended the London Oratory School, then UCL. Avid cricket and rugby fan, tends to holiday with the Barmy Army on organised tours to watch England overseas.'

'Who are—?'

'Specialist in tax law, particularly in regard to incorporation services for offshore entities. A respected professional in his field, informally known as Andriy Suslov's money wizard. Reputed ties to pan-global money-laundering schemes, including the Azerbaijani Laundromat and, now it turns out, the mirror-trading scandal. Get the point yet?'

'No. Who—?'

'I'd never heard of you until this time yesterday. Now I know what you had for breakfast. By the end of the day, I'll know shit you don't know about yourself.'

'You're a journalist, like the other one?'

'No, Simon. I work for Suslov, same as you.'

Shelby put his head down and stepped around him to go. Stringer put his arm out to stop him. 'I said I work for Suslov, Simon. You're not walking away from that.'

Shelby looked sideways at him, eyes jumping from place to place. 'What is this about?'

'Jamie Tan.'

Shelby's mouth curled downward before he could stop it.

'You admit knowing him, then? Good.'

'I never said—'

'The people that killed him used a car registered to Withshaw. Suslov to you to Tan – make the connections for me.'

'I'm leaving now. If you touch me again I'm calling the police.'

'You move and I'll torch your house. Look at me and think about whether I mean it.'

Shelby stared at Stringer's chest, paralysed. Trying to summon the will to move, the simple action of putting one foot in front of the other now a gamble he couldn't bring himself to take. He rubbed his forehead with his palm. 'I'm aware of that name but nothing more.'

'You're a director of Withshaw.'

Shelby looked incredulous, rocking on stilt legs. 'I'm a paper-director for numerous companies, it's the nature of what I do.'

Stringer shook his head. 'Suslov hired me to compromise Jamie Tan. Tan was moving money out of Russia wholesale – that puts him firmly in your sandbox. What's Suslov's interest in him?'

'I have no idea.'

'Where is Suslov now?'

'I wouldn't know. New York, Paris, Dubai...'

'Then you get him here for a meeting.'

'Impossible. Andriy doesn't come to you, you go to Andriy. He's dragged me halfway around the world for a five-minute meeting before.'

Stringer looked at the man's face, the sun reflecting white off his glasses.

He grabbed him by the back of the neck and rammed his head into the black railings next to them.

Shelby let out a cry like a dying animal. Stringer kept hold of his collar and wheeled him back around to face him, checking the street as he did so; still empty. Shelby's glasses had fallen to the pavement and there was a line of blood trickling into his right eye.

'Would he come to London if he heard you'd been killed, Simon?'

Shelby tried to blink the blood away, his face bleached of any colour, making the crimson rivulets on his forehead all the more vivid.

'Find a way to get him here. Do not mention my name. You have until the end of the day.' He stuffed a piece of paper with a phone number on it in his suit pocket. 'Text me on this number with the details.'

Lydia worked through every combination of Goddard and Suslov's names she could think of, Google bringing up nothing to confirm they'd ever met.

The email chain between their people stopped with the offer

of a time and place and no confirmation from the other side, leaving open the possibility the meet had never happened. Even if it did, what did it mean? A three-year-old meeting that opened up another front in the Goddard investigation did nothing to help her understand why Jamie Tan was murdered. And even with everything Goddard symbolised to her – corruption, graft, unchecked power – murder was a whole different universe.

She called Dietmar again, the second time she'd tried him, wanting him to flesh out the relationship between Suslov and Shelby. Everything she'd learned about Suslov marked him out as ruthless, but even the Russian link provided no hint of a motive, and there was still nothing to directly connect him to Withshaw or Jamie Tan.

Unless the connection was Michael.

She checked the time on her screen, noticing the noise level in the office had crept up as people started arriving for the day. She had to get out of there, cabin fever and the threat of prying eyes driving her towards the door. She squared off the travel pack Stephen had given her, suddenly realising she hadn't noticed whether he'd left or not. Strange he wouldn't have checked in on her.

A printout of the Suslov-Goddard emails was spread across her desk and she gathered it up into a neat pile. She stood it in front of her, ready to fold it away but stopped. It was out of sequence and the sheet on top was one of the earlier mails in the chain. Right there, staring at her...

A name that meant nothing, but maybe everything.

CHAPTER 48

The phone buzzed in his hand and Stringer brought it up to read. The message was succinct:

Andriy will meet you at 10.00 p.m. in Docklands. Exact location to be supplied thirty minutes before.

He slipped off the edge of the bed and walked to the window. His castle in the sky. The room in the Helipad Crowne Plaza was executive bland – neutral carpets and off-white walls, a glass coffee table with high-end London guides scattered across it, a mid-century modern desk with headed notepaper in the drawer. The bed was large and comfortable, the hotel catering to a clientele far enough up its own arse that a pillow menu was provided on the bedside table. It was the kind of anonymous hideout that he normally relished because it enabled him to sleep like the dead. So he took no pleasure in the irony of having spent three hours staring at the ceiling, exhaustion a companion that shadowed but never seized him.

He tapped the screen to text back his answer: *Okay*

He stood at the window and looked at his watch. Ten hours to wait, a stretch of time that felt like a prison sentence. The pro and con of the message coming sooner than he expected, Shelby wasting no time setting him up.

If his fears about Suslov were right, he'd be walking into a death trap. On the slim chance he was wrong, still Suslov would surely bring reinforcements, a beating the least he could expect for threatening the man's money wizard. He looked down at the water, the Thames reflecting the blue-grey sky from his viewpoint. A luxury yacht crept out of the inlet on the opposite bank, a short channel between the high-rises that surrounded Chelsea Harbour, home to a handful of big-money boats. It turned east to head downriver, leaving a v-shaped wake in its trail.

Then the wake started to break up, a helicopter swooping in overhead. He felt it before he heard it, the bass vibrations of the rotors coursing through his fingertips on the glass. Then the thumping sound, audible even through the triple-glazing. It crossed in front of the sun; in silhouette, like a carrion bird circling over a corpse.

It came lower and he could see the craft was red and white with commercial markings, a sightseeing operator returning from a trip across the capital. There was a bustle of activity on the helipad below, and he watched the stick figures moving everything into place. He took it all in, finding focus in concentrating on the details.

When the wheels touched the tarmac, he checked his watch again.

Cawthorne Probert's offices were five minutes' walk from HFB, although Lydia only recognised the proximity of the two banks when the cab dropped her outside.

She pushed through Probert's double glass doors and found herself in the vaulting reception area. It was different to HFB and similar at the same time – the European architectural flourishes swapped for chino-and-blazer American conservatism, the contrasting styles unified in the trappings of wealth they conveyed.

There were four receptionists spaced along a low granite desk. She went up to the oldest, a man in his late forties, her phone in her hand with the profile shot on screen. 'Hi, I'm hoping you can help me. This is really random but my friend used to work here and we lost touch, I just wondered if she still does?' She turned her phone around for the man to see.

He looked at it and spread his hands. 'Sorry, nope. I don't recognise her.'

'It was about three years ago the last time we spoke. Her name's Alicia Crowley.'

The woman next to him leaned over. 'I remember Alicia.'

Lydia flashed a hopeful smile, angling the phone towards her.

The receptionist nodded, pointing to the screen that showed Alicia Tan's LinkedIn picture. 'Yeah. She left a good while back I'm afraid, couldn't tell you where she went.'

Lydia shrugged, stepping back slowly and fighting to keep the breezy smile on her face until she turned for the exit. 'Thanks.'

Confirmation. Alicia Tan, née Crowley, was one of the Cawthorne Probert staff exchanging emails with Peter Goddard three years before, trying to set up a meeting with the mayor's office on behalf of their client, Andriy Suslov.

CHAPTER 49

Stringer stood listening.

The darkness inside the toilet cubicle was complete, heightening his sense of hearing, every creak and hum laced with foreboding. The boat had made the short journey across the river and now was idling alongside the helipad, engine noise filling the blackness, as palpable as tar. He brought his hands to his mouth, to reassure himself they were still there and to quash the sense he was suffocating. He felt his breath coursing silently past his fingers and thought of Ellie blowing the head off a dandelion. He held on to the image.

A new sound came from outside, rotor blades descending closer. He touched the knife in his jacket pocket for reassurance. Getting onto the yacht proved easier than he could have hoped. He'd watched it slip into Chelsea Harbour, the layup point while it waited for Suslov's helicopter to arrive, and that was his cue to race across the river. When he got to the marina, the captain was at the other end of the dock, talking to another skipper, allowing Stringer to slip aboard unseen under the cover of dusk. All his cover stories and plans redundant, it turned out; the arrogance of money working in his favour for once.

The rotor noise peaked and subsided. He took his phones out of his pocket and made sure they were switched off. He counted off the minutes, trying to remember how long it'd taken between landing and embarking when he'd accompanied Suslov before.

He heard the cabin door open and close outside. Sooner than he'd expected – or maybe not, his sense of time as disoriented as everything else. He listened for voices but there were none, just the sound of someone moving around the cabin. Then even that stopped. But the presence was unmistakable, the primal sense of another human in proximity, only the width of a flimsy door separating them. He waited until the boat moved off, the engine noise ramping up, then took the knife out of his pocket and stepped out of the cubicle.

Suslov looked up too late, Stringer's blade already at his throat. The shift into the light was dazzling him, but he held steady, his finger to his lips as an instruction. For his part,

Suslov didn't even move his head, looking up at Stringer through his eyebrows, his expression caught between shock and fury. Then, slowly, his hand reached for his chest, discomfort spreading across his face.

Stringer glanced at the porthole in the cabin door, the bodyguard in place but not looking their way. He pulled Suslov up by the lapel and shoved him onto the seats opposite, out of sight of the window. He bent close to his ear. 'Just fucking breathe.'

Suslov massaged his chest, shooting a look that could eviscerate.

'You make a sound and I'll cut your throat.'

'You're already dead.'

'Then I've got nothing to lose. Why did you set me up?'

Suslov's breathing started to level off. 'What?'

'Keep your voice down. You call to that meathead by the door and you're dead before he turns the handle. Why did you set me up?'

'Set you up? I wouldn't waste my time.'

He dug the blade deeper into his throat. 'The answers you give determine whether you come off this boat alive or dead.'

Suslov tensed every muscle in his neck, his voice coming out as a rasp. 'If I die tonight, everyone in your family will be hurt by it. Your sister, her child, your parents. I make that promise to you.'

His arm trembled, Suslov glancing down at it. He swallowed, a try at keeping it all together. 'We can both still walk away from this. Tell me why you killed Tan.'

'Is this money? You want your idiot money? You threatened to kill Shelby over thirty thousand?'

'No, to get you here.'

'What?' Suslov pressed himself back against the seat. 'What for?'

'Because this ends tonight.'

'I told you already, Tan only had value to me alive.'

'I believed that until you told Dalton to put a gun to my head.'

Suslov's expression contorted, confused. 'I don't know what you're talking about.'

'Don't...' Stringer felt the first creep of doubt in his guts. 'Don't fucking lie to me.'

'Dalton? Look outside, I have many others I would send with a gun before him.'

The knife was suddenly heavy in his hand. 'You were listening on the phone. Dalton took me into a car park with two of your men...'

'Not my instructions.'

'You didn't know?'

'What motive would I have? Have you considered this?'

'I know about Withshaw. It's yours, isn't it?'

'Yes. And?'

There was nothing in his voice, in his tone, his expression even more twisted in confusion. A fucking question mark where the guilt should be. Stringer lifted the knife so it was no longer touching Suslov's skin. 'The men that killed Jamie Tan used a car registered to Withshaw.'

'No.'

'The fuck is "no"?'

'No. Impossible. They're my goddamn cars.'

'I've seen the CCTV.'

'Then you saw wrong. Why would I?'

Stringer stared at him, his vision tunnelling. 'Because

someone told you to shut down Tan's scheme. The money coming out of Russia.'

'Shut it down?'

'Mirror trades.'

'You know that much and still you think I would kill him? You are a blind man.'

Stringer cycled through questions in his head, calibrating for the possibility he'd got everything wrong. 'He ran the scheme at HFB. You wanted him compromised – why?'

'He's got ten billion dollars a year passing through his fingers and you ask me why I do these things.'

'Money? You wanted a cut?'

'Not a cut. Jesus.'

'Then what?'

'The end destination. Once the money's out in the wild, it needs to find a home. People don't take all those risks so it can sit around doing nothing.'

'Your investment funds.'

'Of course. Control Tan, control the destination.'

'Ten billion a year flowing into your coffers. You taking your percentage.'

'My business feeds on cash, the same as any other. More so.'

Stringer ducked down to look out the window, gauging how far they'd travelled. He saw Tower Bridge coming up, maybe only ten minutes more until they reached Docklands.

'Say again about the cars,' Suslov said. 'Withshaw.'

'A black Honda SUV, registration LD16—'

Suslov was shaking his head. 'I own cars on three continents. I don't know the plates.'

'Registered name is Andrew Pitts.'

He kept shaking. 'I don't know the name of everyone that works for me.'

'Does Dalton?'

'Yes. But he wouldn't know which end to hold a gun.'

'He had men with him who did.'

'Impossible. He has no authority. He is my fucking bag carrier.'

Stringer let his gaze stray to the water, everything out of focus. 'Where is he?'

'I don't know.'

'Get him to meet us in Docklands.'

'He already knows you are here tonight. I told him to arrange a car to have me picked up.'

'Then he knows he's blown.' The scene was shifting so fast he couldn't stay on top of it. 'Why would he fuck you over?'

Suslov pushed the knife away from his throat already hanging low. 'There is no way.'

'There's CCTV of Jamie Tan being put into your car. I'm the only person can put this together for you.'

Suslov loosened his tie and unfastened his top button. 'You come for me with a knife and now you want to help me.'

'Dalton set you up for Tan's murder. Your house, your cars.' Stringer held the knife up, then made a show of slipping it into his pocket. 'You underestimated him.'

Suslov stared at him, a fire raging behind his eyes.

CHAPTER 50

Lydia pressed the buzzer again. When no one answered, she rattled the driveway gate, the black metal barely moving. 'Alicia...'

She cupped her hands around her mouth. 'Alicia Tan, I need to speak to you. It's about Jamie.'

The Tans' house loomed over her in the gloaming. Using his name was low, but it came from acceptance that Alicia wasn't there; *we let ourselves down the most when we think no one's watching*. Next door, a light came on in an upstairs room, a shadow visible behind the drapes.

She crossed the pavement and opened the back door of the cab, holding it while she took out her phone. She'd missed four calls from Stephen, the time gap between each one growing shorter, the sense that she'd finally pushed him too far. She brought up her call list and dialled Michael's number again.

The driver turned around to look at her. 'Where we headed?'

She ducked into the cab and raised her hand apologetically to him, phone to her ear. 'Two seconds.' She stood up again, hearing the automated voicemail message kick in.

She redialled, getting the same result. This time she let the automated voice finish; then the beep and a yawning silence.

'It's me, where the hell are you? I know...' She looked up, grasping for the words. 'I can link Tan and Andriy Suslov going back three years. You already knew that, because I'm pretty sure you work for Suslov and I want to hear you say it. Call me back, you lying fucking coward.'

The voice was her own, but not the emotion. The words were fierce, angry, but what she felt inside was only disappointment. The knowledge she'd betrayed her judgement, her instincts.

She bent over to fold herself into the cab's back seat.

The driver looked at her in the mirror. 'All set?'

'Palgrave Estate on Cranbourne Street, please. It's near Euston.'

The bodyguard threw Stringer onto the deck. He couldn't get his hands out to break his fall, landing on his elbow, pain shooting up his arm. The man stamped on his ankle, pinning him down with his foot. Then Suslov came up behind, a hand on the man's shoulder to restrain him. Canary Wharf stood silent above them, its outline as hard and sharp as the point of a sword in the night.

Suslov circled around and stopped by his feet, a glance at the riverbank, the gentle sound of water slapping against wooden pilings. True to his word, there was no greeting party there to meet them. He really had come in good faith – or whatever the right term was for him showing up in the belief he was protecting Shelby. There was no good faith, no good intentions, in this fucking sinkhole.

Suslov took his phone from his ear. 'He does not answer.'

Stringer turned his body, trying to ease the pressure on his ankle. 'He's not here. He knows.'

Suslov motioned for the bodyguard to lift his foot, then spoke to him in Ukrainian. Stringer grabbed his ankle, writhing on the deck. He made out the word 'Dalton' and nothing more, but Suslov's tone was vicious. When he finished, the man kicked Stringer and motioned for him to get to his feet.

'Just give me a place to start,' Stringer said, almost pleading. 'Where does he live?'

'This is no longer your concern,' Suslov said. He looked at the bodyguard again. 'Get him inside and get everything out of him. What happened.' He switched to Ukrainian and added something else. Stringer got it straight away.

Get him inside the boat no one had seen him board. The boat no one knew he was on. He glanced around, Docklands deserted at this hour, no witnesses on the riverbank either. 'Wait...'

The bodyguard grabbed his arm and pulled him up. Then he twisted it behind him and started walking him back into the cabin, Stringer's elbow exploding.

'Somebody bought Dalton off,' Stringer shouted over his shoulder. 'I'm the only one who can put it all together.'

Suslov had his eyes on his phone, typing something, ignoring him.

'They got to him and they're coming for you.'

The bodyguard stopped, hesitating as he reached to open the cabin door, waiting for confirmation to continue.

'Fucking think...'

Suslov looked up, a crack forming, the bodyguard still looking to him.

'Someone powerful enough that he'd even fuck you over. And I can find them.'

Suslov held up a hand. 'How?'

'I need my phone.'

Suslov considered it, then nodded warily for the man to let him go. Stringer took it out of his pocket and held the power button to turn it on – slow, deliberate movements.

His phone came alive and the notifications rained in. A voicemail message and four emails. The top one was from Milos – the first line showing in the notification bubble. The call log from Dalton's phone – he'd come through with it. He opened the attachment, his eyes flicking back and forth between the screen and the oligarch.

The bodyguard asked something in Ukrainian, but Suslov shook his head, an expression that said *not yet*.

'This is Dalton's call list.' Skimming it, tripping over his words. There: one that lasted twenty-six minutes and change, corresponding to the date and time they'd been in the underground garage. Much longer than the rest of his calls, obvious for it. 'I've got the mobile number he was taking instructions from.' Before Suslov could say anything, Stringer dialled it, holding the phone out between them to show it wasn't a trick.

He put it on speaker as it started ringing. Suslov had his own phone in his hand, and it remained silent and still – likely confirmation he'd been telling the truth.

The phone rang for another thirty seconds before it finally cut out. No voicemail message, no name.

Suslov took a step towards him. 'How can I trust this? Everything you do is telling lies.'

'The risk I took tonight. I thought it was you.'

'And now you know you were wrong.'

Stringer looked away, no defence he could offer.

Suslov put his hands on his hips. 'This man. If he exists, he is the one ordered Tan's death.'

Stringer nodded once. 'With Dalton's help.'

'So.'

A single word that offered a lifeline. What he wanted obvious, nothing more to be said.

The city glowed in the distance upriver, red lights flaring in the dark. Stringer put his phone away and looked at Suslov again. 'They tried to kill me. Let me find them and I'll square it for both of us.'

Lydia hauled herself out of the cab and looked across the estate. She hit the button to redial Michael's mobile, but after a silent pause it went straight to voicemail, same as before. She kept her phone in her hand and made her way along the passage that cut between the blocks into the central courtyard.

It was surrounded on three sides and the buildings seemed to absorb the noise of the outside world. Her shoe clipped a piece of broken glass and sent it skittering across the gravel, the sound ringing out like a bell. A man crossed in front of the block across from her, a weary-looking dog padding next to him, the pair alternating between light and shadow as they passed under the security lamps mounted on the wall above.

It was all inside her, she knew that. But it wasn't fear jangling her nerves, it was the sense she didn't belong. The irony of feeling like she was intruding in Michael's life when he'd trampled all over hers. Readying to confront him over Suslov, despite the risk to herself.

She stopped in front of the block called Palgrave and looked up at the fourth floor, counting doorways from the left end of the balcony until she got to the one she'd seen him go into. She went over to the intercom panel and buzzed number forty-five.

The speaker crackled into life, catching her unready. She brought her mouth closer to speak...

The system beeped to indicate she'd been buzzed in. She pulled the heavy blue door open and entered the stairwell.

Stringer came down the escalator at Canary Wharf station, the moon framed in the giant, glass latticework dome above his head. He had his phone pressed to his ear, Lydia's message playing out, straight fire coming out of the speaker. She'd clicked about him and Suslov, she intimated as much; but the other thing she said was new – a link between Suslov and Tan going back three years.

She'd been on his heels the whole way, none of his lies throwing her off course for long – and now she'd overtaken him. She was as smart and tenacious as anyone he knew, and it wrecked him to think she'd never trust him again.

He deleted the voicemail but as he did, the screen burst into life with a call – Milos.

'Yeah?'

'Bro, it's me.'

'I know.'

'You get my stuff?'

'Yeah, you did good.'

'Cool, cool. Listen, that other thing we was talking about...'

'What?'

'Mans nosing in your shit.'

The line started to break up as he reached the concourse at the bottom of the escalator. He jumped off and ran a few steps back up the staircase to try and keep the signal. 'What about it?'

'I spoke to someone who was into it.'

'Who?'

'Chatroom thing, just a username innit.'

'And?'

'Thing is ... Listen, this ain't right, that's why I wanted to tell you...'

'Fuck's sake, say it.'

'The thing the buyer wanted most was deets on your family.'

Stringer gripped the metal handrail. In his mind he saw the glass high above splinter and break and rain down on him, a blizzard of razor shards that sliced him into a mush of skin and blood. Milos's voice pierced the vision, a young couple on the adjacent escalator staring at the lunatic on the staircase looking up as if the sky was falling.

'Bro, you there?'

'Yeah. I'm here. How much did they know?'

'Not sure, I couldn't ask that. But look, I'm saying, you got anyone you care about, maybe get them to be somewhere else for a while, hear me?'

The staircase was bare brick, no numbers on the landings to indicate which floor she was on. Lydia counted four sets of stairs and went out onto the communal balcony. A lock turned somewhere along it, and a cone of light spread on the concrete where someone had opened their front door.

A woman craned her head out, looking at her, then peering past.

Lydia stopped a few paces short and the woman focused on her again.

'Did you just buzz my flat?'

Lydia nodded. 'I'm looking for Michael.'

The woman stepped over the threshold and wrapped her arms around herself. 'What for?'

Lydia looked at her and knew she'd got it wrong. She had the same blue-grey eyes, the same high cheekbones; the family resemblance was easy to see, even in the dull light.

'My name's Lydia Wright, we're working on a story together.'

'A story? You're the journalist.'

Lydia frowned. 'He's told you about me?'

The woman looked out across the estate and back. 'In passing. Can't you call him on his mobile?'

'He's not answering.'

The woman re-wrapped her arms around herself. 'What is it you want him for?'

'It's just to do with the story.'

'Which is what exactly?'

Lydia glanced at her feet. 'How much has he told you?'

'Enough. Enough that when a stranger knocks on my door at ten o'clock at night I know to worry.'

'Were you expecting him? When you let me in?'

She shrugged. 'I just assumed.'

'Do you know where he is?'

The woman didn't answer, disappearing back inside. Lydia stepped forward far enough to see she'd gone into the kitchen, off to one side just inside the doorway, and was looking at a phone charging on the counter. She put it to her ear, eyeing Lydia with a look that said to stay where she was. From the concentration on her face, it was obvious she was listening to a voicemail.

The woman hung up, touched the screen and put it to her ear again. 'Mike, call me when you get this. Thanks.'

Lydia planted her hand on the wall. 'What did he say?'

The woman came out onto the balcony again. She leaned on the rail and looked out, scouring the courtyard and the grass and the parking spaces below, all of them occupied. She turned back to Lydia. 'What paper do you work for?'

'The *Examiner*. Here...' She took her card out and held it up to catch the light, a circular yellow fitting above their head.

The woman brought it towards her to look at, then let go. 'Come in for a minute, yeah?'

Lydia followed her inside. The woman directed her into the

kitchen while she locked the front door. It was long and narrow, a large window looking out onto the balcony and the flats opposite.

Lydia leaned against the countertop. 'Listen, I don't mean to be pushy, but what did his message say?'

The woman held up a finger, already calling someone else. 'Dad, it's me. Has Mike been there?'

Lydia looked her over again, the same slim frame, the 'dad' clinching it – brother and sister.

'Okay, thanks. Look, will you call me if he shows up? No, I just need to talk to him. Give Mum a hug from me.'

She put the phone down on the counter, staring at the wall as if it was on fire. 'What the hell is going on with my brother?'

'How much has he told you?'

'I know someone died. I know that person was into something bad.'

'And the message?'

She looked away, swiping an imaginary film of dust off the countertop. 'He said he's on his way here now.'

'Okay.' Lydia was nodding. 'Okay, cool.'

The woman sleepwalked across the room to the kettle. 'Do you want a tea?'

'I'm fine. Thanks.'

She flicked it on but seemed to forget about it as soon as she did. 'Why did you come here tonight? Because this is really starting to mess with me.'

'I couldn't get hold of him, and ... I need to talk to him. I didn't know what else to try.'

'I know he's in danger.'

Lydia held her stare, seeing tiredness and apprehension. 'Did he say who from?'

The sister closed her eyes. 'If you know Mike, you know the answer to that.'

'What's your name?'

'He didn't tell you?'

'Like you said, he doesn't talk much.'

The woman gave a quiet laugh, rueful. 'Abi. That's why it was weird he told me about you.'

'What did he say?'

'That you were caught up but didn't know how bad it really was.'

'Patronising bastard.'

That brought a genuine smile to her face. 'Yeah.'

The kettle finished boiling and clicked off, and the silence stretched between them. Lydia opened the top of her bag to check her phone screen.

'Anything?'

A knock at the door startled them both.

Abi leaned over the sink to look sidelong out the kitchen window. She brought herself back slowly.

'What is it?'

'It's not him.' She stepped into the hallway to stand by the door. 'Yes?'

Lydia came over and stationed herself behind her.

'Police, Miss Howton. Open the door please.'

Abi snapped around to look at her, eyes dancing with uncertainty. She spoke to the door again. 'What's it about?'

'Your brother. Open up and we can talk.'

Abi took hold of the handle but hesitated. She slipped the security chain on and opened it a crack, not showing herself. 'You got some ID?'

'Yep.' There was a pause, each waiting for the other to speak. 'I'm not going to put my hand through there, though.'

Lydia found herself creeping slowly backward. Abi glanced around at her, haunted, seeing her backpedalling. She gave a slight nod. Then she turned to the front again. 'Put it up against the kitchen window. It's the one on your right.'

Lydia reached the end of the hallway and found herself in the living room. She stepped off to the side, craning to look.

Abi turned back to her again, shooting her a question with her eyes. Lydia shook her head, mouthing, *No*—

The door crashed inwards. Lydia jumped back in shock, hearing Abi cry out and then fall silent. She could hear a man's voice in the hallway. Someone turned the catch to lock the front door.

Lydia glanced around, shaking. There was a reclining chair at an angle across one corner. Without making a sound, she stepped on the cushion and climbed over the back of it, pulling herself into a ball and screaming in her head.

Then she saw the toys.

There were crates of stuffed animals and plastic dolls and action figures of TV characters. There was a kiddy's table, pretend food and miniature cups and plates arranged across it. She looked up at the ceiling, feeling like she was seeing through it. *Fuck fuck fuck fuck.*

The man's voice was muffled and she couldn't make out his words. She peeled the flap back on her bag, her phone right there, and dialled 999. Then she heard footsteps coming down the hall. She jabbed the red disconnect symbol just as Abi and the man came into the room.

'All I want is to talk to him. Your brother understands how this works.'

The voice wasn't what she expected, the man well spoken. She could just see them through the gap between the chair and the sofa next to it, but only as high as their waists. He was wearing a dark suit and polished black shoes. As she watched, the man lowered his hand to his side. He was holding a gun.

She couldn't breathe.

Did the call connect? If it did and the cops called back now...

She waited a second until one of them spoke again – Abi. 'I don't know where he is, I swear to god.'

Lydia swiped her screen in silence and turned on airplane mode. She pressed her eyes shut tight—

There was a thump from upstairs. Everything stopped.

'What the fuck was...?' He raised the gun again.

Abi took rasping breaths.

The man was silent, and she could picture him doing the same as she had – seeing the toys, the jigsaws...

He moved across her line of vision and out of sight, her only sense of where he was the sound of measured footsteps when carpet gave way to laminate. Then they stopped.

'Hello, sweetheart. Why don't you come down and see your mummy?'

CHAPTER 51

Stringer ran up the stairs at Euston already calling Abi's number.

He turned left out of the Tube entrance and bombed along Euston Road towards her flat. Her phone kept ringing until the voicemail kicked in. He swore and looked at his watch – 10.30. Nowhere else she'd be that time of night, her phone normally switched off if she'd gone to bed. He pushed on faster.

Lydia was on her knees, her head just above the chair back, craning her neck so she could look down the hall. The man was out of sight but she could see Abi in the doorway, peering up at the top of the stairs through the banisters.

'It's alright. Just go back to bed, poppet.'

'Your mum's just joking; don't listen to her – come down.'

There was a shuffling sound, then it went to shit.

Abi charged forward, screaming, 'Don't you fucking dare!'

Lydia scrambled to her feet, just in time to see Abi crash into him, clawing at his head. He grabbed her wrist with his free hand, trying to wrestle her off, but Abi screeched, slashing at his face with her nails and drawing blood on his cheek. Before Lydia could move, he threw Abi back and she stumbled to the floor, her skull hitting the laminate like a gavel.

He aimed the gun at Abi, his fingers probing the wound on his face with his free hand. 'You crazy fucking...'

Lydia had already dropped out of sight again. It was over in a heartbeat. She swore at herself for not doing something, and again for thinking it would've helped.

The man spoke again, calling up the stairs. 'Come down here now. Please.'

Abi said something to him under her breath she couldn't catch. Then she spoke again, louder: 'Just go back to bed, sweetheart, everything's going to be okay, I promise.'

'Mummy, I can't sleep. It's too noisy.'

'Please, honey, just go to your room and—'

'Enough. You, down here, now.'

Abi dropped her voice, slow and guttural now. 'I will kill you if you touch her.'

'Just shut up. Get her down here and she can stay with you where I can see her. Then we'll get him round here to sort this out. Where's your phone?'

Lydia clamped her hands around her head, cursing herself. Trying to think straight was like seeing through smoke. Her whole life, searching for the edge; and now it'd found her she could barely move. She wasn't ready for this. Never had been. Her the only one that couldn't see it.

'Tell her. I won't say it again.'

And if he turned the gun on the kid? That had to be the red line. If he aimed at the kid she had to be in front of it. She dug her nails into her skull, her fingers already going cold at the thought.

A buzzer sounded, a grating tone, resounding in the quiet.

Lydia's heart stopped. She heard the kid cry out, startled. Then her footsteps, light and fast, up a couple of steps, and across the ceiling above her.

'Shit. What was that?'

Abi's voice: 'The entry phone.'

'Who are you expecting?'

Abi didn't reply.

'Him?'

The silence was loaded, could only mean he'd guessed right.

'Answer it.'

She heard Abi rising to her feet.

Lydia looked behind her, the windows just above her head but too high and looking out the wrong way to see into the courtyard. She took her phone off airplane mode, typed a message to Michael:

In your sister flat. Man with gun here

She cradled the phone in her hands, waiting for an acknowledgement.

Stringer walked along the balcony to Abi's door. He stopped just short, something nagging—

She'd answered the intercom. Sounding throaty, as if he'd woken her up. But she'd answered. Normally she just buzzed him in if she was expecting him.

He looked ahead, the light on in the kitchen, the glow blossoming from the window. He stopped to listen, hearing a car passing along the road outside the estate, echoed snatches of a teenager talking on his phone somewhere unseen below.

He knocked on the door. 'It's me.'

Movement inside and then it cracked open. Straightaway something wrong, Abi's expression off, her eyes downcast. Then the door opened the rest of the way and Dalton was standing behind her, hands out of view but her face clueing him to what he was holding. 'Inside.'

Stringer stepped onto the doormat as Dalton backed up with Abi. The door swung shut behind him and Dalton prodded Abi forward to lock it again. 'Where's Ellie?'

Abi raised her eyes to the ceiling, indicating the bedroom. Dalton waved him down the hallway with the gun, then manoeuvred Abi around so she was at the foot of the stairs, his back to the door. 'Call her.'

Stringer held his palms up, slow and calm. 'You've still got options, Dalton. There are ways we all walk from this. But if something happens to either of them, all those options disappear.'

A sniff at the top of the stairs made them all look up. Ellie was standing there in bright-green princess pyjamas, clutching her bunny toy. 'Uncle Mike, I can't sleep.'

'It's alright, kiddo.'

Dalton beckoned her and she waited a few seconds then started down the steps, slipping her feet over the edge of each one until she dropped onto the next, an agonising procession until she stopped halfway down.

'Why don't you tell me what you want,' Stringer said.

'The wife.'

Stringer looked from Dalton to Abi and back. 'Alicia Tan?'

Dalton nodded. The same thing he'd wanted in the garage; his assumption that was a test starting to break up. The significance a mystery. 'What does she matter?'

'You met with Andriy tonight?'

Stringer nodded.

'And now you're here, so you must have talked him onside. So you think you're in the clear.'

Ellie started moving again, lingering on each step. When she got to the last one, she pressed herself against the wall, eyeballing Dalton with the directness only a child can muster. Abi called her over, and she thought about it, then made the short dash to her. Abi scooped her up in her arms and turned her away from the weapon. She started to move into the kitchen.

Dalton trained the gun on them. 'Where are you going?'

'Let me get her some milk,' Abi said. 'Please.'

Dalton stared at her, then flicked the gun to say she could go. He swapped to Stringer. 'You too.'

Stringer didn't move. 'Just keep that pointed on me. Leave them out of this.'

'Go.'

'Mike, please, do what he says.'

There was desperation in her voice. He took a few steps forward and stopped in the kitchen doorway, putting himself between the girls and Dalton.

'Did he send you here to kill me?' Dalton said.

'You're the one with the gun.'

'He's still using you. You know that, don't you?'

'We're all being used.'

'Where is the wife? I know you got to her.'

'What happens if I tell you?'

'I walk out that door.'

Stringer spread his hands, keeping them by his sides. 'You can walk out right now, I'll come with you. You get what you want when we're downstairs.'

'Mike...' He could feel Abi's eyes on his back.

Dalton came two steps closer, their faces a metre apart. He spoke in a near-whisper. 'I didn't want to be here tonight. Don't make me do this.'

'Go out that door and we can talk. I don't owe Alicia Tan anything.'

Dalton stared at him, his bottom teeth showing, close enough that he could hear his breath catching on dry lips. He closed his eyes for an instant and opened them again. 'I can't.' Then he swung his arm.

Stringer was on the kitchen floor looking up before he knew what'd happened. A stabbing pain blasted through his head and he heard Abi cry out behind him. He reached up with his hand and felt blood where Dalton had smashed him with the gun butt, a knot already forming. He glanced over his shoulder, Abi shaking and pressing Ellie's face to her chest.

Dalton stood over him just inside the doorway. 'This is the last time I'm going to ask: where is she?'

'I don't know.'

'Stop fucking lying to me.'

'I don't know.' Stringer dipped his head, the movement making him feel sick. 'On my life. I had her stashed and she disappeared.'

'Mike, don't—'

Dalton flicked his eyes up. 'Shut up.'

'She's gone. She could be anywhere in the whole fucking world.'

Dalton stared at him, his breathing fast and shallow. Then he aimed the gun at Abi.

She spun away from him, shielding Ellie again, her neck twisted to look at Dalton. 'You'll hit her if you do. Can you live with that?'

His arm was dead still, but his eyes were glazed. Stringer saw a man afraid enough to do anything.

He slipped his finger inside the trigger guard. 'We all disappoint ourselves in the end.'

A blur moved behind him and Dalton toppled forward to the floor. The shock froze Stringer for a heartbeat, then he dived for Dalton's gun arm, grabbing the wrist with both hands and ramming it into the floor until the gun shook free. Dalton surged forward to ram him with the top of his head, and both men fell sideways. Dalton got his wrist free again. He snatched the gun up and put it to Stringer's eye.

Lydia Wright reared up behind him and brought the ornament down on his head with two hands.

Lydia put the brass elephant on the kitchen counter, some manifestation of shock making her square its feet with the edge. She ran her fingers over it, feeling the dimples across its surface, her eyes on the floor. The man Michael had called Dalton was face down, unmoving. 'Shit...'

Abi swept past her, carrying the kid out of the room.

Michael propped himself on his elbow, reaching for his head, blood matted in his hair.

Lydia felt the trembles in her chest start to build. 'Is he dead?'

He stared at her like she'd walked out of a nightmare. 'Where the hell did you come from?'

'I sent you a message. I was looking for you.'

He hauled himself around so he could prop his back against a cupboard.

Looking now, she could see Dalton was still breathing. 'Who is he?'

Abi came back into the kitchen and reached across Lydia to snatch her phone from the charger cable.

'You okay?' Michael said to her.

'Fine.' She started back down the hall. 'I'm calling the police.'

Michael got his feet under him, swaying as he stood up. 'Wait.' He stepped over the body going after her. 'Abi...'

'What?'

'Just wait.'

'What for?'

Lydia watched them, Stringer with his hand against the wall to steady himself as he picked his way along. 'He's part of something bigger. Just a second.'

She saw Abi glaring at him, her phone in her hand. Then she turned and went into the living room, out of sight. Comforting the girl.

'Who is he?' Lydia called down to him.

Michael came slowly back up the hall. He looked at her and away, reaching down to the body and pressing his fingers to the man's neck. He put his foot on the gun and slid it away across the floor, then knelt down and patted the man's pockets. He found something and reached inside to get it, producing his phone.

'Michael?'

'He's Andriy Suslov's man.'

'So are you.'

He stopped still.

'You told him you met with Suslov earlier. I was in there, I heard what you said. He was your mysterious fucking client, wasn't he?'

'It's not how it looks.'

'Why don't you want the police here?'

'You want to do this right now?'

'Yeah, before you can make up more lies.'

'I swear to god I'll tell you everything. But I need to know.'

'Know what?'

'Who sent him. He screwed Suslov.' He took Dalton's hand and pressed his thumb against the home button to unlock the phone. He got his own phone out and brought a number up on screen, then typed it into Dalton's.

'Who are you calling?'

Michael said nothing and hit dial. Lydia stared at him, this wire of a man kneeling on the floor and gripping the phone like he was pleading for his own life.

It sounded like someone answered and Michael jagged it away from his ear as if it was burning him, recognition on his face. He pressed the disconnect button and held the phone at arm's length, staring at the ended call. 'Jesus Christ. Jesus fucking Christ.'

Stringer stepped over Dalton and went into the sitting room. Abi was cradling Ellie across her lap, the girl staring up at her with hollow eyes.

'So what now?' she said.

'I don't know.' He came closer, reaching out to stroke Ellie's hair.

'You don't know? Well then you've got five seconds to make your mind up or I'm making the call.'

'We can't do that.'

'Why the f—' She bit her lip, stopping herself, glancing down at Ellie. 'Why not?'

'The people he works for ... they're connected.'

'What do you mean? Connected to who?'

'Establishment.'

'Establishment?' She slipped one hand over Ellie's ear. 'If you're thinking about protecting him to run an angle...'

'I'm not.'

'I know how your mind works. Don't lie to me – if you put money over her safety, we're through.'

'Never.' He bent down to one knee, unsteady, to be at her eye level. 'Never. But we need to be smart.'

'I can't handle this.'

'I'll get him out of here.'

'Yeah? And what happens when these people come looking for him?'

'I'll put you in a hotel for a few days. Just while I take care of them.'

'You're telling me the police can't deal with this but you can?' She pushed his hand away from Ellie. 'You're off your head, Mike. Whatever you're thinking, do it now. I want all of you gone.'

'I'm sorry. If I'd known...'

'I don't want to hear it.'

Her anger was like a house fire, the heat driving him back.

'Michael...' He wheeled around, Lydia leaning out of the kitchen doorway to call him. 'He just moved.'

He went back to where she stood, flitting from one line of thought to the next. As he got there Dalton made a grunting sound. His face creased and then his fingers twitched.

Stringer pulled the sleeve of his coat over his hand and crouched down to pick up the gun. He pocketed it and looked up at Lydia, watching him. 'Can you drive?'

CHAPTER 52

Lydia left the engine running and buzzed Abi's flat. Michael answered straightaway. 'Coming now.'

It'd been a thirty-minute round trip to his place in Holloway, a smart development rising up just behind the Tube station. A cab took her there in a daze, her head a raging froth that wouldn't settle, but by the time she found his car in the garage under his flats, she was starting to think straight. And the thought it coalesced around was this: she'd never know what might've been said between him and Dalton in the time she was gone.

Now she got back in the driver's seat and gripped the wheel, waiting for Michael to appear. She concentrated on her hands, something real and known, a comfort when she was so far past normality's vanishing point.

Dalton came out of the communal door first with Michael behind him, checking both ways. Michael bundled him into the back seat and pushed him across so he could get in the same side. Lydia saw he'd tied his hands with a length of cord.

She watched them in the mirror. 'What now?'

'Head north.'

'Where are we going?'

'I'm working on it.'

She turned around. Dalton was listing in his seat, head slumped against the window. 'Is your niece alright?' she said.

'They're gone, I put them in a cab. They're safe.' He broke off from her stare. 'They'll be okay.'

She pulled away and steered the car through the narrow entranceway. She stopped at the junction with the main road, the indicator ticking in the quiet. 'Before we go anywhere, I want to know who he is.'

'He's Suslov's man. He fucked him over.'

'You said that already. What does it mean?'

'Keep driving.'

'I'll drive when you start talking.'

She heard him take a breath, steeling himself. 'Suslov was the one hired me to compromise Tan.'

'I worked that out.'

'Everything else I told you was true.'

'Except you never fucking mentioned you were working for the number-one suspect.'

'Because I knew how it looked.'

She pressed the accelerator and turned into the road. 'And?'

'I went after Suslov tonight, but he had no idea about the link to Withshaw.'

'He told you that?'

'Yes.'

'Do you believe him?'

'He needed Tan alive. Tan was supposed to funnel the mirror-trade proceeds into Suslov's hedge funds. Make himself the go-to investment house for the Russians once their money was laundered. That's why he hired me in the first place – so he could force Tan to convince them to push the clean cash his way.' She saw Michael look along the passenger seat to Dalton. 'Now fill in the rest,' he told him.

Dalton brought his hands up, cupped together, and rubbed his eyes with his knuckles.

'Why did you kill Tan?'

'I didn't,' Dalton said. 'You saw the video.'

The last word jolted her.

'You arranged it,' Michael said.

Dalton turned his gaze to the window, dark houses passing by outside.

Lydia gripped the wheel tighter, every word in high clarity now. She tried to keep her eyes on the road, but she kept flicking to the rearview, looking at him.

'Tell me,' Michael said.

The buzz in her head got louder, one question repeating over and over...

She swerved to the kerb and jammed the brakes, whipping off her seatbelt. 'What happened to the woman who took the video?'

Dalton kept his eyes down.

She turned around and surged between the seats, slapping his leg to make him look. 'What happened to her?'

'I don't know.'

'Is she dead?'

'I don't know anything about her.'

'Tell me. Fucking tell me.'

Michael got in front of her. 'Easy.'

She struggled against him a second, finally letting herself fall back onto the seat, shaking. 'I'm taking this piece of shit to the police.'

Michael pulled himself forward on the passenger seat so she could see his face. 'Okay.'

'Okay?'

'I just need twelve hours.'

CHAPTER 53

Stringer adjusted his shirt cuffs on the ride up, the air in the lift warm and stale like he was the morning's first passenger.

The receptionist flashed a smile at him as he came over, looking uncertain.

'I'm here to see Sir Oliver.'

She looked down as if she was checking his diary on the screen, but already starting to speak. 'I'm afraid Sir Oliver has appointments all morning...'

'Tell him Michael Stringer is here about Dalton. He'll squeeze me in.'

Kent met him by the door to his office with a smile and a handshake. Stringer took up a position in front of the desk, waiting for him to go around it and sit down – expecting a show of deference to put him at ease.

Instead, he came to stand in front of him. 'I had a feeling.'

'About what?'

Kent picked up a pen, absently. 'That it was you calling last night from Dalton's phone. I was starting to lose faith.'

'In?'

'You.'

Stringer put his hands in his pockets. 'I've got Dalton.'

'That's already understood. He's still alive?'

He nodded. 'And talking.'

Kent tapped the pen on the table. 'I've no doubt about that. The trouble is he struggles with the truth.'

'Tell me your version then.'

'There is no version. There's only what happened, what didn't, and what can be proved.'

Stringer stepped closer. 'What happened is that Dalton came after my family.'

Kent put a hand on his shoulder. 'I can promise you I had no involvement in that. None.'

'You were on the phone when he tried to kill me though.'

Kent stared at him, choosing his words. 'What are you here for, Michael? Why don't we gloss over the accusations and get to the part where you tell me what you want. Because if you do have Dalton and he's not dead or in custody, then you've made the smart move by coming to make a deal.'

'Dalton came to you about Jamie Tan.'

Kent pursed his lips.

'He told you Andriy Suslov had hired me and was going after Tan,' Stringer said. 'You had him killed to keep him out of Suslov's reach. So Tan was originally working for you.'

Kent laid the pen down, staring at it while he chose his words. 'It's an interesting theory.'

'Don't insult me. It's no secret Russian money floods into the London property market. Your play was going to the source. Billions in dirty roubles, washed clean through mirror trades – but once it's out, there's the age-old problem: what to do with all that cash? Then you swoop in with a solution: why not invest in building my luxury developments? Jamie Tan as your salesman – who better than the financial wizard they'd trusted to get their cash out in the first place? And then you sell the finished apartments back to the same kind of people. You win twice.'

'If that were true, I'd have to have extensive contacts in Russia. People who'd be very unhappy with anyone who became an impediment to their prosperity.'

'You don't need to threaten me, I've seen what you're capable of. I wouldn't be here if I was trying to pick a fight.'

Kent put his arm across his stomach and propped his elbow on it. 'Good. Because there is scope for a deal here, if you don't overplay your hand.'

'Why did you pick me for the Carlton job?'

'Any number of reasons.'

'Indulge me.'

'Nigel will be a useful man to know.'

'But why me?'

'Perhaps I wanted to see your work. The job offer I made you was real.'

'Then why didn't you just clue me in on the Tan thing? You bought off Dalton, why not me?'

Kent squinted at him. 'A matter as sensitive as that? Dalton already knew the details when he brought them to me, you did not.'

'How did he know about your involvement?'

'Tan told him. It was supposed to be a *hands-off* message to your friend Suslov – a warning that Tan was protected – but Dalton cut him out and came to me instead. To make his own deal.'

Stringer looked at the floor, nodding.

'I sense you came here with a proposal in mind,' Kent said.

Stringer kept his gaze down, reaching for his inside pocket. He passed the slip of paper to Kent. 'A hundred grand, in this account by lunchtime.'

Kent took it without looking. 'And what are you offering?'

'Dalton. But I want him taken off the board.'

Kent looked at the piece of paper in his hand, details of an account held in the British Virgin Islands. 'I was hoping for more.'

Stringer looked up. 'Such as what?'

Kent stared at him, looking for something in his eyes. Not finding it, he blinked and broke off, leaving it unspoken – Stringer with a growing sense of what it might be. 'Midnight tonight. You'll be contacted with a location.'

'If the money isn't there, I'm dust.'

'It'll be there.'

Stringer turned to go.

'Keep in mind what I said, Michael. You're under my patronage now, as are the people close to you. It's vital you understand what that means.'

Stringer looked at him, getting it. A threat proffered as an arm around the shoulder. A razorblade dressed in a suit.

CHAPTER 54

Lydia jumped up when she heard the keys turning in the lock.

The door cracked open, crunching as it caught on the security chain. 'Let me in.'

Michael's voice. She peered through the opening to see he was alone and slipped the chain off. 'Where did you go?'

'To speak to Dalton's boss.' He passed her, went into the front room. 'Any problems?'

She followed him and stopped in the middle of the floor. 'How can you ask me that like I'm cat-sitting or something? I'm climbing the walls here.'

He turned and fixed her with his eyes. 'It's almost over.'

'Over how?'

He poured a glass of water and went to check the bedroom, finding it shut. 'You closed the door?'

'I couldn't look at him anymore.'

'Did you check on him?'

'A while back.'

Michael opened the bedroom, Dalton slumped in the corner tied to a radiator pipe. He looked up at them. 'I need a piss.'

Lydia spun around and walked away, her hands pressed to her mouth. He'd asked for twelve hours before she called the cops and she'd taken him at his word. But nine hours in, here she was playing prison guard to a man lashed to a radiator. Not just illegal but immoral. Michael – this man she barely knew – off cooking up a deal with Dalton's boss. His sister's words from the night before ringing in her ears – 'I know how your mind works' – fearful he'd put money over his family's safety. No telling what he was capable of when it came to strangers.

Something she couldn't be part of.

She took her phone out and stood by the window, staring at the screen, traffic snarled up in a queue of buses coming out of Finsbury Park station down the road. She checked over her shoulder to be sure Michael was still in the bedroom, then started typing.

CHAPTER 55

The clock said fourteen minutes to midnight.

The industrial estate was on the outskirts of Borehamwood, close to the junction of the M1 and M25. Stringer understood why they'd chosen it for the handover – good links, fast access in and out.

A slip road took them in. Commercial premises lined one side of it, a rutted car park for each one on the other, their entrances marked by goalpost-style gates that seemed redundant when there wasn't a car in sight. Half the units were abandoned, all of them dilapidated; only the signs on the front of the going concerns differentiated them from the rest – a tile warehouse, a self-store place, an insurance outfit. All of them were shuttered for the night. There were white security lights beaming at their forecourts, but the car parks were dark.

Stringer guided Lydia to the third one along. He was on the back seat, next to Dalton. She'd avoided making eye contact with him in the mirror the whole drive.

Dalton straightened in his seat as the car slowed. 'When are you going to tell me what you want?'

Stringer ignored him, scanning the far end of the slip road.

Lydia turned her head. 'What now?'

He glanced at his watch. 'Couple of minutes.'

Dalton looked from one to the other. Then he brought his hands up, still tied, and jammed them into the headrest in front. 'You've made your point; tell me what you fucking want.'

Stringer looked at him. 'You're done.'

'No, you're fucking yourself over. Listen to me, Suslov's lying to you, I know the real story and I'll cut a deal with you.'

'I don't need anything from you.'

'If you give me up, Suslov will kill me.'

'You made your choices.'

'No. Fucking no; be smart.' Dalton turned in his seat and bent towards him, grabbing Stringer's shoulder. 'Money. I can get you paid properly – not the shit Suslov's got you dancing for. Real money.'

Stringer shrugged him off. 'Earlier today Sir Oliver Kent gave me a hundred grand. That kind of money?'

Dalton froze, his mouth slack, a line of saliva stretched from one lip to the other.

'Who were the two men on the Tan hit?' Stringer said.

Dalton righted himself slowly, hollow eyes turning to look out the back window. 'He sold me out?'

'You must've seen it coming. Kent doesn't need you anymore.' Stringer clicked his fingers to get his attention. 'Who did the job?'

Dalton was shaking his head. 'Sergei and Oleg, I don't even fucking know. They flew them in from Kiev or somewhere. They were on the first flight out again the next morning.'

'Where's the body?'

'They're ex-special forces.' He shook his head, resigned. 'It's long gone.'

'Where?'

'As if I'd ask them that.'

Stringer felt Lydia's eyes burning into the side of his face now. 'And you provided them with transport. Pointing the finger at Suslov in the process.'

'I'm not saying another fucking word until you get me out of here.'

'What happened to the witness, Dalton?'

'I don't know. I swear I didn't know anything about it until you showed up with the video. They must've got her.'

Another car came off the motorway in the distance, turning on to the slip road, its headlights tracking slowly towards them.

It pulled into the same car park and made a wide loop around to stop twenty feet away, lighting them up.

Dalton stared over at it. 'Who's this?'

Lydia reached back and grabbed him. 'What about Tammy Hodgson? Who killed her?'

'They did,' Dalton said, desperate. 'She got too close.' He squirmed away from her grip. 'I had no idea they were gonna come after her. Or you.'

'Fuck you.'

'There's more, just get me away from here. Suslov takes his orders from the Russians...'

'It's too late for that.' Stringer opened his door and got out.

Dalton started bucking and shouting, the sound spilling out through Lydia's open window.

As he passed it, she reached for his sleeve. 'Michael...'

He looked down at her.

'This is wrong.'

'Trust me.'

She jammed her head against the wheel, screwing her eyes shut. Then she lifted it again and jumped out of the car and came around in front of him. 'Whatever he did, we can't just hand him over to be killed. The police should be dealing with this.' He tried to go around her and she moved in front of him again. 'You promised me.'

The passenger door of the other car opened and her gaze snapped to the man that got out – tall and well built, a black Superdry jacket accentuating his bulk.

Stringer put his hand on the roof and leaned close to her. 'Trust me.'

He started walking towards the other car.

The man in the Superdry jacket had come around to the front to meet him, his legs strafed by his own headlights. Davey. Years since he'd seen him, his body thicker and his hair thinner, eyes deeper set, harder than he remembered.

'So you were serious?'

Stringer nodded. He handed over a Ziploc bag with Dalton's gun in it. 'He's in the back seat.'

'I can hear.' Davey turned the bag over in his hands, examining the weapon as he said it.

'He waved that in my sister's face, and her little one.'

'And you're still willing to give him up?'

'He can give you the others.'

He stared at him.

'What?'

Davey shrugged. 'You hear things over the years is all.'

'About?'

'About you. What you're doing now.'

'What does that mean?'

'Thought maybe you'd be settling your own scores these days.'

'I am.'

A thud came from Stringer's car and they both looked over.

It was rocking slightly, Dalton panicking, trying to boot the door open from the inside. Davey signalled to his partner to go and collect him. He looked at Stringer again. 'And he's good for murder?'

'Accessory at least. You'll have to talk to him about the extent of his involvement, but he provided the killers with transport.'

'He's talked then?'

'Some. He's holding some stuff back to use, but he'll give it up for protective custody.'

'And the threat to his life?'

'Is genuine. I wouldn't have called you otherwise.'

'Yeah.' He nodded. 'Yeah, okay.' He looked past Stringer, watching the other officer cross the tarmac. 'Who's the girl?'

'No one.'

'Mike?'

'No one. She was never here.'

'You're asking a lot.'

'I'm giving a lot.'

'We'll see.' Davey shot him a look as he said it. 'Is this some kind of recompense then?'

'For what?'

'Not a word in six years, Mike. Now you call me out of the blue.'

'So?'

'I thought maybe you'd had time to reflect. Guilty conscience eating at you.'

'I'm trying to save his life, that's all.'

'You don't ever think about the old days?'

He shook his head. 'Not like that. I followed the orders I was given.'

Davey put his hands in his jacket pockets. 'And the rest.'

Stringer took a step back. 'You can't be a bit undercover. I did the job I was asked.'

'Don't give me that. We're not talking about breaking a few rules *in the line of duty*. You fucking crossed over.'

'I didn't come here for this.' He turned and started back to the car.

Davey called after him. 'And what've you done since you left the force? A blag artist for the high and mighty?'

Lydia had her phone to her ear as he approached, talking fast, but she took it away when he came close. She stared at him, eyes like a spooked animal. He went past her to the back door, Davey's partner trying to coax Dalton out. He was lying on his back in a heap of sweat and spittle where he'd been trying to boot the door open. He bolted up when Stringer appeared. 'I don't know about the witness but you want the rest, there's shit you can't even imagine—'

'Just get out.'

Suddenly there were more headlights coming fast down the slip road. Stringer whipped around and saw another set coming from the other end.

Davey's partner had clocked them too. 'What's this?'

Stringer let his gaze linger a second more, then he slammed Dalton's door shut and yanked Lydia's open for her. 'Get in the car.'

She looked at him, not moving.

'Come on.'

The silver paintwork came into view just as they put their lights on, washing everything in flickering blue. Three cars; two stopped to block the car park entrance, the third pulling up behind them. Uniforms spilled out, and two men in suits – one Asian, one white.

'POLICE. Everyone away from the vehicles right now.'

He saw Lydia glance back at him once as she ran towards them.

CHAPTER 56

One Week Later

Lydia flicked through the *Standard* while she waited.

The message had made her feel ill when it first came up on her phone; it made her confront feelings that were still raw and visceral; easier to just box them off in her head. But by the time she steeled herself to read it a second time, she realised the tone was different to the ones that had preceded it, and the language too. That was when she allowed for the possibility it could be genuine.

She'd messaged the sender back, asking them to prove they really were Paulina Dobriska, and within a minute she received a selfie that was unmistakably her. After that, they'd talked over FaceTime twice before she finally agreed to meet in person. She did it the right way this time: a crowded cafe on Oxford Street in the middle of the lunchtime rush. The chair opposite her was the only free one in the place, and she had to bat off interest in it every few seconds, spreading the newspaper to make the table look less inviting.

Lydia turned the page and found what she was looking for. She wasn't expecting a splash to mark Sir Oliver Kent's death, but two columns on page twelve seemed stingy. The article covered the basics and not much else, noting that the respected businessman and former councillor and London Assembly member had been found dead at his home at the age of sixty-three. The police had made a statement that there were no indications of foul play, but the coroner was investigating to determine the exact cause of death.

It was code for suicide. The journos she'd spoken to behind the scenes said he'd taken an overdose of prescription pills. He had left a note, but the contents were still a matter of speculation.

She looked up when the door opened, Paulina Dobriska edging in sheepishly, scanning around for a stranger's face she'd only seen on an iPhone. Lydia got up to wave her over. When she came close, Lydia felt tears filming over her eyes and tried to blink them away, a last ditch at salvaging some veneer of professionalism.

'I'm so pleased to meet you.'

Stringer knocked on the door and stood back so he'd be visible through the spyhole.

The street looked a little less grubby in the daylight, a window box holding purple flowers lending a splash of colour to the front of the house. He heard music from inside, electronic beats he didn't recognise, in competition with the sound of at least one radio coming from a window upstairs.

Angie Cross opened the door and smiled when she saw him. 'Alright. What're you doing here?'

'I've got something for you.'

'You wanna come in?'

He shook his head gently. 'I can't stay.' He took the slip of paper from his pocket and gave it to her. 'This is an offshore account with a hundred grand in it. It's yours.'

She stared at the account details and passcodes, glancing at him with a half-smile as if it was a joke. 'Are you taking the piss?'

'No. I can help you bring it back into the country.'

'Who's this from?'

'Someone who won't miss it.'

'Anyone would miss that much money. Is it yours?'

He shook his head. 'No one knows you have it, except me. You earned it.'

She looked up, her mouth ajar.

He ran his hand over his stubble and glanced to the side. 'Look, there's something else. When we met, the way things were for you...'

'With Malcolm?' – the insurance big shot who'd beaten her half to death.

'Yeah. When you said no police...' Grasping for the right words – Lydia's condemnation had sowed doubt that'd taken root. 'The way we settled it – I don't know that was right.'

'What are you...?'

'If you want to press charges, I'll back you all the way.'

'I don't get...' She closed her eyes, shaking her head as if she was trying to clear it. 'What's that got to do with this?'

'Like I said, you earned it. Taking this doesn't stop you going to the police. It's between us.'

She stared at the slip a second longer. Then she handed it back to him. 'I don't want it.'

'What? Why not?'

'I made my choices, I'll live with them. Not with this.'

He took a half-step back. 'Slow down a minute. Why don't you take some time...'

She lifted her eyes to meet his, the look of disbelief slowly ebbing. 'No, honestly. I don't want to sound like a bitch. I appreciate it and all, but...' She cracked a nervous smile. 'I need to stand on my own two feet. This is someone else's.'

'You can. This is just...'

He searched her face, seeing a resoluteness behind her words. He thought about how she'd gone wrong before, how men handing her money brought about nothing but dependency, and then he got it. The understanding passed unspoken, her smile getting broader, and he found himself matching it.

She punched him in the chest playfully. 'Anyway, you can't get rid of me that easily.'

CHAPTER 57

Stephen took his jacket off and sat down on the bed. Lydia closed the door and stood with her back to it.

She'd come home to a pile of post on the doormat and an empty bedroom next to hers. Chloe had called to break the news, and she couldn't blame her; no one wants to live with a flatmate who tells you out of the blue it's not safe to go home. Without someone to share the rent, though, it probably meant she'd have to move; another item to add to the list of things that needed sorting, a list that could be shortened to one entry: *my life*.

'So? How did it go with Paulina?'

Lydia smiled, remembering the meeting. 'Really good. She's been through it, though.'

'Did she go into detail?'

She nodded. 'She was terrified. Like, absolutely terrified. She posted the video everywhere she could as soon as she took it because she thought they were going to kill her. Her way of trying to tell what'd happened, if she didn't make it. But then she dropped her phone when she was trying to get away and she freaked out.'

'That's awful.'

'Her first thought was that she always had a tab open for Amazon, so they'd have her address right there if they found it. The only family she's got is a cousin in Manchester, so she took a load of cash out and went to hide at his place.'

'Why didn't she tell anyone?'

'No one to tell. She's got friends in town but her family are in Poland. And she had no phone – all her contacts were in it.'

'What about the police?'

'She called Crimestoppers, anonymously, but she was too afraid to go in person. She thought they wouldn't believe her.'

He crossed his legs. 'You know what I'm going to ask next...'

'Interview?'

He nodded.

'I don't know. She's pretty shaken.' She folded her arms, mirroring him. 'Are you saying I've still got a job?'

'Do you still want it?'

'What does that mean?'

'You know, what you were saying on the phone. About starting over.'

'That was right after everything. I was all over the place...'

'I understand.'

'But I've been thinking about it some more. I think what I want now is stability.'

He got up and came across to her. 'You're bloody good at what you do, Lydia. That hasn't changed.' He scratched his cheek. 'They've got a suspect for Tammy's murder – you heard that?'

She nodded. The same man Michael had photographed in her kitchen. The papers named him as Kyle Curtis, a repeat offender with a history of violent crime, his whereabouts currently unknown. She'd been piecing it together as much as she could; the theory that best fit what she knew was that the Russian end of the operation had approved Jamie Tan's murder, sending professional killers directly, Dalton acting as point man. The rest were recruited by Dalton and Kent in the aftermath, Curtis among them.

Some days she wanted Curtis dead – the days she couldn't stop thinking about Tammy. Her own guilt spurred it. At some point she'd stumbled on the idea that if she'd just said no in the first place, ignored the email, the whole thing would've fizzled out, and Tammy would still be alive. It was senseless, she knew that deep down. Didn't stop her beating herself up with it anyway.

'So this thing is over now, right?' Stephen said.

'I don't know. If they identify the hitmen who killed Tan, and if they are Russian nationals, that'll be a massive diplomatic blow-up. Especially when Russia refuses to extradite them.'

He put his hand on her arm. 'I meant for you.'

'Singh and Wheldon keep coming back with more questions, but...' She could sense his frustration and she slipped away from him, nodding to give him the answer he wanted. The promise of a return to normal life.

She went to the window to look out. The daylight was almost gone, the street and the houses opposite falling to the dusk. But the sunlight was still catching the highest branches of one of the trees, the last rays bathing them in a golden light that she would have sworn was receding even as she watched. The promise of something better, slipping away.

CHAPTER 58

Stringer leaned on the wall of the pub opposite Lydia Wright's office, the drinkers around him in shirts and no jackets looking uncomfortable. The temperature had dropped ten degrees overnight, a hard break with summer that'd caught London unawares.

He hadn't spoken to her since Borehamwood, too afraid even to try. If he had his way, he'd get one more chance to sit down with her and set the record straight – allay all those fears she had about him that'd led her to go to the police. He couldn't say for sure why he cared so much; or maybe he could but just didn't want to admit it.

It would never happen, and he would live with that.

In the end it was his own fault. A miscalculation; telling her about Kent and his deal to give up Dalton, without telling her what was really going down. A notion that she'd be safer if she believed Dalton was dead and buried at Kent's hands. That she'd go back to a normal life while the authorities broke him down and used him to go after the real players, maybe even make inroads on the Russian end of the scheme. It made sense at the time, fresh from people pointing guns at everyone he cared about, when he still believed there was hope if he could just make the right moves.

Now, with the benefit of distance and reflection, the dull autumn light exposed it for the self-deception it had always been. That Lydia's moral compass could ever be as broken as his own.

He watched the main entrance, grey rain beginning to fall like a judgement on all of them. He stood there with impunity because he knew she wasn't inside the building; she hadn't been back to work since it happened. But the man he wanted was.

Stephen Langham came out of the doors and crossed the road, tacking around the traffic. Stringer slipped into his trail, following him all the way to London Bridge Tube before he approached.

'Stephen?'

Langham glanced back, still walking, but Stringer caught his eye and he stopped. 'Yeah?'

'You don't remember me, Stephen?'

Langham stared at him, looking blank, about to say something when he cut him off.

'No, you wouldn't. It was brief – Sir Oliver Kent's office.'

'Sir Oliver's? No, sorry.'

'Sure. But I remember you.'

'Okay. You are?'

'Sir Oliver was into some very bad shit, and then I see you there, on first-name terms with him. I think you know what I'm talking about.'

'No, I don't. And this conversation is over.' Scrabbling to get away.

'Stephen, I know who you are.' He stepped closer, the crowd dynamic coming into play now, Langham looking like he wanted to melt into the pavement but too embarrassed to make a scene. 'I know you better than you know yourself. In thrall to money and the men that control it. Trying to work out if you hate them for having it as much as you hate yourself for craving it.'

'What is this psychobabble?'

'I've worked for people like Oliver Kent for years. They use people like us, and they only keep us around as long as we're useful. I've bought off more journalists than I can remember, but Kent went one better, didn't he? No need to bother with a fixer when you can just buy off the whole newspaper. Just got to find the right man on the inside.' He nodded his head towards Langham in faux appreciation.

Langham came towards him, a sense of urgency creeping into the crowd as the rain fell harder. 'Who the fuck are you?'

'I know what Kent was into, probably know more about it than you do. Maybe you thought it was just some white-collar shit – rich fuckers moving their money around the world, so who cares? But I've seen the real cost, and it's people getting killed and people pointing guns at innocent women and children. I know the scale of what you were hiding for him by keeping his name out of your papers. I want you to keep that in mind when I tell you this.'

'I don't work for Oliver Kent. You don't know what you're talking about so get the fuck out of my face before I put you on the—'

Stringer held up one finger to silence him, and Langham's bravado evaporated. 'Kent's dead, but there are others and they'll pick up where he left off. They'll find you, if you're not in with them already. I don't care what you do for them, or what stories you write or get quashed on their behalf, but I want you to keep one name in mind: Lydia Wright. If you hurt her, or her career, or she gets hurt because of you, I'll take you apart. I'll be watching. You think you can knock people down with your newspapers, you haven't got a clue what I can do to you.'

CHAPTER 59

Lydia stepped out of the lift into a small, well-lit landing. The carpet underfoot was new, still had that smell about it, and the walls had been recently painted a powder grey. It was bland, anonymous, and safe; at last, after the fact, one of her assumptions about him was on the nose.

Michael answered the door a few seconds after she knocked. It was the first time she'd seen him caught off-guard. It brought a half-smile to her face, to know she'd wrong-footed him for once.

'Hi.'

He was standing there in jeans and a shirt, barefoot. He looked strange in anything other than a suit – younger, less stressed. 'If you'd rather I go...'

He leaned on the edge of the open door. 'Go?'

'I wasn't sure if you'd be pissed off at me.'

He looked down, shaking his head. 'No. No, of course not.'

'Can I come in?'

He straightened up, faltering opening his arm out. 'Sure.'

She walked down the hall into an open-plan living room. The décor was different from the Finsbury Park flat, but just as impersonal. There was an empty glass on the table and a laptop on the kitchen counter, but nothing else on display – no pictures, no personal effects. A pair of doors were open, leading onto a small private balcony that caught the sunlight, the jagged London skyline in the distance beyond it. 'Nice view.'

'How are you?'

She tilted her head. 'I'm okay.'

'How did you...?'

'Your car. I've been here before, remember? The flat numbers are on the parking spaces.' She drifted back to the end of the counter where he was standing. She pointed to the laptop screen. 'Florida Keys – nice. Thinking of a holiday?'

He flipped the screen shut, a look on his face she couldn't read. 'One day. Not yet.'

'If you're looking at getaways, should I be worried?'

'About?'

'Retribution.'

He planted his hands on the countertop. 'Honestly? I don't know. But that's not why I was looking. I'm not running away.'

'What does Andriy Suslov think about that?'

'I don't know. He knows I did him a favour though, so...'

'You think he's happy Dalton's in custody? He probably doesn't want him talking any more than Kent did.'

He was already shaking his head. 'Dalton was a nobody to Suslov, that's why he was trying to move up by latching on to Kent. I don't think he can say anything to hurt him.'

She closed her eyes, nodding. 'Is your sister okay? And her kid?'

'Yeah.' He looked away. 'Ellie hasn't spoken about it once. We're hoping she thought the whole thing was a bad dream, but maybe she's burying it. Abi's shook up but she's the toughest person I know. She'll come through it.'

'I feel for them. I wish ... I could've done more.'

'You saved their lives. And mine.'

'We're quits then.' She shrugged saying it, enjoying his discomfort when he looked down and nodded. 'You heard about Sir Oliver Kent?'

'Yeah. Suicide.'

'You buy it?'

'Do you?'

'Not for a second.'

She gripped the end of the counter. 'I'm breezing around your flat like we're old friends and you haven't even asked me what I'm here for.'

'I'm not sure I've got the right to ask you anything.'

'You know you fucked up, then. That's a start.'

'I made missteps. I don't blame you.'

'I didn't mean to get you in trouble. If that's worth anything.'

'You didn't.'

'No charges?'

He shook his head. 'Not so far. Davey – DCI Davidson – vouched for my actions that night.'

'How much does he know?'

'Less than you and me.'

'And Dalton?'

'They wouldn't tell me even if I asked. He'll be co-operating though – it's his only out.'

She looked at him looking at her; she'd never known another human being so comfortable in a pointed silence. 'Why didn't you tell me you're ex-police?'

'What difference would it have made?'

'Maybe would've been easier to trust you.'

'It was a long time ago. It's irrelevant.'

She looked at the wall, clearly more to the story. The man never gave anything away for free, but there was a note of shame in his voice that hinted at the truth. 'I wouldn't have called Singh and Wheldon in if you'd been honest with me. If I'd known what you were planning.'

'I thought...' He ran his hand over the laptop absently, regrouping. 'I thought I was protecting you.'

'By making me think you were giving him up to be killed?'

'I already said I got it wrong.'

She leaned over the countertop. 'I think you've got a problem with telling the truth. I think you default to lies because it keeps you in control. So that only Michael Stringer can know the real story.'

He took a breath to say something but then looked at her as if he was thinking about it. 'I don't know what to say to that.'

'Don't look so crestfallen. It's an observation, not a moral indictment.'

She started to smile and he mirrored her, but embarrassed, bowing his head in a way that said she'd understood him better than he understood himself.

'Are you back at work now?' he said. The abrupt change of subject confirmation of his embarrassment.

'I will be, soon. Why?'

'There's something you need to know.'

She straightened up, his tone making her wary – not the idle distraction she'd thought.

'Your boss, Stephen Langham.'

Her hairs on end now. 'How do you know who...?' She shook her head, remembering who she was dealing with. Eyed him, waiting.

'He was on Oliver Kent's payroll.'

'What? How...?' She closed her eyes, trying to make sense. 'How could you possibly know that?'

'I saw them together. So I asked him about it.'

'You ... And he just admitted it, did he?'

'Of course not. But as good as.'

Holding on to the counter for dear life now. 'What ... I don't understand, what for? Access?'

'Denial of. Kent probably had someone at the top of every paper – shooting down stories to keep his name and his dodgy schemes out of the news. Usually they use a fixer or a middleman, but I guess the stakes were higher for him.'

'Shooting down stories': the phrase stopped her dead. Exactly what had happened to her, Stephen quick to shift the blame onto management. The implications cascading – Goddard and Oliver Kent collaborating on various deals over the years. Goddard trampling planning rules so developers and investors would make more money... 'Jesus Christ.'

'I know, it's a lot to take in, but...'

'No, it's ... it's not that.'

He looked at her, waiting for more, concern on his face. 'What?'

A picture coming together, incomplete but taking shape. 'About Oliver Kent,' she said, 'I keep turning it over.'

He came alert now, the first signs of the old intensity in his bearing. 'Go on.'

'Kent and his backers had Tan killed to keep Suslov from getting him, right?'

He said nothing, watching her.

'But I keep thinking, if Jamie Tan was running the whole scheme, why would they kill him? Doesn't that cause them more problems than it solves?'

'I had the same thought.'

'But then Kent turns up dead, supposedly suicide. So what's your best guess on what really happened there?'

'Someone on the Russian end wanted him silenced. Maybe serves as a warning to Dalton, too.'

'You don't sound convinced.'

He tilted his head, sloughing off his own theory. 'We know they've got more than one scheme moving money out of Russia. Tan's replaceable, Kent less so if he's the facilitator on the UK end.'

'Exactly. The backers are the ultimate power here. The people with the money.' She traced a circle on the countertop. 'So what about this: what about if Jamie Tan wasn't the brains behind the mirror trades? What if he fronted it, carried out the actual transactions and stuff, but there was someone more valuable behind him, out of sight? Someone who made the connections, brought in the clients, brokered the deals.'

He was nodding as she said it. 'That would mean the scheme could carry on. No interruptions.'

'And if that person had cut their own deal with Suslov, with the approval of the Russians, then Oliver Kent becomes yesterday's man. Expendable.'

'More than that – a loose end. A threat to expose them.'

Michael was watching her – blue-grey eyes resonating with the same certainty she felt. 'Say her name,' he said.

'Alicia Tan.'

CHAPTER 60

Stringer parked his car across the driveway gates. Straightaway he noticed Alicia's Lexus was in a different position on the gravel.

Lydia jumped out before he'd even stopped the engine, holding down the buzzer on the entry panel. Stringer came to stand behind her.

The front door opened and a man in a suit with an open collar came across the drive. He was cut from the same cloth as Suslov's bodyguard on the boat.

'Yes?' His accent was Eastern European.

'My name's Lydia Wright, I'd like to see Mrs Tan. It's in her interest to talk to us.'

Alicia appeared in the doorway, hesitating as she looked out. She made eye contact with Stringer and held his stare. Then she called out to the bodyguard, her voice strong but quiet. 'It's alright.'

The man looked back at her for confirmation and she nodded.

Silence. Then a buzz as the electric motor came to life, the gate sliding open.

The man shadowed them across the driveway.

Alicia Tan stepped back to wait for them inside. Lydia went in first, but it was Stringer she kept her eyes on as they came close. When they were through the door, the bodyguard closed it behind them and only then did Alicia speak. 'You promised me if I walked out of that flat I'd never see you again.'

'Things change,' Stringer said. 'I wanted to be sure you were still alive.'

She opened her hands out, fingers splayed. 'Then you've got what you came for.'

He shook his head. 'Not yet. I need to know if this ends with Oliver Kent.'

She crossed one foot in front of the other. 'I don't understand.'

Lydia swore under her breath. 'Oliver Kent had Jamie killed as a warning to you. He knew Suslov was trying to squeeze him out, and he thought that would scare you back into line. He underestimated you, and you defected to Suslov anyway, taking all your influence over the mirror trades with you. You and Suslov go back, from when he was your client at Cawthorne Probert.'

Alicia was a pro; Lydia had gone in all guns blazing and she showed no reaction to any of it. She looked at Stringer. 'Is she always this friendly?'

'I just want to establish that we're on an even footing when it comes to information,' Lydia said.

'I don't even know who you are.'

'Lydia Wright. I'm a journalist.'

'A journalist.' She glanced at Stringer again. 'The one with the video?'

Lydia nodded and Alicia shot her a look. 'Five minutes of fame off the back of my husband's murder.'

'You chose your life. I didn't ask for any of this.'

Alicia's mouth fell open. 'Are you honestly standing in my house telling me my husband deserved it?'

'No. I'm saying you both knew the risks.'

'Who the fuck do you think you are?'

Stringer cut in. 'This act would be a lot more convincing if you'd gone to the police like you said you did, Alicia.'

She breathed out slowly, uneven.

'I should've worked it out then,' Stringer said, 'in the flat. You owe me for that, if nothing else.'

'Owe you, how?'

'I bought you time and space to work out your deal with Suslov. Unwittingly, but it was a godsend for you. Disappear off the fucking earth at just the right time. Kent was looking everywhere for you.' He thought back to the underground garage, Dalton's questions about Alicia's whereabouts, Kent probing him for the same in his office. Giveaways he should've recognised at the time.

'You must feel so used,' Alicia said.

'I'll live.'

'If you came here for money, I think you know I'm not the person to threaten.'

The bodyguard took a step closer to her, apparently oblivious to the whole different scale of protection she was referring to, stretching two thousand miles to the east.

'He's already told you what we want,' Lydia said. 'Does it end with Kent?'

'You don't know what you're talking about.'

Lydia drew nearer. 'Look, I don't give a shit about you or your scheme, or any of the other bullshit. I just want my life back, and to know I can walk around without looking over my shoulder.'

'Then my best advice to you would be to keep a very low profile.'

'That costs you more.'

Alicia started backing away. 'This really isn't a negotiation—'

'Peter Goddard,' Lydia said. 'Three years ago you were trying to arrange a meeting between him and Andriy Suslov. Tell me what was discussed, and I'll forget I ever heard of you.'

Alicia stared at her, showing no reaction.

Stringer watched the bodyguard, his hand slipping to his pocket.

Alicia blinked and said, 'Come into the kitchen.'

She talked without emotion or eye contact. At first the phrase 'ice queen' kept running through Lydia's head, but as Alicia went on, even that label didn't fit quite right – too caricatured and stylised. This was a businesswoman engaging in a business transaction – a dispassionate exchange of information for a perceived advantage.

Andriy Suslov had been her client at Cawthorne Probert and that had brought Peter Goddard to her door. Goddard talked up a business opportunity he was fronting, aimed at super-rich foreigners: investment in luxury London developments on preferential terms – the kind of terms only Goddard and his political cronies could deliver. Goddard talked up his construction partners, and introduced them to his liaison with the industry – Sir Oliver Kent. 'Goddard used to say the name as if it was a synonym for probity. The overseas guys loved it – they'd hear "Sir" and think "establishment". As if that was some stamp of officialdom that made it all legitimate – even when we all knew it wasn't.'

Suslov had given them an audience, but ultimately decided to pass – for the reason that only a billionaire could turn down the chance to make an easy couple of mil: 'It's not enough. It's not worth my time.'

But Alicia had recognised an opportunity none of the others could see; something she'd been working on in the background ever since she first helped Andriy Suslov get his money out of Russia: mirror trades. And in Sir Oliver Kent, she'd found the last piece she needed: someone crooked enough to funnel the money to, who could offer a return to make it worthwhile. He'd near enough bitten her hand off to get involved, and once they'd put everything in place, it all ran smoothly for a couple of years – that was until Andriy Suslov got wind of it all and decided to muscle Kent out.

Michael asked a question then, but Lydia couldn't concentrate on what he was saying. All she could think about was Stephen's betrayal.

All the time spent doubting herself. The self-recrimination. The sanctimonious fucking lectures about how she needed to learn patience. All of it a lie, in truth him spiking the Goddard story to protect Oliver Kent. She felt sick at the thought she'd let this man into her bed. Into her life. Violated by the person she trusted the most.

Alicia was speaking about Jamie Tan – answering Michael's question. How easy it'd been to talk Jamie into being the front man for the scheme while Alicia stepped back from the industry for cover. 'Greed was Jamie's North Star. He hated himself for it but he wasn't strong enough to change or do anything about it – except light a few candles.'

Lydia tuned her out again, sick of all of them – Jamie and Alicia, Suslov, Kent – rich people willing to trample over anyone and anything to take even more. Attended by simpering fucks like Stephen Langham. Tammy came into her mind then, all the rumours that she'd turned into a crackpot, cutting her career off at the knees, and wondered if he'd been behind that too. Destroying the best investigative reporter of her generation just to protect his masters – and covering up for them when they had her killed.

Everything she'd worked for, everything she'd believed in, everyone she'd trusted, ground to dust.

Stringer climbed behind the wheel, Lydia looking straight ahead through the windscreen.

'She doesn't know about Dalton,' he said.

'Nope. She's screwed.' She sounded faraway, her jaw set like she was ready to go to war.

The details Alicia provided didn't mean much to him, but the gist was easy enough to grasp – Goddard touting preferential terms on large-scale property developments to selected investors. Terms he was able to secure by using his clout in City Hall. Its significance to Lydia was harder to gauge. 'Is it enough?'

'Enough for what?'

'To get him?'

She lifted her eyes, focusing on the light playing off the treetops like it was an answer to a question only she knew. 'Fuck getting him. Let's make some money.'

ACKNOWLEDGEMENTS

My sincere gratitude goes to everyone who helped in the creation of this book. In particular, I'd like to thank:

My agent, Jane Gregory, her editor, Stephanie Glencross, and the whole team at David Higham Associates for all their input and encouragement with this manuscript as it evolved.

My publisher, Karen Sullivan, for seeing the potential in this book, and the wonderful team at Orenda Books.

Beverley Fox and all the staff at Weybridge Library, for the truly amazing support they've shown me – it makes such an incredible difference.

Richard King, for his invaluable help with all matters financial (and time-zone related).

Mark, Flick, Laura, Hannah, Sara, Megan and the rest of the crew, for keeping me sane by trying to kill me twice a week.

My fellow crime authors: writing can be a lonely business, and the encouragement and comradeship from the crime community is invaluable.

My family, for putting up with the endless hours of me sitting at a laptop staring at the wall.

And most of all, my readers, who have come with me through four books now, and I hope will join me for many more.

If you loved *Blood Red City*, you'll enjoy...

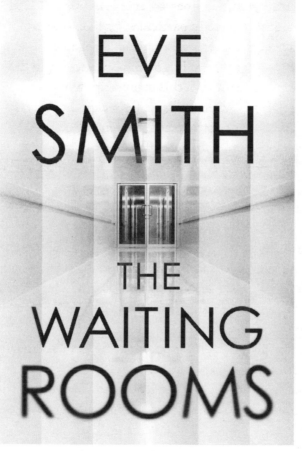

EVE
SMITH

THE
WAITING
ROOMS

Decades of spiralling drug resistance have unleashed a global antibiotic crisis. Ordinary infections are untreatable, and a sacrifice is required: no one over seventy is allowed new antibiotics. The elderly are sent to hospitals nicknamed 'The Waiting Rooms' ... hospitals where no one ever gets well...

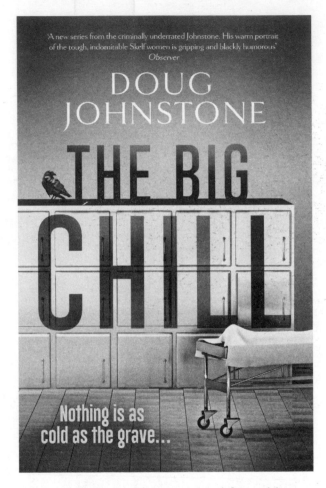

DOUG JOHNSTONE

THE BIG CHILL

Nothing is as cold as the grave...

Running private-investigator and funeral-home businesses means trouble is never far away for the Skelf women, as they take on their most perplexing, chilling cases yet in book two of this darkly funny, devastatingly tense and addictive new series.